PATTON'S WAY

Cattleman's Club 1

Jenny Penn

D0723350

EROTIC ROMANCE

Siren Publishing, Inc.
www.SirenPublishing.com

A SIREN PUBLISHING BOOK
IMPRINT: Erotic Romance

PATTON'S WAY
Cattleman's Club 1
Copyright © 2008 by Jenny Penn

ISBN-10: 1-60601-159-6
ISBN-13: 978-1-60601-159-1

First Publication: November 2008

Cover design by Jenny Penn
All cover art and logo copyright © 2008 by Siren Publishing, Inc.

ALL RIGHTS RESERVED: This literary work may not be reproduced or transmitted in any form or by any means, including electronic or photographic reproduction, in whole or in part, without express written permission.

All characters and events in this book are fictitious. Any resemblance to actual persons living or dead is strictly coincidental.

Printed in the U.S.A.

PUBLISHER
Siren Publishing, Inc.
www.SirenPublishing.com

DEDICATION

To Cindy for all her help and support.

PATTON'S WAY

Cattleman's Club 1

Jenny Penn
Copyright © 2008

Chapter 1

Pink flowers flowed down to her ankles, white turtleneck folded up to her chin, and a ponytail, smooth and slick. A little mascara and a touch of lip-gloss, the gold cross they had given her on her sixteenth birthday and the diamond studs they'd given her on her twenty-first, right along with the champagne glasses filled with apple cider.

If only they knew how shit faced I got the following weekend celebrating with my friends.

Patton snickered to herself and shook her head at the image staring back at her. The outfit would have done a twelve-year-old girl proud. Too bad she was twenty-three.

I look like a high-classed call girl dressed up for a kinky client.

That wasn't far off. She'd dressed up for the Davis boys and they were definitely kinky. A shame they wouldn't be showing her any of their tricks. Then perhaps the thong hidden beneath the billowing folds of her skirt would serve more purpose than just covering her up.

Patton smiled with the knowledge of her barely-there bra. She might be done up like a doll, but underneath breathed the desires of a flesh and blood woman. If the Davis boys couldn't recognize that fact, perhaps she needed to find a few good men who did.

I've been looking for those men for the past six years and what do I have to show for it? A box full of vibrators.

So perhaps it was her problem the Davis brothers still looked at her as if she was twelve. The clothes didn't help. They perpetuated the image, just how the brothers wanted it. Patton grimaced imagining what they would do if she showed up dressed in one of her tight, little outfits.

Chase might actually bust one of those blood vessels that always throbbed out from his temple whenever he yelled at her. Chase Davis was the oldest of the pack. The self-anointed man of the house, he assumed the role of the stern, unbending authority figure with the ease of a man born to wield power.

He was such a hunk. Patton sighed. He always walked around in those faded, hip-hugging jeans. When he wore a shirt, he always wore a black and tight t-shirt. Personally, she liked him better without a shirt. All those muscles, all that tanned skin, Patton wanted to do all sorts of things to that hard, thick body. Hell, all the brothers rippled with muscles that Patton would love to get more than just her hands on.

The man had a model perfect face except for the bump in his nose, thanks to breaking it more than once. Even that minor flaw attracted her. When he had to go out into the fields, he'd put on his Stetson and pull it down slightly so that the curved edges made his rugged features look more strong and angular.

Just like his brothers, Chase had the straight eyebrows, a strong jaw line, just rounded enough not to be square. His lips haunted Patton. The brothers all had the same not too full and not too thin, perfect lips meant to tease a woman to insanity.

The only differences between the three were their eye colors and the length of their hair. Chase had dark blue eyes and kept his light brown hair short, neatly trimmed.

Slade's lighter blue eyes were as piercing as Chase's were mesmerizing. Just as Chase's stormy, blue eyes fit his temperamental personality, just as Slade's fit his perceptive one.

Slade's lighter brown hair curled around the edges of his collar and ears, letting the chocolate color highlight the smooth, tan skin of his neck. It softened the hard edges of his features, but a woman would be a fool to mistake that illusion for reality.

Devin, the youngest, had smoky gray bedroom eyes that darkened with humor or pleasure and lightened with his anger. The charming, reckless younger brother, his shaggy hair cut annoyed Chase and proclaimed to the world his rebel status. Just to irritate Chase further, Devin normally let it grow long enough to fall down around his eyes.

"You look ridiculous," Casey snickered from Patton's doorway.

"Gee, thanks." Patton turned from the mirror. "I'm so grateful for your moral support."

"You want support, why don't you slip into that black sheath dress you wore to Allen's party the other night and put on your five inch stilettos and walk into that house demanding what is yours?"

"Because that might actually get me put over Chase's knee."

"Leave the panties off and I'll guarantee you'll get more than a spanking." Casey came into the room and settled on the bed. "When are you going to let them boys see who you really are?"

"It's not that easy and you know it."

Casey, Patton's best friend and business partner, knew all about Patton and her obsession with the Davis brothers. Having met the three Southern raised bad boys, the feisty red head now completely understood Patton's predicament.

Arrogant, demanding, and with a healthy dose of sexism thrown in, the Davis brothers wanted their lovers hot and wild and their so-called "sister" sweet and demure. Two things Patton would never be, sweet or demure, but she could pretend. She either played along or risked losing them all together.

When her dad had died leaving her parentless, Wanda Davis had stepped in. She'd taken Patton into her home and raised her as the daughter she'd always wanted. Though Wanda had never formally adopted Patton, she had secured a deathbed promise from her sons to finish raising Patton.

They'd fulfilled that promise. Now she was all grown up and the promise didn't need to be adhered to. A fact Patton was all too aware of. That hadn't occurred to the brothers though. A blessing or a curse, Patton didn't know how to break the spell either way.

"I see you're packing some heat here." Casey lifted up a pair of tight fitting leather pants. "Got plans?"

"Just want to be prepared if Hailey's around. I might sneak out to some clubs."

"You planning on being gone long?" Casey asked as she continued to root through Patton's bag.

"A week max."

"So what is this impromptu trip about?"

"Chase said he wanted to discuss my graduation gift." Patton zipped up her laptop.

"Jesus, Patton. When are you going to tell them that you didn't go to college?"

"Uh, never." Patton cut Casey a sideways look. "I may not be ed-juma-cated, but I ain't dumb."

"This is like a bad sitcom." Casey rolled her eyes. "Dare I ask how you're going to fake the graduation ceremony?"

"I'm not going. Unfortunately, you and I are taking a celebratory trip to the Bahamas. So, our diplomas will be mailed to us."

"And when this diploma doesn't show up?"

"It will. I ordered up a rendition—"

"A fake."

"So? None of them went to college. They wouldn't know the difference." Patton zipped up her suitcase.

"Lord have mercy on you if those boys ever find out what you really do for a living." Casey stood and lifted Patton's suitcase for her.

"That's never going to happen."

"And if it does?"

"I'll change my name and move to Alaska."

* * * *

I am going to spank that ass until she can't sit down for a whole fucking week.

Chase pivoted at the refrigerator.

Then I'm going to hunt down that bastard and beat him to a bloody pulp.

He turned at the counter.

I'm going to hang him by his toenails from the front oak as warning and lock her in her room 'til she's ninety.

Every time he thought about those photographs, his blood boiled. That was his Patton. His Patton. There for the world to see naked and sweaty with some disease-infested playboy licking her damn stomach.

I'll rip his tongue right out of his head!

Chase pivoted at the refrigerator.

How could she!

"Pacing isn't going to get her here any faster."

Slade's annoyed tone shifted Chase's attention from thoughts escalating the need for violence in his muscles. His younger brother sighed and his expression clearly stated his annoyance.

"I can't believe she did this," Devin muttered, drawing Chase's eyes to the laptop.

He didn't need to see the image of the auburn beauty wearing nothing more than a thong. His eyes though couldn't tear themselves away from the image. The woman wore nothing but a tiny black thong. Her gorgeous locks hung down over her shoulders and barely covered her nipples.

The chains hanging down all around her, caressing against her naked body made the image darkly erotic and lead a man's cock to pulse with the fantasy of having her tied up for his mercy.

Devin clicked the mouse and a new picture flowed down the screen. At least she wore a bra in this one even if the little scrap could barely be called such. Sitting on a saddle with a black Stetson pulled down, concealing most of her face. Not her smile though. The seductive little twist of her full sensual lips promised all sorts of forbidden things.

Those hot, irresistible curves made a man's hands burn with the need to touch her. The glint of her belly button ring promised things a man couldn't resist. She had another though, one guaranteed to drive a man wild with lust.

The subtle glint of silver peeking through the sheer fabric of her panties required a man to truly study the image to notice the small detail. Of course, the hand slipping under the elastic edge of her panties assured a man spent his time studying that portion of her anatomy.

Chase's dick went from semi-hard to trying to push its way through zipper and denim. Damnit. He shouldn't think things like that. Not about Patton.

He'd helped raise her from a girl scared of monsters under the bed to the carefree woman she had become. *Carefree*, Chase snorted to himself. *More like impulsive, reckless and completely lacking in any common sense.* Of all her wild antics, this one ranked as the worst.

She'd given them many nights of worry, concerned that one day she would get hurt. If not hurt then she'd end up chained to their bed, because there was only so much a man could take. The last time she'd been home, they'd almost all collectively snapped because of that damn belly button ring.

It had driven him crazy. He'd caught Devin staring at Patton more than once with a boner the size to make a horse jealous. That need had driven Devin right out of the house and he'd spent most of Christmas running through the available women down at Cattleman's Club.

Chase hadn't fared much better. Instead of driving his cock into every wet and willing cunt he could find, he'd been short tempered and moody. At one point, he'd completely lost it and demanded Patton take the damn thing out.

Patton, being Patton, had refused and gone nose to nose with him. He'd lost the battle because he couldn't very well admit to her that it gave him an erection that couldn't be eased with a little hand stroking in the shower.

Chase just wanted to keep on pretending Patton was a little girl. He could deny his perverse instincts if he saw her as the naïve innocent running around in pigtails.

As a woman, Patton would be fair game. It would be open season for not just him, but all three brothers. They knew just how to reduce a woman from proud to begging, where to touch, kiss, and stroke to make her come apart as one orgasm after another ripped her control away and left only them as masters of her desire.

Chase had never felt ashamed or embarrassed by what he and his brothers did to a woman. They'd never hurt one or left any unsatisfied. Patton was different, or at least, she was supposed to be.

Devin clicked on the next page of the on-line lingerie catalog and Chase turned away. He didn't want to see pictures of her in an intimate embrace with another man, even if they were pretend. It had better damn well be pretend.

"Will you stop staring at those photographs?" Chase slammed down the laptop monitor, drawing a dark look from Devin.

"You're going to go blind," Slade snickered.

"Or break your zipper."

"You're one to talk," Devin retorted. "Or was I mistaken when I heard Charlotte going off on you for calling her Patton while you fucked her last night?"

"Screw you, Devin."

"At least when I'm pretending she's Patton, I remember to call her 'baby' and 'sweetheart'. I don't make you starve just because I can't keep a name straight and the damn woman wouldn't even cook us breakfast."

"It's those damn pictures."

"Bullshit. You've been hot to pump that pussy since she was eighteen."

"Don't talk about Patton that way!"

"Why not? It's the truth. She's a beautiful fuckable woman and we all want a piece of her."

Chase was barely aware of Slade jumping out of the way, as he dove over the counter and knocked Devin to the floor. Unleashing all his pent up rage, he tried to beat his younger brother straight through the floorboards.

Chapter 2

Patton blinked as she took in Devin's appearance. His eye had already swelled, his lip busted and his nose looked as if it had recently leaked a little blood. No big surprise, Devin had greeted her many times before with a face full of bruises and handful of busted knuckles. With his smart mouth and quick fist, Devin had a reputation for getting into fights.

"Devin, I keep telling you when a woman says no, she means no." Patton shook her head sadly.

Devin didn't grin. He didn't come back at her with his customary smart assed retort. He just stood there with one eye narrowed on her as he blocked the door. A trickle of unease moved down her spine. Devin always greeted her with a smile and a quick hug before he disappeared, busy with something or somebody.

Patton tried again to evoke a response. "Are you going to let me in or are you waiting for a tip?"

"Come in." Devin stepped back, still unsmiling.

Whatever was wrong with the youngest of the Davis boys must have been contagious. Charlotte, the boys' so-called housekeeper, came to a momentary stop as she rounded a corner carrying a large load of wash. Another set of eyes narrowed on Patton. Without a word, the petite brunette stomped into the kitchen.

Well, this is going to be a fun trip.

To add more joy to her homecoming, Chase stepped out of den. His swollen and bruised face ended the mystery of whom Devin had gotten into it with. Not a big shock there.

Devin shared Patton's passion for reckless behavior and her predilection for earning Chase's ire. On more than one occasion, Patton had thought Chase would have gone fist to fist with her if she were a man.

Like now, if the dark look he gave her was any indication. Trouble was definitely afoot and she appeared to be at the center of it.

"In here." Chase jerked his head toward the study.

The sound of the door shutting off her only exit followed his command. Not that Patton would have fled, but a more sensible person would have considered it. Instead, she smiled at Chase and walked up to give him a chaste kiss on his cheek.

"Hello to you too, Chase."

Patton turned to see Slade sitting on the large leather sofa. A family affair, that could only mean big trouble. The Davis brothers only ganged up on her when she'd really pushed the limits.

Of course, their definition of the line was a lot more conservative than hers. Like when she was in the seventh grade and had failed to mention Mary Beth's birthday party was actually a boy/girl party. They'd tagged teamed her for that one.

Or the time she'd gotten Chase's permission to go to the Metallica concert when she was in high school. She hadn't said they were holding it in Panama City. Where they had come by that impression she didn't know.

Nor had she lied about spending the night with Hailey. They had spent a lovely evening in the downtown Atlanta Marriott. She'd never said she intended to sleep over at Hailey's house. If they had failed to comprehend what she said, that wasn't her fault, but she had paid for their mistake and paid dearly.

After all those years, the idea of being in trouble made her stomach churn. Some things never changed. Patton didn't let her nerves or her doubts show as she greeted Slade with a sisterly peck on his cheek before settling down onto the sofa beside him.

Chase took his seat behind the desk as she crossed her ankles and clasped her hands in her lap for good measure. Patton played to the demure image of her clothes in a desperate ploy to settle their nerves.

From beneath lowered lashes, she studied Chase. The little vein in his neck pounded away. God but he was seriously hot when he was mad. What it would be like to have him refocus all that aggression into fucking her, pounding harder, deeper into her body while she screamed and bucked beneath him in ecstasy?

Patton shivered at the image, her eyes flicking over to Slade, adding him to the image. Broad shouldered, lean hips and nothing but tight muscles between, all three Davis brothers had been cut from the same cloth. It made her pussy weep just to look at them.

"How's school?" Slade broke the silence, his tone calm and reasonable.

"Fine." Patton smiled easily with the lie.

"Enjoying your last round of classes?"

"Yep."

"What are you taking again?"

"Just some business classes."

Slade always showed interest in Patton's studies, but this line of questioning did not feel like his normal conversational filler questioning. He wanted something, digging for it and he only did that when he knew exactly what he was looking for.

"Some business classes, huh?"

"Yep."

"Excited to graduate?"

"Who wouldn't be?"

Patton wanted to squirm. Thing looked worse than she'd anticipated moments before. He couldn't possibly know the truth about her college experience. If he did—Patton's eyes shifted back to Chase—she really should run.

"After four years, I guess you're pretty anxious to get a job and move on in life, huh?"

Carefully she avoided adding any more lies to the pot. "It's been four long years."

"Yeah." Slade nodded, pausing as if thinking for a moment. "How many credits does it take to graduate?"

"A lot."

"You don't know, do you?"

"There are so many it's hard to keep track."

"I see."

The contemplative silence came again. The significance of Slade being the one to question her wasn't lost on Patton. Things were terminal when Chase couldn't be trusted to speak. Though if history proved to be any indicator, his silence wouldn't last.

Once Slade went in for the kill, Chase would erupt. Then it would be shouting and cussing and the 'I'm the head of this family and you will show me respect' speech all nightlong. Devin would come in, adding his scathing, sarcastic comments to the bonfire.

"That's a nice outfit."

"I thought you would like it."

"Is that what all the college kids are wearing these days?"

"Better to be a trend setter than a follower." Patton smiled sweetly. "Besides, you taught me to be myself and not conform to social pressures."

"Social pressures? I imagine there are a lot of those at school."

"I don't worry about it."

"Pressures to drink, have sex, get tattoos and piercings, things like that?"

"For some, I guess."

"So you would never get a tattoo. Would you, Patton?"

"That's a real commitment and you know how indecisive I can be."

"A piercing isn't a commitment."

"No, it's not."

"But you wouldn't get one of those either."

"You know my belly button's pierced."

Patton kept her expression relaxed. The sick feeling in her stomach didn't make it easy. That was Classic Slade. A teaser question, one he knew the answer too, asked only to gauge her response.

"But nothing else is. Right?" Slade pressed, silently daring her to lie.

Ah, shit. How could they know about that?

"Why? Do you have a spot you want to recommend?"

"That's it!" Chase's hands slammed onto his desk as he rose to Patton's bait. "Answer the damn question."

"What question?" Patton blinked in false confusion.

Damned anyway, she had two options right now. Let Chase boil and suffer a long, drawn out argument or fuel the fire and hope for a quick explosion. She'd had a long five-hour drive through the traffic-laden interstate and into the back roads of lower Alabama. Dressed as a kid and generally cranky, option two best suited her mood.

"Do you have anything else pierced?"

"Why, Chase, what else would a lady pierce?"

"Don't fucking give me that shit, Patton," Chase snarled, his hands clenching into white knuckled fists. "We know."

"You know," Patton repeated drawling out the words. "What do you know, Chase?"

"About it all. Please tell me you did not pierce your..." His voice faltered and his finger came up to point at her crotch.

"Pierce my what?" Never before had she seen that particular color of red staining Chase's tanned cheeks. "My tits?"

"Don't use that kind of language."

"Oh, well, I guess I can't tell you what I got pierced, because I'm sure you'll find that word even more objectionable."

"Oh, God." That plaintive sound came from Devin and she caught him staring at her lap with a forlorn look.

"Maybe you'll let Devin tell you since he seems to have figured it out. I know for a fact, you let him say the word pussy all he wants." Bow shot. Direct hit. That got him out of his seat.

"God damnit, Patton! I should wash your mouth out with soap. A proper lady doesn't talk like that."

"Could you be any more antiquated in your attitudes, Chase?" Patton matched his stance, jumping off the couch with a full sail of indignant anger. "It's such a shame to see a man so young acting so old. Next thing you know you'll be talking about the good old days when women couldn't read or vote."

"Don't you try to turn this on me. I'm not the one who's been lying four years."

"Lying?" Patton placed an insulted hand over her chest.

"We *know*, Patton," Chase growled like a dog ready to bite.

Ah, hell. She had both feet in her grave now she might as well lie down and get buried. Following that goal she turned and hooked two fingers in the waistband of her skirt and pulled it down just enough to give them a tantalizing view of the top string of her thong, before Slade intervened.

"What are you doing?"

"Showing you the piercing," Patton responded as if it were the most natural thing to do.

* * * *

Chase swallowed hard, unable to tear his eyes away from the bright-red string that dipped down and disappeared beneath the edge of her skirt. He couldn't stop his mind from following that string down through her firm ass cheeks to the sweet heat waiting for the pleasures of stroking fingers, velvet tongues, for the invasion of harden dick that would pound her into a screaming orgasm.

"No!"

Chase charged her like a bull in heat. Another second of looking at her smooth flesh broken by the line of her thong would break not only his control but that of his brothers as well. Then there would be no mercy for sweet, little Patton.

"How could you do that?" Chase grabbed her by the arms and yanked her back around. "Decent young women don't get their...their..."

"Clitoris."

"Pierced," Chase could barely get the word out. He knew she didn't have any idea all the dirty thoughts and images that were feeding so much blood to his cock it threatened to burst straight out of his jeans. Hell, she'd probably faint dead away if she could see some of the visions he could.

Visions of her tied spread eagle to a bed as one of his brothers fed his cock into her mouth as she sucked with carnal abandonment. Chase would have his head buried between her soft thighs, devouring her pussy, showing her just how much pleasure a skilled tongue on her piercing could give her.

She'd buck up and it wouldn't be long before he had his cock buried balls deep into the wet, clinging depths of her pussy while one of his brothers fucked her tight ass, filling her snug, little body so full of cock that she screamed and begged for her release as they pounded into her.

"Maybe I'm not as decent as you wish, Chase." Patton's taunt tore him from his fantasies, making him focus on the flesh and blood beauty before him.

"You better be."

"Or what? What are you going to do, cowboy? Spank me?"

Slade jumped in, saving Chase before the argument took a dangerous turn and he acted before he thought. "You don't understand, Patton. Men think certain thing about women who have a piercing like that."

"Oh, I think I do."

Patton's smug smile held too much knowledge for Chase's comfort. Instantly the images from the web flashed through his mind. Apparently, Patton wasn't done slinging the sledgehammer at his tenuous control. She had only just begun.

"I knew it would tease the guys. Just like, I got my new piercing to tease me. You see I knew this guy who had his tongue pierced and found certain…pleasures to be had because of that little piercing. But you can't expect every guy you like to go pierce his tongue, so I took matters into my own hands or my own—"

"That's enough!"

Chase barely managed to get the words out. Her words flared a primal instinct to life in him. It demanded he kill, kill and claim. If her tongue pierced boyfriend had been around, that's exactly what he would have done. He'd have used his fists to eradicate his rival. Then he'd drag Patton to the floor and take what belonged to him.

Tension filled the air as he fought to control his more base desires. He could sense his brothers fighting against the same need, the need to see what she had done. Had she gotten a little ball, perhaps a ring or maybe a little bar? He had to fight against every impulse of his body demanding he discover just what Patton had hidden between her legs.

"Enough? Given your 'I know everything' attitude, I'm assuming you're upset about more than just a piercing. So, what else is eating at you?"

"Don't, Patton," Slade warned her, speaking when Chase could not. "You've told enough lies these past four years to set a record. I thought we raised you better than that."

Chapter 3

"Don't try to guilt me, Slade."

It might be time for the truth, but there would be no weeping, pleading or playing the bad little girl for them. She had accomplished something great in the last four years, something better than a college degree.

She had single handedly built her business from the ground up. At twenty-three she had accomplished a lot, becoming financially independent, securing her future. The Davis brothers weren't going to make her feel guilty for that.

"You forced me into lying to you. I told you four years ago that I didn't want to go to college. Did you listen to me? No."

"So, you're admitting you're not in college." Finally a hint of anger, a tinge of aggression seeped into Slade's tone. "You've been lying to us all this time."

"Technically you never asked if I was *in* school. You just asked about school," Patton corrected.

"Don't," Chase snarled, drawing her attention back to him. His jaw clenched so tight it amazed her he didn't break a tooth. If she had been a man, he'd have already hit her by now. "Don't try to manipulate this and don't think I'm going to let you get away with blaming us for your deceptions."

She should have taken Casey's earlier question more seriously. The truth be told, she didn't have an answer. Every time she'd thought about telling the truth, doom and death had come to mind. Now the time had come and she had to do or say something.

Changing the past was impossible and she wouldn't do it if she could. She'd made her decision. It had been the right one. Patton didn't feel guilt over that. The only thing that bothered her was having deceived them and having stolen from them.

Without a word, Patton walked back over to the couch and picked up her purse. Pulling out her personal checkbook, she headed to the desk for a pen.

"What are you doing?" Devin finally joined the conversation.

"I'm writing you a check." Patton bent over to do just that.

"This isn't about money. You lied to us, deceived us."

"I know." She ripped the check from the book and flipped to the register as she continued speaking. "I'm a grown woman. That's something you don't want to see me as. I made the mistake of pretending to be what you wanted so that you would be happy, but that's over now."

Patton straightened and slapped the check against Chase's chest. "That's a hundred grand. Should reimburse you with some interest."

"It's not about the money," Chase snarled, ignoring the check to snatch her wrist. "It's about the lying."

"What was I supposed to do? I told you I didn't want to go to college. You didn't want to listen to anything I had to say." Patton yanked her arm back, letting the check drop to the floor. "I found what I love to do and I am successful at it."

"Is that what happened? You found out you like having people take naked pictures of you as some diseased whore eats strawberries from your belly button?"

The words built up momentum, coming faster and louder. His red face contrasted with the purple vein throbbing angrily away from his temple.

"Naked pictures? I never took any naked pictures."

"We saw the website, Patton." That pearl came from Slade.

"If you are referring to the Barely There Creations website, I'm not naked in those pictures and Allen is a good friend."

"Allen?" Resentment laced Devin's tone. "Who the hell is this Allen?"

"A good friend," Patton repeated.

"How good?" Devin stepped forward.

"A *very* good friend." A very gay one too, but she wasn't about to let Devin dismiss Allen on that principle.

"Are you sleeping with him?" It sounded more like an accusation than a question.

"Oh, God's sake, Chase. I'm not about to go into the details of my sex life with you."

"What sex life?" Slade grabbed her arm this time, yanking her around to face him.

"That's none of your business," Patton retorted haughtily. They'd probably be ecstatic to know she had no sex life, but she'd never admit that to them.

"We're responsible for you."

"I'm legal in all fifty states, Chase. Your responsibility has ended."

"So that gives you the right to post pornographic pictures on the web where any scum with a hard-on can see your…" Chase stumbled again, looking too mad to get the words out.

"Get a grip, Chase." Patton tossed her hair as she scowled at him. "Nobody can see anything."

"They can see everything!"

"Please, some of the girls that you have out to your pool parties wear less and I don't see you complaining."

"They're not you."

"Oh, I see, so there is a special rule that says every other woman can flaunt her body but I got be covered from head to toe."

Chase took a threatening step toward her, but Slade interfered. He threw a hand onto Chase's chest, holding him back. Slade might have been more in control than Chase, but not by much. Patton could easily read the anger in his baby blues.

"Enough, Patton. You've managed to sidetrack this argument. The truth is that for over four years you have been lying to us. Would a grown woman do that?"

"You wouldn't have approved."

"We might not have, but an adult would have dealt with our objections."

"Objections?" Patton almost rolled her eyes at that. "You would have forced me to give it up."

"Forced? How can we force a grown woman?"

"You could have cut off the money I needed to start the business." Patton cringed inwardly. Slade had always the hardest to argue with all his rational points. She preferred just yelling with Chase than negotiating the landmines Slade laid out.

"You stole the money. You lied to us. You've put your body on display and mutilated it with piercings. It's as if you're a different person than who we thought you were, Patton."

"I'm just me, Slade," Patton whispered, hating the guilty feeling he forced her to experience. "I know I shouldn't have lied to you or taken the money, but, at the time, I didn't see any other way."

"It's been five years."

"Yeah, well," Patton faltered. Damn him, Slade made her feel as if she were twelve again.

"That's all you have to say?"

"What else is there to say?" Patton fell back on peevish, just as she always had as a kid.

"I'm sorry would be a good place to start."

"Shutting down the Internet site would be a better place," Devin muttered

"That's not in question. She's shutting down that today."

"But you're not, are you?" Slade cut across whatever response Patton had been about to shoot back at Chase. "You think you did what you had to. You would do it again."

Patton glared at Chase, hesitant to let his arrogant command pass without comment. She struggled for a moment, but finally managed to focus on Slade's question.

"Yeah. I'd do it again." Her chin tilted up. "I know you don't approve, but I love what I do. I'm having fun and making money. Isn't that what life is supposed to be about?"

"Having fun?" Chase snarled. "Is that what you call putting yourself on display? Consorting with half naked men? What other kind of fun have you been having, Patton? Drugs? Is that why you've changed?"

"You really don't think much of me, do you?"

"You really haven't given me any reason to."

"Well, for your edification, I don't do drugs. I go to parties, I work on my lingerie, meet with private clients, have a lot of laughs doing the shoots for the website and the catalog—"

"Catalog. You're in the catalog?" Chase's mouth fell open.

"Yeah, I'm in it with some other girls, and you know what, Chase? Half our clients are men who love the damn thing."

Oh, hell. Here it comes.

Patton knew her rash outburst had pushed them too far. All three men's expressions hardened with something more than just anger. It looked like rage, furious, murderous, jealous driven rage.

* * * *

"Move, Slade." Chase shoved at his arm.

"Maybe you should take a breath, Chase," Slade suggested, knowing what the look in Chase's eyes meant. "You don't want to do anything you'll regret."

"Get out of my way."

Slade knew better than push Chase even further over the cliff than his older brother had already fallen so he moved. A second later

Chase had Patton flung over his shoulder like a sack of feed. Patton's screams and curses, kicking and hitting, all to no effect.

Turning on his heel, Chase stormed out of the study leaving Devin and him to listen as Chase's heavy footsteps ascend the stairs to the second level and the bedrooms beyond.

"What do you think he's going to do to her?" Devin asked as they heard a bedroom door slam.

"Hopefully nothing we'll all regret later." Slade's response sounded pained. He didn't know if he'd regret whatever Chase did, but he didn't want that for Patton.

"If he touches her…" Devin's voice trailed off.

Just thinking about what it would mean made his dick harden even more than it already was. God, if Chase touched her, then Slade would finally be able to put to ease the fire that had grown to a constant ache in his body whenever Patton came around, hell even when she wasn't around.

When was the last time he had sex with a woman and hadn't imagined it was Patton? That wasn't the worst part. The worst part was knowing all he'd ever have for the rest of his life was nothing more than a fantasy.

He struggled to believe that once she settled down and married some other man, he'd be free. Perhaps he'd find a woman that fired his blood as she did. In his heart, he recognized the lie. There was only one Patton.

"I'm not sure what I want to have happen."

"What are you saying, Devin?" Slade scowled at his younger brother.

"Foolish thoughts," Devin sighed.

"We agreed, Devin, none of us touches her."

"And what if it's what she wants?" Devin swallowed, but it didn't disguise the hope in his tone. "She is obviously not as innocent as we thought. Who is to say she would object?"

"She's too young to know what she wants." Slade looked away, fighting the temptation of Devin's words. He'd been waging that battle a million times a minute since seeing the catalog. "Don't say that."

"Why?" Devin scowled angrily at him and Slade could read the pain in his gaze. It might be cruel, but Slade had to shatter Devin's hope. No good could come from catering to his younger brother's false hope. "Why can't the decision be hers?"

"Because no matter what she thinks she knows, she isn't prepared to be claimed by us." Slade glared back at Devin. "And you know it."

* * * *

Chase barely held his temper in check as he dumped Patton on the bed. He didn't know what he was doing anymore. All he knew was that her flippant comment about all those men staring at her nearly naked body had blinded him with rage.

It had triggered a primitive, completely feral response in him, one that demanded he punish his woman for her lack of decorum. Her body was for his brothers and him alone. It was not to be shared with others.

But how to punish her?

Strip her naked and put her over my knee for the spanking she so roundly deserves. Then fuck her until she agrees to anything I say.

Chase walked a fine line, inches away from giving his demanding cock just what it begged for. It helped that Slade and Devin hadn't followed him. In his heart he knew he couldn't claim her without them present, but damn if he didn't want to.

He stepped back, hoping the distance would give him the precious control he needed. It didn't. Instead it gave him an eyeful of the hottest spitfire he'd ever wanted to tame.

Her breasts heaved with her fury as she scrambled off the bed. Those amazing navy eyes flashed with blue lightning, warning him that she'd worked up a good mad.

Chase clenched his hands to stop from reaching out to her. Very slowly, reminding himself with every step that this young, beautiful woman was off limits, he advanced on her. She matched his every measured step forward with a step backward.

* * * *

"How dare you treat me as some errant child," Patton spat. "I'm not one of your cheap bimbos who gets all hot and bothered over your Neanderthal routine."

Okay, she lied. The aggression in Chase's action intended to intimidate. Patton wondered what he would think if he knew instead he turned her on. She didn't think she was the only one either. From his nearly black gaze to the bulge in his pants, Patton could tell he was just aroused as her.

Patton wondered if she could get him to do anything with the erection making itself obvious. Given how twisted up everything had become, it just might be possible. He just needed to be pushed past the limits of his control. She had just the thing.

"What's wrong, Chase? Didn't you like the pictures?"

"They are pornographic," Chase snarled. "You're better than that."

"Actually given the number of subscribers we have for the catalog, I don't know how I could be better. They especially love the pictures with the motorcycle. What did you think of those?"

"Don't push me, Patton. You wouldn't like the results," Chase warned her.

"Well, if I'm damned anyway, I guess I might as well fess up to everything and let you know that's my bike."

That news struck him hard if the way he came to a sudden stop was any indication. "No."

"No?" Patton forced a smile. "Yes, it is. I have the key right here in my purse."

"Give it to me."

She ignored his demand. "I had to rent a car just to drive down here."

"Give me the keys, Patton." He took a step forward that she matched with a step back.

"I always wanted a bike. When I finally had enough spending money, the first thing I bought was that bike."

"Now, Patton!"

"I won't." Patton raised her chin up defiantly.

"You will."

"You can't make me."

"Wanna bet?"

She'd come even with the bathroom door when an idea hit her. She moved her purse protectively behind her and gave him a slight smile.

"I'm not giving you anything. You want it, you'll have to take it."

"Don't, Patton."

"Don't what? You're not really going to spank me."

With that, he lunged at her. He moved fast, but Patton reacted faster. She managed to slam the bathroom door and throw the lock before he could shove it back open.

Chapter 4

Patton ignored Chase pounding on the door. She worked fast, knowing the bathroom door wouldn't hold for long. Upending her purse on the counter, she snatched up her key ring and wiggled the bike key off. She'd barely managed to secure the key in its hiding place when the bathroom door splintered open and Chase stormed in.

It wouldn't surprise her to see steam coming out of his ears. He looked that enraged. His eyes surveyed the litter on the countertop before narrowing back on her. Patton felt the moisture leaking out of her pussy kicking into high gear as he raked his eyes up and down her body.

"Where is the key, Patton?"

He asked the question, but as his eyes stayed fixed on her, Patton suspected Chase already knew where he had to look. For the first time, a doubt whispered through her.

Stupid, stupid girl. Do I even know what I am doing? Am I really prepared for what he is about to do to me?

"I hid it."

"Give it to me."

"Come and get it."

Chase didn't need any more of an invitation than that. Patton shrieked when he snatched her up by the waist and threw her over his shoulder. She should have been screaming, kicking, fighting for her release. Instead, amazingly, he heard her giggle.

He knew in that instant he'd been played. Played by Patton. His sweet, innocent Patton played grown-up games now. She had to pay for that. Only one punishment seemed appropriate. He hoped that when it came time, he'd be able to stop.

He tossed Patton onto the bed. Her hair fanned out as she bounced to a stop. He could see by the rapid rise and fall of her breasts that her breathing had accelerated, her heart pounding faster now. Her nipples hardened under his gaze as he raked his eyes down her body, giving her every indication of what he intended.

"This is your last chance, Patton." He watched her eyes darkened more at the sound of his roughened voice. "If we go down this road, I promise you, you won't like where it ends."

Patton's crossed her arms beneath her breasts and tilted her chin up in response. Chase clenched his jaw against the image she made. Her auburn hair a beautiful wave of fire across the rumpled bed sheet. Her navy eyes near black with wild shards of pure energy crackling through them. The hem of her long skirt crumpled up, revealing smooth, tanned legs.

Chase shook his head, ridding it of the more perverse thoughts that clamored to take control. *Punishment,* he silently repeated the word to himself. He couldn't let his control slip for a second. If he did, then there would be no stopping him. No pleading on her part would save her from her fate.

Would she plead? Maybe not now, not here with just him. Later on when Slade and Devin joined in, she'd realize her mistake. Then it would be too late. They would bring her pleasure and take their own, but at what cost?

"You scared, cowboy?" Patton's smug smile tested his resolve. "Because you don't look too sure if you're up to the challenge of finding the key."

Her smiled dipped when he lifted one knee up and pushed her legs open as he came over her on the bed. As he grabbed both her hands in his own, the tempting curl of her lips faded completely away.

He had to pull her arms out from under her breasts and made sure the backs of his hands rubbed against the soft undersides of her globes. The slight touch made her jerk, her nipples furling into even tighter points revealed by the sheer fabric of her shirt.

Chase bit back a moan and stilled while he fought the urge to guide his hand over her swollen flesh and under the edge of her turtleneck to touch her skin to skin. That way laid doom.

He had to keep to his plan. With that thought and a fortifying breath, he straightened her arms over her head. His big calloused thumbs began rubbing circles in her tender palms, teaching her that she was sensitive even there. She learned the lesson, he was assured by the way she twisted into his touch, her legs falling open.

With gentle firmness, his hands slid slowly down her arms. Chase watched as her eyes darkened more. A whimper, one he was sure she tried to hold back, escaped between her delectable parted lips. The sound drove the demon inside of him.

Again he forced himself to pause, to fight for control. His hands tightened around her forearms, holding steady despite the urge to rip her shirt out of the way and bare her to his gaze, his touch, and his kiss.

Slowly, moron, this is punishment. Punishment.

Chase chanted that word repeatedly, silently to himself. After a long, tense moment he managed to rein in his more base desires, just barely bringing himself back under control to continue the slow, sensual glide of his hands down her sides, enjoying the feel of her stomach muscles quivering beneath his touch.

Hooking his thumbs under the edge of her shirt, he indulged in the feel of her soft flesh beneath his hands. Her skin felt like the finest of silks. Chase smiled inwardly at the thought.

The only silk he'd ever felt was a pair of boxers an ex had bought for him a long time back. Those damn boxers had felt so good against his balls they'd kept him constantly hard, though not nearly as hard as touching Patton made him.

The tips of his fingers began to slip under the edge of her top, pushing it up and out of his way. He teased the sides of her breasts, holding back a groan when he saw the skimpy, see through fabric barely holding back her lush globes. Thankfully, they were piercing free. Chase couldn't have handled a surprise like that.

Patton sucked in an audible breath when his fingertips brushed against the pebbled ridge of her nipples, sending visible shocks streaking through her body that had her arching up into his touch. Her stomach muscles trembled and he smelled the spicy sent of feminine arousal in the air.

* * * *

All thoughts of teasing Chase into losing control disappeared as his hands continued their gentle exploration. Others had played with her breasts, pawing and sucking on them, but none of those experiences prepared her for the feel of Chase's slow progression over them. She was in agony feeling his hands where she wanted them, but not doing the things she wanted done.

"Please."

"Please what, Patton?" Chase's rough and rusty voice caressed her in ways a simple touch couldn't.

"Touch me." Patton's hands came to cover his, forcing them to pinch and roll her nipples as she thrust them harder into his palms.

The show demand must have broken his resistance. As if of their own violation, his hands began moving, teaching her new ways to enjoy his touch.

She jerked, letting out a harsh cry as he began to use the flat of his palm to roll her nipples, over and over, faster and faster. One of her hands shot up, entwining in his hair and jerking him hard down toward her breasts.

He didn't resist the invitation. His tongue sneaked out for a lick— a taste, one quick taste, and then another longer one that soon escalated into a devouring. When he sucked the hard nub through his teeth into his mouth she cried out, her hand tightening in his hair as her body began to writhe with need.

He drove her insane, Patton thought as she panted for breath. He sucked on her, nibbled at her with those hard teeth, and what he did with his tongue, twirling and licking the sensitive tips had her eyes rolling back into her head.

He went from breast to breast, tormenting her as his hand shoved her skirt up past her knees. His motions, no longer smooth and controlled, had become rough and hurried, sending thrills racing through her and making her muscles contract and quiver.

Her legs wrapped around his hips. Patton ground herself against the thick length of his erection, impatient for the feel of hardness against her aching softness. The rough fabric of his jeans cut through the flimsy lace of her panties, biting into her clit, tweaking her piercing and making her cry out as she moved faster, harder against him.

* * * *

Chase felt the heat of her desire through his jeans. The smell of her arousal drugged him. Goddamn, if she wanted to be stroked to an orgasm, it would be by his hand.

He slid his hand under the elastic edge of her panties. When his hand met with the smooth, soft flesh of her bare cunt, Chase sucked in a hard breath and fought the need to unzip and slam into her tight pussy with all his strength.

He desperately tried to regain control. Patton ruined the attempt when she tilted her hips, trying to force his hand lower as she begged.

"Please touch me."

Chase lost it again. He plunged his hand down, slipping two fingers into her tight channel as his thumb stroked up to tease her clit. The smooth feel of a little metal bar dangling from her clit had him matching her moan.

Rolling the bar with his thumb, he matched the motion of his hand on her breasts, swirling both sensitive buds in motion. He sucked her other tit, scraping his teeth along it in rhythm with the fingers plunging into her sopping wet cunt.

"Fuck me, Chase," Patton screamed. "Fuck me now!"

"Are you sure, Patton?" Chase asked raggedly, barely able to catch his breath at the beautiful sight of Patton flushed with passion beneath him.

"For the love of God, I need you, Chase."

Chase stared down at her as he slowly moved his hands over her hips. A part of him knew this was wrong, that he should stop. He couldn't fuck Patton, but this girl wasn't the Patton he knew. She was the one from his dreams and fantasies with her auburn hair wild, her eyes black with lust, her skin pink with desire, her breasts heaving while her pussy wept, wept for him.

He wrapped his fingers around the edge of her panties intent on ripping the material from her body. Seconds from claiming the woman of his dreams, he felt the cold touch of metal and the hard slam of reality. Looking he saw a key wrapped around the elastic string of her panties, nestled against the flare of her hips.

The glint of the silver brought him back to the moment. He hadn't dragged Patton to this room for sex. He brought her here because she'd lied to them, deceived them and stolen money. She'd put her body on display and bought that damn motorcycle.

Don't stop now, his dick screamed at him.

No! Chase shook his head, trying to block out the painful, throbbing demands of his cock. His fingers gripped the key, pulling it free to use as a magical salve to his insanity.

Chase threw himself off her, knowing that in another second his mind would lose the war with his dick. Then he'd rip Patton's panties off and give her the fucking she begged for. Before night fell she'd find herself shared, getting fucked by both Slade and Devin, separately, together, tied up, anyway they wanted it, whenever they wanted it.

That was what it would mean to claim her and Patton just didn't understand that fact.

Patton sat up, spitting fire. "Where the hell do you think you're going?"

Chase took a deep breath. He had to do something, say something to stop her from pursuing this, him or any of his brothers. Looking her square in the eyes and knowing he was about to hurt her, he told himself he did it for her own good.

"Consider yourself punished, Patton."

He made it out the door before she could respond. The second it clicked closed he heard her scream and something slam against the other side of the door. Taking in a deep breath of fresh air, Chase repeated that he had done the right thing no matter what his heart said.

Patton screamed, driven almost completely out of her mind. She felt as if her body was being stretched thinner and thinner. At any moment, she'd shatter into a million pieces. She wanted that release, needed it, and he'd left her.

When his hands slid out of her, she had delighted over the loss, anticipating something harder, thicker to soon replace it. When his weight had lifted off her, she'd opened her eyes to watch, wanting to see him as he undressed.

What had the coward done? He'd turned tail and ran, leaving her in a state of wild need. Well, if he thought she was going to take that without protest then the man was in for a rude awakening.

Patton didn't need him. She could handle this problem herself. When she did she'd be back to good and out for blood.

* * * *

Chase stood there unable to move as the door supported his weight. The part of him that had dreamed of this day, longed for it, wouldn't let him walk away so easily. The rational side told him he'd really screwed up.

He should never have touched her. Now the taste of her, the sight of breasts swollen with arousal, her naked pussy dripping wet and ready to be played with, eaten, fucked...

Oh, hell, don't think about that. Think about slugs in slime, shoveling shit, anything but watching as one of your brothers fucked her lovely little cunt.

Chase shook his head, trying to clear the images from his mind, but they refused to disappear. They were burned permanently into him.

His fingers, still sticky from Patton's juices, and knowing he should wipe them on his jeans, he couldn't stop himself from taking a taste, just one taste of the forbidden fruit. Chase closed his eyes as his fingers slid past his lips and the sweet and spicy taste of Patton imprinted itself forever on his taste buds.

He was doomed. Chase held his head in his hands knowing he had come out of the bedroom even more scared than when he went in. He knew that when Devin and Slade fucked other women they thought of Patton, because he did the same. It had been easy to close his eyes and see her in his mind, but now he had a gut deep feeling that time had past. Now he knew what she tasted like, looked like, felt like and there would be no fooling himself in the future.

The safe thing to do was to flee. The decent thing to do was to go back in and apologize. Either way he had to get Patton far, far away from his brothers and him. Forgiving her for everything and rushing her out of the house sounded like the best plan.

Chase took a deep breath and counted to ten before reaching for the doorknob. Concerned about more flying objects, Chase opened it cautiously and peeked in. He froze at the sight that greeted him.

Patton still lay on the bed, her legs splayed wide with her knees drawn up. The position gave him a perfect view of her hand working rapidly in and out of her pussy. He could hear the squishy sounds as she fucked herself. She gasped and writhed as she used her free hand to pull and pinch her nipples.

It was the most amazing sight he'd ever seen. As she neared her climax she got louder, her hand pistoning faster and faster into her pink, little cunt as her hips thrust up in rhythm to take her fingers as deep and hard as it could go.

Chase's eyes began to burn and water, reminding him to blink. He didn't want to, didn't want to lose the amazing sight of Patton pleasuring herself. Mesmerized, he remained rooted in his spot until she cried out and fell onto the bed shuddering.

Not trusting himself to do the right thing, Chase turned and fled. Slade stood in the doorway to the study, a question in his eyes. Chase ignored him, slamming out of the house and heading for his truck. He needed a drink, a drink and a woman, any damn woman. He needed the Cattleman's Club.

* * * *

Patton watched Chase's truck kick up dirt all the way down the long drive before disappearing around a curve in the pasture. Her fist curled as she accurately guessed where he was headed. Chase had made it clear. He didn't want her. He had gone to find a different woman to wear out his erection with.

Well, fine. Fuck him. It's not as if he's the only man whose cock gets hard.

She had waited a long time and turned down many opportunities in the delusional hope that one day the Davis brothers would be hers. It was clear that wasn't going to happen.

They all had their panties in a twist because of some racy pictures, when she knew for a fact that their kinks were way more bent than that. That hadn't stopped them from getting holier than thou with her.

Punish me, will he? I'll show that arrogant asshole.

Patton would be damned if she was just going to sit in her childhood bedroom as Chase went out there and fucked his way through the female population of Pittsfield. She'd show him, she'd show them all, they couldn't control her.

With that in mind, she righted her clothes, collected her purse and opened the window. It had been a long time since she had jumped out her old second story window, but it all came back to her with ease.

Chapter 5

Hailey couldn't stop laughing. It was either infectious or Patton had too much to drink because she joined in. It had taken her nearly an hour to walk to Hailey's house. Her childhood friend had been shocked to see her standing on the doorstep, but had agreed instantly to a trip into Dothan for some much-needed clothes shopping.

Patton had left her suitcase full of clothes in the foyer of the Davis brothers' house and damn if she was going back there. Besides she hadn't packed much of the real Patton into the bag, just one outfit, a pair of leather pants and a nice tight sweater to go with it.

She'd spent a bundle buying a new wardrobe filled with her favorite types of clothes, tight, short and sexy. That perfectly described the sundress she'd changed into before they'd left the mall. None of it had shocked Hailey who knew all about Patton's secret life. Just like Casey, Hailey knew all the dirty details of Patton's predicament with Chase, Slade and Devin.

Unlike Casey, Hailey didn't root for her to go for it. Hailey didn't care much for Patton's self-appointed guardians. That probably had a lot to do with the brothers' habit of playing big brother to Hailey who already had her own older brothers to deal with.

Brett and Mike, the twins from hell, had long ago left town for a life of seeing the world with the marines. They'd asked the Davis boys to "keep an eye" on their kid sister. They took the role seriously, a little too seriously as far as Hailey was a concerned.

The two women had bought all the necessities for makeovers and a pizza before returning to Hailey's house for some much needed girl time. That had been three hours and almost a whole twelve-pack ago.

Now they stretched out on the loungers in Hailey's backyard, letting their toenails dry while they stared up at the stars.

"Now, you know when a man walks in on you fucking yourself and doesn't offer you a hand that he's not interested."

"I don't know." Hailey still hadn't stopped giggling. "Maybe it has something to do with him being your brother."

"Don't start with that crap. Chase is not even my step-brother," Patton corrected quickly. "We're not related."

"Technically, but he probably still thinks of himself as your protector." Hailey belched after making that declaration. "They're not related to me either, but they still manage to drive me insane with their pompous attitude."

"Pompous." Patton snickered. "I'd say it was more as if it were a God complex. They think they rule the world and we should be happy to be allowed into their kingdom."

"They treat us as if we're still eight."

"Eight-year-olds don't have boobs like these." Patton pointed to her chest.

"Some do. Some of them fashion cover models aren't old enough to drive. Of course, most of them probably aren't virgins by the time they start to drive."

"Gee, thanks, Hailey." Patton gave her friend an insincere smile. "Make me feel better, why don't you?"

"Hey, don't whine to me. You don't have to be a virgin. You could have had the whole alphabet from Adam to Zack if you wanted by now."

"I'm waiting for the right man." Patton began to pick at the label on her bottle, venting her annoyance on the stubborn sticker.

"Technically three men, which makes you the sluttiest virgin I've ever heard of."

"I love Chase, Slade and Devin, but if it isn't to be, I guess I'll find myself three other hunks to gang bang me. God knows there are enough ripped men running around Atlanta to scratch any kind of itch."

"Really? Then why haven't you?"

Patton's shoulders slumped. "I guess I just wanted to be in love with a guy before we had sex."

"That's sweet."

"It's stupid."

"No, it isn't. Following three men around like a love sick puppy when all they do is pat you on the head and tell you 'good, girl', that's stupid."

"I do not follow them around like a puppy."

"Please, spare me. You're the strongest, hard-willed woman I know, but when it comes to the Davis brothers, you turn into some weak, little woman, doing whatever they want, whatever they say."

"I do not!"

"Yeah? So you regularly wear skirts that come down to your ankles and turtle necks all the way up to your chin?"

"Screw you, Hailey."

"Let me ask you this, if it had been any other man than Chase, what would you have done to him for walking out on you like he did today?"

She would have tracked his ass down, pinned him to the wall and ripped him a new one. She might have gone to an adult toy store and bought a pump to send him with a too sweet note apologizing for not recognizing his problem. All sorts of vindictive, mean spirited ideas came to mind.

"That's what I thought."

"I didn't say anything."

"You didn't have to. Your expression said it all. You would have hurt and humiliated the bastard, but what did you do with Chase? Jumped out a window and ran away. Why don't you just keep on running, Patton? Run all the way back to Atlanta, to the life you built there and just admit defeat."

Admit defeat? Never.

* * * *

Both girls were too involved in their conversation to notice Devin moving past the open garden gate or see his head appearing briefly before he ducked back out of sight. Still thinking that they were alone, their conversation went on uncensored.

Devin closed his eyes and banged his head against the fence. He didn't need to hear this. From finding out that she was a virgin, to knowing that she wanted not just one, but all three of them to make her a woman, it was just too much.

The idea that she intended to give up, go to looking for three other men to take her innocence made his blood boil. He didn't direct his anger at Patton though. He aimed it at his two hardheaded brothers for putting them all in this situation.

Patton had been right when she said that they weren't her brothers. They weren't, not by blood, not by marriage, not by law. They were her self-appointed guardians, nothing more.

It had started seventeen years ago. Charley Jones, Patton's father, had worked on the Davis ranch as foreman for as long as anybody could remember. Charley had been best friends with Devin's dad, Mitch.

When Charley's wife just left one day, Devin's mother had pretty much assumed the role of looking after Patton while Charley worked out in the fields. For a mother of three boys, it had been Devin's mom's dream come true to have a little girl to teach to sew and cook.

Then one night, Charley and Mitch had drunk a little too much and gotten into a fight. When the men had been separated, Charley lay dead on the floor from a puncture to the heart. Mitch had delivered the wound with the knife he always wore strapped to his thigh.

Whatever happened between Mitch and Charley, nobody knew. Mitch had never explained and Charley couldn't. As the cops had walked Mitch out, he had turned to his wife and asked that she look after Patton.

The little six-year-old had moved into the Davis farmhouse and driven Devin insane with her silliness. He had been ten and wanted to be out riding the horses and tending the cattle with his older brothers. Instead, he'd been stuck playing with the pesky little girl.

Forced to play everything from Barbie to dress up, over the years, their relationship had grown from antagonistic to close. When Patton had started to develop, Devin had taken notice. If it hadn't been for Chase and Slade threatening him, he'd have done something about it, too.

Chase and Slade saw her as their little girl lost. They'd played the role of protector to her for so long, they'd refused to accept the notion of her as woman. Slade had always been there helping her with her homework, teaching her how to ride horses and drive a car. Chase had been the father figure, setting curfews and enforcing the rules of the house.

Patton's voice broke through Devin's thoughts. "I refuse to admit defeat."

"Then you're going to die a virgin."

"Maybe that's the problem."

"That's what I've been telling you."

"No, I mean. Maybe if I had some experience, it would help me figure out how to seduce Chase, Slade and Devin."

"It's like watching a horse beat its head into a stall door."

"I'm serious. What I need is a throw away guy."

"A throw away guy?"

"Yeah, a friend with benefits."

"That's never going to work."

"Why not?"

"Because you're not the type of woman."

"I could be."

"You'll fall in love and then be in a worse spot for loving four men."

"Are you going to help or sit there and make pithy little remarks?"

"Fine, you want a throw away guy, I know just the man."

"You do?"

"Trust me on this one. I'll give him a call and we'll get that cherry popped before the end of the week."

Devin took that cue to end this party. He needed to get Patton back home before Chase got there and realized she'd slipped out on him. When he and Slade found out she'd disappeared from her room, they had thought she'd be back before dark.

Then the sun went down and the brothers started to worry. Neither knew what had happened between Chase and Patton, but they knew what Chase would do if he learned about her escape.

Slade had gone off to the club to make sure Chase stayed out while Devin hunted Patton down. Not that it had been hard to find her. There weren't many places in Pittsfield where she could go. Hailey's had been the first on his list.

"Does this hunk come with friends? You know after all these years of fantasizing about being taken by three men at once, I'm not sure only one will do."

"Excuse me," Devin spoke louder than necessary. "It's time to come home, Patton."

His sudden appearance didn't get so much as a squeak of surprise from the two women. They both turned rounded, glazed eyes on him. The empty beer bottles littered around the loungers told him all he needed to know.

"I'm not going anywhere with you, Devin Davis. I'm done with you and your bossy brothers." Patton waggled a finger at him.

"Is that right?" Devin sighed.

"That' right." Patton nodded. "I'm staying here."

"Is that what you think?" Devin didn't falter as he closed in on her.

"That's what I—" Patton's words ended in a shriek as Devin hoisted her over his shoulder. "Damn you, Devin! Put me down!"

"In just a moment, sweetheart." Devin paused long enough to tell Hailey goodnight before he carried his squiggling armload out of the yard and off to his truck.

* * * *

Patton sulked the whole way home, refusing to talk to Devin. She pointedly stared out into the blackness as he drove. As far as punishments went, this was the worst and Devin shifted in his seat uncomfortably.

So many things existed between them now. It went beyond just her deceptions over the past few years. Patton wanted him, wanted all three of them. How she knew that possibility even existed befuddled him. It didn't matter though.

No matter what she knew, she would still be ill prepared for the type of dominating, rough sex the brothers liked. It was time to explain a few facts of life to her. His brothers would probably kick his ass for telling her what he intended to. For that matter, given Patton's current mood, she might kick his ass too.

She slammed out of the truck the moment he pulled up the handbrake. He caught her as she went storming through the front door. She turned narrowed eyes on him and pointedly looked at his arm.

"Let me go, Devin."

"I think we need to talk."

"I don't want to talk to you." Patton tried yanking her arm free.

"Too bad." Devin tightened his hold. Before she could argue further, a sound drew both their attention toward the kitchen. Charlotte stood there, her eyes fuming as she stared at the couple.

"Charlotte, what are you doing here?"

Before the woman could speak, Patton answered for her, "She's waiting for one of her masters to fuck her, dumbass."

"Patton!"

"What? That's your collar on her, isn't it? She's your little pet, isn't she?"

"How did you—?"

"What? Do you think I don't know all your little secrets, Devin?" Patton turned on him. "Giving me shit about some racy pictures when you are getting paid to make women into sex slaves, talk about hypocritical.

"Speaking of which," Patton looked over at Charlotte. "Aren't you supposed to be out back in the barn, all tied up and waiting for your masters' orders? You must not have trained her right, Devin."

"That's enough, Patton." Devin shoved her toward the study. "Get into the study now."

"Boy, I'm not your servant to boss around." Patton turned on him, her hands going to her hips.

"Don't test me, Patton. You may not like the results," Devin growled.

* * * *

The words didn't give Patton pause, but Devin's tone did. He had always been the relaxed brother, quick with a smile and a joke. While she had gotten aroused watching him discipline women without mercy, he had never, not once, used that kind of tone on her.

A solid body of muscle backed the hard tone. Devin looked so good. His dark brown hair went a little wild, curling under the brim of his Stetson. Instead of detracting from his harsh tone, the slightly boyish charm of those stray tresses added to it.

They highlighted his blazing eyes and led her eyes to his lips pulled tight with displeasure, his hard jaw and down over his soft black t-shirt that hung to every ripple his well-muscled body.

Just the sight of him all tensed and ready for battle did funny things to her. Despite the weakening of her muscles, she didn't let anything show on her face. Turning she slammed into the study.

Hailey's comment about being a coward echoed through her head, making her tense with annoyance. The comment had irritated her more than normal, because she feared Hailey was right.

She'd gone out on a limb today with Chase and it had backfired horribly. The fear of failure, the urge to give up ate at the inside of her stomach making bile taste come to her mouth.

What she needed was a plan. That's how she built up her lingerie business. Plan, enact, succeed, had been her motto and it had served her well. She just needed to apply the same technique to luring the Davis brothers into her bed.

She needed a solid plan, something that had no risk of failure, like divide and conquer. The idea sprung to life inside her and her mind started whirling with how hard it would be to split the men up, who was the weakest.

The soft click of the study door closing had her twirling around to find Devin leaning against it. His eyes lit with a heat that Patton couldn't distinguish between anger or desire. The large erection pressing against his jeans indicated the latter.

"What was that all about, Patton?"

"What was what all about?" Patton gave him an innocent look, switching from anger to nonchalance in the determined attempt to keep him off balance.

"What you just said about Charlotte, about collars and training women to be sex slaves. Where did you come up with that idea?"

"Come up with it? I didn't come up with it. You guys did." Patton hoped her smile was seductive. "Or did you think I didn't know what goes on in the back barn?"

"You knew?" His tanned skin paled at that news.

"You guys went through great pains to keep me away from that barn. What do you think that did to a little girl like me, as nosey and curious as I am?"

"Jesus, Patton." Devin closed his eyes, his face twisted as if he were in pain. "Did you see a lot?"

"Enough." Patton sensed her advantage and moved in closer. "Enough to know that you like your women to submit to your every desire."

"Patton—"

"It made me hot, imagining that I was one of those women."

Without any warning, she pinned him against the door and did just that. Devin didn't put up any resistance. She thought he might be in shock. It didn't last long. In moments, he took over the kiss.

When Devin felt Patton's warm breath against his lips, he could resist temptation no more. Committing the shape of her lips to memory, Devin slowly, toughly traced the sensitive edges of her lips with the tip of his tongue until Patton murmured unintelligently and opened her mouth.

He'd been trying to go slow, to control the fiery burn of his blood, but when she deftly sucked his tongue into her mouth, all thoughts of gentleness stripped away. Repeatedly he plundered the sweet, moist depths of her mouth.

Patton was no voyeur in the play. Her tongue stroked his. She sucked his tongue until he thought his dick would burst through his pants trying to get to the feel of those lips on his hot, hardened flesh.

Devin didn't know when he moved. He only knew that suddenly Patton was pinned beneath him, her legs wrapping around his waist as she pushed herself up against the bulge of his erection. Even through his jeans, he could feel the heat of her wetness, smell her arousal filling the air and he knew that he had to have taste, just one taste.

He'd promised his brothers he wouldn't take Patton's innocence, but that was all. He could do other things, many things, things he hadn't promised not to do. As Devin began to kiss his way down her neck, slipping the straps of her dress aside to bare her breasts, he promised himself he'd stay in control.

Patton closed her eyes and groaned as she felt Devin's large, warm hands engulf her breasts. Those magical hands gently caressed their way up the sides of her breasts to the tips. Lightly at first and then with growing pressure, he toyed with her nipples, rolling, pinching, tugging on them until she cried out and arched her back begging for more.

His mouth, hot and wet, followed the trail of his hands. When those firm lips closed over the first peak, Patton couldn't stop the whimper of need that escaped. At first just his tongue toyed with her nipple, then his teeth slid down its sensitive edges before finally his entire mouth closed over her and he began to torment her in earnest.

Patton had never felt this hot and desperate before. She writhed and thrashed beneath him trying to get more of his touches, his kisses. As nice as his mouth felt on her breast she wanted it elsewhere, knew that she would do to get her wish as his hands roughly began to push up under her dress.

Her legs instinctively widened as his hands caressed their way up her thighs. By the time his knuckles scraped over her panties, they were soaked through with her cream. Patton gasped at the pleasure of his touch, thrusting her hips further, aching for a deeper touch.

"Please," she panted when he hesitated. "Touch me."

The plaintive plea appeared to have no effect as he stayed still. She didn't care, too consumed with her own need. The urge to touch blended with the need to be touch.

"No." Devin drew back. His hands closed over hers as she reached for his jeans zipper.

That one word had the effect of an entire bucket of ice being tossed over her. Patton froze, her mind reeling with the implications. She'd have rolled away, escaping him, but as if sensing the direction of her thoughts, Devin settled back down on her, pinning her to the floor with his superior weight.

"Let me go!" Patton twisted and bucked beneath him, desperate to escape the humiliation of the moment.

"Not 'til you listen to me." Devin didn't budge.

"I don't want to hear anything you have to say."

Two times in one day, a Davis brother had toyed with her affections and she had allowed it, begged for it. Any sane woman would consider murder.

Patton fought him, slapping at his shoulders until he grabbed both her wrists in one hand and held them high above her head. One of his rock hard knees split the seam of her own softer thighs, spreading them until he settled nicely between her legs. He had her good and truly stuck.

* * * *

It had been a test of Devin's control, the hardest one he had ever faced, to stop when all he wanted to do was strip her naked and fuck her right there on the study's floor. The only thing that had reeled him in was the distant voice whispering that she was a virgin.

Patton deserved more than to have her innocence taken by a quick rut. She deserved more than anything he could honestly offer, but that fact didn't dissuade him. He'd give her as much as she could take and let her decide what she wanted.

Patton had said she'd seen what they were capable, indicated it had turned her on, but that wasn't the same thing as wanting it. Nobody could know if they enjoyed submission without trying it first.

"Are you ready to listen to me?" Devin asked the panting woman underneath him.

"Go to hell."

"I'll take that as a yes."

"Take it anyway you want. Just get off me."

"You say you know about what Chase, Slade and I are into, but you don't have any real experience do you, Patton?"

"I have tons of experience! Years of it!" Patton spat. "I've fucked so many guys, I've forgotten their names."

"You're lying, Patton. I heard you talking to Hailey. I know you're a virgin."

"Go screw yourself, Devin."

"Not 'til I tell you the truth. First about the barn and the women, you're right. We did train women there. The farm hadn't been in the greatest financial position after Mom died. Chase had several military friends who knew women from other countries who wanted to come here."

Patton froze. "You're not talking about the human slave markets, are you?"

"No." Devin scowled, offended by the idea. "You know Chase would never force a woman. These women already...used their bodies to get what they wanted. They were willing, but when they came here, they wanted to...fine-tune their skills.

"So, they paid Chase and eventually Slade and me to get those skills. It was a very lucrative arrangement for all parties." Devin paused, letting her digest what he'd just explained.

He knew it was a lot for her to take in. In Patton's life, the brothers had always tried to be gentle, loving, supportive, whatever she needed. Even if she'd grown up to see them as men, her view of them was still colored by the past. None of them could afford that kind of delusion anymore.

"So, do you guys still..." Patton's voice wavered for a moment.

"Train women?" Devin didn't exactly know how to explain about the Cattleman's Club. It was best not to try. Devin ducked the direct question. "The barn is still set up as a...toy house. Everything we need to train or entertain women is in there, from harnesses to ties to sex toys."

"I see."

"We kept it from you to protect you."

"Spare me your moral high ground." Patton sneered. "Are we done? Because if we are, then get off me."

"No, we're not done. You need to understand."

"Understand what? I understand you have your little toy room and your little plaything waiting. You don't need me."

"Damn it. Listen to me." Devin tensed again as she began to struggle once more in his hold. He waited until she settled back down, accepting the futility of her circumstance. "Are you ready to listen?"

"Say what you have to say."

"Those women never meant anything to us. None of them ever will. We—"

"Not even Charlotte?" Patton interrupted. Her annoyance obvious in her tone, but Devin could also see the hurt shadowing the bright light of anger in her eyes. It bothered him as nothing else could have.

"Not even her."

"Bullshit. You put a collar on her. I may not know much about the world of domination, but I know what that means. You claimed her."

"Not permanently, we didn't. That's why she's so mad."

"Whatever." Patton's tone told him clearly enough that she didn't believe him for a moment.

"It's not a whatever," Devin snapped back. "Charlotte knows the truth."

"What truth? That you're lying dirt bags that rut with any willing woman?"

Chapter 6

Devin ground his teeth together and closed his eyes. He would not let her antagonize him into a rage. What he had to say was too important for him to be sidetracked now. Oh, but he was tempted.

Devin began after a deep breath. "Way back when you were seventeen, you dated a guy named Bo. Remember him?"

"Of course."

"You remember that night you got busted making out with him by the sheriff's deputy and he brought you home?"

"How could I forget? Chase grounded me for three months, that hypocritical bastard."

"Yeah, he got mad. We all did. It concerned us that you might be…sleeping with Bo and we didn't like that fact. More than didn't like it, hated it in a way that made us want to hurt him."

"Bo?" Patton scowled at him with that look she normally reserved for Chase. The one that said he was clearly overreacting. "You wanted to hurt him? You three guys against a scrawny sixteen-year-old doesn't exactly seem fair."

"Yeah, we wanted to pound him into the ground and that's when we realized that our feelings went beyond the matter of just being the protective guardians. It became impossible for us to deny any longer that we wanted you."

"You have a funny way of showing it," Patton snapped. "I keep hearing no."

"That's because we want to protect you."

"From what?"

"From our lifestyle. You—"

"Why?"

"Why?" Devin paused. He was genuinely confused by the question.

"Yeah, why? If what you do isn't wrong, doesn't hurt those women, why would you need to protect me from being one of them?"

"Because they knew what they wanted. You're just an innocent girl. We want you to have a normal life, to get married and have kids and a husband who adored you. A normal life with one husband, not three who had perverted you to their own ends."

"I see." He could hear the faint grind of her teeth as she clenched her jaw for a moment, obviously fighting back the urge to rip him apart. "So you decide now what is normal? What is best for me? I don't have any rights, any choices in the matter?"

"Not then, but now—"

"Now what?"

"Now I'm going to tell you about the pact Chase, Slade and I made that night after the deputy brought you home."

"The pact?" Patton rolled her eyes. "You guys really are drama queens."

"You have to understand, Patton, that we all love you, want you, to the point where if only one of us had you it would destroy all of us."

"Then I guess you better get off me before Chase and Slade end up killing you."

Again he ignored her attempt to entice him into a different argument, one he knew she thought she could control. "We couldn't let that happen and we agreed that if any of one of us took you to bed, we would all claim you. Chase would marry you, but you'd be wife to all of us."

"You agreed." The laugh that he got sounded a little too close to hysterical for Devin's comfort. "You three got together and made a decision about my future? A little arrogant, isn't it? A little presumptuous? What if I don't want to marry you and I just want to fuck you? Hmm? What then?"

"It doesn't work that way, Patton." Devin didn't flinch under her murderous glare. "So you consider your next course of action real well because we'll love you, adore you and rule you."

"Rule me. Jesus. You seriously think you could ever pull that off?"

"A lot of strong women like to be dominated, Patton. Don't knock it if you haven't tried it."

"Try it? What are you going to do? Lend me out to some pervert to give me a lesson?"

She was pushing, but Devin refused to snap. "No."

* * * *

With a suddenness that shocked her, Devin rolled aside and stood up. She blinked for a moment before her mind kicked in and she scrambled to her feet. With jerky movements, she righted her dress while Devin patiently waited.

"Come on." He held out his hand.

"What?" She didn't move, too surprised at the change in his demeanor. "Where?"

"Come here, Patton." Devin kept his hand out expectantly.

"No." She dug her heels in, crossing her arms beneath her breasts. "I'm not going anywhere with you."

Devin gave a long-suffering sigh. He moved with a quickness that caught her totally off guard. One moment she stood on her own legs and the next she was lifted into the air again. This was getting annoying.

"What the hell are you doing?"

"Taking you to the barn." He sounded decidedly cheery about that fact.

"Put me down now or I'll scream for Slade and Chase," she snarled, curling her fist to pummel his back with greater force.

"Wouldn't do you any good. They're not here."

"Stop this now, Devin." She became more panicked as he shouldered his way out the kitchen door.

"Hush up, sweetheart." His hand that had been holding her secure across the buttocks gave her a little pat that had her growling. "We're almost there."

"Damnit, Devin! You can't do this to me!"

"Why not? You do want us to fuck you, don't you?"

Yes, she did. She had dreamed of this moment, but now that it was here, Patton was having some serious issues. In theory this moment was supposed to be filled with thrills and excitement, not fear and anxiety. Devin's next comment didn't help her condition one bit.

"Don't worry, sweetheart. I'm not going to fuck you. I'm just going to train you to fuck." His still cheery tone ramped up her nerves. What had she gotten herself into?

"Ah, here we are."

Patton's stomach tied itself into knots. She had pushed for this, fantasized about this, but now that he carried her into the darkened confines of the small barn, she wished she'd considered the matter a little more seriously.

It was too late. Devin carried her straight through the unused barn to the room in the back. From her upside down position, Patton could see the glint of metal and the warm hues of wood as Devin snapped on the light. She'd seen all the things in the small room, but from the outside.

The hooks embedded in the ceiling and walls with their rope ties and pulley system seemed more menacing from this side. So did the large wardrobe where Patton knew they kept a wealth of toys stored.

Devin dropped her unceremoniously on the well-kept bed in the back. The rings on the four posts with ties were attached to the spindles of the headboard. Patton knew exactly what they used them for.

Dumbfounded she watched as he closed up the door, padlocking it from the inside. Belatedly she scrambled off the bed, realizing exactly where he had placed her and what he intended. She needed a little more time to think about this, needed him to be less like the man she spied on and more like the man she'd fallen in love with. The ache to have Devin soothe her was nearly painful, but as he swirled the dial on the combination lock and turned back toward her, Patton knew she was no longer dealing with the Devin she knew.

When Devin turned around to find Patton still standing there, glaring at him from the darkened corner, he had to hold back a smile. The little innocent still thought she could bluster her way out of this situation. That was fine. He'd be glad to straighten her out.

"What the hell do you think you're doing?" Her attempt at an indignant tone failed horribly.

"Giving you a sample."

"You're kidding. You're not…"

"But I am," Devin assured her and watched the shiver race down her body in response. It was a better response than he could have hoped for. "Now, I put you on that bed and you are to remain where I put you."

"You can't be serious." Patton winced and he knew the reason. Her breathy voice held the sound of desire despite the words.

"Can't I?" He moved toward her, holding himself tall and tense to maintain the image of a man in complete control.

"But you said that you couldn't fuck me because of the pact."

"Oh, but there are so many other things we can and will do besides fucking, sweetheart. Now, on the bed."

"I'm not one of your playthings to be ordered about."

"But you are my plaything for tonight," he corrected. "And as such you should be aware that there are consequences for disobedience."

"Consequences?" she strangled on the word, her voice cracking.

"Punishment," Devin clarified. "I believe that Chase introduced you to the concept earlier today. Of course, he let you off easy by leaving you unbound so you could masturbate away your unfilled desires. I'm not going to be so lenient."

Patton paled at his words. "How did you…"

"Know that you masturbated?" At her weak nod, he smiled. "Because I overheard you talking to Hailey. I must admit that I envy him the sight of your beautiful legs opened wide, your pink little pussy glistening with desire as you pleasured yourself to orgasm. Tell me, did you use a toy, or those skinny little fingers?"

"That's none of your business."

"That's another punishment you've earned."

"You are seriously deluded if you think I'm going to tell you how I masturbate."

"Why? Chase will tell me."

At her strangled shriek, he knew that he'd embarrassed her. The hitch and then the sound of her breathing faster told him that wasn't all his words had done.

Devin knew women well enough to recognize the signs of desire. It was part of being a competent master to be able to read a woman's body and know what she needed. Embarrassment aside, his words, the image they inspired in her mind, made her hot.

"Don't be embarrassed, little one." He caressed her hot cheek, feeling her labored breath against him palm. "I can assure you that if you do decide to let us claim you, you will be putting on many shows for our entertainment. There's just something about watching a woman pleasure herself that makes a man ache to fuck her."

"I wouldn't do that," she whispered.

"But you like it, the idea of us watching you." Devin leaned down until his lips almost touched her own. "Don't you, Patton?"

"I…I…"

She couldn't think of an answer. The idea made her ache with a strange desire to comply, but she couldn't tell him that. Not under these circumstances. He just might ask her for a show. Then what would she do?

"Chase shouldn't tell you anything."

"Why not? We have no secrets from each other." Devin began to slowly rub her trembling lips. The gentle, teasing caress was at odds with his words. "He'll tell Slade and me everything. Tomorrow I tell Chase and Slade about tonight."

"You wouldn't."

"Of course I would and I will." Devin's hands slid down her neck to rest on her madly beating pulse.

"That's not very gentlemanly of you." Patton's voice broke as he began to place small, lingering kisses along her jaw line.

"Then it will be Slade's turn. He wouldn't be able to resist you." He kissed his way down her neck and her head tilted back under its own steam, silently offering more of herself to him.

"Soon we'll all go mad with desire and the only thing standing in our way will be your choice. Things will end whatever way you want, Patton. Don't you want to make an educated decision?"

"Devin…"

"Get on the bed."

He stepped back, leaving her feeling bereft, almost unable to stand on legs that had turned to jelly. His tone lost some of its smoothness, taking on a hard edge when he issued his command again.

"I'm not going to ask you again, Patton."

The implied threat wasn't lost on Patton. He didn't need to say the words for her to know he threatened her with discipline, punishment. The unwanted memory of Chase's punishment sprung to her mind. It had been horrible to be left in that condition, but at least she had been able to take care of the matter. As much as she wanted to avoid being punished, her body trembled so much with the combined effects of desire and fear that she couldn't move.

"I can't," she finally admitted in a faint tone.

"Sure you can, sweetheart. Just sit down." Devin's tone held no hint of sympathy and a good deal of humor.

Knowing that she amused him helped her regain some of her fight. She took a deep calming breath and crossed her arms over her breasts. Tilting her chin up in defiance, she glared at him.

She caught his slight smile before the world rotated and she flew through the air again. Patton's surprised yelp was cut short as her stomach hit two hard thighs. At the last second, she threw her hands out to catch herself before her head could bang into the floor.

Before she could think to protest, her dress was lifted out of the way, her underwear pulled down to the top of her thighs. Patton's breath caught as she felt the cool night air on her naked ass. She tried to rear up but his arm across her lower back held her down.

"Oh, God, don't."

Smack!

Chapter 7

Patton squealed as the first blow landed sharply against her right cheek. The slap stung and her butt lit alive with fire. A rough hand stroked over where it had just injured her tender skin, trapping the heated flames against her tender skin.

The feel of that rough hand lightly smoothing over her sensitive flesh sent the piercing shards of heat straight through her ass into her pussy. The pain and humiliation of being spanked did not compare to the embarrassing revelation that she got turned on by his barbaric treatment.

"Please, Devin." Patton hated herself for begging. "Please, let's talk about this."

"Too late, sweetheart."

With that, he spanked her until her butt felt like a living inferno and she could feel the wetness leaking out of her pussy to the top of her thighs. She tightened her legs, squeezing her thighs tightly together to hide the evidence of her desire.

"Lord, woman, I have never seen a finer ass." Devin's words so reverently and softly spoken sounded like a prayer.

Devin smiled as she squirmed harder under the gentle caress of his hand as he soothed her blushing ass. He should punish her for the wiggling she'd done while he spanked her but felt in a forgiving mood. After all, this was only a sample.

At least one of his questions had been answered. He'd been a little concerned when he pulled Patton across his lap that she'd not take to the spanking. Not every woman enjoyed discipline.

Patton had. Between all the movements, he'd heard her gasps and muffled groans, seen the way her rear rose slightly with anticipation. If that didn't tell him enough, he could smell her arousal despite her attempts to hide it from him.

"Did you enjoy your punishment, Patton?" He wanted to hear her admit it. Doing so was an important step in her introduction to his world.

"No," she answered raggedly. "Now let me up, you deviant."

"I think you're lying, Patton." Devin chuckled and shook his head. "Lying to your master earns you more punishment."

"No, please," she whimpered.

"Hmm, first let's see if punishment is in order."

Devin slid one finger down the inviting crease between her cheeks and further until he touched the warm, wet evidence of her desire. Patton gasped at the feel of that lone finger running along the length of her sensitive nether lips.

"You seem awfully wet for a lady who didn't enjoy being punished, sweetheart." He stroked her soft, inviting flesh. "Yes, indeed. You want to change your answer?"

"No," Patton croaked. It didn't matter if he knew the truth. She wouldn't give him the satisfaction of hearing it.

"Hmm, let me see what I can do about changing your mind."

He eased a finger between the wet folds of her sex, circling her opening in a maddening caress before sliding the thick digit into the very core of her being. Patton couldn't stop her moan of desire at the intrusion. Her thighs relaxed of their own volition, allowing him room to deepen the caress.

Devin took immediate advantage as he repeatedly stroked into her hot, inviting flesh. He inserted a second finger, widening her tight sheath. Her response was instantaneous as she groaned and pumped her hips back, trying to take in more of his questing fingers.

He obliged, thrusting his fingers deeper, rotating them until he pressed against her magic spot. Instantly Patton bucked and cried out, her channel cramping down on his fingers. Devin chuckled unsteadily above her and pressed again.

"Oh, please." Patton shuddered, unsure if she could take much more.

"You like that, baby?" Devin whispered as his thumb slid up to find the hard, pierced nub of her clitoris. "What about this?"

He rolled the little bar piercing as he pressed down on her sweet spot.

"Oh, God, yes! Do it again."

Patton knew that one more caress would send her over the edge, triggering the strongest orgasm she'd ever had. Desperately she lifted her hips, grinding her pelvis into his hand as she tried to force him to her will.

"No!" she cried out as she felt his hands leaving her. "What are you doing?"

"I'm waiting to hear the truth from you, sweetheart," he explained patiently.

"Truth?" She tried to focus. "What truth?"

"You enjoyed being spanked, didn't you, Patton? It got you hot."

"Yes, you bastard! It got me hot and wet. Now finish it," she spat, near delirious with desire.

He chuckled at her declaration before raising her panties. She stilled as he lowered her dress but began to fight when he lifted her back on to her feet.

"Wait. What are you doing?" she asked raggedly. "You can't leave me like this. Damn you, Devin!"

"All in good time, sweetheart. Now, strip for me."

Her mind screamed at her to deny him. Her pussy yelled just as loud not to. The decision was made by her ass. It did not want to be put back over his knee. It hurt and couldn't take another round.

With fingers that trembled as much from nervousness as from desire, she reached for the buttons on her sundress. Devin leaned back, obviously getting comfortable to enjoy the show. The movement emphasized the enormous bulge just beneath his belt buckle. He was not as cool and removed as he'd like her to believe and an idea occurred to her.

Despite her inexperience in these kinds of games, she struck out on her own. Patton slowly undid the buttons of her dress all the way down to her navel. The dress gaped open to reveal the rounded sides of her breasts and her flat stomach.

She watched him from under lowered lashes, gauging his reaction as her hands slid up the edges of her dress. Her fingers slipped under the fabric to tease her nipples before continuing to slide further up to the straps.

She slid first the right and then the left one down. They caught on her upper arms allowing the top of her dress to sag. The material bunched on her breasts, concealing the pointed tips in the floral folds.

"I didn't ask for a show, Patton."

Devin's growl surprised her. Her hands stilled as she gazed at him in confusion.

"Don't you like—"

"That's not the point." Devin's feet hit the floor. "It works like this. I tell you what to do and you do it. No improvising."

"Okay," she responded slowly, more than a little intimidated by the way he towered over her.

This man was so different than the easygoing Devin she knew. The things he said and did were foreign to her. Nothing of the dreams and fantasies she had translated into reality. It was both more and too much.

"I'll take it off." Patton didn't recognize the sound of her own voice anymore. Soft, hesitant, a little watery, it betrayed her apprehension.

"Too late."

That was all the warning she got before he yanked the dress straight up and off her. Instantly she felt cold and vulnerable standing in nothing more than her pink thong. She hadn't worn a bra with the outfit because the dress had come with built in cups.

Her nipples puckered to hard points as much from the chilly air as from his heated perusal. Without considering the consequences, she instinctively crossed her arms over her chest. The action drew a sigh from Devin.

"Did I tell you to move?" Devin reached out to tug her arms back to her sides. "That's twice you have acted without permission. You've earned another punishment."

"What?" Patton blinked. "That's not fair."

"This isn't about fairness, Patton." Devin wrapped a finger around one of the silky locks teasing the side of her breast, but did not actually touch her. "It's about control and obedience."

"You're going to spank me again."

"Close your eyes."

Patton took a deep breath and did as he instructed. The loss of sight added to her building apprehension. So did the sounds of him dragging things across the floor. Whatever Devin prepared, Patton didn't think that she would get another spanking.

Mentally she reviewed some of the images she had witnessed when she had been too young to truly comprehend them. Images of women suspended in harnesses, of them blindfolded and moaning as one brother fucked them or another used a toy on them. Hot memories flooded her mind, and for a moment, she forgot to fear her upcoming punishment and lost herself in the excitement of her own lustful thoughts.

The callused feel of Devin's hands jarred her back to reality. He wouldn't fuck her. That went against his precious rules. Punishment didn't and hadn't she asked for it?

It had been her actions that forced Devin and her into a situation that she had always claimed she wanted. This was what she wanted. Even if she wasn't in control, things were going her way.

"Don't worry, Patton. You'll enjoy this."

His hot, husky voice lulled her into a moment of peace with her decision and she allowed him to lead her across the room. Whatever she had expected, being seated on his lap wasn't it. He settled her against his chest. Beneath the soft cotton of his shirt, the warmth of his hard muscles heated her back.

The rough denim of his jeans chafed the insides of her legs as he pushed his thighs between hers. A moment later, he widened his legs, forcing hers to split until she felt the cool air on every crevice of her exposed cunt.

"Have you ever watched yourself while you masturbated?"

The sudden intimate question had her swallowing hard. No, the idea was perverse, dirty, and just the suggestion made her hot. She was so lost in the idea of his question that she forgot his rule about hesitating.

The sharp, stinging slap to her pussy had fire shooting straight up her stomach and racing across her back to engulf her entire body in the unexpected inferno. Shivers of pained pleasure coursed through her, making goose bumps break out all over her skin.

"I asked you a question."

"No."

Patton barely managed to get her lips to form the word and it came out mumbled and hoarse. The second smack hit her clit straight on and sent a lightning bolt ripping through her, searing every nerve ending until no part of her didn't tingle.

Her brain couldn't compute the overwhelming sensations. In the chaos, it constricted the function of her lungs and increased the speed of her heart. The conflicting order left her light headed and fearing she might faint.

"No, what?"

Patton didn't understand the question. Devin didn't give her the time to figure it out. He brought his open palm down for a third hard hit. Her whole body bowed under the impact as the first spider webs of rapture spun across her body.

"No, what, Patton?"

"Please," she cried, not sure if she could take any more of the extreme sensations. "I can't think when you do that."

"Then learn."

His growl had barely finished vibrating through his chest when he struck again. He didn't pause this time as the blows came fast and hard. Patton screamed as small flares of ecstasy began to detonate through her body. They grew stronger, combining into a growing mass that threatened to tear her apart at the seams.

He stopped suddenly, leaving her quivering on the edge of orgasm. Her fingers bit tightly into his thighs, needing his strength to hold her up or else she'd melt right off his lap and pool at his feet in a limp puddle.

"Do you want to come?"

"Yes. Please, Devin, I need it."

"Do you remember the question I asked you?"

"No," Patton whined. She knew he wanted a different answer, but she had no other to give him.

"Open your eyes, Patton."

She did as he instructed, slowly relaxing her scrunched features. The first thing she saw was herself. Her swollen breasts flushed as her eyes dipped lower to spread legs, the pink folds of her pussy wet and glistening with cream. The image in the mirror was so sinfully erotic that she instinctively started to close her lids, not ready to accept this new reality.

"Don't."

Devin's hard command stilled her motions and she sought his gaze. He stared at her body, his heated gaze devouring every inch of her bared flesh, making her feel even more vulnerable. She was open and completely exposed to him. The stark contrast of their different states of dress made the scene in the mirror more dark and forbidden.

"Does this jog your memory?" With his question, he lifted his hand and Patton's breath caught at the sight of the toy he held.

"Yes," she whispered.

"Yes, what?"

"Yes, I remember." She did. Her face burned with embarrassment as her mind skipped to where this conversation ended. He wouldn't make her do that, he couldn't.

"And?"

"No."

"Patton."

"No, I've never watched myself masturbate."

"This is your punishment."

"Devin—"

"Take the dildo, Patton. I want to see you use it."

Chapter 8

Devin could see her hand shaking as she reached for the dildo and knew that if Patton could escape this moment, she would. He didn't leave her any choice.

The concepts he was trying to teach her might be difficult for her, but that didn't mean she wasn't excited. He could see the evidence of her arousal glistening along the swollen lips of her pussy, smell the sweet scent of her excitement in the air. Her nipples were puckered, her eyes glazed with lust, her lips parted as her breath panted in and out. It was more than he had expected, could have hoped for and all the permission he needed to continue.

Her fingers bent around the curved edge of the phallus, but as he began to let go, he could feel the heavy object slip. She'd have dropped the thing if he hadn't closed his fingers over hers, lending her his strength.

With his guidance, her arm bent, her hand lowered and he watched in the mirror as the bulbous head began to part her little cunt. Patton didn't have the strength to bear even the sight of what was happening and he saw her lids drift down to cover her eyes.

"Watch."

She forced her eyes to open, glazed, rounded and watery. Even if she couldn't force her eyes to focus, Devin could. He watched with intense fascination as her tiny opening expanded, swallowing the hard cock inch by inch as he forced her hand to feed the full length of the toy into her pussy.

Patton trembled too much to do anything. Devin really should pull the dildo out and punish her for her disobedience. The problem was the more punishment he gave her, the less likely she was to be of any assistance.

He'd never faced this problem before. All the women he'd ever trained had been professional or at least women with a wide variety of experience. This was new to Patton. She didn't have a history to help her adjust to the extreme circumstances he forced her into.

He could foresee spending the entire night punishing her. Then she'd have no satisfaction, just more frustration. He didn't want her to leave with that impression. If they had a future, then he would need to make sure she became addicted to the pleasure he could give her. He had to make her helpless but to return to his embrace for more.

With that single thought, he took control of her hand. Forcing her to fuck herself with rapid motions, he pounded the toy deep into her. She writhed on his lap, moaning her desire as her entire body contorted with her impending release.

Devin would have let her have it despite her failure to ask for permission, but then she closed her eyes and he brought all motion to a stop. He didn't want to disappoint her. Nor did he want to give her the illusion that this wasn't very serious business.

If she became their woman, absolute obedience would be required.

"No," Patton shrieked, her eyes popping back open. "Don't stop!"

"You closed your eyes." Devin kept his tone inflexible. "And I didn't give you permission to come."

"I'm sorry." Patton's apology rushed out and Devin could hear the truth. He had pushed her beyond concern for pride or dignity. "Please Devin, let me come."

"No."

Devin pulled the toy out slowly, feeling the resistance as her internal muscles tightened down, unwilling to release the dildo. It popped free with an audible sound, telling him how wet and hot she had been, as if he couldn't see or smell the sweet overpowering scent of her desire.

It made him ache to replace the fake dick with his own cock. The urge became so strong it was painful and he had to pause or lose control the desire flooding his dick with more blood than it had ever received before. He couldn't do it, but he had to do something before his control snapped.

"Please, Devin." Patton squirmed. "I promise I learned my lesson. Don't leave me like this."

"You've displeased me with your disobedience."

"I know. I'm sorry, Devin. It won't happen again."

"We'll see." Devin lifted a hand to her chin and forced her head to turn. "You want to come?"

"Yes. I'll do anything you ask."

"Anything?" Devin bit back a smile. She made this too easy.

"Please don't punish me anymore. I can't take it."

"Hmm." Devin appeared to contemplate that, but he already knew his response. She had inadvertently played right into his hands. "No more punishments. Now you have to earn your pleasure."

"Earn it?" she blinked, delightfully innocent.

"On your knees."

Devin didn't give her a chance to obey his command but instead forced her down between his legs until she knelt before him, eye level with the enormous bulge in his jeans. The feral look in his eyes told her what he wanted, told her he wouldn't be patient about getting it either.

What amazed her was that she wanted to. Sucking cock had always been something Patton had done for the guys, something to make up for the fact that though she had been willing to fool around, but hadn't been willing to have sex. Now though the idea excited her, added to her own state of arousal.

Licking her lips, she worked first to undo his belt and then to lower his fly, not an easy task given the tension in the zipper thanks to the large erection pressing against it. Spreading his jeans open, she nuzzled her face against the cool cotton boxers still concealing his rock hard cock.

His dick jerked against her cheek, slipping through the opening in his underwear. The pearl drops of his desires leaked out of the blind hole on top. Tentatively she licked up the taste of his arousal before dipping her head to lick the entire head. Devin flinched under the teasing assault, his cock leaking more pre-come.

"Don't tease me, Patton," he growled. "Suck it."

Her hands slipped into the opening of his boxers, freeing the entire length of his erection. Sliding down, her cool fingers explored his balls, weighing them before rolling them in maddening turns.

He groaned in response and Patton thrilled over the way his legs tensed around her. She looked up from beneath her lashes and found him watching her. With their gazes locked, she licked her way down the length of his shaft, letting her tongue tease his balls.

She felt her pussy clench and then begin to weep at the feral look of pleasure that hardened his face. The eroticism of watching him while she explored his cock had an effect not just on her but on him as well. Patton could sense his control fading away.

His breathing labored, his body jerked at every teasing touch of her tongue. Amazingly, the already long shaft before her grew harder, the head going purple with blood. She thrilled at the idea of pushing him beyond, turning him into the primitive male animal he could be.

With that in mind, she worked her way back down to his testicles, pausing for a moment before sucking one heavy sac into her mouth. His hands tightened in her hair with a fierce grip and he jerked her back up to the top of his cock.

"Suck it now, Patton." His hips thrust up slightly with his demand.

Patton grinned before she took him into her mouth. She thrilled at the way he groaned and forced her down over his entire length. Devin took over, guiding her motion, using his hold on her hair to pump her mouth over his shaft with growing speed. In minutes, he shook, crying out his pleasure as he came.

Swallowing down the liquid proof of his release, she continued to suck and lick him until his movement slowed and still. Only then did she raise her head. Catching his look, she licked her lips again, wiping away all evidence of his come.

Devin's eyes narrowed at the movement. Jesus, despite having some of the best-trained women suck him off, he'd never experienced anything like she'd just given him. It went beyond a matter of skill or talent, but love and giving. Patton had enjoyed sucking him off. She hadn't done it just because he'd demanded it.

She'd done it because it pleased him and it pleased her. Devin wanted to return the favor. He'd told her she had to earn her pleasure. Well, she'd earned a whole night of it.

"On the bed."

Patton didn't hesitate this time. She scrambled up and scurried off toward the bed. Devin carefully tucked himself back into his jeans before following her. Best not to leave that out lest he forgot himself and put his dick to use later on.

When he stood, he noticed that she had obeyed his order. She lay on the small mattress with her legs slightly parted. That wouldn't do. Not for what he had planned.

"Legs wide, bend your knees over the edge of the bed," he ordered as he moved to the foot of the bed. "Try to touch your feet to the floor."

Patton swallowed but obeyed. Whatever embarrassment she had over being exposed to his view had obviously waned back in front of that mirror, but was not completely lost if the color in her cheeks was any indication. Devin smiled. She was learning.

Patton didn't want to do anything to screw it up. Especially not when he crawled between her splayed thighs and settled his face barely inches from her pussy. Oh, God, this was her favorite thing.

Of course, she didn't have much to compare it with, but she found it hard to believe that anything could feel as good as having her pussy eaten, especially if the man was talented.

The air caught in her throat when she felt the warm brush of breath against her over stimulated pussy. Before she could draw breath, a warm soft tongue licked her. With long, slow strokes, it lapped at her cream, deviling into her core before flicking up to rasp against her clit.

Delicately he tasted her, his forays becoming slowly deeper, more intimate. She arched into the talented tongue slowly trying to drive her insane. Slow, deep spasms began to rock through her body, growing in intensity.

She could take no more of his teasing. His maddening tongue swirled over her clit in a repeated rasping caress that had a blaze of colors exploding behind her closed lids. All the rules and consequences forgotten, she buried her hands into his hair.

Devin didn't think about obedience and punishments either. His focus was squarely on devouring the most delectable cunt he'd ever tasted. With a surprisingly strong grip, she forced him closer.

Writhing beneath him, she moaned demands between panting breaths. Poor baby, she really thought she could force him to obey her commands. Devin would have smiled at her arrogance if his lips weren't already busy.

Training her would be a challenge. An endeavor that could last a lifetime and Devin was more than willing to dedicate himself to the task, just as he did now.

He separated her folds with his fingers, sliding his tongue down to tease the entrance of her tight sheath. From her scream and the way she bucked upward, he knew she approved. He began to fuck his tongue in and out of her hot core.

"Oh, God. Oh, please. Devin!"

Her head thrashed back and forth on the pillow. Her internal muscles clamped down on his tongue, trying to suck him in deeper, but he had no more to give her. Lifting his mouth, he slid his fingers deep into her.

He wanted to push her beyond any previous pleasure she'd known, to erase the memory of all others from her mind and her heart. That need cut through his control and unleashed the primitive man lurking beneath his skin.

His lips closed over her clit and he sucked on the little piercing. He stretched her spasming sheath wide, swirling his fingers to tease her sweet spot while he flicked her piercing with his tongue.

Heat whorled and whipped out from her pussy, searing through her body to incinerate her in its consuming embrace. She wouldn't survive this. That thought echoed through her on the crest of a release so explosive she swore she could feel her bones fracturing from the detonation.

Time skipped away from her as her entire body convulsed with the most devastating release she'd ever experienced. Only the pain in her chest and the need to breathe brought her back to reality.

She lay there, sweaty and trembling as he crawled up her body. Every one of her limbs felt like dough, sticky and limp. She didn't have the energy to return the tender kiss Devin placed on her lips.

When he drew back, Patton blinked her eyes open. He had that arrogant male smile, the one that said he'd done good and he knew it. Amusement gleamed in his desire-darkened eyes and she could well guess the turn of his thoughts.

"Want more, baby? I do."

Before she could respond to that, he slid the long forgotten toy deep into her. She wasn't ready for this, but that didn't stop him. He intended to kill her with sex. That was Patton's last rational thought of the night.

Chapter 9

The sounds of morning slowly penetrated Patton's drowsy mind. The sweet harmony of the ranch filled the air—the hollers of men, the whinnying of horses, the steady pound of cattle on the move.

The scent of leather and musk drugged her and she snuggled deeper into the pillow, allowing the odor to lull her back to sleep. A thick arm pulling her tighter against a hard body had her eyes opening. For a moment, she blinked dully as the past night's memory filtered through her mind.

Oh, God. What have I done?

Patton knew well what she'd done. She'd played slave to Devin's desires and had the most exciting night ever. She'd never had so many climaxes or such powerful orgasms before. All her greedy, horny body could think about was doing it again.

"Morning, sweetheart," Devin rumbled huskily in her ear, sending shivers down her spine. "Cold?"

"No," Patton whispered, unsure of how to handle the moment. She had gotten her way, gotten Devin into bed, finally tasted the forbidden fruit. Gloating, though, didn't seem appropriate.

"Hmm." Devin pulled her closer. The hard, ridge of his morning erection nestled against her ass. The rough denim scratched the smooth skin of her butt, reminding her that she was naked and he was fully clothed.

"Want some more?" He began nibbling on the side of her neck. "I do."

That was all the warning she got before his hand slid down between her legs and started rubbing against her clit. Patton gasped and wiggled, allowing him to drag her leg up over his thighs and open her completely to his touch.

Within minutes, she swam through a sea of ecstasy, trying hard not to cry out. Devin brought her to one delicious climax and then another before rolling her on her back. With three fingers still fucking steadily into her weeping cunt, he began to kiss his way down her body.

He paused long enough to toy with her breast, sucking the tip into his mouth and rolling it around with his tongue. Patton moaned a complaint when his mouth left her sensitized nipple to kiss the undersides of her breasts. As he continued further down, her breath caught, realizing what exactly Devin wanted more of.

With no encouragement, she spread her legs wider, allowing him to settle between them. His fingers slipped out of her to hold her folds open so that he could press his tongue into her core. Her body convulsed with electricity that radiated out from her pelvis.

His questing tongue licked upward to slide across her clit and latched onto her little piercing. Devin sucked her tender little nub into his mouth and lapped at her piercing. He slid three fingers deep into her and began pumping her hard and fast.

Patton came the same way. The tension tightening in her spiraled completely out of control until she snapped. She screamed as her body convulsed with hard spasms.

"Patton!" Chase's shout sent ice water through her veins. The sounds of somebody trying to open the door had her shrieking again and diving for the covers.

"He always did have lousy timing," Devin muttered.

"What hell is going on in there?" Chase roared. "Devin, are you in there?"

"Yeah," Devin hollered back.

"Oh, God," Patton whimpered from under the blanket.

"Open up!"

* * * *

"I'll be there in a moment."

Devin was just as annoyed. Gently he pulled back the edge of the blanket to reveal Patton's flaming face. She looked ready to pass out from embarrassment.

"So much for my blow job, huh?"

"How can you joke at a time like this?" Patton whispered harshly, as if scared Chase would hear.

"What else are we going to do?" Devin shrugged. "Besides who said it was a joke?"

"Devin," she gasped.

"Devin!" Chase yelled banging hard on the door. "Damn it. Open up."

"Give us a moment to get decent."

"How could you say that?" Patton shrieked.

"What?" Devin gave her a puzzled look. "It's not as if he doesn't know what we were doing. There is only one thing that goes on in this room."

"He's going to kill us," Patton moaned. Holding the blanket up as a shield she, looked around frantically.

"There's no other way out, Patton. No window to jump through that isn't nailed shut already."

"You have less than a minute, Devin, or I'm taking this door out."

"He means that." Devin sighed as he rolled off the bed. "You better get dressed."

Devin reached down to grab her dress off the floor and tossed it to her before he headed toward the door and the devil pounding on it. Patton barely had enough time to scramble into the thing before the door bounced against the wall as Chase slammed it open.

She tried to hide in the shadows toward the back, but Chase's eyes cut through the dimly lit room to find where she cowered. He wasn't alone. Slade filled the rest of the space behind him.

Patton's pulse kicked into sonic mode as she watched Slade's gaze fall to the floor where her pink panties lay like a beacon against the dark wood floor. Gasping in horror, she quickly scooped them up, as if that would somehow erase the guilt she could feel being pressed into the room by the two large Davis brothers filling the door.

"Slade, take Patton back to the house." Chase turned his murderous glare on Devin. "I need to have a word with our little brother."

Slade didn't hesitate to follow Chase's order. A second later he had her arm in a secure hold and started dragging her past Devin's smirk and Chase's dark scowl.

"You better carry her, Slade," Devin called out. "She doesn't have any shoes."

Before Patton could protest, Slade swept her up into his arms. For a second she thought about resisting but realized the stupidity of that action. The barn floor was littered with debris. She didn't need a cut on the bottom of the foot to make this morning even better.

She buried her face in his shoulder and hid from the looks they got from the ranch hands, certain they all knew what she had been caught doing. They had to know. Things had gotten decidedly quieter since Chase had roared her name.

It was bad enough that Chase and Slade had walked in on them. Having the whole ranch know about it just completed her humiliation.

Without a word, Slade carried her into the kitchen, depositing her on a stool. When he stepped back, she got her first look at his grim features. His gray eyes were a stormy mixture of speculation, anticipation and anger. Patton blushed under the intensity of his perusal.

Slade finally broke the silence. "Were you two doing what I think you were?"

"Why do you want to know?" Patton crossed her arms over her breasts, just as much to hide the pointed tips as to appear defiant.

"Just answer the question." Slade's growl sounded more like Chase than the normally reasonable tone he used with her.

"No."

"Damnit, Patton!"

"It's none of your business." Patton raised her chin.

"It's my business." Slade's sharp retort forced its way through clenched teeth.

"You just want to know if Devin fucked me because then it can be your turn to take me upstairs and give me a morning ride."

Charlotte rounded the corner at that moment. She came to a dead stop at Patton's words, her eyes darting from the rumpled state of Patton's dress to Slade's obvious erection. Without a word, she turned and stormed back out.

"I think she's going to be giving you back that collar."

"Excuse me?" Slade's hands curled into white knuckled fists.

"Don't play dumb with me, Slade." Patton smiled slightly. "I know all about your little master and pet game."

"I was referring to that it's my turn comment," Slade snapped.

"Oh." Patton shrugged, pretending she couldn't care less. "Devin told me all about your little pact."

"He did, did he? What else did Devin tell you?"

"Tell me, not much, but he showed me a few things."

"Stop it, Patton." Slade took a deep breath, obviously fighting to regain control of himself as well as the conversation. "I know you might think you have a right to be difficult, but just drop the attitude and tell me—"

"What?" Patton cut him off. "How I know all about your side business? About how I knew what the supposedly unused barn was really used for before Devin took me into the back room and showed me last night? That despite your attempt at making me feel guilty yesterday for lying, your secrets are just so much more interesting than mine. What? What do you want me to tell you that you don't already know?"

Slade's mouth opened and closed several times as he thought of one response after another, but none of them seemed appropriate. For the first time in a long time, he was at a complete loss for what to say. She was right about everything, but all that seemed irrelevant in the face of what she and Devin might have done out there in the barn.

What might have happened? What did happen? Slade wasn't sure he was ready for the answer. He felt pulled in opposite directions, anger at Devin for violating Chase and his wishes and anticipation that Patton was now theirs.

"Would it make a difference if I paid you?"

"Excuse me?" Slade felt the tips of his ears start to burn.

"Paid you." Patton jumped off the seat, her arms dramatizing her words. "I could be like your client. You could teach me all your tricks."

"Don't even—"

"It's perfect. No attachments, no stupid pack, just sex."

"This isn't a joke," Slade snarled, snatching her arms in his fists. He squeezed her slender limbs tight with his anger, fighting the urge not to shake her as well.

"I wasn't kidding."

Patton jerked out of his hold. Slade could see the mask of anger begin to crumple and the pain she tried not to reveal. Tears grew, glistening in her big violet eyes and making them shine. Taking a deep breath and gathering herself in a cloak of coldness that made him bristle, she turned away.

"Patton?" Slade's voice brought her to a pause in the doorway.

"Ask Devin your questions. He seems more than willing to go into the details."

Patton didn't allow him to expand his question, nor did she look at him. Slade let her go, watching her worriedly. It was cowardly, but he was grateful she spared him the sight of her tears falling. If only one had fallen, it would have tracked a bloody whip mark through his very soul.

Chapter 10

"You have exactly one minute to explain yourself before I take you apart piece by piece." Chase stepped into his not so little brother's space.

"Perhaps then I should start with we didn't have sex." Devin smirked, not the least bit intimidated.

"Then what exactly did you have?"

"An educational experience on the positive aspects of being sexually dominated," Devin answered succinctly.

"Don't push me, Devin. I want to know what happened here last night."

Devin told him, leaving nothing out. When he finished, he watched as Chase's fist clenched and knew his brother fought hard not to punch him. He'd have welcomed the punch—anything to rid Chase of his anger and get him to think rationally.

"Don't you see," Devin implored, catching Chase by the arm before he could turn and storm away. "She now knows all she needs to make a decision."

"The decision is not hers." Chase shook Devin free.

"It should be," Devin snapped. "She's not a child and if she wants to be with us, knowing all that we are and accepting it, why shouldn't she? Why should we all suffer, denying ourselves what we want?"

"Because it's not right. We're her guardians."

"No, we're not. Patton's all grown up now. She is an adult, capable of making her own decisions." Devin's own anger rose.

"I can't." Chase unclenched his fist. "I promised our mother to take care of her and make sure she was happy, not pervert her and put her into service for our sexual desires."

"What if being with us is what makes her happy? Then by denying her, aren't you breaking your vow?"

"If mother was still alive, what do you think she'd do if she found out about this?"

"That's not a fair question."

"You know the answer. That's why my answer has to be no." Chase turned and stalked out.

* * * *

Chase would have liked nothing better to do than to pound his younger sibling into the ground for pulling this stunt. He didn't have time for that though. He had to stop this before things spiraled out of control. He had to undo what had been done and convince Patton there would be no repeat performance of what had happened between Devin and her.

He found Patton sitting at her vanity brushing her hair. He paused, his mind flashing back to when he had built the small table for her. She'd been young then, not even been a double digit. The chair legs were nicked and deformed by her attempts to help him.

He could almost see her still, sitting there and babbling on about how Hailey liked Collin, furious that Matt had put gum in her hair at recess and Chase had cut it out, or how Mrs. Rollins, the creature teacher, made her read a note she had passed to Shelly in front of the whole class.

She would sit in that chair and tell him all her problems. Back then she told him everything. Her violet eyes would shine up at him in complete faith that he could solve her problems. Chase's heart ached at the loss of those days.

It had been years since she had confided in him, years since she had seen him as her protector and not her adversary. His fist clenched with the need to hit something. Devin made a perfect target, but he wasn't there. Devin had crossed the line.

Thanks to Devin's rash actions, Chase held no hope of those days coming back now. He'd never be able to look at her without imagining what had happened in the barn last night, pained by the fact that it hadn't been him with her. That was his greatest fantasy to see Patton kneeling naked and subservient before him.

Nothing more than a fantasy, Chase reminded himself. He couldn't risk trying to make it a reality. If everything blew up, his family would be decimated and he would lose Patton forever. He wouldn't let that happen.

Chase had already talked his decision over with Slade and Devin in the kitchen. He had expected Slade to back him up, but he'd hesitated. His will to resist had been tested by Devin's description of the night before. Chase could see it in his eyes. Slade wouldn't be able to withstand temptation for much longer. If Slade caved, then Devin would be completely unleashed.

He had to put an end to this before things with Patton went too far. He couldn't rely on Slade or Devin to comply with his decision for long. He needed to get her back to Atlanta, even if it was to run a lingerie business and pose in some racy catalog. He would just pretend that reality didn't exist.

Most importantly, he had to remain calm and rational, make her see reason. He didn't feel either of those things around Patton. He felt like a leashed dog fighting for its freedom, all pent up aggression and frustration.

Just watching her now made his dick so hard it hurt. His heart pounded as his palms became sweaty. He felt like he was sixteen again, trying to talk to the girl he liked. At thirty-one, it both humbled and annoyed him. The feeling wouldn't go away so he might as well work through it.

"Patton." He forced his legs to carry him slowly forward as she turned around.

He could see the moment of happiness at the sight of him in her eyes. Almost immediately, she lowered her head, hiding from him. He should have expected it, but that didn't stop it from hurting.

"Hello, Chase." When had her voice become so low and sultry sounding? Last night when she was with Devin? Was she remembering? Was she fantasizing about being that way with him?

"Um." Chase swallowed hard forcing his thoughts back onto the here and now. "We need to talk."

"Is this going to be another lecture?" Patton didn't look up, but she tensed, clenching the brush in her hands.

"No. It's an apology."

Her head snapped up. "For what?"

"You were right. I did force you to go to college." Chase sat down on the edge of her bed and met her wide eyes head on. "You used to always talk about being a fashion designer. I remember when you were younger and we gave you mom's sewing machine. You saved up all your money, bought that god-awful fabric, and made us all those lopsided shirts. Do you remember that?"

"You wore them anyway." She smiled sadly.

"It made you happy." Chase shrugged. "It always made you happy and I always encouraged it because of that. Then when it came time to go to school, you insisted that you wanted to be a fashion designer and I insisted that you go for a real degree. I shouldn't have done that. I should have let you go to a design school. Perhaps if I had, things would have turned out differently."

"You say that like they turned out wrong, but they didn't. I have a great business, Chase. I am happy. The thing that bothered me was having to lie to you, but I don't have to do that anymore."

"No, you don't. I'm glad you're happy and I was wrong to call you down here. I think you should go back to Atlanta and continue with your business." It almost hurt to say those words and sound sincere, but he managed.

"You do?" Patton studied him for a moment. "What is this?"

"What is what?"

"This." She waved her hand at him. "This crap you're forcing out of your mouth."

"It's not crap." Chase bristled. Damn the woman. Did she have to argue over everything? "I'm telling you that I shouldn't have interfered with your life and you should go back to it. I'd think you would be happy. I'm apologizing. You won."

"It depends on why you're saying it."

"What?"

"Whether or not I'm happy depends on why you are saying it." Patton's eyes narrowed on him. "You have another woman, don't you?"

"Another woman? What are you talking about?" Chase's head started to ache.

"I'm talking about the way you stormed out of here yesterday. You met somebody last night, didn't you?" She leveled the hairbrush at him. "Didn't you?"

"No." Chase wanted to snatch the brush right out of her hand. He hated when she pointed things at him.

Worse yet, when she poked him in the chest with her finger it made his control bow and strain with the stress of holding back his more base desires—desires to punish and dominate, desires that would lead her to being straddled naked across his lap, with his cock buried deep inside her wet, clinging cunt. He wouldn't fuck her.

No, he'd have her take those beautiful, delicate hands and play with her clit, tease her tits, maybe even suck one. He'd love to watch her pleasure herself, feel her tighten all around him as she came screaming apart all over him. Then he'd put his hands on her hips and begin to pound—

"Do I look stupid?" she demanded, snapping him back to the reality of a pissed off Patton and that damn hairbrush waving in front of his face. "I know what this is about. You want me out of the way so you can have an orgy with whatever whore you picked up last night."

"Damn it, Patton." He snatched the hair brush right out of her hands. It was that or do something really stupid. "I didn't pick up any woman last night."

"Really?" She tilted her head with obvious disbelief. "Then what did you do with your hard-on?"

"My..." Chase blinked. How the hell was he supposed to answer that question?

"Don't look at me like that," she snapped. "You had a massive erection when you played your little game yesterday. Are you telling me that you didn't take it for a dip in a—"

"Patton!"

Chase shook with the urge to yell at her, but he managed to control himself. She did this on purpose, picking a fight. He had to get this conversation back on track.

Chase forced his jaw to relax, taking his time before continuing. He had a hard enough time pushing her toward something he didn't want her to do, but her attitude made it almost impossible. It was well over a minute before he spoke again.

"Not that it is any of your business, but I drank it away."

"Hmm." She pursed her lips, considering him for a moment. She must have realized she hit a dead end, but she changed topics. "Then what is this about?"

"This is about doing what is best for you."

"Best for me?"

"You wanted to be a designer and now you are one, a successful one. Go back to that life and enjoy it."

"What if I don't want to go back?" Patton didn't buy a word of what he said. It would have helped if he sounded the least bit sincere, but that was kind of hard given how tightly his jaw was clenched.

"Why wouldn't you?"

"You." Very carefully, trying to control the trembling in her hands, Patton prepared to risk it all.

"Me?" Chase flinched as if she had lashed him with her tone.

"I could work from here. Run my business from the ranch."

"Don't you have a shop in Atlanta?"

"That's Casey's, my partner's, side. I do the designs and manufacturing. She handles the shop and catalog sales. So technically I can work from anywhere."

"I think it would be better if you left."

"I don't. I want to come home. I want to live and be with the men that I love." Patton rushed out the statement before fear and nerves got the better of her.

"You're young and you have options. You shouldn't tie yourself down to a decision so quickly." Chase dragged his hand through his hair.

"You mean I shouldn't tie you down to one."

"I'm just thinking about what is best for you."

"No. You're thinking about what is best for you." She turned her back on him.

"Listen to me, Patton." Chase stood, going to her and forcing her to turn back to him. "We're hard men, who take what we want when we want it. You deserve better than that. We enjoy things that might seem novel to you now, but that will wear off. Then what will happen? You deserve to be with a man who can love you with gentleness and care."

"What if I prefer hard?"

"You're a virgin," Chase dismissed. "You don't know what you prefer."

"You have all the answers, don't you, Chase? Why are you fighting me so hard?" Patton demanded, unable to keep the hurt out of her tone.

"Oh, baby, it's me I'm fighting."

Chase couldn't stop himself from touching her. He cupped her face in his palm. Rubbing his fingertips over her lips, they trembled beneath his touch.

"I want you so bad it's hard for me to even see straight, but I have to think about what is best for you."

"You don't have the right to decide what is best for me. I'm a grown woman." Patton jerked her chin out of his grip.

"Patton—"

"Oh, shut up!" She jumped up. "I'm tired of listening to your excuses."

With that, she stormed out of the room. Chase watched her leave, feeling completely helpless. He had gotten what he wanted, hadn't he? All he had to do was stay strong when she returned and she would see that it was pointless to remain here.

Chase's shoulders slumped as he thought about what that meant, going back to the long, empty days and nights filled with temporary physical relief. His mind multiplied the days into weeks, the weeks into months, the months into years. It was a grim view, but an honest one and it would all be worth it to know that Patton was happy.

Chapter 11

Slade stepped out onto the back porch to gaze across the yard to the lone figure sitting on the tall white fence bordering the corral. Jean clad legs looped around the slats, slender arms braced along the top, the girl could have been a figment dredged from his memories.

She wasn't. This wasn't the sixteen year old Patton looking out on the world. It was the twenty-three year old version. How things had changed in the years since, Slade sighed. Still with her white t-shirt loose and the Stetson perched on her head, it was almost impossible to see the changes from behind.

Shoving his hands into his pockets, Slade braced himself for what was coming and ambled down the steps and through the short grass toward the only woman who ever meant anything to him.

Slade would have avoided the conversation they were about to have if he could have, but escaping the confrontation was not an option. Chase needed his help. Patton, too, but he doubted she would see it as such.

"Hey."

Patton didn't respond to his greeting, didn't even look at him. Slade hadn't expected anything less. She always got quiet when she was mad at him. He didn't force the conversation onward. Pulling his hands free, he looped his arms around the fence at her side and waited.

Distantly he wondered how they had come to this moment. When had it all changed? Where had his sweet innocent Patton gone? Slade smiled sadly at the question. Sweet and innocent and Patton didn't really belong in the same sentence.

Patton may have a heart as big as the entire state of Alabama, but she'd never really been sweet. Not in that bubble gum and lace way. At her core, she'd always been a fighter, diving in head first to chase down what she wanted.

It had been amusing when she'd been little. Now it scared him, because what she wanted could wreck their family. Despite what had happened between Devin and her, Patton was still innocent.

A virgin, the idea seared him, bringing a strange mixture of comfort and dread. None of them had been a woman's first. With their sexual appetites, it was best that way.

The things they desired, what they did to a woman, it demanded more than a virgin could give. They weren't gentle, tender lovers, but greedy bastards that drove a woman's passion with a single minded determination that took them all to the pinnacle of rapture's peak.

He wanted nothing more than to show those heights to Patton, but not at the expense of her heart, of her laughter, of the very essence of her spirit. He feared that would be the price they all paid.

Slade couldn't deny that Devin's description of what had happened in the barn last night tested the very limits of his control, but Chase was right. Enjoying a night of domination did not a submissive make. Patton didn't even begin to understand the meaning of the word submissive.

"Did you agree to his edict?"

Slade didn't wonder whom she was talking about or what she was referring to. Still it was best to be clear. "Who? Chase?"

"Is any other man arrogant enough to issue an edict around here?"

"He's just doing what he thinks is best. We all are."

"And to hell with what I think."

"We're just worried you're not thinking."

"Screw you, Slade."

"You know you have a tendency to act on emotion, not to think things through."

"I'm not a little girl anymore, Slade. Just because I didn't come to the same conclusion you did doesn't mean I haven't thought about this, thought about this for a really long time."

He could hear the defensive anger in her tone and knew from Chase the way his conversation had gone with Patton. It didn't lead to a happy conclusion. There might be no way to get to one, but Slade tried anyway. He just chose another track.

"And all that thinking, did you ever allow us the right to make our own decisions?"

"Excuse me?"

"You're mad because you don't think we're letting you make your own decisions, but you aren't allowing us ours either."

"You have some nerve, you know that."

"Yeah." Slade grinned. "So you've told me on a few occasions."

"Are you seriously standing there telling me you don't love me, don't want me in your bed and your life?"

"I do love you. I'll always love you, Patton, and want you in my life. You're just going to stay out of my bed."

"You'd rather pack it full of sluts, close your eyes and pretend that it was me instead."

Direct hit, Slade flinched, but held his ground. "That's my choice."

"Your choice sucks. Your choice is to make everybody unhappy and what kind of decision is that? Tell me how rational and well thought out it is to chose to live your life miserable and force me to live mine the same way."

"Better than taking you to bed only to discover you don't enjoy the same things we do. Better to error on the side of caution."

"Cowardly more like."

"You're not going to insult me into changing my mind."

Patton growled softly beside him and hopped down from the fence. In her tradition of storming off mad, she turned and stomped toward the ranch. Slade didn't follow, fully expecting her to slam into the house.

If she thought to seek out Devin for some comforting, she was going to be disappointed to learn that Chase had sent him away. Neither of the older brothers trusted their youngest to control himself anymore. Not after what had happened last night.

Patton's words shocked him into turning around. "It's never mattered to you, what I want. All my life it's been you guys deciding what is best for me. That ends now, Slade. I'm going to get what I want. With or without your consent, I'm going to have things my way."

"If you do, it will be the last time, Patton. You think about that. If you win this argument and we claim you, we'll dominate and control every aspect of your life.

"What you wear, eat, how you spend your days, who you hang out with, we'll control everything. Your catalogue, your website, your whole damn lingerie business will be over. We wouldn't allow it. You get your way in this and it'll be the last time you get your way in anything. Best you understand that before you go doing anything rash."

Patton's chin raised to the challenge. "We'll see about that Slade Davis."

With that ominous threat, she turned and finished storming off.

* * * *

Patton slammed her bedroom door, then opened it to slam it again. That felt good. It would have felt better to take her anger out on something other than an old wooden door. A fist to Chase's arrogant face would have been perfect.

She sighed and looked around the girly bedroom. It was so different than her room back in Atlanta. The brothers had designed this room for her when she'd been a little girl. They'd leashed her image, too.

A princess bed with canopy, pink bedspread, pink walls, stuffed animals and soft lacy accents, it all irritated her enough to consider going on a rampage and wrecking every damn thing in the room. Instead, she clenched her fists and screamed.

Screamed until her throat hurt and all the anger and anguish inside had been temporarily vented. The emotions still swirled within her, but room had been made for rational thought now. That was what she needed to do now, think.

Slade and his stupid arrogance, control her—Patton snorted. *As if.* He thought very highly of himself and his barbaric brothers if he thought they could ever control her beyond the bedroom. Oh, she could admit that when it came to sex, she'd enjoyed Devin's taste to a degree that had surprised and shocked her.

She wanted more even if the butterflies that set to flight in her stomach at the idea were any indication. That didn't mean she was going to let them pick out cutesy little outfits for her and force her into giving up the business she had slaved to build. No, Patton wanted it all.

She would get what she wanted. Period. There was no room for argument as far as she was concerned. All she had to do was come up with a plan, something that ended the way she wanted things to end.

Patton slumped down onto the bed and glared at the gossamer fabric overhead. Her hands itched to reach up and tear the sheer fabric to shreds. The sight of it enraged her and she scrunched her eyes closed, taking deep breaths to focus.

There were two battles to be waged, one for the brothers and the other for the life she wanted with them. Perhaps it would be better to separate the two. Fighting to convince the men that she could learn to be submissive in the bedroom and that they could learn to be accepting of her interest outside of it, might be taxing for their primitive brains.

If building her business had taught her anything, it had been to pick her battles and fight them one at a time. That meant convincing Chase, Slade and Devin to break and take her to bed came first. After she'd solidified her position as their woman, she'd show them that they couldn't control her in all things.

Patton hoped she could show them that. They were operating in pack mode right now, but the pack was breaking, she could feel it. Devin had already created a fissure between them. She just needed to apply a little more pressure to truly shatter their control.

Once that happened though, they'd regroup. United under the new pack law, the brothers would be very difficult to manipulate. It would be a problem, one she didn't even know how to grasp given her complete lack of knowledge of what it would truly mean to be their woman.

Still, Patton was confident that once she attained that precious position, she'd figure out a way around their overbearing commands. Once they learned that they couldn't control every aspect of her life, things would settle down and they could live happily ever after.

Patton snorted at her own thoughts. Maybe not happily ever after all the time. No doubt, she'd test the limits of their authority and they'd test the limits of her patience for the rest of their lives, but it would be a good life, one filled with love, happiness and the occasional fight.

All she had to do was get them over the hump. How was she supposed to show them that she could be what they wanted in a lover? Telling them was a dead end. Even showing them hadn't panned out. Perhaps she shouldn't even bother to try.

Patton's eyes snapped open as the idea began to swirl in her head. This time she didn't see the girly canopy above, but the visions dancing in her head. The corners of her mouth lifted even as she sat up. It was perfect.

She'd give them exactly what they wanted, but not at the safe distance all the way back in Atlanta. They wanted her to move on, go back to her business and find a new man to love. That's exactly what she would do, but she was going to do it here in Pittsview. Right where they could see her.

If her teenage years were any basis for comparison, it would drive them crazy. It wouldn't be long before jealousy and lust combined to break their will and deliver to her bed all three Davis brothers.

Patton laughed and immediately clamped her hand over her mouth to muzzle the sound. It wouldn't work if she gave them any indication that she'd planned it all. That would just solidify their resistance.

No. It had to be a surprise attack. It would also require her to make a trip back to Atlanta to get everything settled on that end. Then she could move back here. Not to the ranch, that would never work. She'd have to find somewhere else to stay and she had just an idea where to look.

Bounding off the bed, she looked around her room. Nothing here was worth taking. Pinning a note of the expected kind, she picked up her purse and rushed out of the ranch and into her future.

Chapter 12

"That's sexy." Hailey leaned in to watch Patton's drawing come up on the monitor as the scanner finished.

"Yeah. I hope the client likes it." Patton bent over to save the sketch as a file and open her email account.

"Client? That's not part of your collection?" Hailey sat down on the other side of the kitchen table.

Patton had moved in with her four days ago. Hailey had been glad for the company. Her three-bedroom house had always seemed a little big, but then Patton had driven to Atlanta and brought back a ton of stuff. The place suddenly seemed much smaller. Not that Hailey minded.

"No, it's a specialty order piece."

"I didn't realize some women ordered custom-made underwear." Not that it shocked Hailey, but Patton's response did.

"I guess they consider it a business investment."

"You're not... I mean, you don't mean..."

"Call girls?" Patton looked up with a smile. "Don't look so shocked, Hailey."

"It's just I didn't realize you catered to that kind of clientele." Hailey popped open her soda can.

"When you need money, you can't be picky about your clients. Besides," Patton shrugged, "I'm a woman trying to convince three brothers to have an intimate relationship with me. I'm not exactly prudish myself."

"I thought you had given up on that." Hailey scowled. "Isn't that why you're staying here?"

"Nope. I'm staying here because I want those boys to suffer the consequences of their decision."

"You're punishing them?"

"Yeah." Patton grinned. "I'm punishing them. They think they're the masters, doling out punishment as they see fit. Well, I'm the new mistress in town."

"You said they threw you out."

"No, I said Chase told me to leave," Patton corrected her, looking at her laptop as it searched for an Internet connection. "He wants me to go back to Atlanta. He wants me to find happiness with another man, fine. But I'm not going to give him the satisfaction of hiding the reality of what that means five hours away in Atlanta. I'm going to do it right here, right in front of them."

"That sounds kind of mean," Hailey scowled, looking uncomfortable with Patton's comments. "I mean, you're basically going to try and make them jealous, right?"

"I like the way I said it better." The computer beeped and Hailey watched silently for a moment as Patton typed away at the keys.

"Well, you can dress it up any way you want, Patton, but it's still a petty thing to do."

"I thought you wanted me to start dating other men."

"I do, but not in such a way that you end up creating a disaster. I mean, think about this. Let's just say your plan works, and they're driven insane with jealousy, who's to say they just don't beat the shit out of the man you're dating? Then you end up without the brothers and with a man in the hospital. What does that get you?"

Patton scoffed. "I wouldn't let them beat anybody up."

"I respect the fact that you think you can control them, but you can't." Hailey paused as if to consider how to say what she had to say. "I love you as a sister, you know that."

"Yeah, I know it."

"And you've been hot for those men since you were sixteen."

"A long time." She drew out the words, still on the letter she was writing.

"And I know you think you know about their unique proclivities, but you don't know everything."

"I know all about their particular interests, Hailey. Trust me."

"I'm not just talking about domination games and sharing, Patton. There are other rumors."

"What rumors?" Her hands stilled as she looked up, finally focusing on Hailey.

"It's not just them."

"You know something." Patton stared at Hailey in shock. "What do you know?"

"When you told me about their side business, it gave credence to some of the rumors I've heard but never believed. See, people whisper that they share with more than each other. There's a group of men that are into that."

"A group?"

"Like a club."

"You're serious."

"You remember the old, run-down lodge by PB Pond?"

"Yeah."

"Chase bought it a few years ago and fixed it up. Nobody really knows what goes on down there, but there is an awful lot of activity."

"Are you trying to tell me they expanded their business outside the barn and to the lodge?"

"I don't know. There is a lot of talk and you see a lot of women around town with…chokers on. Most of them are here for a short time and then they leave."

"I can't believe this."

"Whatever it is, it's kept real quiet between whoever is involved. The rumors stem off the men seen with the women wearing the…chokers, off the trucks people can identify parked in front of the lodge, but that means half the men in this town. Hell, all the sheriff's deputies and the mayor, too."

"And you didn't see fit to tell me this before? Why?"

"I didn't know if it was true. You know how people are in this town. They like to talk. Ain't got much else to do at night but to drink, fuck and gossip. So who the hell knows what the truth is?"

Patton stared at Hailey, absorbing what she had said. Maybe the brothers had just given up the financial aspects of it and moved on to training women for the fun of it. That wasn't such a far stretch. Women who needed those types of skills were still around, probably more abundant than ever with the growing economy in Atlanta catering to convention goers and world travelers.

Ah hell, that would explain how they found out about her business. Patton knew a few of her clients catered to just such type of customer. She'd certainly made very specialty outfits for them. What if one of her clients had been one of the brothers' clients?

Hailey pulled her attention away from her thoughts. "I'm just saying, what if the man you pick is part of their group? There could be some serious backlash to that."

"If what you're saying is true, then that is probably one of the reasons they want me out of town so bad."

"But it doesn't change your mind." Hailey slumped back in her chair, fiddling with her soda can.

"Hell, no, sweetheart. It just makes everything better. Chase wouldn't train me, but I'm betting one of his buddies will. Just think how that will go over with the Davis boys."

"Yeah, well, what if they put the word out not to touch you?"

"What does their word mean to a bunch of horny men?" Patton snickered.

"It means I have to go to Dothan to find a date," Hailey shot back. "I'm telling you, Patton, this is a dangerous town to play games in. We're not in a position of power here."

"Hmm." Patton shrugged after a moment. "What else am I supposed to do, Hailey? I'm in love and I'm hurting."

"I know you are." Hailey reached out to cover her hand with her own.

"I'd like to say that I'm better than getting even, but the truth is, I'm not. I want them to suffer." Patton smiled sadly. "I've wanted them to know what it is like to see the person you love go out with one woman after another and then go home to an empty bed and lay there being eaten alive with jealousy."

"Well, if you're going to start dating women..." Hailey smiled.

"You know what I meant." Patton rolled her eyes.

"I know and I understand." Hailey squeezed her hand before letting go. "Hell, I'm as human as you are, but that doesn't mean I'm not worried about your plans."

"The truth? I'm worried, too." Patton sighed. "I'm not sure what I'm doing anymore. I got nothing but emotion driving me forward."

"Driving without brakes, huh?"

"Destination—crash, site—Stanley's Spring Break Bash this afternoon, be there or be square." Patton retorted with a smirk.

Hailey smiled slightly. "In that case, I better get my bathing suit on. Just don't land me in jail. Okay?"

"Friends to the end?"

"To the grave." Hailey gave her a sharp look. "Just don't get me arrested."

* * * *

"Are you sure you want to do this?" The doubt in Hailey's eyes as she cast a quick glance Patton's way was as evident as it was in the question.

"They wanted a war, they got one," Patton stated dispassionately as she looked around at the pool party in full swing.

The hot sun shined down on the Saturday, adding to the allure of the sparkling water that tempted the partygoers to cool off. Most of the town had shown up for Stanley's normal Spring Break Bash. While Spring Break might have been a traditional celebration for the children and teenagers, Stanley's bash catered only to adults, thanks to the open bar that assured a long and wild party.

Patton had never been, but when she'd hear about it, she had known she'd found the perfect venue for her coming out. When she had gone back to Atlanta to pick up her sewing machine and some supplies, she had stopped in at a favorite boutique that specialized in swimwear.

Her bathing suit didn't reveal as much as the thongs many of the women wore, but it was still an attention getter. The one thing Patton had learned with her designs, sexy wasn't so much a matter of how much you revealed, as it was about how it was revealed.

"Come on, let's go see if there are any free loungers."

Patton didn't wait to see if Hailey followed but began cutting through the crowd. With what Hailey had told her the other day, Patton looked at the people with new eyes. As old friends and acquaintances greeted her, she noticed that some wore chokers. A lot of women that Patton didn't know wore the specialized neckwear. The only other thing they all had in common, they were hot. Figured.

Finding a set of loungers still available, Hailey and Patton dropped their bags. Hailey took off to get some beers while Patton began to unveil her masterpiece. She had just begun to lift her shirt when two strong hands covered hers and halted their process.

"Need some help?" a deep, rough voice asked.

Turning her head, Patton stared at the tall and well-toned man. He smelled of leather, sun and male, a combination created to drive women into heat. If that wasn't weapon enough, the stud had been graced with the brightest green eyes, a perfect set of white teeth and a double set of dimples destined to give women heart palpitations.

He was almost good enough to distract her from her main intention. Almost, but not quite. He was definitely worth keeping in mind. If things didn't work out the way she wanted over the next few days, she'd use him as a consolation prize.

That thought made her grin. Her smile was all the permission he appeared to need. The man used his hold on her waist to pull her closer into the heat and hardness of his body.

"My mama taught me not to let strangers undress me."

"I'm Cole. Cole Jackson."

As if that declaration gave him rights, he curled his fingers under her T-shirt and lifted. Reflexively her arms lifted, allowing him to slide the soft cotton up. For a moment, he hesitated and Patton was blinded, bound by her own shirt.

A second later she was free and narrowing her eyes on Mr. Cole Jackson. He gave her a slow smile, letting his hands come back to her waist. Something dark in those green eyes swirled to life, something aggressive and predatory.

Patton shivered under his gaze, feeling the tingles of awareness begin to awaken her body. A revelation for her, Patton wondered in that moment if her response to Devin that night in the barn had been solely because he had been dominating her, or if she were the type who would enjoyed submitting to a man's sexual desires.

Her body's response to Cole gave her hope. If she couldn't have the men she wanted, she could at least have some of what she wanted.

"What did you say your name was, sweet thing?" Cole drawled, letting his work roughened thumbs sensually tease the sensitive skin of her lower back. The touch was electric and Patton arched slightly under the caress.

"Patton," her voice had gone soft, husky. "Patton Jo—"

Her words cut off as Cole got yanked suddenly away and thrown aside to reveal the fire-breathing dragon known as Devin Davis.

"Get your hands off her, Jackson!" Devin roared as he pushed the man back.

Men and women moved out of the way, their conversation stilling as their attention diverted to what looked to be the beginning of the first fight of the bash.

"What the hell, Davis," Cole snapped, shoving Devin a mere inch back over the foot that Devin had thrown him.

"Keep your hands off her!" Devin snarled, stepping into the younger man.

"What's it to you? I don't see your name branded on the little woman."

"She's my sister."

"Ah, shit," Cole groaned. He knew Devin well enough to know the other man could throw down with the best of them. Not that Cole would back away from a fight, but if the little miss was his sister, Devin was in the right.

Cole could understand, even respected Davis's stance. He had a younger sister himself. The last thing he'd ever want was for Chelsea to become involved with a Cattleman.

Davis wouldn't stop him. Cole would just have to be discreet about his pursuit, find a time when the little Patton wasn't so well protected. He wouldn't bother if the woman didn't appear interested, but he'd seen the flare of desire in those captivating violet eyes.

"My mistake." Cole held his hands up in surrender. "I didn't mean any disrespect. I didn't know you had a sister, Davis."

"I am not his sister," Patton snapped, coming between the two. "Don't you be telling anybody that I am, Devin. We're not related by flesh or law and you know that."

"I'll deal with you in a moment, Patton."

"Deal with me?" Patton's eyes went wide. "I don't think so."

"Patton."

"Don't Patton me." Patton's eyes cut over his shoulder to catch sight of Charlotte. The other woman glared hatefully back at her. "Why don't you just go back to your games and plaything, Devin, and leave the real men and women to their business?"

A perfect exit line, Patton turned, planning to flounce off in high indignation. She ran smack into the naked wall of Slade's chest. Before she could react, he latched a hand around hers.

"Devin, why don't you have a talk with Cole? I'll take care of Patton."

It hadn't been a suggestion. It had been order. While Devin might have bowed to Slade's authority, Patton didn't feel so compelled. She yanked on her hand, but he just tightened his grip until it hurt.

"Settle down, Patton. We don't want a scene," Slade whispered for her ears alone.

"You might not, but I don't care."

"You force a scene and I'll give you one." Slade's hard tone warned her that he had not just issued an idle threat. "I'll put you right over my knees and paddle your ass in the middle of this party. Now get your bag."

Chapter 13

"Let me go," Patton snarled softly as Slade used his hold on her to force her through the crowd toward the large yard where all the cars were parked.

"Smile, Patton."

"You're such a bastard," she stated with a big smile.

"Why are you here?" Slade demanded, ignoring her insult.

"Because I was invited," she snapped back obnoxiously.

"I meant in this town," Slade growled through his fake smile. "You are supposed to be in Atlanta."

"Who says?"

"The note you left with Charlotte last Sunday."

"My note said goodbye, Slade. Not I'm going to Atlanta."

"Stop playing games. Just say what you mean."

"I did. I said goodbye, as in good riddance. I'm done with you three assholes. I've got better things to do with my time and better men to do it with."

Patton's words struck deep. Rage boiled through Slade and he yanked on her arm harder than he intended. She stumbled and yanked back.

"You're not going to find those men here."

"Says you, but from the rumors I'm hearing I think I'm going to find a perfect replacement for you, with ropes, toy rooms and all. Isn't that right, Slade?"

That brought him to a stop. He turned on her so suddenly she walked right into him. Stepping back, she rubbed her nose as she glared with at him.

"What rumors?"

"You know what rumors. The barn wasn't enough for you, was it? Chase had to go buy a whole frigging lodge for you boys to play nasty in."

"You know about that?" Slade felt his stomach drop.

"Know?" Her eyes widened with her exaggerated tone. "Know about how you made your little side business into some dirty club where all the local guys are free to join. All they need is the attitude and big enough dick, right?"

"I can explain."

"Don't bother." Patton's smile made his inside go cold. "I really should be thanking you."

"Thanking me?" Slade's eyes narrowed on her. "Why?"

"For giving me so many options, duh." Patton rolled her eyes. "I did like that sample Devin gave me. Since that was a one time only deal, you can imagine how excited I am to be in a town full of dominant men. All trained in the fine art of pleasing a woman, thanks to you."

Slade clenched his jaw, too afraid of what he might say in response to that bit of logic. It couldn't happen. No matter what Patton thought, not one single man in their club would touch her.

He would see to that. He'd start with Cole Jackson. When he had seen Jackson pull off her shirt, Slade had seen red. That little stunt of binding her with the fabric had been a classic warm up move. It would be Cole's last move on Patton.

Jackson was a well-respected Cattleman. He'd earned his full membership status quicker than most, but Slade didn't see that in a favorable light at this moment. Cole could be slippery when it came to getting what he wanted. There could be no doubt what that Cattleman wanted.

A primitive animal instinct flared to life in him. He'd almost lost it watching the young stud holding her close, touching Patton's bare flesh. He wanted to rip Patton out of Cole's arms and beat the man to a pulp.

He wanted to push Patton down and fuck her right there in the middle of the party. He wanted to make her scream with pleasure so that every man there knew she was his. If Devin hadn't interfered first, the very least Slade would have done was punch the Jackson bastard.

"Where are you taking me?" Patton dug her heels into the grass when he pulled her up to the side of her truck He was close to breaking. One more push from Patton would tumble his control.

"Get in the truck, Patton."

"No." She yanked her arms free and backed away. "You don't own me Slade. I don't have to do a damn thing you say."

"Don't push me. I'm on my last thread here."

"Oh?" She widened her eyes. "Is that supposed to scare me? What are you going to do, Slade?"

"You don't want to find out," he warned, advancing on her.

"You're not going to do anything. You're all talk and no action. That's all you've ever been. A lot of hot air and empty threats. Face it, Slade, you're just not man enough to control me."

The worst thing she could have said to him, it figured she'd say it. She seemed completely unaware of how vulnerable she was with her breasts barely contained in the small cups of her bikini. The low riding wrap skirt revealed the smooth, tanned flesh of her stomach with the little belly button ring glinting in the sun. She was a banquet for his starving eyes.

Not man enough? Control? He'd show her exactly what he could do.

Patton's mouth opened to blast him again. Whatever she had been about to say, it turned into a startled shriek as he lifted her up and shoved her onto the seat.

Her wrap skirt twisted about her, coming undone to reveal her tiny bikini bottoms. The two halves held together by little strings tore easily under his hands. Patton must have realized she had pushed him too far.

She began slapping at his hands, cussing him and trying to squirm away. She was no match for his superior strength. He held her still with one hand on her thigh and ripped the bikini bottoms out of his way.

His eyes feasted on the swollen, pink folds of her cunt. Despite her threats and demands, her naked flesh glistened with the evidence of her desire. The smell of her arousal drugged him, transfixing him on a single goal.

Nothing restrained him. She had said she wanted a man to treat her this way. The only man who was going to do that was him. Dragging her across the seat, he forced her legs wide. Without hesitation, he buried his head between her soft thighs and began to devour her weeping pussy.

* * * *

Patton jumped when the tip of tongue slid up her pussy and brushed against her clit. Slade did not bother with a gentle, seductive build-up to the moment. He attacked her clit, lapping repeatedly at it. He swirled his tongue around and around, working her little nub into a firestorm of sensation.

Patton arched her back, bucking toward his mouth and giving him enough room to slide his hand under her bottom. He held her still as he continued to torment her over sensitized bud. It was too much and Patton snapped.

Patton writhed in Slade's hold as mindless pleasure swamped her body. Slade appeared unaware of her condition, never pausing as he continued to work his rough tongue over her clit.

Her body shook with the pleasure he forced on her. Her orgasm felt never ending as it flowed from her pussy over her limbs, encircling her hard nipples. Those hard little tips ached for attention.

Patton felt like a bitch in heat, desperate for the touch and feel of a man's hands on her body. Slade's hands gripped her hip and butt, but her tits needed to be played with.

Patton grabbed her breasts and began pulling, rolling, tormenting her nipples, trying to match the rhythm of his tongue. She trashed under the combined effects of his mouth eating her pussy and her hands on her breasts.

When she hit the right speed, rolling both her tips with the flat of her palm in the same motion he used to roll her clit, her body shattered under a great, rippling wave of ecstasy. Wave after wave of rapture rolled through her, echoing from her toes to her head.

The intense pleasure wouldn't stop, not with Slade's tongue continuing to torment her. Her body was one huge mass of intense pleasure that refused to be contained. Her heart raced as she tried to draw enough oxygen into her lungs to keep from passing out.

Her muscles ached as they contracted again, threatening to shred under the pressure. Still he kept going, kept pushing her harder. Patton sobbed as his tongue flicked her over stimulated clit, begging for just a moment of peace. Her cries fell on deaf ears.

Slade might have seemed unaware of Patton's cries, but he heard every single one. They fed the animalistic lust driving him. Poor thing, she had to be the loudest woman he'd ever tongue fucked. A little training could fix that, but Slade wouldn't bother.

Her cries could be heard throughout the yard, probably back into the house. Anybody who heard them would know what they were doing. They would know that she was his and none would dare to get between them. A raw growl sounded in the back of his throat with that primitive thought.

Slade pierced the shuddering depths of her tight, virgin pussy, eating into her pulsing sheath with the desperation of a starved man. He could not get enough. Spearing his tongue into the exquisite clench of her inner muscles, he fucked her with deep, greedy strokes until she flooded him with another wave of lush, sweet cream.

Patton screamed out her release as she rode his mouth. Her hands, clenched around his tresses to force him closer, his tongue deeper. He rewarded her demand by fucking into her with fast, hard strokes, wiggling his tongue until he found the sweet spot hidden in her depths.

Tickling her G-spot in rhythm with his thumb on her clit sent her right into another explosion. The aftershocks of her last climax fueled the inferno that threatened to consume her body in its fiery embrace.

He growled, the sound vibrating against her flesh. Lapping up the liquid proof her climax, he became more aggressive. His fingers bit into her thighs, trying to force them wider. He licked back up her slit to find the hard bundle of nerves and nip it with his teeth.

Patton squealed at the sudden assault. The sudden zing of pained pleasure sent a shock through her body. The sensation was almost immediately drowned in a rush of ecstasy as he thrust his fingers back into her clenching pussy while his tongue laved at her clit.

This time when her climax broke, she shot straight up, her hips arching so high his finger slid from her spasming sheath. Slade growled and slammed her back down, apparently not yet done with his treat.

Boldly, with dark intent, he slid his finger down from her dripping cunt to the tight, entrance of her ass. Patton cried out in surprise, immediately trying to squirm away. His held her in place, keeping her pinned as his fingers circled the rim of her anus.

Without any hesitation, he pressed his thick digit into her clenched, untried channel. Pain blurred with the intense pleasure electrifying her body. Even as her mind revolted against the forbidden act, her body responded.

The walls of her passage tried to grip his finger, tightening around it to increase the sensation of being stretched. Slade reveled in the way her body shivered and shook as he stretched her back entrance.

He kept his mouth firmly latched onto her clit, making sure she received pleasure as well as the pain. He drove her straight through one orgasm and into another, and kept on going.

He could spend hours, days, years with his head buried in her softness. She was so sweet, so hot. The only thing better would to have his cock buried deep into her tight little cunt, pounding into her hard and fast.

He needed that and he needed it now.

"God damnit, Slade!" Chase's roar washed over the couple a second before Slade was ripped violently away from her.

The motion jarred her so hard Patton rolled off the seat and slammed her head into the dashboard on her way to the floor. Chase shoved her legs upward and slammed the truck door with enough force to shake the large vehicle.

Patton blinked, her mind having trouble focusing. Her mind might be having problems functioning, but her ears weren't. The words being shouted just outside the window registered, bringing a harsh does of reality with them.

Chapter 14

"What the hell do you think you're doing?" Chase roared as he shoved Slade.

Slade stumbled back, still dazed with lust, and crashed to the ground. The jarring impact snapped him back to reality. Chase stood over him, white-knuckled fists and flaring nostrils.

"Are you going to answer me?" Chase snarled. "Or do I have to beat it out of you?"

Slade explained quickly, about Cole and Patton's comments on finding another guy, everything that had driven him pass his tolerance and ignited the primitive male urge in him to claim what was his.

"Jesus." Chase swallowed.

Chase's anger appeared to shift. Slade knew where it was refocusing. On the same person his own anger had been aimed at, Cole. The younger man had dared to touch Patton. He could do something about that, but not about the fact that someday some man would be touching Patton and it wouldn't be him.

"What a mess."

"She's changed, Chase." Slade hesitantly gained his feet. He felt pretty sure his brother wouldn't hit him now. "She's not our little girl anymore."

"Don't you think I know that?" Chase snapped. "But this is too much, we can't have her running around town inciting the Cattlemen. Despite what you said, there isn't any guarantee that one of them wouldn't take her up on her offer."

"There's only one way to stop that from happening."

"Don't say it, Slade. Don't even think it."

"Why the hell not? It's what we want, what she wants—"

"Patton doesn't know what the fuck she wants!" Chase roared. "Think with your head, not your dick."

"I'm thinking with my heart, you asshole." Slade's hands curled into fists. "I love her and I know both Devin and you do, too. The only reason we ever held back is because of the fear it wouldn't be what Patton wanted, but now we know it is. Jesus, Chase, why fight it?"

"She got some romantic, girlish notions and that's it. Once she realizes how rough it gets, she'll be changing her tune."

"And what if you're wrong? What if she doesn't change her tune? What if she loves it and begs for more?"

"Loves it? Patton might enjoy playing games for a night, but for a lifetime? It wouldn't take long before the she realized that it isn't a game and then what? It will wear thin on her."

"I don't think it will, Chase."

"You really think Patton will accept obeying us in every way?"

"In every way?" Slade shook his head. "We could try that thing called compromise. Pick our battles, let her have her way on some things."

"On some things?" Chase snickered. "Let me ask you this. What you do think about those pictures on the Internet? Her little catalog?" When Slade didn't answer, Chase smirked. "That's right, the first thing that would have to go is that. You think Patton's going to just bend over and accept that?"

"She might." Slade didn't believe it himself.

"What if she doesn't? I would tear my heart out and serve it to her on a platter if it would make her happy, Slade. You know this."

"But what we're doing is tearing hers out. We're denying her ourselves, not giving her a chance."

"She's too young, damn it. She's a goddamn virgin. How the hell does she doesn't know what she wants."

"The hell with that excuse. She's a grown woman."

"The fact is that Patton is innocent and she doesn't know what's she getting herself into. I can't do what Devin did and give her only a sample. Can you do it? Can you have Patton and then just let her go?"

"I don't think she'll leave," Slade stubbornly insisted.

"I can't take that risk. I wouldn't risk hurting Patton." Chase's shoulders slumped, the fight appearing to drain right out of him.

"You're already hurting her," Slade stated softly.

"Think about what is best for Patton. If you love her, you wouldn't force this on her. You wouldn't seduce her into chains, Slade. You'll let her go free."

With that, Chase turned on his heals and stomped away. Slade frowned at his brother's retreating back in concern. It wasn't uncommon for Chase to lose his temper or go fist to fist with his brothers, but the pain he'd seen in Chase's eyes had been a sight he'd never before seen in his older brother.

Was he being selfish? Maybe Chase was right. Patton was a virgin. No matter the sample Devin gave her, it couldn't be the same thing as having three men dominate her. They wouldn't contain it just to the bedroom, either. Chase had a right to be worried about that.

Patton was a bossy, determined woman. Her reaction to orders had always been the same, instant rejection. There was no quit in her when she put her mind to something, no extreme too far to go to attain her goals.

It was what made her both desirable and maddening. If they did claim her, they'd probably have to spend the rest of their lives taming her. Even then, they had no guarantee of success, but it would be a fun ride.

Or would it? Would she grow to hate and resent them? Would it change her from wild and carefree to bitter and conniving? Slade scowled. That question bothered him and he knew it bothered Chase, too.

Slade turned toward the truck and hesitated. They'd forgotten all about the fact that she was in there, listening to their argument. Slade didn't need to imagine what her response would be.

Ah, hell. I'm about to get it.

Bracing himself for Patton's fury, he opened the door to find the cab empty. Slade scowled as he looked straight through the truck and out into the yard revealed by the open driver's side door.

In the distance he heard a motorcycle engine fire to life. Slade closed his eyes and prayed that wasn't the same bike Patton had taunted Chase with only days before.

* * * *

"Another." Patton shook her empty bottle at Riley before letting the glass donk into the hard wooden surface of the bar. With a sigh, she rolled her feet over the edge of the stool and glared at nothing in particular.

She hadn't been in the mood to return back to Hailey's empty house and going back to the party hadn't been an option. Despite her unusual get up or the early hour, Patton had decided to spend her time brooding at The Pub.

Torn between excitement and disappointment, Patton didn't even know what she felt. Today she could claim one small victory. Her plan to make the Davis brothers jealous had worked. The outcome had been exactly what she hoped for.

Right up until Chase's appearance on the scene. Spoiled sport had ruined all her fun. She had never doubted that Chase would be the biggest obstacle to overcome. It had been her hope to turn Devin and Slade against him and thus outnumber him to a victory.

The problem was, she was horny and nobody was around to scratch her itch. She could just go home and do it herself, but that idea held little appeal when compared to the amazing orgasms Slade had given her with his mouth. No dildo could compare. Patton's head dropped.

At least she had the bar to herself. Nobody was around to witness her dreadful condition but Riley, until the jingle about the front door rang out its cheery greeting. Apparently, another person in town thought hanging out in a dark bar in the middle of a sunlit spring afternoon sounded like a good idea.

Patton wondered what other lost soul had made his way into Riley's boring day. Her interest didn't prod her into looking up, even when she heard the stool beside her creak and a large, denim covered thigh broke into her lowered view.

Figured. The jerk probably saw a woman dressed in a bikini sitting at the bar and thought he hit the jackpot. A few well-placed words should dissuade him of that notion. She better be quick with her rebuttal before the man got any bad ideas.

"Well, that was a disaster, huh?" Patton's head snapped up to look straight into Devin's eyes. He grinned at her before looking toward Riley. "Bring me one of what the lady's having."

"What are you doing here?"

"Looking for you, duh." Devin rolled his eyes.

"You naturally assumed I would be here, in a bar."

"Where else?" Devin turned that damn double dimple grin back on her. "Given the way your day is going, stands to reason having a drink would sound like a good idea."

"You're in an awfully good mood." The hiss of a bottle losing its top echoed the plaintive sound in her tone.

"Why wouldn't I be?"

"I don't know." Patton shrugged. "Last time I saw you, you were threatening bodily harm to a man who looked like he could hold his own in a fight."

"Cole and I settle our disagreement with words. No need for fists."

He appeared unconcerned by the fight he almost had. Instead he focused on nodding his thanks to Riley as the bartender set two fresh beers in front of them. Devin's large, solid shoulder bumped into hers as he leaned to the side to pull his wallet out from his back pocket. Patton made a dirty face, not that either man paid her any mind. With annoyance, she shifted out of his way.

"Seriously, Devin." Patton pushed once Riley turned back to cleaning behind the bar.

"Seriously, Patton." He faked an injured expression that had Patton rolling her eyes. "I can do more than throw punches, you know."

Patton let that slide and an uneasy silence thickened between them. She was probably the only one who thought of it that way. Devin sprawled back in his stool, as comfortable as he pleased, that stupid grin reflecting back at her in the mirror behind the bar.

"So how did you find me?"

"Riley called and told me."

"Rat." Patton shot Riley a disgusted look. The barkeep just smirked and shrugged before he began pulling out packs of beer from one of the coolers.

"You didn't call anybody else, did you?"

"Like who?" Riley looked up for a moment to give her the best innocent look his rugged features would allow.

"Like Chase."

"That's who I called in the first place."

"I answered the phone," Devin supplied before Patton could ask.

"Why?"

"He wasn't in any condition to do it himself."

"You going to make me drag this out of you, bit by bit, huh?"

"He was busy."

"I can imagine with what."

"Your perverted brain would come up with the wrong answer." Devin took a drag on his bottle before lowering it to rest against his hard stomach. The move drew Patton's eyes downward to admire the well-muscled body beneath his shirt. She could hardly miss the erection pushing against his jeans below his belt buckle either. She wasn't the only pervert sitting at the bar.

"Chase was one sheet short of being three to the wind and working hard to catch up fast though."

"Slade? He ain't going to show up next is he?"

"Doubt it. After the spectacular blow up between Chase and him, he hopped in his truck and threw dirt on his way down the drive. I imagine right now he's at home—"

"Beating the hell out of Charlotte's ass and wishing it was mine," Patton muttered.

"There you go again, letting the pervert inside rule. Charlotte's back at the party, probably praying Chase doesn't get so drunk as to be totally useless."

"That's the positive thought I need to brighten my day." Patton raised her bottle to him.

"Ah, don't worry about it, little one. Even if Chase doesn't drink enough to need the help of his brothers carrying his passed out ass to bed, he wouldn't make Charlotte's prayers come true."

"Says who?"

"Says me and I know. Chase wouldn't fuck Charlotte."

"Why not? That's what you keep her around for."

"Not this past week. Not any of us."

The quite seriousness to Devin's tone made goose bumps prickle down her arms. With those few words, he said so much more. For the first time, in a long time, Patton felt special, loved. The sensation should have been welcome. Instead it highlighted the aching loneliness inside her heart.

She dropped her head, unable to stop the pout or the words that came out of her mouth. "I should believe that, why?"

"Because I've never lied to you."

He hit Patton hard with that one. Whatever else she could say about the brothers, they'd always been honest with her, even if they hadn't told her everything. It was more than could be said about her. She shied away from that guilt.

"Slade's home pouting, Chase is off getting shit faced, all fighters back in their corners, huh?"

"Disappointed?"

"What the hell does that mean?"

"It's just a question." It wasn't and his tone belied that fact.

"Yeah, well, take your questions elsewhere," Patton retorted. "You're disturbing my solitude."

"Ah, that's what this is and here I thought you were having a beer while you plotted your next scheme."

"Excuse me?"

"You know, the next round in this master plan that is unfolding."

"I do not know what you are talking about."

"Oh, don't play innocent with me." Devin's empty bottle smacked the bar top with the first signs of aggression. "I may not have Slade's smarts, but I ain't dumb. I know you, Patton. You didn't just accidentally forget to tell us you were staying with Hailey in town. Nor do I consider it coincidence that you showed up at the biggest party and five minutes later had another man's hands all over you."

"You're suggesting I planned this."

"Artfully staged by the mistress of manipulation." Devin waved the empty bottle to emphasize his grand pronouncement.

"And Cole?"

"Just another helpless pawn in your game. An innocent bystander that jumped into a situation he had no idea had been fabricated to attain the results that you wanted."

"I don't think the words Cole and innocent belong together."

"Rarely, but in this case…"

Patton glared at him. "If that is what you think, why are you smiling?"

"Well, one, because I figured it out and Slade and Chase didn't. Two, because I'm game."

"You're game?"

"I'm wishing you nothing but success, sweetheart."

"Well, hell, then why are we sitting her talking when we could be wasting the afternoon away in other, more pleasurable, pursuits?"

"I wish, believe me." Devin gave her a long look that sent heat bombs off through her body. "I really do, but that's not the rules of the game. You know that."

"The rules are what we make them."

"Yeah, but I'd like to live to enjoy the fruits of your success. If I go against both Slade and Chase, one of them will kill me."

"So, you're not going to help?"

"Look at it this way, I'm not going to get in the way."

"You already did with Cole."

"With good reason. If I hadn't been first on the scene, that man would have ended the day with a broken nose at least. Besides, you got what you wanted out of the deal."

"Did I?"

"Slade saw red and whatever happened in the yard sounded good poolside."

"It did?" Patton paled, her voice becoming a high-pitched squeak. "You could hear?"

"Sounded like some woman got fucked good." Devin smirked. "Of course, if that had been the case we wouldn't be sitting here and Slade and Chase would be looking to have a much better night."

"No fun for nobody."

"I wouldn't go that far. You could have some fun."

She picked up at those words. "Another taste of the forbidden?"

"Ah, I like my skin on my body." Devin gave her an apologetic smile. "I think dinner and a movie would be more appropriate."

"If that's all I can get."

"Come on, Patton. Why does it all have to be about sex?"

"Because I've never gotten any and I'm getting damn tired of it?"

"It's been a long time since we just hung out and had fun and I'm getting damned tired of that."

"You're a pain."

"Are you going to sit here in this boring bar making sharp comments or get off that lazy ass and take me out to eat, woman?"

"You're paying." Patton slid off her stool.

Chapter 15

"Don't I always?" Devin stood, looping an arm around her shoulders.

It was an old gesture. One that held new meaning to him now and despite the 'just hanging out' comment, when Patton snuggled into his side, Devin didn't say a word.

It felt right in more ways than he'd admit at that moment. Instinctively his arm tightened, bringing her in closer as he escorted her toward the door. They paused only long enough to say goodbye to Riley.

"We need to stop by Hailey's so I can change."

Patton's comment drew his eyes straight down and they lingered on the sight of her smooth, golden globes enticingly cupped by her bikini. "Why? I like what you got on."

"Friends, Devin, remember?"

"Fine." He sighed in disappointment. "Whose stupid idea was that anyway?"

"Yours."

Yeah, it would have to be his dumb ass that suggested something so obscene. Devin smirked at his own thoughts. He was being noble and damn if that wasn't completely out of character. Too bad his brothers weren't around to appreciate the moment.

Devin's good humor evaporated the instant they turned the corner of bar and into the parking lot that The Pub shared with the small florist on the other side of the lot. When he'd parked, there had been two other cars in the lot. While neither had looked like the rental

Patton had driven down, he'd assumed she'd gotten a new rental or actually brought her car.

He'd assumed wrong.

Devin's feet ground to a halt as he stared at the stripped down black motorcycle parked in the lot, the only other vehicle left besides his truck. The owner had pulled it around so that instead of having to back out of the space, the bike could be driven straight out. The position left the Georgia license tag staring him in the face, the words Fulton across the bottom.

"What's wrong?"

"You weren't just screwing with Chase."

"What?" Devin sensed Patton's head turning toward him, but he couldn't tear his eyes off the bike to glare back at her. "Oh, yeah. No, I wasn't screwing with him. That's my bike. What do you think?"

The question asked in that cheery, excited tone had him growling out his answer. "I think you need to be put over a man's knees and paddled until some sense echoes in that empty head of yours."

"Excuse me?"

"Did you really drive that thing here? Today? In nothing more than a bikini and flip flops?"

"That's really none of your business, Devin. I'm my own woman and I do what I want. If you have a problem with that then you can just get in your truck and get the hell out of here."

With that grand pronouncement, she turned to flounce off toward the deadly black beast, leaving Devin with only three options. He could let her get on the damn thing and ride off to her doom. His heart clenched painfully at that thought.

He could do what he most wanted to and snatch her up and paddle her ass for being so difficult, then smash her bike with his truck. That choice would only lead to her hating him or him fucking her. Either one would be an unacceptable conclusion, at least for now.

That left him with only one thing to do. Rein in his tempter, make amends, huddle her into the truck and make damn sure she arrived home safely. It was going to be difficult, but Devin had no choice.

"Hold on." Devin snatched her back by the arm.

"Yes?"

"I'm sorry."

"You could say it like you mean it."

"Well, I don't mean it, but I'm saying it anyway." Devin snapped. "I'm sorry, Patton. I love you and I don't want to see you maimed, dismembered or killed. Forgive me."

"I'm not going to be hurt, Devin." The way she rolled her eyes had his hand tightening around her arm with the need to shake her. "I know how to ride the bike. I took lessons."

"Yeah, what about all the other assholes on the road?"

"It's called defensive driving."

"It's called, 'I don't want to argue about this, so get in the truck and I'll take you to dinner'."

"We could take my bike. I'll let you sit in the bitch seat."

"Don't push it, Patton."

She eyed him for a moment before she held her hand out to him. "Give me your cell phone."

"What?"

"Give me your cell phone and I'll get in the truck."

"Why should I give you my phone?"

"So that while we're out having a great time as friends, you're not tempted to sneak into the bathroom and call anybody. When this night is over, I expect my bike to be in one piece, right here, where I left it."

Devin hadn't thought of that, but he would have. Glaring at her, he unclipped his phone from his belt and slapped it into her hands. "Happy now?"

"Glowing with joy, let's go eat."

* * * *

The ride back to Hailey's place was tense and Patton considered backing out of the evening. As she changed her clothes, she admitted that it wasn't all Devin's fault. Half of the truck had been filled with her annoyance with him.

He had tried to control her and it irked. If she got her way though, she'd spend the rest of her life dealing with moments like these. It would either be a miserable life as Chase constantly pointed out or she had to learn a new way with handling these kinds of problems.

Compromise, the word floated through her head. Hated and annoying, the concept had never been easy for her. Still, for the Davis brothers and the hope of future with them, she would have to learn. So would they. That thought picked up her spirits.

Pulling her purse over her shoulder and plastering a smile on her face, she walked back to where Devin waited for her in the living room. He flipped through her sketchbook with that look on his face.

"Like what you see?"

Devin's heated gaze lifted up. "Not bad."

"Not bad." Patton snorted. "That's why you're threatening to bust your zipper?"

"Hard wired reaction."

"I'm really good at what I do, Devin."

"I can see that, but don't you ever want to move beyond the thong and...I don't know, design dresses or something more...well, less revealing?"

"I might," this time it was her turn to shrug, "one day."

"Hmm."

Compromise, the word whispered through her again. "Let's not argue about it now. No point in it really. We're just friends and so you don't have much a say about what I do."

Devin's eyes narrowed and Patton couldn't resist a smile. He might know her game, but that didn't make him invulnerable to her tricks. That was the beauty of emotions—reason didn't count for much.

"Fine." Devin gestured to the door. "Shall we?"

Dinner was a pleasant affair. It didn't take Devin long to get over his annoyance, which was one of the things Patton loved about him. It was easy come and easy go with him.

Both of them made an attempt to steer the conversation from the three hot zones, her business, her bike and her plans to lure Chase and Slade into her clutches. Instead they focused on old stories from their childhood, good times then that led to remembered laughter now.

They even managed to talk about new stories, Devin's antics on the ranch and Patton's life in Atlanta. Everything went good as long as neither strayed toward the off limit topics.

Patton tried, really tried to stay clear of the danger zones, but it was hard. After an hour of good food, good wine and good conversation, she couldn't resist falling back into the dark hole.

"I just have to know," Patton started after the waitress had carried off their desert plates. "What do you have against the motorcycle? I thought you always wanted one?"

Devin took a moment, his smile fading away. "I did, but this is different."

"Different? How?"

"Because I don't want to see you get hurt."

"You think I want to see you get hurt?"

"Oh, don't even try that."

"Why not? It's a valid question."

"No, it's not. It's not the same at all."

"Why? Because you're a man."

"Yeah." Devin nodded, goaded out of his shame over his sexist attitude. "I'm a man and we can handle motorcycles."

"You respond better in an instant to crisis."

"Yeah, we do."

"You're stronger, more capable of controlling the machine."

"I can bench press two twenty, can you?"

"You're not as likely to get hurt."

"If you know all the answers, why ask the question?"

"You don't even know how to ride a bike."

Devin glared sulkily at her. "I could learn."

"I could teach you."

That brought him up short. Patton enjoyed the moment. He remained silent as the waitress reappeared to hand him the small black leather folder with the check inside. Shooting her a skeptical look, Devin turned to handle the check.

Patton bit back her smile. He had reason to doubt her motives. It wasn't out of the goodness of her heart that she tempted him with her bike. No, she had high hopes for this scheme. In teaching him how to ride, he would be forced to defer to her knowledge. That would set into the motion the idea that she was competent enough to be trusted with a motorcycle.

Better yet, maybe she could arouse his interest to the point where he bought his own. If it was something they did together, it would create a strong bond. One that, hopefully, could be relied on to hold when Chase came crashing down on their heads.

Hell, maybe she could even lure Slade onto two wheels. Then it would be a short trip to get Chase out on the road with them. The vision of all four of them taking a ride on a lazy Sunday made her sigh with longing.

It would be nice to share something like that with the brothers. Maybe if they shared it with her, they'd ease up on the macho bullshit. Perhaps that was the winning hand or perhaps they'd take off on their bikes and leave her at home, locked in the bedroom.

"You're serious?" Devin's question drew her back to the moment and it took a second to refocus.

"On teaching you to ride? Yeah. It would be great to have somebody to ride with and I can't think of anybody I'd like to take off on an adventure more than you."

"Sweet talk, nice touch." Devin pursed his lips, obviously torn.

"Come on, Devin. It'll be fun."

"If I agree to this, Chase will want my head mounted in the study."

"If you don't, you'll do something else that'll tick him off. Why waste the opportunity to be in trouble on something small. I say go big."

That got a laugh. "You always do."

"So do you. Come on, it'll be fun."

"All right." Devin shook his head. "I must be insane, but I'll give you tomorrow afternoon to see how well this goes."

"Great!" Patton almost giggled with her joy.

"If it doesn't go well…"

Patton knew exactly what he left unsaid and quickly rushed to assure Devin. "It will. It will go fabulously."

"Okay."

He didn't sound all that happy with his own decision, but she knew once committed, he wouldn't back out. Now it was up to her to show him that she knew how to handle a motorcycle.

"Let's get moving or we'll be late for the movie." Devin pushed his chair back, but instead of getting up to help her with her chair, he hesitated. "I have to use the restroom. I'll meet you out by the truck."

Something about the way he said it gave her pause. Her internal alarm went off, but she had no way to accuse him of anything and not look like a fool. Puzzled and concerned, she waited for him in the lobby, just in case she caught him doing something he shouldn't be doing—like talking to another woman.

When he came down the hall from the bathrooms, he still looked tense and uneasy. He forced a smile and Patton knew then that something was definitely up.

Chapter 16

By the time Devin pulled the truck back into The Pub's parking lot, he had begun to sweat. Despite his attempts to contact Cole Jackson both at the restaurant and the movie theater, the bastard hadn't answered his phone. With Patton still holding his cell hostage, he was out of opportunities and beginning to dread what was about to happen in the next few minutes.

He should have never called Cole from Hailey's. It had been a moment of anger and annoyance that had led him to do something so rash. Now that Patton had extended some kind of peace offering on the issue of her motorcycle, things were about to blow up.

The lot was mostly empty, the Cattlemen no doubt enjoying their evening in the safety of the club instead of the public domain of the town's watering hole. With an internal sigh of doom, Devin parked his truck next to Patton's bike and consoled himself that at least the scene to come wouldn't be played out in front of an audience.

"Well, that was fun."

It should have been. Devin had spent the last two hours with his arm around his dream girl while she snuggled into his side and ate popcorn out of his lap. He should have been on cloud nine except he'd have gotten cast out of heaven for the dirty thoughts making his boner hard enough to be mistaken for an exoskeleton.

Not much could make Devin's dick wilt, especially around Patton. Fear of her reaction and the coming confrontation worked magic on the least obedient member of his body.

He tried to smile. "Yeah. It was a good movie."

"Better company." Patton's suggestive tone, her seductive smile, they warned him what came next.

"Uh, Patton."

"Hmm?" She wiggled closer to him across the bench seat.

"We're out as friends, remember?" He hated to say it and it showed in his tone.

"So? A little friendly goodnight kiss wouldn't hurt."

As if he could stop there. Devin started when a warm hand settled on his knee. Almost too quickly for him to catch, it slid up his thigh, leaving a trail of heated longing that jumped started his cock's interest.

Flattening her hand beneath his, he gave an unsteady laugh. "We know we can't do this, Patton."

"Mmm." Her breath warmed his neck before she took a little nip of his sensitive flesh. "Just a little taste."

"Damn it, Patton." Unsteady himself, he managed to find the strength to force her back. "Behave yourself."

"Or what? You going to spank me, cowboy?"

"I might."

"You forget, Devin, I liked to be spanked."

Ah, hell. She just had to remind him of that and undermine all his best intentions. The woman was dangerous and Devin had the unusual sensation of suddenly being the prey instead of the hunter.

"I liked everything we did." The husky sound of her sensual voice stroked his heated senses. "Don't you remember, Devin? How you spanked me, made me touch myself?"

Her actions matched her words. Devin watched mesmerized as her hands came up to cup and fondle her breasts. He swallowed hard as a voice, a very distant voice, beat back against the whirlwind of lust creating static through his head.

He couldn't let this happen. He couldn't touch her either. His control wouldn't last a second then. That only left retreat. He, Devin Davis, trainer of women, turned tail and ran.

Shoving open the door, he leapt from the truck as if Satan himself tried to seduce him. Patton's lusty laugher followed him out into the fresh night air. Taking a deep breath, he turned to see her leaning against her hands as she stretched half-way out on the bench seat.

"I can see why you enjoy being in control, Devin," Patton purred. "It's very…exhilarating to be the aggressor."

Devin schooled his features and pulled out his strongest master's tone. "That's enough, Patton."

"I don't know why you bother to fight me, Devin." She wasn't impressed or intimidated. "You know I always get things my way."

"There are other things I can do besides spanking you if you don't start behaving," Devin warned. "I've only begun to show you the tricks in my bag. Some of them are not so pleasant."

"And that is supposed to dissuade me?"

"Patton."

"Fine." She gave over with a complete lack of grace and scrambled out of the open door. Devin stepped back to give her more room than necessary. "Just remember, tomorrow I'm in control."

"Of the motorcycle lesson," Devin qualified.

"Whatever you want to call it." Patton winked at him before stretching up to give him a quick kiss on the cheek. "Good night, Devin."

"Night."

Even though he bid her farewell, he didn't bother to get back in the truck. Instead he watched her pull a helmet out of the back saddle bag and strap it to her head before throwing a leg over the bike.

Patton didn't question why he stood there. She knew his tradition of watching women safely off before taking his own leave. That was true and he would have stayed still even if he hadn't been expecting what was about to come.

Patton turned the key, but nothing happened. She did again, then again, one last time before she turned furious eyes on him. Devin stood still, but inside he cringed.

* * * *

"Well, how bad is it?" Patton glared at Hailey over her soda as her friend walked into the kitchen. "Give it to me straight."

"They pulled your spark plugs."

"What?"

"The spark plug, the thing that conducts an electrical current and causes the gas to ignite in the cylinder and thus creates pressure that pushes the piston down and makes the engine run."

"I know what a spark plug is," Patton snapped.

Though she didn't really know what it did. Hailey did. Hailey knew all about engines and had her own shop set up behind her house, which was just why Patton had called her last night instead of taking Devin up on his offer to have her bike towed to Cole's shop to be looked at.

Bastard. She knew he'd done this. Somehow, someway, despite his protests of innocence, Devin had one of his friends break her bike so she couldn't ride it. It would serve him right if she didn't teach him how to ride, but that would just be stabbing herself in the back.

Her plan was still a good one. She couldn't let a little obstacle dissuade her from her goal. All she had to do was get the bike back to running. Well, Hailey had to get the bike back to running.

"So, how long will it take to fix?"

"How long will it take to go to the bike shop in Dothan and get some plugs?"

"That's all?"

"That and screwing them back into the cylinder head."

"Great! We can head out after you had some breakfast."

"I get to eat before we go? How gracious of you."

Hailey's snide tone wasn't lost on Patton. "I'm sorry, Hailey. I'm just really excited to get my plan back on track."

"The one where you teach the man who sabotaged your bike to ride?"

"When you say it like that, it sounds stupid."

"Gee, I wonder why that is."

"Hailey."

"I'll give you this. It's better than your plan to make them jealous."

"I haven't given that one up."

"Oh, God." Hailey's head dropped.

"I've even picked out the guy I'm going to use."

"This should be good."

"What do you know about Cole Jackson?"

"Are you out of your mind?"

"Probably, but tell me the details anyway."

"He owns a car repair shop, does custom builds and restorations. He rides in a few of the regional motorcycle races. Fucked about everything in town—"

"Including you?"

"I haven't had my shots yet," Hailey stated with a sneer.

"He's one of those they talk about, isn't he?"

"Oh, yeah. He's got two sidekicks to go along with him." Hailey paused. "Just your number."

"You don't like this guy, do you?"

"Don't mean anything to me."

"You know a lot about him for him to mean nothing to you."

"Okay, he's a cocky, arrogant, son-of-a-bitch, with fast hands and an entitled attitude. Rubs me the wrong way."

"You guys gone out or something?"

"No." Hailey slammed the refrigerator door open. "I wouldn't waste five minutes on that slime and you shouldn't either."

"Sorry." Patton held up her hands in surrender. "You just have a strong opinion about the man, makes me wonder why that is."

"He touched my car."

"Oh." Patton nodded in understanding. Hailey was very possessive of her baby. Not even Patton was allowed to drive it.

"He had the audacity to tell me to bring it to his shop and he'd fixed the paint job."

"Hmm." Hailey had painted the baby herself and took great pride in the work.

"Then he tells me he thinks he hears an arc."

"An ark?"

"Electrical misfire," Hailey explained. "Thinks he needs to check under my hood. He says to let him take her for a test drive and he'll have her fined tuned and running right."

"I can see why you're upset." Patton wondered if perhaps Hailey had missed the implied come-on in Cole's words.

"He's lucky I didn't run him over."

"Then you don't mind if he gets hit." Perhaps, it was better that Hailey didn't like Cole. Patton couldn't use a man Hailey was interested in as bait in her game. Cole made perfect bait.

"Just as long as I don't end up in jail for it."

"You got a fear of bars, you know that?"

"Yeah, well the last time an old high school friend came to town I ended up behind them. That's an experience I do not intend to repeat."

"I'm not Angelina."

"You're not far off."

* * * *

Patton looked at her watch and scowled. Three thirty, Devin was a half hour late. She tapped her foot against the railing as she went over the conversation they'd had earlier. He'd seemed shocked, but happy that she'd gotten her bike fixed and had assured her he would be there for his lesson at three.

Well it was past three now and where the hell was he? She could feel the knots in her stomach twist tighter at the thought that he might stand her up. It didn't just concern her that her plan might be failing. Disappointment pressed down on her. Patton had been looking forward to spending more time with him.

The other night had been nice. It had reminded her just how much she enjoyed being with Devin, even if it wasn't sexual. The night had been sweet right up to the end. Then things had kind of exploded between them, with her yelling and him getting defensive.

She felt much better now that she knew he hadn't actually wrecked her bike but played more of a practical joke on her. She could deal with a practical joke. He'd certainly played enough of them on her over the years. If she didn't have a bigger game to run, Patton would have taken the time to return the favor. She still might.

The sound of a truck engine coming down the road had her looking up expectantly. Her hopes changed to confusion as Slade pulled his Ford into the driveway behind Hailey's Studebaker. As he pushed open his door, Patton's feet dropped down to the wooden planks that made up Hailey's front porch and stood.

"Where is Devin?"

"Been a change of plans." Slade stalked toward the front porch looking too handsome and very dangerous.

"Chase."

"Good guess, but wrong. If Chase had gotten wind of what you two were up to, you'd have gotten a call to come visit Devin in the hospital before he died."

"It's not that bad."

"I don't want to hear it." Slade stopped at the bottom step. "Believe it or not, Patton, I didn't come out here to argue."

"No? Then why did you come? Why didn't Devin call?"

"He's busy doing chores."

"I thought he'd finished his chores."

"But not mine."

"Oh."

Patton didn't know what to say to that. After the way things had ended yesterday, she felt somewhat nervous around him. A feeling Slade made hard to shake. Chase made her so damn mad she easily got over any embarrassment. Devin had just the opposite effect on her. Charming and sweet, he made it easy for her to smile and wish for another round. The way Slade stared at her though, made her fidget.

"Let's go for a ride," he finally spoke.

"Where?"

"I've got to run to Dothan to pick up some fresh produce."

"Oh." Again he left her feeling uncertain. When he gestured for her to come down the steps and precede him down the path to his truck, Patton didn't know what else to do but obey the silent command.

Chapter 17

Slade's mind whirled and churned, pushing out useless though after pointless idea. When he'd caught Devin heading out the door, it had been easy enough to get him to talk. His younger brother had obviously been torn between the devil on one shoulder and the angel on the other.

Actually he'd been torn between Patton's tempting offer and knowing how wrong he'd be to give in. He had to hand it to Patton. She played the game at whole new level of sophistication. When she'd been younger, she'd been easy to read, quick to respond and it made it simple to control her more outlandish schemes.

Not anymore. Tempting Devin with motorcycle lessons, returning to town so she could force them to watch her date her way through the male population, the whole scheme was outright brilliant. Checkmate hovered in the air, and if he didn't figure out a way to save his queen, the kings would be lost.

The problem was he didn't have any control over the situation anymore, no control over Patton that was for sure. She was an adult, completely free to do as she wanted. As for that, so were the members of the Cattleman's Club. Chase could issue all the orders he wanted, but when it came to a group of dominating men being teased into a rut by a sexy filly…

"You're going to break the steering wheel."

"What?" Slade cut a quick look at Patton.

"You're going to break the steering wheel if you don't let up on the poor thing. I know you're wishing it was my neck, but you need the wheel to drive this truck."

"I don't want to wring your neck," Slade muttered. He wanted to wring the neck of whatever asshole took her virginity.

"It's obvious, Slade."

"What's obvious, Patton?" He used her same annoyed tone.

"That you want to yell at me. Just get it over. I know. I was wrong to offer Devin riding lessons. It's horrible of me to move back in town without telling you. I'm just evil bitch."

"I didn't say that."

"You're thinking it."

"I never thought of you as a bitch."

"But evil?"

Well... "No, just…"

"Just what?"

"Too damn tempting by half." Slade went back to muttering and wringing the steering wheel trapped in his grip.

"I'm sorry I'm pretty."

That did it. It broke Slade's mood and a laugh escaped. Damn her, how did she always manage to do that to him? He was mad at her, had a right to be mad. Somehow though Patton always managed with a bat of her eyelashes and some quick comeback to break through his anger.

"You want, I'll dip my face in acid, eat a thousand donuts until I'm too big to fit through the truck door and you have to haul me around in the bed."

"I don't think you have to go that far."

"Maybe you should try it."

"Try it?"

"Yeah. We could shave your head. Not in a stylish way, but in a way that made you look like you were going bald. Then you could beef up on jerky and ding dongs until you had no less than four necks."

"You think that would help? You would stop chasing me if I got fat and went bald?"

"No." The teasing tone in her voice receded and he caught a glimpse of her turning her head toward the window. "I'll always want you, Slade. I love you."

In a blink, she brought the tension back. Damn her for twisting him like a string. She pulled him taut with needs and wants, then released him from the binds, but only for a moment, only for as long as it took her to twist him up all over again.

He needed a way to break the cycle, a way to send her from Pittsview and back toward Atlanta. Pushing her never worked. Patton's contrary personality saw force as reason to dig in. No, it had to be her idea or it wouldn't work.

How to convince her that she couldn't get her way in this, Slade didn't know. He worked the problem over and over again, but nothing came to mind. He got stuck going with his gut, a situation he didn't like.

"I love you, too, Patton." Slade reached a hand across the bench seat to give hers a squeeze. "Like a sister."

Boy, was that ever a lie. If it wasn't, then he was one seriously sick fuck. Patton apparently saw through his desperate attempt to put distance between them if her snort was any indication.

"You always wanted a sister whose pussy you could eat?"

"*Patton!*"

"I'm just asking." Her tone went flat, too calm and very annoying. "That's pretty sick, Slade. That could actually change the way I feel about you."

"We are not talking about that."

"Why not?"

"It's not appropriate." And it made him too hot by far to be thinking about how sweet she tasted, how sexy she looked, how much more he wanted when she sat merely two feet away.

"I see. It's appropriate to pin me to the seat and force one orgasm after another on me while you lick my clit—"

"Damn it, Patton. Shut up!"

"Outside a pool party where anybody could catch us, like Chase."

"I'm warning you, Patton."

"He's just jealous. I bet he regrets not taking a taste when he had me pinned to the bed. Of course he got to watch me fuck myself—"

"I'll put you over my knee if you don't stop, right now."

"I bet that's a sight you'd like to see. Devin certainly did."

"That's it!"

Slade slammed down on the brakes so hard the truck fishtailed as it came to a screeching halt along the grassy shoulder. Chest heaving with potent mixture of lust and anger, he turned on the woman doing her damndest to drive him insane.

"No more, Patton."

"What?" She slid closer and Slade couldn't stop from flinching backward. "Are you really going to spank me? Didn't Devin tell you how much I enjoyed that, how wet I got, how it made me willing to do anything he wanted?"

The hard, uneven surface of the door cut into his back while soft, sweet woman pressed into his front. Slade told himself to flee, that his resistance wouldn't hold, but she nuzzled his neck, her hand stroking up his thigh, captivating him within her spell.

"I want you, Slade."

Her hand covered his erection, burning him through the denim as her grip tightened, molding itself to his hardened length. He should stop her. This was wrong. That thought was overshadowed by the sound of a zipper being lowered.

A second later warm, slender fingers curled around his aching flesh. She squeezed and Slade didn't know what happened next. Overdosed on lust, everything blurred into a frenzy of kissing, touching, pushing clothes haphazardly out of the way.

She tasted so sweet, felt so soft, but he needed more, he needed to be buried deep inside her wet heat. That was the only way to banish the insanity that ripped him apart from the inside out. The desire that had eaten him through the night demanded that he finish what he had started the other afternoon.

Only when he felt her liquid desire creaming along the ultra sensitive length of his cock, her plump folds parting and the tight ring of muscles of her cunt squeezing along his dick head, that Slade could finally breathe. His back arched, his muscles tensed, reading themselves to plunge full force into the sweet utopia of Patton's body.

The blare of a horn as a car flew snapped the world back into place. Slade saw Patton beneath him. Her violet eyes almost black with desire, her breasts rosy, brighter red in the areas that had obviously been mauled. Mauled by his mouth, the sight shocked Slade to his core.

This couldn't happen. That truth echoed through him, beating back the waves of demand emanating from his cock. He didn't know if he actually spoke the words aloud, but from the widening of her eyes, Slade knew Patton had heard them. The spell she'd cast over him broke.

In a sudden rush for control, they both moved. Beneath him, Patton arched, trying to force him further into her hot, clinging, cunt. In response, under their own will, his hips flexed, meeting her and feeding another inch into her tight channel.

His hands moved faster. Stripping off his belt, he looped it around her wrist and then through the handle bar above her window. A hard tug and a quick knot pulled her tempting heat from him and left her tied to the side of the cab.

Mustering the last vestige of his strength, Slade threw himself across the distance and to what little safety the other side of the cab offered him. For long moments neither spoke. Both breathed raggedly and glared at each other—two warriors intent on victory, eyeing each other across the battlefield of the vinyl seat between them.

The fight was unfairly weighted in Patton's favor, thanks to the single-minded determination of his cock. Damn traitor. Slade gingerly put the tyrant back in its denim cage before it could do anymore damage.

It hurt to do. The need in his balls had built to a painful level. If Patton hadn't been present, he would have taken himself in hand. Slade wouldn't give her that satisfaction. She would see it as a sign of weakness.

The vixen already smelled blood in the water. One could only imagine what she might do next with even a little encouragement. As if to prove his point, her tone purred out, stretching across the seat to inflame his already burning senses.

"I don't know why you're bothering to fight it, Slade. You know I'm going to get my way."

Slade closed his eyes, blocking out the sight of an almost naked Patton, bound and waiting for her pleasure. His head hit the window as good warred with the devil beating at his jeans zipper.

"I should have left you at Hailey's."

* * * *

Patton scowled at that comment. Perhaps she had overplayed her hand. He had been so close though. So close and now so empty. Damn, but she needed something filling her aching insides. At this moment, she'd have even accepted another man. She was that desperate.

Later she would regret it, reason forced its way between the breaks in her slowly receding desire. Patton sighed, recognizing the truth. Mimicking Slade's position, her head thumped into the window as she rested it against the cool glass.

Her plan had a serious flaw. That much had become obvious. She might be able to seduce the brothers into fucking her, but she couldn't seduce them into feeling right about it afterward.

They had to make the decision for themselves or the results could be disastrous. That didn't mean she should pack her bags and admit defeat. It might sound like an attempt to make them jealous, but they needed to face the reality of their current position, the reality of her with another man.

More was needed though. If all her plan consisted of was making them jealous, they'd just scare off her dates and it would be a draw. The scales needed to be weighed by more than sex. She needed to remind the brothers their relationship encompassed more than just sex. More than adversity existed between them, happy memories of Christmases and Easter egg hunts, of ridding horses through the pastures and watching horror movies late into the night. They shared laughter and quiet times and above all else, love.

That was the bait that she needed to be using, not her body. As fine as she knew she looked, she knew plenty of women who looked better. Many of them had been running around at the pool party in collars. The Davis brothers hadn't chosen even one of them, because they weren't her.

They wanted her for more than her body. They wanted her for the rest of their lives. That truth lay in the heart of their pact. Their love for her would be their greatest weakness.

"I'm sorry."

The beginning, the one she needed to start fresh with, was an apology. Patton turned to look at Slade. He still slumped into the side of the door, chest heaving, erection at full staff beneath his jeans. One eye slitted open as he assessed her and she could read the obvious doubt in the gesture.

"I'm sorry, Slade. I shouldn't have done that."

"No, you shouldn't have."

"I shouldn't have pushed you yesterday either. It wouldn't happen again."

All that got her was a grunt and his other eye opening. He watched her the way a cow watched a wolf.

"I mean it. I may want more, but you've made your decision. I should respect that, just as I want you to respect mine."

"What game are you playing now, Patton?"

"No games. I love you, Slade. I want you in my life any way I can have you. If pushing you to do something you'll regret means damaging what we already have then I'll back off. I don't want to lose you."

That heartfelt statement appeared to penetrate his doubt. Slade straightened up and cocked his head.

"I almost believe you meant that."

"I do mean it. Chase, Devin and you are the most important people in my life. I can't imagine it without you in it. Not even for sex would I risk the bond we share."

"Hmmm."

"Come on, Slade, untie me. I promise not to rape you."

That got a laugh, one that bubbled over into a fit that his head dropping to the steering wheel. It must have been a release of some form, because, before her eyes, he laughed until he cried. As the chuckles wore down they seemed to drain his body of all energy. His head rolled to the side and he glanced at her out the corner of his eye.

"I'll untie you," he stated. "Any more funny stuff and that's it though. Got it?"

"Got it." Patton nodded. "No more funny stuff. We'll just have a nice relaxing day like we used to."

"I still think you're up to something," Slade muttered, but he gave her the benefit of the doubt, like he all ways did, and reached to undo the belt chaining her to the window.

Patton was intensely aware of his scrutiny as she righted her clothes. He'd grown tense again, as if expecting her to pounce on him or, perhaps, trying to guess at her motives for offering a truce. Let him guess. He couldn't do anything even if he did figure it out. That was the beauty of her plan. No countermove.

With a smile, she turned toward him. "Well, are we going to sit here all day or get moving? I'm hungry."

Chapter 18

The rest of the day passed event free. Patton lived up to her end of the bargain, acting like nothing had happened between them. Slade really tried to go along with the pretense that things were back to normal.

He might have convinced Patton of his act, but inside he remained twisted in knots. Glimpses and fragments of images played out in chaotic order through his mind, giving him momentary insight into the insanity of those heated moments when he had nearly claimed Patton. It drove him nuts, especially with Patton being all sweet and relaxed.

It reminded him of the way things used to be, when it had been easier for him to control his lusts and refocus them onto some faceless, nameless substitute. He feared now that time had past and nothing would bring it back.

The problem was, Slade didn't know where to go from here. There appeared to be only two possible futures, one with Patton and one without her. The idea of not having Patton in his life disturbed him too much to contemplate.

The idea of having Patton around while she dated her way through Pittsview until she settled down to marry some other man and raise his children hurt so bad it made Slade want to kill whatever son-of-a-bitch touched his Patton.

He couldn't win. The hope of getting Patton back to Atlanta and out of temptation's reach had dimmed during their chat over lunch. He tried to remind her of all the things she'd left behind in Atlanta by asking about her life there. As big as her smile had gotten as she'd talked about her friends and business, when he had asked if she missed it, Patton had shrugged and said she missed being home more.

"I can't imagine Pittsview can possibly compare to a city like Atlanta." Slade had pushed while the waitress cleaned away their plates.

"Depends on what you want out of life." Patton smiled. "I don't deny that it was exciting being in a big city, but I'm just a small town girl at heart. I like the peace and quiet. Besides I can go back to Atlanta as much as I want to visit."

"What about your friends there?"

"I have better friends here, longer, closer, childhood friends."

"Don't you need to be there for your business?"

He'd been that desperate. The last thing Slade wanted was to have her resume her racy career, but if it meant getting her far enough away that he didn't have to watch her with another man, he'd do it. He'd do it for Patton, because she deserved better than what he and his brothers could offer her.

What little hope he held that he'd cornered her with that one had been smashed as Patton explained how she could do her designing from Pittsview. She had it all planned out, how she could go back to Atlanta for meetings with private clients and communicate on-line with her business partner to keep up with the store, catalog and on-line sales.

Her partner handled most of the actual business matters, the books, scheduling and coordinating sales with fulfillment orders from the manufacturers. All Patton did was the designs, made prototypes for the manufactures to copy and handled any issues that came up with production. She also sewed custom orders for her special clients.

She just needed was a house big enough to offer her studio space. She'd already moved the bulk of her stuff into Hailey's and had contacted a realtor to help her find her own place. Patton had come home to stay.

It was a nightmare and a fantasy all rolled into one.

Slade rubbed his eyes, fighting back the headache that had been building behind his eyes all day.

"Tired?" Patton asked him from the respectable distance of her seat on the other side of the cab.

"A little."

"Been busy lately, huh?"

"Yeah, I think it's time for a quiet night at home."

"That sounds like fun. What about heading back to the ranch for dinner and then we can veg out on the couch and watch some movies?"

That was a bad idea. A whole night spent with Patton? Slade almost cringed. All four of them together pretending to be one happy family, ignoring the slow march to disaster that they were all on, Slade didn't think he could survive the night.

The excitement in her voice doomed him and he heard words coming out of his mouth that hadn't been authorized by his brain. Words like, 'yeah, that sounds like fun' and 'what kind of movies are you in the mood for?' That was Patton's power over him. She could always get him to react without thinking and it frightened him on some fundamental level.

"So what are you going to do with all this food you bought?"

"What?" He should have been prepared for that question.

"The corn, the tomatoes, onions, sweet potatoes, you know all the food you have overflowing their boxes in the back of the truck? You aren't stock piling for a nuclear war, so what's it for?"

"Oh, it's just for some friends who are throwing a party," Slade explained nonchalantly. At least, he hoped he sounded unconcerned.

"Really? What party? I love a good time."

"It's by invitation only." That came out too quickly and he caught the motion of her head turning. Damnit! Now he'd caught her curiosity and a curious Patton was a dangerous Patton.

No way could he tell her the truth. That the food was for the Cattleman's Club Bash at the end of the week when even nonmember males were invited to join in the festivities and check out the club. The only women allowed were members or dates of Cattlemen.

Over the next two days, there would be a rush of women flooding into the town. The club's extra cabins were already overbooked. Normally the cattlemen would put up the extra females in their homes, several would stay at the ranch much to the delight of the hands. Not this year. Not when Patton could suddenly drop in and surprise everyone. That meant new plans would have to be made.

Thankfully, Patton didn't ask anymore questions and the conversation turned back to trivial things. Slade let out a relieved sigh when he turned down the drive toward the ranch. He needed to get out of the truck and breathe air not scented with the sweet smell of Patton, just a few minutes to get his head cleared and let his muscles unwind.

The front door of their two-story house banged open and Chase stormed out onto the porch as Slade brought the truck to a stop in front of the old wooden structure. He could easily read the annoyance in his big brother's eyes and knew he was about to get it for being late, for bringing the food back to the ranch and not to the lodge where GD waited to help him unload the boxes.

Whatever Chase had been about to say, the words stalled out as his eyes cut to Patton jumping out of the cab and hollering out a hello. Chase's eyes jerked back to Slade, narrowing on him, and he knew Chase wanted to rage at him for bringing her here, back into the lion's den.

"Hey, Chase. What's for dinner?"

"Dinner?" Slade heard Chase echo that word as if it were foreign to his existence. Before he could respond further to her question, Patton gave him a big hug and damned if Chase didn't look as uncomfortable as if a man actually hugged him.

"It's going to be a great time," Patton babbled on. "We're going to have dinner and watch some movies like the old days. What do you say? Oh, Devin, hey."

Patton's attention and hug turned toward their youngest brother, who had no problems with hugging her back. As the two of them talked, deciding what to eat and picking out movies to watch, Chase turned his scowl loose on Slade.

He just shrugged it off. If Chase didn't have the heart to tell Patton no, what did he expect Slade to do?

* * * *

Dinner turned out to be a haphazard affair. After Chase dismissed Charlotte for the rest of the night, the brothers floundered over who would do the actual cooking. Since none of them had developed that skill and were obviously reluctant to eat anything Patton might have prepared, it had almost come to pizza before Devin suggested grilling up 'some grub'.

Chase had commandeered control over the coals and spent all of his time focused on moving the meat and vegetable around, chasing hot spots and avoiding them. Patton knew it wasn't just his normal need to be in control that drove him to hover over the bar-b-que.

He was actively avoiding her. They'd grilled out enough times over the years and he'd always had the time to play horseshoes with them, to stand around the gates of the pasture, drinking a beer and shooting the shit. Not today. Not even through dinner did he involve himself in the conversation. He barely spared her a glance and when it came time to clean up, he quickly excused himself, mumbling something about the horses in the barn.

For their part Slade and Devin ignored Chase's surly mood. Patton though couldn't let it go. Despite Slade's scowl and the shake of Devin's head, she followed Chase out to the barn.

It was new. The brown wood not yet gray with the aging of years. It sat on the opposite side of the yard from the old run down one that had last been used when their mother had still been alive. All the structures now dominated the clearing of the main house.

New barns, sheds, and the rows of small apartments where the hands stayed speckled the south field. The area was safer than the north field that backed into a small forest and the possibility of a tree falling during a storm. What made the area better also made it worse. Without the shade of the trees, the buildings were left unprotected under the sun's harsh glare.

As Patton cleared the side entry and walked down the short alley made by the side of the office and a stall the sweet smells of freshly cut grass gave way to the musty odor of wood and leather. The warmth of the day had become a stale humidity trapping and magnifying the scents of hay and manure within the wooden walls.

"That's my pretty girl. There you go."

Patton stilled at the soothing, gentle sound of Chase's voice. His words were followed by a crisp chomp and Patton smiled. She peered around the corner of the stall and spied Chase doing just what she had suspected a few stalls down.

A glint of steel caught her eye as he cut another slice of apple away from the core. Guinevere neighed and nudged his hand. Chase laughed, a deep, husky sound that warmed the anger out Patton.

"Such a greedy little girl, aren't you?" Chase asked the animal in as cooing a tone as the big man could muster.

There had been a time when he'd talked to her like that. Underneath all the hard layers and stern mask, Chase had a tender heart. His big, callused hands were capable of the softest of caresses.

Patton watched with such envy that it was physical pain as Chase rubbed the horse's head, his hands smoothing down her neck. From the way Guinevere leaned into his touch, she obviously liked the caress.

It had been so long since he had touched her like that. The sight of his open affection cut deep, reminding her of everything she'd already lost. The reality that she might never find it again was too much to contemplate. She had to win this battle they were currently locked in. She just had to.

Mustering up her courage, she stepped out into the main aisle. "I think the horse is in love with you."

Chase's head snapped around. Before her eyes, his expression hardened back into a guarded mask. "Patton, what are you doing here?"

"I thought maybe we could talk."

"What do we have to talk about?"

"I don't know, maybe why you are being so cold to me?"

He turned back to Guinevere. "I just have a lot on my mind."

"Maybe I can help."

"Help? I don't think so."

"You never know."

"I know."

"Not everything, Chase."

That got her another dark look. "I know enough, Patton."

"Did I do something?" That sounded stupid. What hadn't she done? Still she wasn't prepared for his emotionless response.

"Why are you standing here?"

"What do mean by that?" The words barely made it out over the pain constricting her chest like a powerful band trying to squeeze the life out of her.

"I thought it was fairly obvious. Do you really need me to say it?"

"You want me gone."

"I can't figure out why you haven't left yet."

"You know why," Patton whispered.

Chase turned to face her fully then and she saw that more than just his tone had gone cold, but his eyes as well. "There is nothing for you here, Patton."

"Don't say that."

"Why? It's the truth."

"No, it's not. My family is here. You're my family." He flinched at that, showing a chink in his armor. Patton couldn't help herself but to push. "Come on, Chase, can't we—"

"Don't, Patton," he cut her off. "Don't tell me what we can or can't do. There is no we."

"I didn't mean—"

"Yes you did and you need to understand this very clearly. There is you and there is me."

"It doesn't have to be like that."

"Yes it does. That's the way you made it."

"I didn't."

"As you are so fond of telling me, you're all grown up and capable of making your own decisions. You made the decision to risk your life on a motorcycle, regardless of my concerns. You chose to pursue a questionable career where you flaunt your body, despite the fact that I know you are better than that.

"Now you have decided to move back here and torment us with other men. There is nothing I can do about it, about any of it. There is nothing you can do about how that makes me feel. I have the right to make my own decisions, too, Patton."

"Just because you don't approve of what I've done doesn't mean things have to be so…harsh between us."

"It doesn't?"

"No."

"How do you want it to be between us?"

"I'd like to be your friend."

"I can't." He shook his head.

"Chase…"

"I'm sorry, Patton." He almost sounded it, too. "When I look at you, all I see is the little girl I used to love and…the woman you've become."

"That's a bad thing."

"Yeah."

"There is nothing I can do to make it better?"

"You can leave."

"But—"

"Leave and don't come back, Patton. Ever."

With that, he turned and walked away. Patton stood there feeling every confidence, every dream, every fiber of her being wilt until she felt like she was dying inside. All she wanted to do was escape, to outrun the horrible sensations eating her from the inside out.

With a muffled sob, she turned and fled.

Chapter 19

Chase wanted to kick something, hit something, beat somebody into an inch of his life—preferably himself. Disgust and self loathing rolled in a great waves through his body, making him feel sick, revolted at being unable to escape his own skin.

He'd seen the hurt his words inflicted on Patton. There had been tears gathering in her big violet eyes. Those eyes that used to glow with such happiness and trust that he felt invincible, now looked at him with wounded sadness and it killed something inside him.

If he had stood there and a single streak had trickled down her cheek, he would have crumbled. He had no defense against tears, especially Patton's tears. Even when she'd been a child, the sight of them falling had rolled lava down his spine, incinerating his strength until he was the weak man only she could ever make him feel like.

That couldn't happen this time. He needed to stay strong, because Slade and Devin's resolve was obviously already eroding away. Chase came to a stop at the corral gate and stared into the empty circle of dirt. That's the way life looked now, emptiness stretching out from weeks into years until his entire life had passed by lonely and unfulfilled.

He had to do it, Chase told himself. He had to do it for Patton. It would be worth whatever pain he suffered to know she was happy. Happiness, life long joy, the one thing he knew he couldn't give her.

Devin's taste test didn't matter. It had been the novelty that had excited Patton, made her accepted Devin's dominance. She wasn't ready for it to span from hours to days to weeks to years. Patton wasn't that type of girl. She was headstrong and controlling. Those personalities made her push now. Nothing like the word 'no' inspired Patton to the fight.

If she won, the ending would be a disastrous. Then Patton would learn what true pain felt like. Her girlish illusions about what life would be like as their woman would be shattered right along with her innocence. The pile of wreckage would grow to include not only his relationship with her, but her relationship with Slade and Devin as well.

What he had done had been a rotten, horrible thing to do, but at least she still had Slade and Devin. Even if he ended up alone, he had done the right thing. He had, Chase repeated softly as he stared down at his hands curled into fists.

He slowly flexed them out. These were not the hands of a tender lover. They were not the hands to soothe a virgin's fears and ease her from girl into womanhood. They were big, calloused and they could never again know the feel of soft, beautiful curves of Patton's body.

But he wanted…Chase looked away from his own hands. Oh, he wanted, more than anything he wanted, wished he was not the type of man he was. If only he could be what Patton deserved, then everything would be different.

* * * *

Slade stepped out onto the porch, half expecting to see what he saw. Patton shot out of the barn like the building was on fire and the devil himself would soon step straight out of the flames. He probably wasn't far off with that thought, now with the way Chase had been acting.

He'd known when Patton had walked out of the kitchen things were about to take a turn for the worse. Despite that Slade was unprepared for the sight of the tears streaming down Patton's face as she raced across the back yard. Muttering a curse, Slade bounded down the porch steps and straight into her path.

Patton slammed into him at full speed, apparently not even having noticed he'd moved. The impact morphed her tears from a silent water weak into rampaging sobs that soaked the front of his shirt in seconds.

The harsh sounds clawed out of her throat and raked through his very soul. He couldn't take the sounds of misery, but was at a complete loss of how to make them stop. His body responded with the ageless reaction of a man confronted with a woman's tears, he squeezed her tight in his embrace.

Slade didn't know if the instinct had been bred into males as nothing more than an attempt to smoother the undesirable tears. If that were true, then the instinct failed. Patton only seemed to cry harder. Her fragile arms wrapped around him and her hands dug into his shirt, clinging to him in desperate need.

Ah, crap. Now it was worse. Now not only could he could he hear her tears, but he could feel the trembling of her body as it pressed as close as clothes could allow. And what was wrong with him?

Patton was beyond upset, completely distraught. None of that mattered to his dick. All it cared about was how soft and warm she felt plastered along his length. She was weak now. It would be easy to tilt her head up and kiss away her tears until his mouth covered hers and he pulled her down to the ground. Then he'd…get a grip.

Slade admonished himself with shake of his head, as if that would knock all the dirty thoughts his dick emitted right out of his ears. It didn't work, and he shook harder. The motion jarred Patton and she leaned back.

In that one sense it worked. Looking down into her tear soaked face, eyes all puffy, cheeks reddened, put a damper on his rousing desires. The sight unleashed a stronger emotion than lust—love.

"Oh, baby." Slade didn't know what else to say.

"I have to leave now." Patton's head dropped.

"You're not in any condition to go anywhere."

"Chase doesn't want me here," she mumbled, a quiver in her voice.

"To hell with him." Slade meant that, too. "Devin is in the house picking out your favorite movies and getting all the snacks together. He's all excited to spend the night making comments with you while devouring salty and sugary foods. You're not going to disappoint him, are you?"

"I don't feel like watching movies right now." Patton sniffed.

"Whatever Chase said, he didn't mean it."

"You don't know what he said."

"I don't need to. I know Chase and so do you. He can be a heartless bastard when he's protecting somebody he loves."

"A selfish one is more like."

"No." Slade gave a half laugh at that. "For all his faults, that's not one of them."

"You weren't there." Patton's head lifted and he could see the tears gathering strength for another round. Her voice wobbled and cracked as she forced the words out, "He told me to leave. To leave and never come back. He said we weren't family anymore."

"Ah, Patton." Slade sighed and cupped her face. His thumbs stroked out to catch the tears as they trickled down. "He's just trying to protect you from himself."

"Yeah, right."

"Chase fears his feelings for you, fears that he will do more damage to you if he gives into the desires in him."

"Don't pretend that he cares if he hurts me. He just proved you wrong."

"No, he didn't. He hurt you to save you from more pain."

"That's bullshit."

"That's the way he sees it."

"He told you that?"

"He doesn't have to. Think Patton, how many times has he said he was 'doing this for your own good'? That you 'might not like his decision, but you'd thank him latter'?"

She stared at him for a moment before her shoulders slumped. "That's classic Chase."

"Yes it is."

"This time was different."

"Only in that this time Chase is honestly scared."

"Scared? Have you been drinking?"

"You've always been his darling, his princess. He wants nothing but the best for you."

"Yeah, right."

"Yeah, right. After mom died and we had no money, he never wanted you to suffer, to go with out. While the rest of us got boots and socks for Christmas, homemade cakes that were barely edible for our birthdays, you were getting stereos and cars and fancy cakes from the bakery."

"I didn't ask for any of that."

"You didn't have to. Don't you see? Chase gave you all the things he could, because he wanted to make you happy, as happy as you made him. Things were really difficult for him—"

"I know that."

"I don't think you do. It may seem easy for him to assume all the responsibility of the farm and the family, like he was born for it, but he had dreams before our father got shipped off to prison and our mother got sick.

"You were too young, but I remember. Did you know Chase wanted to join the marines? He wanted to travel the world. When we were young, he'd look through mother's National Geographic magazines and just stare in fascination at all the strange and exotic places. Did you know that?"

"No." He heard the pout in Patton's voice, but her tears were drying. Slade knew he had started to get through to her.

"I stared with him. I always thought I'd be some great scientific explorer, discovering new plants and animals as I beat my way through the jungle, but when the time came we didn't have money enough for those dreams.

"I gave mine over, just like Chase did, because this ranch, our family needed us. It sucked. I might love this ranch, but when I was young, all I did was dream of escaping. That dream got crushed. That could have crushed my spirit, but it didn't. It didn't break Chase either. You know why?"

Patton didn't answer. Her head dropped toward her chest and Slade reached out to lift it back up, forcing her to meet his eyes. "Because we had you."

"You're trying to make me feel guilty. It's not my fault you didn't get what you wanted in life."

"I'm not saying that." Slade had to bite back his annoyance. "You know when Dad was arrested, Mother cried for days and days. Her whole world had been destroyed. Chase…Chase was so damn mad. He was untouchable. Devin was lost. He withdrew. The boy who had been ready to take the world by storm disappeared.

"This house was full of misery. It smelled of it and all I wanted to do was escape even more. Then one day the social service people cleared all their forms and brought this little girl to our doorstep.

"You didn't smile much that first day or even the day after that, but soon you were running around the house, laughing and getting into mischief. It was all any of us could do to keep up.

"Mother blossomed with having a little girl to teach all her tricks to, how to do hair and sew and cook. You drove Chase insane, making him try to keep you from killing yourself around the horses and the cows. You annoyed Devin right out of the shell he'd been building. I still remember when you made his GI Joe marry your Barbie and live in her little house. I think he was about to shit bricks that time."

Slade's voice faded off as memories of those first few months with a tiny Patton rampaging through the house played through his mind. They made him smile.

"And you?" Her question drew his eyes back to hers.

"Me? I was always the middle brother, too young to be responsible, too old to be irresponsible. In a way, I never really felt...special or needed. Then one night Chase couldn't take it anymore. He tried to help you learn fractions and you drove him nuts. Nobody would ask Devin to help, not with his grades.

"Chase looked at me and said, 'You teach her'. I did. We spent an hour at the kitchen table. When you finally got it, you turned to me and hugged me. You said I was the smartest man alive and I never felt so...special."

"I guess that's why you always helped me with my homework, huh?"

"What I'm trying to tell you, Patton, is that what made this house a home, what made the long hours of work and the stress of barely covering bills worth it, was you. You're the person that brought the joy and happiness to this family."

"Not anymore."

"That's not your fault. Things changed a long time ago. We've just all been pretending they haven't."

"When? When did they change?"

"When you were sixteen."

"That specific, huh?"

"To the day. I remember it clearly. I think we all do. You were showering. Devin got pissed because you were taking too long and he was afraid you'd use up all the hot water. So he flushed the downstairs toilet on you.

"You screamed so loudly and then came storming down the steps in nothing but a towel and wet, angry vengeance. You cussed Devin up one way and down another, poking him in the chest and holding that towel up with a single hand.

"He didn't say a word. He couldn't. All he could do was stare at you and pray that towel slipped. That's all any of us could think. You looked so damn sexy and it was so wrong of us to think that."

"Not that wrong," Patton retorted. "Devin would have been eighteen. Chase and you only barely in your twenties."

"It was wrong because we promised our mother to take care of you, not molest you."

"That's what this is about? A promise you made to your mother?"

"No. Not anymore. It's about the fact that we want better for you. You deserve a man who is romantic, a tender gentle lover. That's not us. I wish it was, but what we like to do to a woman...you're too much of a lady for that kind of treatment."

It hurt to even say the words, but Slade knew they had to be said.

"What if I'm not the lady you want me to be? What if all this suffering is pointless?"

Then they would lose something precious. Hadn't they already lost it though? Not yet, Slade assured himself. They could hold on.

"There is no need to suffer. We're still family, Patton. I still love you. I'll always love you."

"Just not the way I want."

"You'll find happiness." He evaded her comment, but Slade had no more an answer for her than that.

"Hey," Devin's shout broke the moment. "Are we going to watch these movies or what? The ice cream is melting."

Chapter 20

The sky had darkened to black, the moon sitting as lord and master in the middle. Midnight had come and gone before Chase slammed back into the house. He was exhausted, having worn out not only his aggression but all of his energy in chopping wood.

Not that they had much cause for fires, even in the dead of winter, but the split logs would serve another purpose. Come Friday it would be the beginning of the Cattleman's Club weekend long celebration, or orgy, depending on how one looked at it.

The first party would be an outdoor affair with bonfires, roasting pigs, alcohol and women. What better way to start a weekend of sex? Chase could think of only one thing he'd rather be doing or more appropriately one woman he'd rather be doing. Hopefully, she'd left by now.

The muted sounds of explosions and men yelling coming through the den's door warned him she might still be lurking around. Chase told himself to ignore it, to go straight up the stairs and to bed. No good could come from seeing Patton.

He just had to know, had to make sure she'd recovered from the upset he had caused her. The intelligence behind that escaped him, but he was too drained to be running off reason anymore. All he had were raw emotions and they led him to open the den door and look.

Slade's head snapped up, as did Devin's. Patton didn't move an inch. She appeared to be passed out, stretched between his two brothers on the couch. Her shoes were off, her socks possibly missing as her feet were tucked into the warmth of Devin's thighs, right beneath the ridge of his erection. The sight did little for Chase's mood. At least she still had her clothes on, he consoled himself.

Well, mostly clothed. Her shirt was shoved up. The cotton had caught on her bra, folding into bunched layers that not only hid her generous breasts but distorted their appearance thanks to the back of her shirt being higher than the front.

The graceful line of Patton's spine was interrupted by the width of Slade's hand. Her pale skin looked enticingly creamy against his brother's tanned skin. As Slade's hand slowly traced its way down her back, Chase's jaw clenched.

When Patton had first come to stay with them, she'd had nightmares that had made her wake up crying. Their mother had always been there with a hug. She'd rub Patton's back until the little girl fell asleep. It had grown into a habit that extended past the time of bad dreams. Whenever Patton watched TV, she'd stretch out and rest her head on their mother's lap and pester her to rub her back.

When their mother had passed, Patton had taken over bothering Chase, not that he'd minded. She'd curl up and sigh while he rubbed the worry away. It always put her to sleep and he'd have to carry her up to be tucked into bed. Even when she'd been a teenager, they'd maintained that tradition. Right up until she left for college.

It had always been him. Not Slade. Not Devin. Patton had always turned to him for this small comfort. The sight of Slade giving it to her was more than he could stand. Without a word, he stormed across the room and knocked Slade's hand out of the way.

When he lifted Patton into his arms, she sighed and snuggled closer. Ignoring the looks he got from both his brothers, Chase carried her out of the den and down the hall to the stairs.

At the side of her bed, Chase hesitated. He didn't really want to let her go, but he couldn't see any other option. He couldn't really hold her all night like this, no matter how the idea appealed to him.

With a sigh of frustration, he settled her into her bed and tried to straighten up. Patton's body suddenly came alive. Her arms tightened around his neck, her eyes fluttered open and she whispered in that little girl lost voice that never ceased to tug at his heart.

"No, don't let go."

"Shhh." He knew his line. "It's all right, baby. Go to sleep."

He smoothed his hands up her arms and tried to disengage them from around his neck.

"No. Stay."

"Patton—"

"Stay."

The plea in the soft voice had always had him kneeling down on the bed to hold her close until she fell back asleep. Chase was half way there before the insanity of what he was doing struck him. He couldn't do this. He couldn't hold Patton close and not lust for more, not take it from the warm, sleepy body that would surely press itself into his own.

He straightened up. "No, Patton."

"But—"

"Go to sleep."

His harsh tone worked. Quick as if he had burned her, she let go of him. Curling onto her side, she gave him her back. Chase took a deep breath and reminded himself he was doing the right thing.

He made it all the way to the door before the first sniffle chased chills up his back. *Ignore it*, he told himself. *It's just a trick.* Another step, another sniffle. *Ah, hell.*

She was crying. He'd made her cry. The knowledge tore through him and despite all the reasons not to, Chase turned around. He could see her slim little shoulders shaking in the light that cut into the room from the hall.

This was why he'd left the barn that afternoon, because he didn't have the strength to do what he needed to in the face of her tears. Not then and not now. The evidence was in his feet as they carried him back to the side of her bed.

"Patton…" He had no idea what to say.

"Go away." That had sounded more like a sob than anything. "You made it clear. You don't want me here, so just go away."

"I..." Chase wanted to say he didn't mean it. He wanted to take it back, but he feared what might happen if he did. He had to do something to stop those tears.

Words normally failed him. He wasn't good with them, never had been. Instead, Chase fell to his strength. Action. Settling down into the bed with a defeated sigh, he forced Patton to turn around. Her pitiful attempts at struggling were easily subdued.

In short order he had her snuggled into his chest, his hand rubbing up and down here back as he whispered nonsense in a soothing tone into her hair. It never failed to calm her down. It pleased Chase to know, despite everything that had changed, this one thing hadn't.

He was also relieved to realize the blinding lust he had feared didn't manifest itself. Oh, his cock still hardened, but the desire inside him was tempered with a foreign element, tenderness. Never had those two emotions combined within his blood, heating it with a warmth and peace that felt right no matter what his mind said.

"You remember when I used to have nightmares as a child?"

The sudden question startled him and it took him a moment to respond. "I remember."

"You would hold me and I would tell you what I had dreamed about."

"I'd always tell you that they were just dreams and not to worry." Chase smiled at the memorized response.

"You know what my nightmares are now?" He didn't and he didn't want to know. That didn't stop her from telling him. "Now my nightmare is that I'm alone. That I no longer have Slade, Devin or you in my life."

Damn her. Of all the hits she could have dealt him, that was the lowest. He had no defense against her pain, nothing to shield him from the guilt that statement roused in him. He never should have gone into the den.

"That's never going to happen," Chase promised her. He had no other choice.

"But you said—"

"I know what I said and I shouldn't have." With that he was stripped bare. "Don't worry, Patton, you'll always have a place in our family."

"Then you'll try." She sniffed into his neck. "You'll try to be my friend."

"I am your friend, Patton."

"My best friend."

He was doomed. They were all doomed. It was only a matter of time before everything exploded beyond his control. For the life of him, Chase couldn't muster the strength to fight it anymore. However it ended, he'd make sure Patton didn't end up being the one that got scarred. Whatever it took, Chase silently vowed.

The minutes stretched on. Her breathing slowed and deepened. Chase knew she had fallen asleep and he should leave, but he couldn't bring himself to. This was the peace before the storm and Chase intended to savor it.

* * * *

Hailey greeted Patton with a look over as she stepped into the kitchen door the next morning. Patton returned it, unable to keep the smirk off her face. She knew just what Hailey thought. A moment later Hailey confirmed it.

"Well, you're not grinning from ear to ear or doing a victory dance, so I guess your night didn't go as well as it could."

"It went fine, thank you." Patton dropped her purse onto the counter and stepped out of the way as Hailey carried her coffee cup to the table.

"So you plan to make them jealous by spending all day and night with them. I must admit, that's new twist."

"Ha, ha." Patton moved to pull her own cup from the cupboard. "Actually, I am tweaking the plan."

"You are?"

Patton thought back to the scene in the barn yesterday. It still hurt, but time gave her the emotional distance to realize she should have seen it coming. The closer she got to victory, the more cornered Chase would feel and the more he would lash out. She'd have to grow tougher skin if she was going to survive this war.

She'd also going to have bomb him big time instead of steadily working at his control. That thought had led to her current revelation.

"Yeah, I got a new plan."

This one was foolproof.

Chapter 21

Slade stared into the raging bonfire. The flames boomed and popped, racing up into the night sky in a feeble attempt to touch the stars. All around him the field party fought to outshine the fire before him.

The Friday night Cattleman's Club Bash had finally come. Old faces and new ones gathered outside the Cattleman's lodge to relax and talk. There would be no kinky stuff, not tonight. That would come tomorrow evening.

Tonight was a chance for the women who were members to meet the new women and help explain to them the process. A good number of the women associated with the club would leave on Sunday. They would head back to the big cities to put their well-honed skills to use in a more commercial market.

Just like a military training base said goodbye to one class, another round of recruits were already being added to the mix. Most had just gotten in today. Some were here for training, others were there for the novelty of spending their vacation doing something naughty and forbidden.

Either way, all were welcome to the festivities. They would be grand, the grandest of the year to kick off the spring and flow into the summer, which would be a peak time for the club.

A well-known fact the men in the club anticipated and they started the season off with the zealousness of sixteen-year-old boys about to get laid for the first time. They cruised the throng of willing females, making mental lists for the selection process that would begin tomorrow.

Normally all three brothers would be present, checking out as many women as they could. As the founders of the club, they had first pick. They had always reveled in the honor.

Tonight the only thing Slade reveled in was depression. He wasn't alone. Devin was outright sulking. The difference being Devin had boycotted the affair as way of making a very loud statement to Chase.

As usual, Chase didn't pay much attention. His older brother had it in his head that what they needed was a new face and fresh body. What better place to find that then here?

Tomorrow would be the big bang. The party would surpass last year's chaos and set the standard for next year. There would be drinking, cigar smoking, gambling, great food and tons of naked, willing women who would be put to the test before the mock auction that would take place later in the night.

Chase had spent most of the day planning with Dean and GD for that wild night. It would be more than just an excuse for an orgy. The night would be both a graduation and an initiation. Each member would be allotted a number of women based on his ranking in the club.

For him and his brothers, that meant they could chose up to seven women. In the past they had tried to outdo themselves with the outright outrageous things they had done with that many naked bodies. Some of them had been very public displays that had earned them respect beyond what their titles as founders guaranteed them.

There could be eight women for all Slade cared. He wouldn't be participating in tomorrow's sex fest. It just felt wrong. He'd told Chase that. If Patton found out—and knowing Patton, she would—it would devastate her. Even if he could muster up his interest to fuck his way through a pack of nameless, faceless women, Slade wouldn't do that to her.

Things had gone so good this week. Patton had come over everyday. They'd gone swimming in the old pond and ridden horses through the pastures. They'd laughed and bragged as they all tried to best each other in cards or billiards. It had been like old times, but better because they were new times.

All week long the growing temptation to make that happiness permanent, to expand it beyond a simple hello hug or playful tug of her hair, had been growing steadier. Not just in Slade. In all of them, even Chase.

Slade could see it in his eyes. For his part, Chase had put on a happy face and played along. It had cost him though. Well, it cost everybody else when Patton wasn't around and Chase reverted to a snarling, miserable beast.

Chase swore all he needed was to get laid. If that were the truth, he could have easily gone down to the club or taken advantage of Charlotte. Of course he had an excuse for why he hadn't.

He needed somebody new, a fresh girl. Charlotte had walked in on that conversation and looked more hurt than she had all week. Slade knew they would have to let her go. None of the brothers had touched her since Patton's arrival last weekend. For a submissive like Charlotte, that was painful.

Charlotte could share and be shared, but she couldn't be ignored. Not that she hadn't tried her best to be noticed. None of them had taken the bait and she'd taken it personally.

Slade glanced over to where Chase stood talking to a group of Cattlemen. He had his arm around some tall, slender, brunette. She wasn't what Chase wanted, but he never got what he wanted so what was the big deal?

Slade sigh and finished off his beer. This place depressed him. Call him a selfish bastard, but he knew what he wanted and the idea of settling for anything less was abhorrent to him.

* * * *

Hailey looked around the throng of people surrounding her and still couldn't believe she was here. All around her men wearing

Stetsons and women in collars chatted, laughed and some were being a little more friendly.

When they had first arrived, Patton had explained Cole had assured her it would be a tame affair tonight, nothing too outlandish. As Hailey's eyes scanned over some of the couples and triples and even larger groups enjoying each other's company in a very public way, she couldn't help but wonder what Cole's definition of outrageous was.

Even without the public displays of affection, she would have been uncomfortable. Another helpful tidbit Cole had given Patton was to explain the 'dress code'. All male club members wore only black Stetsons. Men looking to join were invited to the party, but were restricted from wearing that prized color.

Shock was too mild an emotion for what Hailey experienced as she realized just how many men were involved in the Davis boys club of kink. Men who held respected positions in town, some elected positions, were running around in black Stetsons acting like oversexed teenagers at an after-prom party.

It repulsed Hailey and all she wanted was to leave. She couldn't, not until she played her part in Patton's little drama. Oh, Patton would owe her big time after this night. The entire plan was a disaster waiting to happen and somehow her friend had sucked her right into the middle of the storm.

She checked her watch. It had been thirty minutes. Patton had asked for forty-five. She was going to get thirty plus however long it took to find either Slade or Devin. God, she hoped they weren't doing anything embarrassing. Patton had wanted her to find Chase to recite her lines to, but Hailey valued her life.

It was impossible to find anybody in this crowd, especially with all the men so similarly dressed. Hailey worked her way around the bonfires, trying to distinguish one of the Davis brothers in the sea of denim clad, t-shirt wearing men.

Nobody spared her a glance. Why would they? Compared to the skimpy, sexy outfits all the women were wearing, Hailey looked more like a man in her jeans and soft-weight, button-down flannel shirt. She hadn't even let Patton unbutton it low enough for her bra to peek out. As far as Hailey was concerned, the top button being undone was enough.

Sighing in frustration, Hailey turned and ran smack into a hard wall of muscle. The soft cotton shirt was almost hot to the touch, scented with aftershave and leather. The combination sparked to life a part of her she had often tried to be above.

"Well, well, well," Kyle Harding drawled in an all too familiar southern accent as his hands latched onto her arms, allowing her to step back, but not flee.

If ever she had an arch nemesis, Kyle was it. Though she hadn't seen or spoke to him in years, the torment he had put her through during high school had never been forgotten. He'd been the lead dick in the clique of motor heads who had objected to having a woman in their auto shop class. At first he'd treated her with arrogant distain, talking down to her and cracking sexist jokes. When she had started getting straight A's and showing up him and his buddies, he'd escalated his pestering to practical jokes she hadn't found the least bit funny.

Duct taping her books to the workbench, wiring her locker with a car alarm, rewiring her projects, changing jets in her carburetors, anything and everything to drive her insane for three years straight.

"Kyle," Hailey responded with all the venom stored in her heart just for him.

"Hailey Mathews at a Cattleman's event, will life ever cease to surprise?"

"It already did," Hailey retorted. "I'm not the least bit shocked to find you here."

"I must say," Kyle ignored her obvious distaste to run his eyes down her body. "You're looking very tempting tonight, Hailey."

What the hell? He was flirting with her. Kyle Harding flirting with her, apparently life didn't cease to amaze. The most shocking thing was her own body's response to the heated glimmer darkening his hazel eyes to liquid chocolate.

Kyle had always been handsome. Even in high school, he'd seemed to have the hard body of a grown man. With those hazel eyes, chocolate hair and slow, shit eating grin, he'd made many rounds through the female population.

That had only ever made Hailey dislike him more. The fact that he now unleashed that charm on her made her nipples harden, her belly quiver and her temper flare white hot. Hailey crossed her arms over her chest, not about to give him the satisfaction of knowing his effect on her.

She disguised the move by narrowing her eyes and cocking her hip. "You look as plum ugly as ever."

He laughed at her insult, the sound deep and husky. "I see your charm hasn't changed either, nor your fashion sense."

"Never did take to the street walker style."

"Hmm." The sound rumbled out of his chest as his eyes did another slow dance down her length. "Didn't your mama ever tell you, covering everything up just makes a man itch to unwrap you? But," his finger reached out to stroke down her neck and Hailey flinched backward from the electric caress, "you seem to be missing something."

"Don't touch me."

"Ah, but you're so soft."

"I also have teeth and trust me my bite is a lot worse than my bark."

"I love a woman who bites and screams and bucks with her passion."

"Passionate hatred."

"You protest a lot for somebody who could just walk away."

That hit her hard. He was right. Why the hell was she putting up with this? With a growl she shoved past him and stomped off into the night with that damn sexy laugh of his chasing after her.

It was true. When you stopped looking, you found what you had been searching for. As Hailey stormed through the crowds, intent on getting to her car and escaping this insanity, she ran smack into Slade.

Chapter 22

"Hailey?" The sight of the little redhead so shocked Slade he dropped his beer.

"Slade." From her tone, the surprise was mutual.

"What are you doing here?"

"Enjoying the party?"

That would have been more believable if she looked the slightest bit happy. Not that it mattered. Hailey shouldn't be here even if she was having the greatest time of her life. She was hands-off and every Cattleman knew that.

"This is an invitation only party. How did you get past the gate?"

"I had an invitation."

Well, duh. "Who invited...Patton." Slade didn't need an answer to figure that out. He didn't even need to ask the question. Who else would have dragged straight-laced Hailey to this kind of party?

"Who the hell invited her?" Because Slade was going to kick the jackass's ass.

"Who?" Hailey scowled before her eyes suddenly widened. "Oh, my God, you don't know."

"Know?" Slade didn't like the sound of that. Not one bit. "Know what?"

"Oh, wow," Hailey whispered, not appearing to have heard his question despite that he'd fairly snarled it at her. "I mean I just assumed with all the time you've been spending with her, Patton would have mentioned it to you. Then again, she probably didn't want to get into a fight. I mean, with everything—"

"Hailey!" Slade had to stop himself from shaking her and settle for gripping her by the arms to get her attention. "What didn't Patton tell me?"

"That she's been seeing Cole Jackson."

"No."

"No? Yes. They've seen each other everyday this past week."

Seeing each other…everyday…Cole and Patton, the horrifying stammer of thoughts froze his blood. It all started to make sense now. Why Patton hadn't pushed to stay later when they ended her daily trips to the ranch early. Why she'd show up late, sometimes disheveled. Why she hadn't pushed once for something more than friendship.

Patton was dating Cole. She already had her something-more-than-friends man. She'd done what they'd asked and moved on. The reality of that fact cut straight through him, leaving a devastating hole growing in his heart.

Cole? That hadn't been what they wanted for her. Cole with all his perversions and his addiction to sharing wasn't any better than they were. He was worse. Cole didn't love Patton. He couldn't, not the way they did.

This was the conclusion of the all the suffering they'd endured? Cole was the man they'd saved Patton for? No. It couldn't happen. Not unless it already had.

"Are they sleeping together?" The words were almost impossible to get out over the rock of denial crushing down on his chest.

"No. Not yet." Slade breathed again with that answer. The relief was short lived as Hailey checked her watch. "Well, maybe by now."

"Where is she?"

Slade didn't expect an answer, didn't wait for one. Releasing Hailey, he turned to find the lovebirds himself. Unfortunately, half of that pair was about to get the beat down of a life time. The other half wasn't going to fare much better, though he'd never hit Patton. Maybe a spanking, but not even the good Lord could blame him.

Over the rage of violent thoughts flooding his head and the thundering of his heartbeat, Slade heard Hailey's hesitant response.

"She's not here."

That stopped him, had him turning back toward Hailey. "What do you mean, she'd not here?"

"She and Cole took off a while ago." Hailey winced and shifted backward as her words reeled him in.

"Took off?"

"Yeah, I'm supposed to wait until they get back or…"

"Or?"

"Well, Patton said if she wasn't back in an hour or so, to go home and she'd see me in the morning."

Morning, there could be no doubt about that meant. "Where did they go?"

"I don't think I should—"

"Where?"

"Peter's Point."

"Chase!"

* * * *

"Chase?"

Hailey swallowed, her eyes darting in the direction Slade had turned. Chase stood several feet away. His arm looped around a petite brunette whose ear he was whispering in. Whatever he said, the woman grinned and blushed.

At Slade's roar, he looked up, over and she could clearly see the annoyance in his features. The woman tucked into his side didn't look pleased either. Hailey swallowed again.

"What?" Chase yelled back.

Slade didn't answer, just nodded his head for Chase to come over. With a sigh and a muttered word to the woman with him, he stormed over to Slade.

"What?"

"Patton's with Cole."

She was going to die. Chase would kill her, then Patton, and then definitely Cole. She might love Patton as a sister, but even she wasn't worth the hell that fired to light in Chase's eyes.

It surprised her when all he did was mutter, "So?"

"So?" Slade snarled. "You know what he is like."

Chase's eyes cut to Hailey. "You told him this?"

"I tried to talk her out of it, Chase." Hailey defended herself. "I told her not to do this, but she said that she wanted to…to…you know."

"God damnit." Slade turned to run for his truck, but Chase grabbed him by the arm. "Let me go!"

"Just calm down."

"Calm down?" Slade sounded almost wild now. "Fuck that! You can stand around here with your little brunette, but I'm not going to let Patton ruin her life."

"You're thinking with your dick again. Now just settle down for a moment."

* * * *

Chase didn't release his younger brother as he turned back to study Hailey. After a moment, she began to fidget under his intensive scrutiny. He watched as heat infused her face and knew that it had nothing to do with the fire. Hailey had never been good at these types of games.

"Patton put you up to this, didn't she, Hailey?"

"Up to what?" Hailey tried to sound innocent but failed.

"You're not as good a liar as she is, Hales. So, why don't you just fess up?"

"I'm not lying. Patton and Cole are on their way to Peter's Point."

"I bet they are, just as sure as I am that Patton told you to come and tell us. Right, Hailey?"

"Damnit, Chase," Hailey snapped. "What if she did? Doesn't change the facts, does it? Patton doesn't want to be a virgin no more. Now you're either going fix that problem for her or Cole will. Choice is yours."

With that, Hailey turned and stomped off.

"Over my dead body," Slade snarled. "Cole's not going to fix a damn thing for Patton."

"She's playing us, Slade."

"So? Hailey's right. We either claim her or somebody else will. We have no control over who she picks, including somebody who is rougher than us. Hell, do you really think there is even one other man who will take as good a care of Patton as us?"

Chase went silent for a moment, thinking. Slade had a point. Chase hadn't sacrificed everything so Patton could end up with a man like Cole. He'd done it to save her from the games men like him played. Obviously though, he'd failed. Patton wanted things her way. She always got what she wanted.

It had never dawned on Chase that she would find another man to give it to her. It probably should have, but she had him so twisted up in knots. Truth be told, he was sick and tired of feeling this way, of trying to be a noble gentleman when he really was a bastard.

Slade held himself tense. If Chase didn't come to an answer Slade wanted, then he'd break the pact. He'd take Patton and run off with her. It would destroy their family, but he'd make sure Patton was happy.

"This is what it comes down to," Slade stated roughly. "We didn't give her a choice and now she's not giving us one."

"I don't like to be pushed, Slade."

"Neither do I. I don't like ultimatums either, but sometimes you haven't got any choice but to face them."

"So we got get her and force her to go back to Atlanta."

"Force her? With what?" Slade bit back a sarcastic laugh. "No. It comes to this. I don't want to break my promise to you, but I can't do this anymore. I can't stand by and let another man touch what in my heart I know is mine. I want her and I'm going to have her. You can either be a part of that or not."

"You understand what you are saying?" Chase's eyes narrowed on him.

"I'm breaking the pact. What you do is your choice. Now let me go."

Chase didn't release him but studied him for a long tense moment. "Fine, but after all the games and deceptions, I think Patton deserves a little of what she's dishing out. Don't you?"

"What are you saying?"

"I got an idea."

* * * *

"You know, Devin said he'd kill me if I touched you," Cole commented as he slouched into the truck door.

He turned slightly, facing Patton. The combined moonlight and starlight shining through the truck window only served to make Cole appear even more ruggedly handsome. The sprinkle of light cast his hard features into a sexy combination of shadows beneath the brim of his hat.

"At least, you'll die with a smile on your face." Patton mimicked his position, relaxing against her own door.

"You don't lack for confidence, do you, girl?"

"Never found an advantage to modesty." Patton grinned. "I got the sense you never have either."

"Nope." Cole shook his head. "I never lacked for brains either."

"What? You afraid of Devin?" Patton challenged him.

"I got two rules I obey. I don't touch a friend's sister and I don't touch his woman."

"You know I'm not his sister."

"But are you his woman?"

"If I was, you think I'd have that free time I've been spending with you? That he wouldn't make sure I was taken care of tonight and not running around with you?"

"Hmm." Cole studied her. "It might just be a matter of the heart."

"Excuse me?"

"That boy is wildly jealous over you. You might not be his lover, but I'm thinking he still considers you his."

God, she hoped so. To Cole though she just shrugged. "I'd say that was his problem, wouldn't you?"

"Not if he plans on hitting me, it isn't."

"I must admit, Cole, this sudden concern for you own safety really diminishes your sex appeal."

"Just as you know I hit back."

"Understood."

"I don't mind getting into trouble as long as all parties understand the consequences of what they're getting into."

"Well, you're not getting into anything all the way over there, cowboy."

"Direct, too."

"Never found much reason for subtlety either."

"Well, since you know so much about chokers and collars, then you know you come to me, not the other way around."

"Is that, so?" Patton grinned. "You asking or you telling?"

He didn't respond to that taunt, but raised an eyebrow and waited. Patton couldn't help but giggle. It was a nervous reaction. Here was the moment. It would either be Cole or the Davis brothers.

If they didn't show up, then her heart would be broken but her body would be well satisfied. She knew being with Cole wouldn't be as good as being with Chase, Slade and Devin, but she couldn't spend her whole life a virgin.

Cole made a decent substitute. Hard and demanding enough, she could close her eyes and pretend. With that thought in mind, Patton crawled across the seat toward the hunk waiting for her.

"Very good, sweetheart." Cole ran his hands into her hair. "Now for your reward."

Without waiting for her to respond, he leaned down and took her mouth in a hard, dominating kiss. It shocked Patton. The hot, bold exploration left her panting for breath. She felt burned from the inside out. No other words could describe the inferno of heat and desire that torched through her body as his lips sealed hers.

Her response frightened her. He wasn't the right man, but her body didn't care. Suddenly she doubted her decision. Not sure she wanted to know this about herself, she tried pulled back. The hand threaded through her hair tightened, holding her still as his tongue plundered the moist recesses of her mouth.

He used his whole mouth, lips, tongue, teeth to nibble, lick, stroke her desire until her body trembled and her cunt clenched, weeping out its desire. The kiss seemed to go on forever and Patton began to get lost in the pleasure.

Reality shot back through her when she heard a rip and felt her shirt flap open. Her bra suffered the same fate, being torn in two. The cool night air puckered her nipples and Cole's warm, rough palms came to heat them back up.

"You're one hell of a kisser," Cole whispered raggedly as he broke away from her lips and began placing nibbling, suckling little kisses down her throat.

Patton held her breath, waiting for him to reach her breasts. Her moan of anticipation turned into a startled shriek when the doors of the truck flew open. Cole ripped away from her and she could hear Slade's shout.

"I'm going to kill you!"

"No! Slade!"

Patton went to follow Cole out the driver's door, but a steel band cinched around her waist pulled her back. Patton screamed and struggled as Chase pulled her right across the seat and into his hard embrace.

"Let me go!" Patton struggled against his hold, hearing the horrid sound of several punches being delivered in a row.

"Come on, Patton." Chase shoved her through the door of his truck and pushed her out of the way as he climbed in. Patton tried to go out the other side, but Chase latched onto her waist again, holding her to his side as he popped the idling truck out of park.

"God damnit, Chase. Let me go. Slade's going to kill him."

"He might," Chase agreed in a hard tone and flipped on the headlights. With a quick motion of his wrist, he turned the truck around. "But Cole's got it coming. Devin warned him."

"How can you say that?" Patton shrieked.

"Cause it's true. Now I suggest you stop worrying about your pretty boy toy and start worrying about yourself."

With that ominous warning, Chase spun the truck out of the small dead-end road and took off. Patton turned in his grip to look out to the back window. She could see two men on the ground. The one on top pounded his fist into the one on the bottom.

She shivered with fear at the sight, feeling sick. This wasn't what she had wanted. Sure, she thought Cole might get hit, but not this. Patton closed her eyes and wondered what she had done.

* * * *

Slade looked up as the taillights of Chase's truck disappeared around a bend in the road. They had gone. Falling back onto his butt, he leaned up against the side of his tire and let Cole free.

Cole gave him a hard look, one that said he thought Slade had gone completely insane, and sat up. Slade ignored him to cradle his pained fist. The knuckles were bruised, some of them actually broken open.

"Hurts, don't it?" Cole straightened his shirt.

"It'll heal." Shade shrugged.

"You feeling all right, Slade?"

"Fine. Actually, better than."

"You sure?" Cole raised an eyebrow at that response.

"Best damn day of my life. Why you ask?"

"Oh, I don't know." Cole shrugged. "Perhaps because you just threatened to kill me and then pounded your fist into the ground. Seemed a little odd to me, is all."

"For Patton's benefit."

"Patton?" Cole scowled. "You just scared the shit out of that little girl."

"I certainly hope so."

"I'm missing something, ain't I?"

"She set you up."

"Come again?"

"She and her friend, Hailey, set this up. She got you out here. Hailey made sure we knew."

"Hailey Mathews? The short little redhead?"

"That would be the one."

"They set this up?" Cole blinked, appearing to have a hard time with the concept.

"Played the oldest game a woman can, pitted two men against each other."

Slade had to smile at that. The oldest game and if Chase hadn't stopped Slade from thinking with his heart, it would have worked. Then Cole would have gotten hit for real.

"Well, I'll be damned." Cole shook his head. "That little bitch."

"Hey, watch your language."

"Sorry, man, but what am I supposed to think? If I'm not mistaken, she planned this scenario betting that I'd get hurt."

"Don't take it personally." Shade stood. "I'm sure she thought you could a handle a few punches."

"I can." Cole stood. "Doesn't mean I like them."

"Hell, nobody does." Slade snickered. "Don't worry, we'll take care of Patton."

"And what about her friend, Hailey?"

"Hailey?" Slade shrugged. "Not my problem."

"Well then, she is mine."

"Hold on there a second," Slade stepped forward as Cole turned to climb into the truck. "We watch out for Hailey."

"She your sister?"

"No."

"Your woman?"

"No."

"Then she's fair game."

"Whatever you do to Hailey, just remember that we watch out for her and if you piss her off, you piss Patton off and that pisses me off. Got it?"

"Got it." Cole nodded and climbed into his truck.

"But that ain't going to stop you."

"I've been looking at that woman a long time, Slade," Cole stated evenly. "I know you and yours put a hands-off rule at the club on her, but the way I figure it, you're going to be awfully busy corralling that wildcat your brother packed into his truck. You haven't got time to be watching over little miss Hailey, so I'll take over that responsibility."

"Out of the goodness of your heart, right?"

"I'm full of love, my friend." Cole placed a dramatic hand over his heart.

"You're full of something all right." Slade snorted. "I didn't realize you noticed Hailey's existence."

"Oh, I've noticed that sweet little thing. It just drives me nuts that she wouldn't let me touch that Studebaker of hers."

"Is that what this is all about? A car?"

"Not just any car. She's insulted my skills and now offended my honor. That's just one too many tiny steps over the line."

"You're a weird one, Jackson. You know that?"

"Well, be that as it is, I'm going to be putting my hands on more than just her car." Cole slammed the door to his truck before rolling down the window. "You staying?"

"Patton wouldn't believe I got rid of the body if I show up five minutes later, will she?"

"You're evil, Slade Davis."

Chapter 23

When they reached the farmhouse, Patton jumped out of the truck and ran for the door. She didn't make it to the steps before Chase lifted her into the air and threw her over his shoulder.

"Damn it, Chase," she hollered. "Put me down!"

He didn't respond to her demands or the fists hitting him in the back. Her ranting curses fell on deaf ears, her punches didn't dent the muscles in his back. Patton snarled, bucking and twisting to break his hold.

With ease, he carried her up the steps, across the porch, and into the house. Chase ignored Patton's struggles. Patton was his, theirs. Now that the decision had been made, he wouldn't look back or second-guess it.

This was what she had pushed for. This was what she claimed to want. She would have to face the consequences of that decision. She would understand what that meant starting tonight, now.

He banged into the study with just that intent, surprising Devin who sat at the desk going over some paperwork. Devin looked up, his eyes widening with surprise as Chase dumped a hissing, snarling Patton in the middle of the room.

The moment her feet touched the floor, Patton twirled away from Chase, turning to confront him. She paid little attention to her shirt flapping open to reveal her breasts, apparently far too angered to notice.

Chase noticed. His eyes narrowed in on the smooth flesh. The edges of the round globes hinted at the perfectly shaped breasts hidden beneath the soft cotton fabric. The memory of their soft feel and sweet taste had taunted him over the past week, but no more. Chase's body hardened with the need to see what it had already so intimately touched.

"What in the hell do you think you are doing, Chase?" Patton's hands instinctively went to her hips. The stance widened the gape in her shirt.

"Me?" Chase smiled slightly. With the decision made he could finally relax, take control of the situation, of Patton. "I wasn't the one getting felt up by Cole Jackson."

"No, you were doing the bump and grind with some two bit floozy at the bonfire." Patton's face flushed a bright red with her anger when Chase shrugged aside her comment.

"That's irrelevant."

"Irrelevant?" She gasped. "Boy, you have some nerve. You know that?"

"It's a family trait." Chase shrugged again because he knew how much it would irritate her. The angrier Patton became, the straighter her spine got and the more her shirt gaped open.

"Don't feed me that bullshit. You're the one who told me to go find somebody else. Then the next thing I know, you're busting into his truck like Rambo."

"Should I have come in pretending like I was Mary Poppins?"

"You should have stayed the hell out!"

"Blame Hailey." Chase shrugged again, enjoying the way her eyes widened. "She was so worried about you. After listening to her, Slade just completely lost it."

"Oh, God," Patton whispered, her face paling. He could almost see her mind switching gears from anger to concern to fear. "You don't really think he's going to hurt Cole?"

"Don't worry. Slade wouldn't make the same mistake our dad did." Cole's firm conviction appeared to reassure Patton. He ruined her moment of relief when he added, "He wouldn't get caught."

"What the hell does that mean?" Patton shouted, her fear morphing back into anger in an instant.

"What I said, he'll clean up his mess. Don't look at me that way, Patton. You got more important things to worry about than what's happening to Cole."

"What is more important than the fact that Slade might kill him?"

"Me," Chase stated succinctly, "and what I'm going to do to you."

"Do to me? What the hell did I do? I didn't do anything wrong. You two barbarians had no right to interfere."

"But we did," he assured her smugly. "You're ours and we have a right to interfere in everything you do."

"What?" Patton shrieked. "Oh, hell no! That's not what you've been saying these past two weeks."

"I changed my mind," Chase explained dismissively, making her growl.

"You can't do that," Patton forced out between clenched teeth.

"I can do whatever I want."

"Well it's too damn late, because I changed my mind."

"That's irrelevant."

"Irrelevant?" Patton stared at Chase in open-mouthed amazement.

"We got an echo in here," Chase commented to Devin who had leaned back in the chair to watch and listen.

"Listen here, you smug, arrogant bastard." Patton began advancing on Chase.

"I warned her about her language," Chase said to Devin.

"She's aware of the consequences for disobedience."

"Shut up, Devin," Patton snapped. "This doesn't concern you."

"I don't think she understands."

"It's not me that's having a failure to compute at the moment, it's you. So, listen carefully. I'm not interested anymore. I changed my mind."

"Doesn't work that way," Chase explained calmly.

"You don't make the rules."

"Actually I do. We make the rules. You obey. That's the way it works."

"I'm not about to play lapdog to a jackass like you."

"That's the last time, Patton. You won't get another warning."

"Warning? About what?"

"No more cussing."

"No more cussing," Patton muttered, disgusted with his high handedness. "Well, just so I get this right, what exactly is cussing? Is hell a cuss word? What about SOB? Does that count?"

"You're pushing, Patton."

"How about rat face? Turd breath? What about short-stubbed dick? Or puckered starfish packer?"

"Pucker star—" Chase began to repeat in confusion.

"Ass fucker," Devin explained.

"No cussing!"

"I'd say that counts." Devin shot Chase a quizzical look. "Wouldn't you?"

"Well, hell if that's going to count I might as well go for broke, you wart-dicked, pea-brained, cock sucking, mother...*ahhh*!"

* * * *

Patton screamed as she felt herself whirling through the air. It was like déjà vu when she found her breath slammed out of her body by a set of hard, muscled thighs. This time though they were Chase's thighs and she didn't intend on just sitting still and taking her spanking.

It was one thing to be turned-on experimenting with a little punishment. It was a new level of humiliation to get that way when she was justifiably pissed off. Her anger meant nothing to her body and her pussy had begun to soften, growing steadily wetter as their argument had continued.

A sharp slap turned her cusses into a cry. For a second the stinging blow radiated pain through her tender cheeks. As the sensation moved through her body, it altered, becoming strangely pleasurable.

He didn't give her time to focus on the sensation as more and more blows confused her mind and her body. Pain blended into pleasure until she trembled, her cunt gushing fluids down the top of her thighs. She hadn't noticed when she'd stopped fighting and begun moaning.

"Wow, you were right." Chase's voice broke through Patton's daze.

"Told you." Devin's smug voice brought back the dash of reality she needed.

Damn it!

Patton knew better, given her vulnerable position, than to voice that thought aloud. She was supposed to be resisting, not moaning out her pleasure while offering her ass up for the beating.

Both the arrogant jerks had noticed the change in her demeanor. No doubt, they planned to take advantage of it. At least she wasn't naked. Yet, being the correct word.

"Well, let's see if she likes something a little more adventurous." Chase lifted her back on her feet.

Patton backed away from him as he stood up. She watched, her eyes going wide, as he undid his belt buckle to pull the thick leather strap free. He couldn't be planning on hitting her with that, could he? As if to confirm her fear, Chase ordered her to strip. Patton shook her head in denial backing further away from him.

"I told you to strip, Patton. Is more punishment in order?" He looped the belt around his hand as he spoke.

With a shriek, Patton launched herself at Devin, curling protectively into his lap.

"Please don't let him hit me with that," she pleaded in a soft, little girl voice.

Devin slid a finger under her chin to raise her head up. Before Patton could issue another plea, he kissed her. It started out gentle but quickly flamed out of control.

Time ceased to exist and Patton forgot all about Chase and his belt as Devin continued to ravage her mouth. She barely noticed as he shifted her position so that she knelt over him, straddling his lap.

Large, work roughened hands slid up her ribcage to dip beneath the edges of her shirt to palm her breast. Patton tore her mouth from Devin's, gasping for breath. His wandering mouth began to suck, nip, and lick its way down her neck.

His fingers curled around her hard nipples. They pulled and rolled the tender flesh, sending shards of pleasure radiating outward. Her head tipped back, the movement arched her back, offering up her breasts for his caress.

Patton moaned, unable to stop her hips from rotating, grinding into the hard male lap beneath. Her cunt gushed, clenching in time with the rhythmic pulls on her nipples. Her pussy ached with such desperation to be touched, filled, that Patton barely recognized that a second set of hands tugged at her jeans.

All she cared about was the intense pleasure of her wet folds being parted. A finger slid over her clit, finding the little bar, flicking it, and she cried out as her hips jerked seeking more of the touch.

That questing finger moved on and she whimpered as it gently circled her nether lips. Teasing her with the touches she wanted, but never giving her enough. Patton began to whimper and beg.

Her body was no longer her own. It was at the command of the hands that ruled the pleasure that tormented her. They caressed her breasts, played with her nipples, slid down her arms before skipping over to the sensitive skin of her lower back, but by far the hand buried in between her legs did the most damage to her sanity.

Those maddening fingers toyed with her, making her hips arch and grind against them but always pulling back whenever it started to feel good. Patton didn't know how much more she could take.

Just when she thought, knew, she was about to lose it, a tongue flicked out over the tip of her nipple. Her eyes popped open and she looked down to watch as Devin lapped at the tender tip before sucking it into his mouth.

In perfect rhythm, the fingers buried in her pants began to roll her clit back. Her eyes slid back into her head as her body began to pulse in the ever-quickening beat of the tongue rolling her nipple and the fingers rolling her sensitive bud. Another mouth joined in closing over her other breast.

Patton writhed under the heated caresses, crying out her need until everything exploded. Everything ceased to exist as her body collapsed against Devin, going limp and listless as the aftershocks of her orgasm echoed through her muscles.

She barely noticed that somebody tugged at her shoes, pulling them off along with her socks. As her body was lifted up slightly so that her pants and underwear could be discarded, Patton finally roused herself enough to look down into Devin's lust filled eyes.

"You remember the rule about orgasming without permission?" Devin asked, huskily.

Patton just blinked, her mind unable to compute his words.

Slade's deep voice sounded somewhere over her shoulder. "She's going to have to be punished for that."

It took her a moment before the words sunk in. She tried to gather her wits. Slade had returned, appearing unscathed.

"I think it's your turn, Slade."

"No," Patton whispered hoarsely.

"I'm afraid so, sweetheart," Devin responded just as softly. "You know the rule and you broke it."

"But…" Her words faded off as Devin's warm hand gently caressed the naked skin of her pussy.

The tender touch sent another shudder through her body. So did the realization that she was completely naked. Naked and surrounded by the fully clothed Davis brothers, leaving her totally vulnerable to their eyes, their touch, their punishments. Patton shivered with an exotic mixture of fear and anticipation.

"No buts, sweetheart. You should have asked," Devin instructed her as he continued to rub the back of his fingers against her mound. "You knew."

Patton closed her eyes trying to swallow down the sensations his touch caused her. She tried to bring her arms up to push away from him and only then realized that they had been tied behind her back. Her eyes popped open in alarm and she gazed down at Devin questioningly. Devin seemed to sense the erotic fear that moved through her and smiled slightly.

"We'd never hit you with a belt." Devin confirmed her suspicions. "Just restrain you."

"Come on, sweetheart."

Slade reached around to lift her off Devin's lap. Patton wiggled, whimpering in protest. Expecting to be placed over his legs for another spanking, Patton's heartbeat kicked up speed when carried her out of the study and up the steps toward the bedrooms.

This was what she had wanted, dreamed about. Now that the time had come, she felt apprehensive, unsure if she could go through with it. Patton knew she just needed a moment to calm down.

From the sounds of Chase and Devin pounding up the steps, Patton doubted they intended to give her a moment. Just the opposite.

Slade turned into the large master bedroom. The brothers had never technically used it as a bedroom. After she'd left for Atlanta, they'd turned it into an extension of the barn house playroom.

A little fact Charlotte had explained to her. The venom and hatred in the other woman's tone had been obvious, as had her attempt to create the impression she was more important to the Davis boys than Patton was.

Slade settled down on the edge of the custom-made bed. The mattress was much larger than a king. Patton's eyes took all that in as he arranged her so she straddled his lap. His hands gripping the globes of her ass as he began to gently rub her still stinging flesh.

"Have you ever stretched this pretty little asshole, sweetheart?"

Chapter 24

Patton blinked, his words echoing like a foreign language through her head. If she didn't understand them, she understood the hand he slid down her crack. A lone finger divided her buttocks to brush against the hole hidden in their crease. Instantly Patton tensed, unnerved by the sudden direction things were moving in.

"I'll take that as a no." Slade grinned. "Relax, honey. You knew this would happen. How else are we going to fuck you at the same time?"

Patton swallowed hard, trying to force her body to relax and accept his touch. Yes, she had known this would happen. When she'd been sleeping alone in bed and it had all been a distant idea, the notion had excited her. Now though, sitting naked on Slade's lap, knowing that Devin and Chase watched as he fingered her hidden little hole, she felt more anxious than aroused.

"We're going to have to widen you, sweetheart." Slade let his hand trail further down until he stroked into the wet opening of her pussy. Already sensitive from her recent climax, she gasped as her flesh quivered with renewed interest.

"Chase." Slade looked over her head. "Why don't you get the stuff?"

Patton heard Chase move off and wondered what stuff he was getting. Before that worry could set in, Slade moved again. He stretched out on the bed, lifting her up by the hips.

"Come here, sweetheart." Slade locked gaze with hers.

The feral look in his eyes had her shivering anew. Whatever he planned, he looked forward to it. She didn't have to wonder for long what he intended to do to her. His next command had her cunt clenching around his intruding finger.

"Feed me your pussy, Patton."

Patton wasn't capable of moving. Torn between fear and anticipation, with her hands tied behind her back she could do nothing more than shiver as his strong hands lifted her and began to lower her dripping pussy toward his mouth.

"Such a pretty, bare pussy you have," Slade whispered. "I do so enjoy snacking on it. Arch those hips and feed it to me."

With that command, his tongue slipped out to lick the very tip of her slit. The sudden touch had her crying out, her hips arching as he had commanded to offer up more of herself up for the tasting. He licked the full length of her slit in response.

Patton would have fallen face first onto the bed if Devin hadn't supported her. Kneeling directly in front of her, he held her against his chest. With a hand on her chin, he turned her face toward his.

Devin's lips closed over hers, capturing and swallowing her cries as Slade began to devour her most sensitive flesh. Patton lost the fight for control over her body as Slade sucked her clit and its little piercing into his mouth.

Her world narrowed to the gently pulling rhythm of his lips, the tongue rolling her piercing around and around. Even the feel of a slick finger slowly beginning to penetrate her ass didn't break the sensual spell that trapped her in its erotic embrace.

"Remember," Devin pulled back to whisper. "No coming without permission. We don't want to spend the whole night punishing you."

"But we will," Chase growled dangerously from behind her.

Patton swallowed, unable to respond as Devin backed up, lowering her until she bent over at the waist, her face tenderly cradled in his lap. Slade brought his hands into play. As he pushed first one and then two thick fingers into her, she cried out as the walls of her passage tried to clamp down on them.

A moment later, she felt the smooth, well-greased head of a plastic cock pushing against her back entrance. Patton tensed suddenly realizing what was about to happen. Before she could be overcome by fear, Slade's tongue licked down her slit and trust into her entrance beside his fingers.

Patton gasped. Despite the all the pleasure, it couldn't disguise the painful pressure coming from her ass as Chase eased the thick head of the toy past the tight ring of muscles at her entrance.

It popped through and the pain subsided to an intense aching pressure. The sensation magnified and warped by the pleasure radiating out from her pussy and breasts. Slade moved back up to lick her clit, toying with her piercing.

As Chase eased the length of the toy all the way into her, the escalating throb of ecstasy began to build, growing stronger as Devin slid his hands beneath her to play with her nipples in rhythm with Slade's tongue on her clit. Slade's fingers thrust deep into her, over and over again, pressing back into the dildo stretching her ass wide until Patton couldn't distinguish one caress from another.

She threw her head back and began to thrust her hips in time with those amazing fingers fucking into her. The movement also forced her back onto the toy, heightening her sense of pleasure.

"Oh, God," Patton screamed. "I'm going to come!"

Suddenly they all stopped and she snarled at being left on the brink.

"That's better, baby," Chase whispered in her ear. "But you don't tell us, you ask."

Patton snarled again, fighting the binds on her wrists. So close, just one more touch, one more lick would send her over the edge. She tried shoving her cunt back into Slade's face, forcing him to give her what she needed. It was pointless to fight.

Slade and Devin held her back with their superior strength. A second later, Chase lifted her off Slade's lap and away from possibility of satisfaction. As he moved her, she became increasingly aware of the dildo buried all the way into her ass.

Every little movement of her body magnified and echoed back the shifting dildo until even breathing caused the painful pressure to increase. What started as pain transformed into pleasure, as nerve endings she'd never known of came to life. By the time Chase had adjusted her to lie bent over the bed, Patton ground her teeth to stop from groaning.

"Now it's time to take your punishment." Chase instructed, settling down next to her.

Chase placed one arm over her anticipating her rejection of his statement. For a moment, Patton remained still, trying to adjust to the new sensations overwhelming her body. Then it clicked.

They were about to spank her again. Only this time her ass already burned, stuffed full of plastic cock. She opened her mouth to object, to tell them this was too much but the words came out as a scream as the first blow landed.

The stinging smack made her muscles tighten and clench around the dildo. Pain seared through her followed almost immediately by a pleasurable throb that left her confused. Patton panted as she tried to adjust to the sensation.

Slade didn't give her the time before smacking the other cheek and sending a second round of intense vibrations through her body. The blows came fast and hard after that.

The sensation was completely different than what she'd experienced minutes before. She could feel her body tightening closer and closer to the fine edge of ecstasy. Patton bit her lip trying to hold back her cries. She didn't want them to know how close she was coming. Be damned if it earned her more punishment.

"Do you remember why you're being punished?" Chase whispered in her ear as if reading her thoughts.

"Uh huh," Patton gasped.

"Why?"

"F-for co-coming," Patton sputtered.

"And?" Chase prodded.

"Not asking…oh, God."

"You're about to do it again, aren't you?" Chase chuckled.

"Noooo," Patton groaned as the blows came to a sudden stop. "Don't stop."

"You like that, huh?" Chase reached out to trace her jaw with his finger. "Admit it, Patton. Admit that you like having a dildo shoved up your ass while Slade beats on it."

"Oh, God," Patton groaned and buried her head in the bed.

"Patton?" Chase waited patiently.

"Yes," she croaked into the blanket.

"I want to hear you say it."

Patton swallowed at his words. They did interesting things to her body. The prospect of repeating what he'd said heightened the sensation. She didn't have time to think about that though as Chase tugged on her hair demanding her compliance.

"Yes." Patton forced the words out. "I liked having Slade spank me while I have a dildo shoved up my ass."

"You like it enough to come, don't you?" Chase pushed.

"Yes," Patton squeaked.

"I'm letting you get away with answering into the bed. In the future when I ask you a question, you will look me in the eye and answer clearly. Understand?"

Patton nodded, thankful that he didn't force that on her right now. Everything else was so new, she didn't know if she were ready for anymore.

"Hmm. Well, you got yours but we haven't gotten ours," Chase pointed out as he continued to run his hands through her hair. "Devin tells me you're really good at sucking cock. Want to show me?"

Chase reached back to undo the belt around her wrist. Gentle hands, Chase's hands, messaged the ache out of her arms. He worked over first one and then another before bringing them around to her front.

"Okay, baby, on your knees." He helped her get into the position he wanted. "That's it. Widen your legs, baby. Let the boys see that pretty pussy of yours."

Patton flushed at his words, but did as he asked. His comments reminded her that both Devin and Slade had a full view not only of her dripping pussy, but also the dildo impaling her backside. She secretly wondered if she'd ever grow use to this.

Chase came to kneel in front of her, lowering his zipper and pulling out his cock. She felt her embarrassment fade away at the proof of his arousal. His erection was beautiful, sleek, large, and much larger than she'd have imagined.

The large rounded head brushed against her lips. Looking up into eyes almost black with desire, Patton reached out to run her tongue down its slit. Chase jerked slightly and Patton smiled.

She licked again, little laps that lead to longer, slow exploring caresses. A hand in her hair pushed her down. Closing her mouth over the head, she obeyed the silent command.

Taking him all the way to the back of her throat, Patton used her hand to close over the rest of his length. Her other hand cupped his balls, stroking and rolling them with expert precision. The silky smoothness in her hand hardened even more, growing almost another inch.

Chase hips jerked, then jerked again as she began to suck and lick on him all at the same time. He wanted to cuss as he felt the urge to come quickly overtake him.

The sweet teasing of her tongue, the amazing suction of her mouth, the way she gazed straight up at him made it the most amazing blow job he'd ever endured. His hand tangled in her hair began to force her down and up at an increasing speed as he fucked his cock into her mouth.

It was the most pleasurable hell he'd ever endured and he'd need help maintaining his control. Devin came to his rescue, no doubt remembering his own trial when Patton's mouth had been sucking his cock.

Patton felt the bed depress behind her, a warm breath against the back of her thighs, and still she wasn't prepared for what came next. She choked, losing the rhythm of the cock she sucked on at the first piercing stroke of a tongue through her own wet slit. That teasing tongue swirled around her clit causing her to rear back, pushing her pussy against the mouth that began to tease her most sensitive flesh.

Chase's cock popped out of her mouth as she gasped. Chase chuckled before using his hold on her hair to bring her mouth back down on his erection. Patton didn't have the mind to focus on what she was doing, allowing Chase to control her motions.

She could feel the orgasm building in her. Her hands, her mouth tightened on Chase's cock. She didn't care if they punished her. They could do whatever they wanted to her as long as these sensations didn't stop.

A man only had so much willpower and Patton raced to outlast Chase. She could sense victory when the hand in her hair tightened painful and he forced her pace to quicken, forcing her to take as much of his length as she could. He hit the back of her throat and she swallowed. The sensation broke the last of Chase's control. With a groan, he let go.

Warm, salty fluid spilled down her throat. It felt thick and creamy as he rocked his hips, easing his cock over her tongue. Patton swallowed, the erotic experience heightening her pleasure as she felt three thick fingers swirl into her tightening cunt.

She would have been able to remain in control if somebody hadn't grasped the dildo and rocked it ever so deeper into her ass. The fingers and dildo fucked in and out of her in opposite strokes that had her choking back a scream.

Her world broke apart at the seams as Devin's tongue flicked over the piercing through her clit. She screamed as Chase pulled his cock from her mouth. Her head collapsed onto the bed as her hips arched, trying to follow the fingers slowly leaving her body.

"We're going to have to work on her ability to hold off an orgasm," Devin commented raggedly. His hot breath fanned the aftershocks still pulsing through her cunt.

"That's another punishment," Chase sighed with disappointment.

"At this rate, we'll never get around to the fucking." She could hear the scowl in Devin's voice. If she had the energy, Patton would've smiled. Devin always had been an eat the desert first kind of guy.

"We could just tally them up," Slade suggested. "Then dole all the discipline out at once."

"It'll make it harder for her to learn the lessons that way." Chase didn't actually sound like he objected.

Patton blinked sleepily. She was tired and ready to pass out, but listening to the three men argue over whether to discipline her or fuck her was erotically perverse. She'd vote for sleep, not that anybody asked.

"I say we make an allowance this one time."

"I second that." Slade concurred. "Let's get to the fucking."

Chapter 25

Before Patton caught her breath, hard hands turned her over. She stared at Slade through blurry eyes. He was naked. His cock, hard and straight, pointed right at her. The harsh lines of his features matched his feral gaze as he stared down at her naked, exposed cunt.

Slade spread her thighs wide and settled between them. She could feel smooth rounded head pressing against her weeping opening. He pressed forward slowly, pushing the head of his cock an inch into her snug depths.

Over the shudders wracking her own body, Patton could feel the fine trembling in Slade's hands and knew he fought against the need to thrust deep into the tight, untried depths of her body. His cheek ticked as his eyes watched her breasts lift with her sharp intake of breath as he fed another inch of his hard length into the steaming depths of her pussy.

"Hold on to my shoulders."

The words sounded like gravel and Patton could see the control he exerted for her sake. He felt so much larger, thicker than any toy she'd used and he stretched her almost painfully wide. The pressure caused her tender flesh to quiver, but the throbbing pain mixed with an increasing pleasure.

The dildo pressing against the back wall of her pussy intensified the sensation of being too full. Patton's jaw clenched as his little motions caused a riot of sensation to chorus through her. Want and fear warred within her and she moved slowly to obey him.

Slade tipped her hips toward his cock aligning their bodies into a perfect line. Slowly he eased another inch into her before pulling back only to thrust forward. He gave her a little more with each stroke until her sheath began to adjust, allowing him to move more easily within her.

Beneath him, Patton began to quiver. The tension in her muscles changed from apprehension to pleasure. Still, he went slow and easy until her internal muscles clamped down trying to hold him in her as he pulled back. The small movement broke his control and he plunged forward embedding his entire length into her untried channel. She was so tight, her wet heat burning his cock and he knew he couldn't last long.

He tried to slow his thrust, but her cries of untamed pleasure pushed even that consideration out of his mind. Slade gave in to his need. He fucked her with the wild hunger only she inspired in him.

He heard Patton cry out, her hips arching, lifting her pussy to take every thrust as deep as she could. With his every stroke, her internal muscles pulsed, caressing the sensitive length of his dick in a blatant attempt to seduce his seed from his cock.

The feel of her nails digging into the flesh of his shoulders undid him. Slade knew he was about to come like a randy youth with his first woman. He growled as he fought against the burning sensations in his balls, but couldn't hold it back. He fucked her harder, plunging deeper with every desperate stroke.

"Come for me, Patton."

He needed her to, needed to know she found her pleasure before he took his. When he felt the first lightning strike of release sear through his body he reached down to stroke her clit, flicking the little bar there. He felt her pussy clamp down, milking his cock as she arched back and screamed out her own release.

Her body splintered apart. Once again, Patton felt consumed by the flames of desire. The sensation far stronger, deeper than any of the climaxes she'd ever experienced. The pleasure seared not just her body, but burned straight through her heart into her soul, marking her as his, theirs.

Slade snarled above her, shuddering as his seed filled her body. For long moments, he held himself firmly inside her, pressing his cock as deeply into her as possible as the last of his orgasm played out. With a shudder, he collapsed against her.

Patton only then became aware that her legs had wrapped themselves around him. Her muscles ached with their exertion, still spasming with pleasure as they fell limply aside. She muttered a protest as Slade levered himself up and pushed away from her.

The cool air jarred her and she opened her eyes thinking to issue a protest. The words became trapped in her throat as she saw Devin naked, stepping up to take Slade's place. He lifted and bent her knees, pulling her to the edge of the bed.

She was open, fully exposed as Slade's and her combined juices seeped from her body. Devin's large hands lifted her hips up, as he brought his cock to the dripping opening of her cunt. She whimpered as she felt Devin's cock begin to press into her well-used pussy.

"Am I hurting you?" Devin whispered hoarsely.

"No," Patton moaned amazed that her body could so quickly accept another. Not just accept, but welcome. The aftershocks of her first real climax still tingled through her and they coiled with renewed tension, winding tighter as he forced inch after inch of his thick, hard erection deep into her body.

Devin felt different, his strokes deep and slow, but no less arousing. She felt a mouth settle on her breast to tease and suck the hard nipple. Chase. She gazed glassy eyed at his thick honey hair as he pulled on her nipple in time with Devin's strokes in her body.

Tighter and tighter, the tension coiled in her. Never breaking, the pleasurable ache pushed her higher and higher until she knew when it snapped there would be nothing of her left. A rough hand in her hair rolled her head to the side and the cock waiting for her.

"Lick it clean, sweetheart." Slade's demand held a hard edge that made it impossible for her deny him.

With a whimper, Patton began to lick Slade's dick clean. The taste of their combined flavors added to her pleasure. Without any prodding, she began to suck his hardening dick. The hand buried in her hair tightened as he began to push her up and down along his length.

They all began to pick up speed. Devin strokes became harder, faster, demanding as he fucked into her clenching cunt. Chase matched him as his hand came up to play with her other breast, rolling, pinching and pulling her nipples until Patton bucked wildly under the pleasure of their administrations.

Everything blurred. She could no longer distinguish one sensation from another until her whole world exploded. Patton screamed as the furious spasms ripped through her taut body. Pleasure crashed over her in mind numbing waves, taking her so far out of her body that her world crumpled.

Patton was vaguely aware of Devin's shout of fulfillment mingling with Slade's groan of release as they both shot hot jets of semen into her. She swallowed, trying to take all that Slade had to give her.

She barely managed that simple goal before another set of rough hands flipped her over and dragged her back to the edge of the bed. She had no strength left in her muscles to resist or help as Chase forced her to kneel, pulling her ass over her knees and spreading her legs wide.

The feel of another engorged cock pressing into her pussy pulled a whimpered protest from her. It was too much. She didn't have the energy left for another round. Chase didn't give her the option as he slowly sank his full length into her.

Patton's eyes rounded with the sensation, amazed at how her exhausted body managed to burst alive with pleasure. She shuddered and bucked as the aftermath of her last climax blossomed into the most intense pleasure of the night. He was longer, thicker than his brothers, filling her with such delicious sensations.

Distantly his words echoed in her head. He'd said he was a hard man and he hadn't been lying. Chase had no finesse. Immediately he began to pound into her with enough force to make her body bounce forward. Only his fingers biting into her hips held her in place.

He'd been wrong about one thing. She liked it hard, loved it. She raised up on unsteady arms as high as she could to push back against him, matching his motions thrust for thrust as the inferno building in her cunt flamed out of control and consumed her body.

Chase knew he couldn't last long. This would be the shortest ride he had ever given a woman when all he wanted to do was prolong the experience. It didn't feel right. Patton deserved better.

The God's honest truth, Chase wasn't better. A hard man, he took what his lust demanded he take. He never wanted anything more than he wanted Patton. That had been true before he watched Slade split her cunt wide for her first time ever.

Watching her pink, swollen folds stretch around Slade then Devin's blood darkened cock head had nearly been his undoing. The way her body flushed, her tits tightened, the look in her eyes, the expression on her face, it was all seared into his mind.

It had been the way she wildly bucked, thrusting her hips as she cried out with unbridled passion that matched his own that had Chase almost disgracing himself by shooting his load uselessly all over himself.

He needed this. Nothing had ever felt better than having Patton's tight, hot cunt clamp down on his cock as her internal muscles rippled and pulsed with her climax. That slight rhythmic pressure destroyed him. His hips took on a frenzied, wild rhythm, harder, faster, as his heart raced to keep up. He panted, desperate for breath, but even more desperate for her.

Then it hit him. The white-hot explosion of lightning shot out of his balls and seared through his body as his seed roared from him. Beneath him, Patton screamed as her head hit the bed, her ass still held up high by his hold.

Over the thundering of his heart, the roar of his own climax, Chase slowly became aware of one simple fact. He'd fucked Patton into oblivion. God, he prayed he hadn't hurt her.

Chapter 26

Patton swam through the erotic dreams back toward awareness. She fought waking up, not wanting to give up the dream. It was so good, better than any she'd ever had. The dream had seemed so real she could feel her belly quivering with pleasure, her pussy weeping with need.

The ache in her cunt came to life as a two thick fingers pushed up into her. Patton's eyes popped open with sudden awareness. This was no dream. Two hard, warm male bodies pressed her between them. One leg draped over Slade's thighs left her pussy exposed to his deeply intimate touch while Chase watched with that feral, hungry look in his eyes.

The full thickness of the dildo still filling her ass brought back to vivid life the memories from the past night. She wasn't a virgin anymore. More than that, she was now the Davis brothers' woman.

Chase's hand joined Slade's bringing her back to the present as two more fingers slid into her wet channel. Unwilling to leave any of her untouched, he lowered his head to take one taut nipple into his mouth as Slade took the other into his free hand.

In minutes, they had her moaning and writhing with need. Despite the almost painful stretched sensation in her ass, she rubbed herself against Slade's thick erection hungry to be filled in other ways. Slade chuckled before biting down on her shoulder.

"Sore, baby?" Chase murmured as he pulled his fingers out of her clinging heat to tease the clit hidden at the top of her folds.

"A little," Patton gasped as he played with the bar piercing. "Please."

"Please what, baby?" Chase lifted his head to watch as her head rolled back onto Slade's shoulder, her hips thrusting forward begging for more of the teasing touches they gave her.

"Please, I want..." Patton's words ended in a moan as Slade's finger swirled inside of her, teasing that magical little spot that could shatter her world so effortlessly.

"You want what?" Chase growled. "You want to be fucked?"

"Yes. Oh, God." Patton couldn't control the spasms that had her hips pumping her pussy against Slade's hands.

"Fucked with what? Our fingers, our tongues, or do you want our cocks filling this tight little cunt?"

"Cocks," Patton groaned as their fingers left her.

Her eyes opened but the protest stilled on her lips as she watched Chase line himself up with her wet opening. Slade held her leg higher, giving Chase plenty of room. It filled her with thrills that spiced her pleasure with a darkly erotic element to be fucked by one man while another man held her in position and watched. No doubt, Slade watched.

"Isn't that just the most erotic sight?" Slade's breathed hotly against her ear as Chase slowly fed her clenching pussy one searing inch after another of his silky hardness.

Patton watched with glazed eyes as the blood darkened cock head slipped and disappeared into her much paler flesh. Her swollen cunt lips stretched wide along the width of Chase's erection.

"Look at that pretty, pink pussy glistening with your desire," Slade whispered, his words making her shiver with need and want. "Look how it opens wide to take your lover deep inside you. Tell me, Patton, is he hurting you or is he pleasuring you?"

"Both," Patton groaned.

She spoke the truth. Muscles that had been used for the first time last night ached as they were stretched anew by Chase's thick, hard cock. It was a pleasurable ache, leaving her panting with her need to be full, to have him buried deeply within her body.

"You're to keep that little pussy naked, sweetheart." Slade's deep, husky voice mesmerized her. "I like looking at, like watching it being fucked almost as much as I like fucking into its tight, wet depths. Did you like it, Patton? Did you like it when I fucked you?"

"You know I did," Patton moaned being driven insane by his words and Chase's slow penetration.

"How did it make you feel to know Chase and Devin watched me? To know that I'm watching Chase fuck you now?"

"Hot," Patton gasped as Slade's hands came around to caress and tease her breasts. Instinctively, she arched her back, offering herself up for his teasing.

"You like being watched, don't you?" Slade pulled sharply on her nipples when she failed to respond.

"Yes." Patton had trouble breathing and the word came out choppy and hoarse.

"Yes, what?" Slade demanded with another sharp pull.

"Yes, I like being watched."

"Hmm, I think we should make a new rule then. Maybe we should require you to be naked whenever it's just us. What do you think Chase? Should we keep little Patton naked for our pleasure?"

"Perhaps a little lingerie. A garter belt, stockings and some heels." Chase ground out through clenched teeth.

"And one of those open topped corsets. That way her breasts will always be pushed up and out, ready to be played with. What do you think of that, Patton? Will you make yourself a little outfit for our pleasure?"

"Oh, God," Patton groaned as Chase settled his entire length into her. He paused, his head lowering to nibble along her neck and collarbone. The little nips only added to the delicious pain echoing through her body and she tipped her head back to allow him more access.

"What was that?" One of Slade's hands began to slide down over the quivering muscles of her abdomen to rest at the top of her mound.

"Whatever you want."

"Very good." Slade echoed Chase's chuckle.

"I think she's learning." Slade rewarded her with a single flick of her clit.

"Please," Patton whimpered unable to control the small thrusting movements of her hips as her body begged Slade for another touch, urged Chase to move, anything to relieve the pressure.

"Please what, baby?" Chase continued to leisurely taste her neck.

"Move!" Patton emphasized the demand with a hard jerk of her hips.

"How do you want it, baby?" Chase own hips gave a jerk in response to hers. "Fast and hard or slow and easy?"

"Give it to her hard and fast," Slade answered. "That's what she wants, isn't it, sweetheart?"

"Yes, damnit. Any which way, just fuck me," Patton screeched, drawing another round of chuckles.

"She's cursing." Chase pointed out as he drew slowly back out of her clinging sheath. "She needs more discipline."

"Later. Fuck me first. Discipline me later."

"You can count on it, little one," Chase growled before eliciting a scream of pleasure as he slammed back into her.

He gave it to just as Slade had told him to. Patton bucked and screamed, taking his fierce fuck and returning it thrust for thrust. Her cunt ached a little from all the recent use, her canal stretched to capacity as he violently slammed into her. It felt so good, the sensation nearly driving her over the edge.

Then, as Patton quivered on the brink of orgasm, shaking helplessly with the clenching pre-climax spasms, Chase paused. Patton cried out and thrust her hips desperately against his, trying to force him back onto pace.

Chase couldn't be pressured. When he resumed moving, his strokes remained slow and leisurely causing Patton to snarl at him in frustration.

"You were about to come, baby." Chase smiled smugly. "But I don't remember giving you permission."

"She did that last night with Devin," Slade reminded Chase.

"I guess that's two punishments she earned."

"No, please," Patton whimpered, completely out of her mind with the need to climax.

"I think we need to teach her how to control her climaxes," Chase commented as if he were having a normal conversation.

"Do you want to know how we teach a woman to control her climaxes, Patton?" Slade whispered into her ear.

"Oh, God." Patton didn't want to hear this, knowing instinctively that his words would only add to her already painfully intense desire.

"First we tie her to a bed with her legs spread wide for our pleasure."

"Then," Chase leaned in close to whisper in her other ear, "we bring her to the brink of orgasm again and again and again."

With each word Chase picked up speed until he pounded in and out of her, bringing her right to the verge of the most intense of climaxes.

"Then we stop," Chase matched his actions to his words, "leaving her right there on the edge."

"Please!" Patton screamed unable to stand the teasing anymore.

"That's how we discipline naughty girls who steal climaxes." Chase ignored her desperate cry. "We deny them."

"B-but you de-deny yourselves," Patton stammered trying to think of anything she could do or say to get him to finish what he'd started.

"Oh, no, baby. I can pull out of this tight little cunt and have you finish me off with your beautifully talent mouth. Is that what you want?"

"No," Patton moaned. "Please, don't."

"Why shouldn't he, Patton?" Slade demanded.

"Please, don't leave me like this," Patton wailed. "Let me come."

"All you have to do is ask, baby." Chase kissed her, sealing her cries as he pumped her back up to the pinnacle.

Patton didn't recognize herself anymore. She felt like an animal as she scraped her nails along his back and snarled at him go harder, faster. Her hips fucked him back as hard as he gave it to her.

His balls slapped against her with the force of his movements, pushing her back against Slade's hard length. Slade's erection had settled into the crease of her ass, pushing against the dildo and making her already tight sheath even tighter.

As she approached the apex, Chase kept going until she fell over the edge in the most amazing rush she'd ever experienced. Hot ecstasy cascaded through her body, leaving nothing untouched by the euphoric flames.

Chase thrust harder against her clenching pussy as he rushed toward his own climax. His great, strong body shuddered as he spilled himself into her depths. Behind her Slade groaned and she felt a second wash of warm liquid bathe her butt cheeks.

Patton would have happily passed back out, was halfway asleep when her two lovers pulled away from her leaving her cold and alone. She blinked open her eyes right before Slade pulled her up from the bed. He turned her in the direction of the bathroom.

"Go get cleaned up. Devin will take out the plug." With that command, he gave her a slap on her ass making the dildo shift and send ripples of pleasured pain through her already over sensitized body.

Chapter 27

Patton paused at the door as she listened to the running shower. In the pleasure of waking up with Chase and Slade loving on her, she'd forgotten completely about Devin. Guilt fought to intrude on her bliss, but she shrugged it off as she opened the door and slipped into the steam-filled room.

This whole situation was new to her, not just the sex. She didn't know how three men shared one woman, but figured they'd know what they were doing. After all, they'd done it before.

That thought did not comfort her in the slightest. The fact that she'd be the last woman they shared did. If Devin had told the truth, and she believed he had, then soon she'd be Chase's legal wife and wife to all three of them in private.

The idea gave her a little thrill. If the past night and morning were any indication of what her life would be like from now on, she'd be more than happy to marry the brothers. She smiled at the idea as she moved toward the sink.

"Now that's a beautiful smile," Devin commented as he pulled back the curtain. "You feeling good, sweetheart?"

"Better than."

"Well why don't you come in here and show me?" He held the curtain wide.

"As you wish." Patton gave him a quick kiss on the cheek as she slipped past him.

"As I wish," Devin repeated with a grin. "I like that. What I wish is for you to bend over and grab those dainty little ankles of yours and show me that ass, Patton."

She couldn't mistake the challenge in his tone, nor the desire glittering in his eyes. She hesitated for a moment, unable to control the embarrassment of the idea. Slowly, she moved.

According to Chase and Slade, she'd already earned two punishments. She didn't need a third added to the list. Hopefully they'd forget about the first two. They certainly didn't appear to be in a rush to administer any discipline this morning.

The scene in the bed had taught her one important lesson. They would deny her if she didn't ask to come. It would be hard to remember that in the heat of the moment, but she would try.

Devin's hands caressed her ass, gently dividing the cheeks. Patton hoped he'd think that her skin flamed red from the nearly scalding hot water pouring down over her and not guess how embarrassed she was. Desire mixed in with the embarrassment and she felt her already dripping pussy begin to renew with life.

"Time to take this out." Devin touched the end of the dildo.

The little motion sent ripples of desire through Patton. She bit down on her bottom lip as she felt him slowly pull it out of her body. Embarrassment warred with arousal as the toy finally left her body. The ache that it had caused did not diminish with the toy's removal.

Her ass still felt stretched. A strange throbbing had invaded that most private of areas. The sensation confused her, made her want to cover up and hide until she understood what was happening to her. She gave in to the urge to hide at least some part of herself and began to straighten up without asking permission.

"Patton," Devin smacked her ass in censure. "I didn't tell you to move. Now hands on your ankles. I'm going to clean you."

He hadn't been kidding she realized as she felt a soapy washrag begin to smooth over her exposed backside. Patton squeezed her eyes tightly closed, trying to pretend that this wasn't happening to her. Instead of diminishing her reawakened arousal, the anxiety strengthened it, confusing her even more.

* * * *

Devin could tell she was nervous. Gently he cleaned her ass feeling her tense muscles begin to slowly relax under his tender touch. He took that as a good sign. For their relationship to work she would have to trust them completely.

Trust was earned. Toward that end, everything his brothers and him did to her was intentional despite any appearance to the contrary. Only by being forced into situations that tested her boundaries could she begin to learn to accept their touch, trust in their power over her body.

Of course, ultimately it would be up to Patton. If she couldn't cope, didn't enjoy what they did to her, they would fail. Failure wasn't something Devin would willingly accept. He had to make sure that the pleasure she felt so overwhelmed her all other reservations were swept aside.

Patton started getting dizzy from all the blood rushing to her head. As she felt the rag lift away from her body, she fought the urge to straighten back up, hoping that Devin would ask it of her now that he'd finished. Only he hadn't finished.

His warm, calloused hands slid back down over her ass. Dipping into the crease, he followed the line down, pausing only for a second to press against her small hidden hole. Patton flinched slightly, telling him that she wasn't ready for a deeper caress.

He moved on, sliding his finger all the way down into her hot, creaming cunt. The wetness there had little to do with the water spraying out of the showerhead. Patton couldn't contain the whimper his touch evoked or the way her hips swayed slightly toward his hand.

Patton closed her eyes, trying to keep her balance as she felt him move behind her. She almost lost the battle when she felt the rough stubble of his unshaven cheeks on the ultra sensitive skin of her inner thigh. The sensation overwhelmed her and she fell forward catching herself on the edge of the tub.

She heard Devin chuckle unsteadily before dipping his head. His tongue swiped a burning path through her weeping slit before circling her clit, delivering a rasping caress to her piercing that had a blaze of colors exploding through her eyes.

Devin groaned and slid his tongue down to taste her again. She tasted delicious, her hot, sweet cream the most powerful of drugs. He couldn't get enough. Using his hands, he widened her stance leaving her open for his feasting.

Repeatedly he drove his tongue deep into her cunt, pulling out to trail upward and circle her clit. Above him, Patton started to shake almost violently. When he dipped his finger into her wet aching core she clamped down on it and moaned out her need for more, telling him in stuttered sentence fragments she wanted more fingers, needed something to stroke deeper into her body and send her over the edge to the euphoric never lands.

Devin felt her pussy clench around his finger, trying to hold him there as he slowly drew the digit back out. Her moans turned into a gasp as he replaced it with the tip of his tongue.

He circled the edge of her opening as his finger moved up to mimic the move along the edge of her other hidden hole. She screamed as he plunged both in. Her cunt sucked in his tongue just as her little asshole tightened and puckered along his finger.

He fucked into both tight channels with maddening speed, feeling her body constrict with the intensity of her on-coming climax. She hadn't asked him for permission to come, hadn't warned him that she was about to, and he knew that he should pull out of her body, leaving her wanting for the breach in the rules. He couldn't bring himself to stop, wild with his own desire to bring her to climax.

Instead, he added one then two more fingers into her tight-fisted, back entrance, enjoying the way she thrust her backside against him asking for more. He twisted and scissored his fingers, teasing the nerve endings hidden within.

Patton panted, unable to stop from thrusting back against him. The muscles in her stomach clenched almost painfully tight and she could feel the wave of pleasure beginning to crest. With a cry, she gave herself over to the climax that ripped through her body.

As amazing as the climax had been, she felt empty as she floated back to the reality of the shower. Despite the unfamiliar, slightly uncomfortable feel of the dildo, she wanted to be filled.

If she had any strength left in her muscles she would have turned on Devin, forcing him to give her what she so desperately desired. Unfortunately, her body felt limp. Devin's strength helped her to straighten and stay up on her feet.

"I think you're almost ready to have this pretty little ass packed full cock, sweetheart. What do you think?"

"Yes," Patton didn't consider the ramifications of her words. All she knew was that she ached and that he could ease that ache. "Please, do it now."

"Not yet, sweetheart." Devin lifted her hair over her shoulder to kiss the back of her neck. "Soon though."

"Please, I want it now." Patton rubbed her backside against the hard cock poking her in the back in an attempt to lure him into giving her what she wanted.

"Don't argue," Devin admonished her with a sharp slap to her rear before stepping away from her. "You already earned a punishment for coming just now without permission. You don't want to add to it."

"This game is rigged," Patton muttered.

"What was that?" Devin chuckled.

"Nothing."

"Good." Devin gave her another little kiss. "Now be a good girl and stand still while I wash you."

Devin held true to his words. Instead of using the rag, he lathered up his hands and proceeded to thoroughly wash every part of her body. As his hands firmly rubbed over her, her already limp muscles melted and she had to lean completely against him for support.

By the time his hands worked their way up the inside of her thighs, he had her whimpering, writhing in his embrace. Devin, that bastard, only gave her teasing touches and they drove her insane. As he brushed over the weeping core of her entrance, he pressed his finger lightly inside, but only gave her the first knuckle length before pulling back out.

Her hips bucked, asking for more and she felt his chuckle vibrate through his chest. He gave her one more little taste before slipping his finger up to barely tweak her clit.

"Please."

"Do you want to come, Patton?" Devin asked, as he flicked the little bar pierced through her clit.

"Yes," Patton gasped. "Please, Devin."

"All right." He turned her around forcing her to lean against the tiled wall. "Then do it."

Patton blinked in confusion as he stepped back. Unsure of what he wanted, she watched as his lust filled eyes raked over her body. He adjusted her position so that her wide stance allowed him a full few of her naked pussy. When he didn't reach for her again but continued to study her, she began to squirm nervously.

"I'm waiting." Devin feral gaze finally settled back on her confused one.

"For what?"

"You said you wanted to come, Patton." Devin grin was outright lecherous. "And I want to watch you come. So do it."

"You wa-want me to…to…" Patton couldn't say the words.

"I told you that we liked to watch. You didn't seem to have a problem with the idea in the barn."

That had been different. He had helped, doling almost all of the work. By the time they had gotten to that little show, she'd been awash in so much pleasure she'd barely understood what had been happening. Now though she was all too aware of reality.

"Patton." Devin stepped up close to her, taking her hands into his. "You are the most beautiful woman I've ever seen. I've already watched as you climaxed while I fucked you, watched while Slade ate your beautiful, naked cunt, watched while you sucked Chase's big cock and now I want to watch you pleasure yourself. Okay?"

"Okay," Patton squeaked, not at all sure if she could do this.

"Then close your eyes. Close them, sweetheart." He kissed her eyelids shut before lifting her fingers to his mouth. "And put these beautiful little fingers to work."

He accentuated his words with little kisses on her fingertips before placing one of her hands on her breast and the other on her shaved mound. Then he was gone. Patton took a deep breath in and imagined that she was alone, back in the shower at her apartment.

The situation bordered on being humorous. Her fantasies had always been about them. Now she fantasized about them again, only this time Devin watched her.

She licked her dry lips and moved both hands up and over her breasts, cupping them she ran her thumbs over the engorged tips. Her body arched suggestively as pleasure rushed through her. As she pinched and pulled on one aching tip, she leaned her chin down to let her tongue swirl over the other pink areola.

Devin growled and instinctively moved closer, his cock jerking painfully as he watched her teeth scrape over the harden tip before sucking it into her mouth. His lips curled back in a feral snarl as he watched her alternate breasts.

He looked toward her face to find her amazing violet eyes watching him through her lowered lashes. The small show of trust made Devin's heart swell. God, how he loved this woman. She was more than he ever imagined her to be.

A flash of movement drew his eyes back down. He watched with bated breath as one hand slid down over her slightly rounded stomach toward the bared cunt below. She hesitated, letting one finger slip over her clit to slowly roll it.

Drawing out the moment, Patton watched Devin's eyes darken, riveted on her fingers as she slid two more fingers down past her tingling clit to delve into her clenching cunt. She stroked them in avoiding that magical spot, wanting to prolong her pleasure for Devin to enjoy. Soon, though, her breath shortened to pants as she strained toward climax.

Her touch became firmer, the fingers pulling on one hardened breast tip in time with the thumb rubbing her clit. The squishy sounds of her fingers fucking into her sopping wet cunt could be heard over the prattle of the shower.

Racing, wild, clawing lust took control of her body. Out of control, she arched up as the sizzling heat consuming her bloomed, racking her body with razor sharp pleasure. Patton cried out, shaking in the grip of a climax that she'd brought herself to.

When her hand would have fallen away from her drenched pussy, Devin's reappeared. Covering her slender hand with his own much larger one, he forced her to continue her ministrations. Patton cried out again, sure her already sensitive flesh could take no more stimulation.

He didn't give her the option of stopping. Devin added his own thick fingers to her cunt, filling her with their strength as he joined her in fucking herself. Patton looked down at him on his knees, eyeing her pussy with a hunger that left no doubt of his intentions.

"Suck your tit, Patton."

He watched as her other hand offered up her breast to her mouth. As her lips closed over the tip, his lips matched the motion closing over her clit. As she sucked so did he, hungrily licking and sucking on the hard nub of her arousal.

The climax still riding her body exploded onto a whole new level. Her breast popped out of her mouth as she screamed. Lightning shot through her body, electrifying every nerve ending until no part of her didn't tingle with pleasure.

Her sounds of pleasure cut short as she suddenly felt the head of Devin's cock pushing into her spasming channel. As he stood up, he hooked a thigh over each of his arms and lifted her off her feet. Her back pinned to the wall, she clutched at his neck trying to get good purchase.

He shifted her, lowering slightly as he angled her hips upward. With one hard thrust, he impaled himself to the hilt in her. Capturing her scream with his kiss, he began to pound into her body.

Relentlessly, showing no mercy to the fact that she was still riding the crest of second consecutive orgasm, he fucked her. She'd have thought she would come, quick and intense, but her body was too flooded with pleasure.

"No, please," Patton begged as she felt his hand slide between their bodies and separate the folds of her pussy. He exposed her clit to the rolling motions of his pelvis as he quickened his pace.

"I can't. It's too much."

"Come for me, Patton," Devin panted as he felt his own climax pulling his balls tight. "Come for me now."

He intended to kill her with sex.

That rational thought was her last. Her world exploded and she bucked hard within his strong embrace. Patton was lost in the euphoric haze of primitive lust. As she gasped for breath, she felt thick, fiery jets of semen begin to pulse into her.

Devin collapsed against her, his chest heaving with the aftereffects of his own climax. Exhausted almost to the point of blacking out, her head fell forward into the crook of his neck.

Her legs, still shaking with muscle spasms, slipped down his sides. They were unable to support her weight and she'd have fallen into the tub as nothing more than a puddle to be washed down the drain by the now cool shower water if Devin hadn't pinned her in place.

"I need a nap," Patton mumbled when she finally regained control of her breathing.

Devin laughed, feeling a joy that touched him deep to his soul. He'd never climaxed so hard, felt so complete afterward. A part of him wanted to squeeze her tight to him, to never let her go while another part want to do it all over again. To watch, touch, taste, feel as she came over and over again.

"God, woman. I love you." Devin leaned back to kiss her with all the hunger that ate at his soul. The metallic taste of blood had him pulling back to see the small bite mark her teeth had made in her lip the last time she'd come.

"Oh, baby, what did you do?" Devin kissed the small wound.

"I had to bite my lip to keep from cussing you for making me come that last time."

Her body might have been down for the count, but her mind was already beginning to recover. Devin laughed again and stepped back. Immediately, Patton began to slide down the shower stall wall.

"Upsy daisy, baby girl." Devin caught her before she hit the floor, lifting her in his arms he turned to shut off the water.

"The water is cold," Patton muttered, curling tighter into his warm embrace.

"Yeah. Sucks for Slade and Chase." Devin wasn't the least bit sorry for his brothers.

He carried her out of the stall and set her on the vanity counter. Drying her off, he wrapped her in a towel and carried her back into the bedroom like a little girl. Patton was barely awake when he settled her onto the bed. With a sigh, she rolled onto her side and closed her eyes.

Chapter 28

She'd barely had a moment before somebody pushed her onto her stomach, tugging at her towel to take it away. The cool air-conditioned air chilled her skin and made her shiver.

Patton glanced over her shoulder to see who had been so cruel. Slade grinned back at her. With a glare, she reached for the covers. He stopped her, forcing her down onto her stomach as he moved to straddle her hips.

Slade guessed her intent. "It's not time to go sleep, sweetheart."

"Just a few minutes," Patton demanded into the pillow.

"Now, Patton, you haven't been up a whole hour."

"I'm worn out."

Her comment made him laugh. The sound echoed from across the room. Devin. Cocky bastard, Patton kept that opinion to herself, conceding that he had reason to be cocky. Here she was a limp noodle and from the sounds of it, he was energized and getting dressed.

Well that was just fine. He hadn't climaxed three times in a row. Nor had he started out in bed having two men force him to the edge of climax over and over again, before riding her hard. She wasn't used to so much exercise before she'd even gotten dressed.

The sound of a cap being popped off a bottle right over her head had her eyes opening again. Before she could wonder what he planned, she felt the smooth glide of lotion over her shoulders. Patton sighed, inhaling the scent of her apple scented moisturizer.

"If you want me to stay awake, I wouldn't do that," Patton murmured as her eyes fluttered closed.

"You'll stay awake or be punished." Slade's threat lacked any heat.

His hands didn't. They were hot and slick as he massaged his way down her back. He soothed away the soreness from her tired muscles. Patton moaned in pure satisfaction, not even bothering to fight to stay awake.

He jarred her awake as he turned her on to her back. Laughing at her disgruntled expression, Slade shook his head.

"You fell asleep."

"So?" Patton yawned, already slipping back into oblivion as his hands began to work over the front of her.

"So you've earned a punishment."

"Okay," Patton whispered, not caring.

She awaked sometime later by a sharp stinging bite to her breast. She opened her eyes to find Slade grinning down at her with anticipation in his eyes.

"So you're awake."

Before she could make a comment about how he'd woken her, his head dipped and disappeared between her spread thighs. He held her hips still as he buried his face in her cunt. Like a starving man, he devoured her pussy, hungrily licking and sucking on her already creaming nether lips. He fucked his tongue into her tight core, making her cry out as her hips lifted for more.

Patton found it impossible to believe that her exhausted body could so quickly respond. In less than a minute, he had her panting, begging for more, moaning out her denial as he lifted his face from her steaming center.

"You fell asleep, Patton."

"So?" Patton ran her hands into his hair and tried to force his head back down.

"I told you not to and you disobeyed me."

"That's not fair," Patton cried out. "If you didn't want me to sleep, then why did you give me the massage?"

"Because I want to fuck you, but first I wanted to enjoy touching this beautiful body that now belongs to me."

"Then fuck me already," Patton demanded, arching her hips up. If she couldn't get his face to her pussy, then maybe she could get her pussy to his face.

"First, you have to be disciplined for your disobedience."

Patton opened her mouth to argue but the sound got cut off when Slade's hands came down in a firm slap across her pussy. Patton squealed as the scorching pleasure ripped through her body.

"Did you like that, sweetheart?" Slade growled as he struck again.

This time her clit took the impact, forcing searing heat straight up her spine. She arched upward, electrified by the pleasure from the blows.

"Tell me, Patton, do you like having your pussy slapped?"

As he spoke, he continued to slap her. Harder, faster, until the painful pleasure blended so thoroughly that she couldn't distinguish one hit from the rest. When he stopped, she cried out, writhing on the edge of orgasm.

"Please," Patton whined.

"Tell me if you like having your pussy slapped, Patton, and I'll give you what you want," Slade demanded, adjusting his position so that his thick hard cock rested at the entrance to her body.

"Yes. I like having my pussy slapped. Now make me come!" Patton yelled, uncaring that she was indeed yelling.

"Oh, baby, you just earned another punishment," Slade huskily admonished her.

Before she could respond to that comment, Slade mounted her, shoving his cock all the way in with one rough stroke. Patton screamed at the sudden penetration but he gave her no time to adjust. With a grunt, he began fucking into her tight, clinging sheath.

Patton's eyes flew open amazed at the speed and depth with which Slade moved. He made her feel so sexy and so desirable with his rough loving. The room blurred before her.

It refocused when her gaze found Chase's. He leaned against the bathroom door, his hair wet, his body tense, his eyes hungry as he watched Slade screw her. Those feral orbs locked onto her own lust filled ones, trapping her gaze in his.

Knowing one man watched as another pumped himself between her legs thrilled her, heightening all her senses, making every wave of pleasure crashing through her stronger, sharper, and more intense.

Slade felt some primitive, primal instinct take over his body. A small voice whispered in the back of his mind to be careful, to be gentle. The worry was shouted out by the animal need in him to rut on his mate, to spew his seed into her womb and bind her to him in the most basic way.

He felt her cunt clamp down on him, the first beginning spasms of her oncoming orgasm. Distantly he knew he should stop, make her ask, beg for her release, but he couldn't. He'd never felt so out of control with any woman before.

As he felt her body tensing, reaching the breaking point of pleasure and euphoria, he slammed into her pussy even harder. His balls slapped against her ass as he rode her with rough, dominating precision. He felt ever ripple, every muscle tightening her cunt around his engorged cock until she screamed out her release and bucked against him.

The sound and feel of her own climax snapped his control and he impaled his full length into her. White-hot lightning ripped down his spine as his balls tightened painfully before erupting in a lava flow and he flooded her small channel with his hot seed.

Slade collapsed on top of Patton, completely drained of all his energy. Hell, now he needed a nap. He grinned at the idea, laughing outright at how Patton would respond if he spoke the thought out loud.

Patton murmured, turning her head away from the racket Slade made. She was exhausted and if they would just let her be for five minutes she'd pass right out. That probably wouldn't happen.

She fully expected Slade to move any second and Chase to take his place. Patton blushed as she remembered how she'd stared him straight in the eye as Slade rode her. She'd behaved shamelessly, more so than in the shower with Devin.

The look in his eyes as he watched her…Patton shivered. His gaze had been filled with pure animal lust. That fact should probably scare her, but it didn't. It did just the opposite, turning her on in a way that no simple touch or caress could.

"Come on, sweetheart." Slade levered himself up and off her. "You have to get up."

"Don't want to," Patton pouted, acting like dead weight as he tried to pull her off the bed.

"Patton, if you don't get out of this bed and get that sweet ass of yours in the bathroom to get cleaned up," Slade paused to grin down at her, "well, there's a certain punishment we give naughty little lazy girls like you."

"Fine. I don't care. Punish me all you want. You're going to anyway. You've rigged everything just to make it impossible for me to avoid punishments."

"How many is she due now, Chase?" Slade called back to his older brother.

"Two by me. Devin mentioned owing her one. Add on whatever your count is."

"That's four, Patton."

"Four spankings," Patton snorted. "I guess I'll be sitting on padded seats for a few days."

"You don't want a fifth."

"Go away, Slade. I need my sleep." With that, she yanked the covers up and turned over on her side, dismissing him.

Slade looked over at Chase who just shrugged, but he grinned. His eyes cut back to the dark head of hair barely peeking out from under the covers. He knew just how to get Little Miss Patton out of the bed.

Hopping off the mattress, he jogged down to the kitchen. Rounding the corner into the large room, he came to a sudden stop when he almost ran into Charlotte. Her eyes narrowed accusingly on him. Her gaze immediately dropped to his cock, still hard and glistening with Patton's cream.

He had forgotten about her being in the house. Given all the noise Patton had been making not minutes before and the state of his undress, Charlotte obviously had added up the facts and coming to the correct conclusion.

"Is there something you wanted, master?"

She managed to make the title sound like an insult, as if he were unworthy of it. She was spoiling for a fight, but he didn't want to waste time on having it. What was the point?

It may be harsh, but Charlotte always knew that one day she would have to move on. They had never lied to her about their interest in other women or that her time in their home was limited.

"Ice." Slade stepped past her, ignoring the anger mixed with hurt in her eyes. .

Silently, uncomfortably, Slade ducked back out. As he raced back up to the bedroom, he promised himself they'd find her a good home. Charlotte would be taken care of, he'd make sure of that.

Those thoughts disappeared as he came back into the bedroom. Chase had dressed and Patton had passed out. She didn't stir when he flipped her onto her back and pulled the covers down.

Her shriek a second later could have woken the dead though. She sat straight up, twisting with the motion as he inserted two ice cubes up into her cunt. Slade pinned her back down with his body.

"What the hell?"

"You're awake now." He grinned down at her.

"What did you put in me?" Patton twisted and bucked, trying to throw him off. "That's cold!"

"Ice cubes, sweetheart. Better than caffeine when waking up naughty little girls."

"God! Get them out!" Patton continued to struggle despite the pointlessness of her efforts.

"Okay." Slade slid up so that he knelt over her chest. "Chase, you want to do the honors?"

"Mmm," Chase growled moving toward the bed. "My favorite type of breakfast."

"No, wait—"

Patton's distressed plea cut off as Slade deftly inserted his erection into her mouth. Patton didn't fight him. He wanted to tease her. Well, she could tease him, too.

Relaxing her jaw, she took his cock all the way to back of her throat. Keeping her lips loose, she tried not to suck, but he was so big, so thick it was almost impossible. Instead, she curled her tongue around the large shaft filling her mouth and she licked it as Slade pulled back.

His fingers tightened in her hair, his breathing turning harsh and choppy. The sound filled her with a sense of victory. He might be trying to punish her, but she had the control now.

Chase turned the tide as he buried his head between her legs. His tongue flicked over her clit, making her squirm and Slade laugh as he began to fuck her mouth in earnest. Patton didn't care about winning anymore.

The feel of Chase's tongue spearing into her cunt defined her world. The stark contrast of the ice-cold cubes and his hot tongue made her writhe with pleasure. He sucked one of the cubes right out of her.

Keeping it in his mouth, he brought it up to her clit and began to torment her little bundle of nerves. Patton's eyes rolled back in her head as Chase wound her body tighter and tighter, her climax kept constantly out of reach by the jarring cold of the melting cube.

* * * *

Slade did not have that problem. He didn't bother to fight the need to come, but let the powerful sense of rapture take him over. He lasted three, four more strokes before he felt his climax pierce through his body.

Throwing back his head, he roared out his orgasm for all in the house to hear. Falling limply to his side, Slade sighed. Now that was the best way to start a day. Hands down, Patton gave the best blowjob he'd ever had.

It wasn't just a matter of skill, but the fact that it was Patton. Slade closed his eyes and savored the reality that turned out to be better than any fantasy. Despite al their worries and concerns, Patton had responded at every turn with equal passion to their rough demands.

Slade didn't fool himself into believing that a war wasn't coming. At some point, they were going to have to let her out of bed. Once the fog of lust cleared, Patton would be back to scheming for control. That fact didn't worry Slade.

She could play her games, but there would be no doubt of who the victors were—all of them. In the end, Patton's way would rule, but in her domination she would submit, because that was ultimately what she wanted, what drove her insane with pleasure. Slade would happily be her sex slave, fulfilling every fantasy.

Patton did not feel as relaxed or happy as Slade. No thoughts of the future or the fact that this was her victory entered her head. The moment he rolled off her, Chase stopped, sitting back on his knees. The ice had finally melted and she had been moments away from her own shattering release.

The frustration of its loss fueled her anger and she shot up to grab Chase by his ears.

"I didn't tell you to stop," Patton snarled, making Chase laugh.

"You don't give the orders, Patton." Chase lifted her up and dropped her on her feet by the bed. "That's one punishment, four left. Now unless you want more, I suggest you go get cleaned up."

"Fine." Patton marched off toward the bathroom.

"And Patton," Chase called out as she reached the door. "Don't be pleasuring yourself either. Only we get to bring you to pleasure. No touching or using toys when we're not around."

Patton's jaw clenched and she slammed the door to vent her frustration.

* * * *

Slade chuckled and shook his head. He looked over at Chase and raised a brow.

"What you want to bet that if I walk in there I find her being disobedient?"

"No bet." Chase rolled to his feet.

"You gotta admit, Chase, things are going better than you had anticipated."

"It's only the beginning." Chase's eyes caught on the bathroom door and Slade watched the happiness drain out of them. "Wait until we ask her to give up her business and then we'll see how well things are going."

"Have you ever heard of the word compromise, Chase?"

"Compro—what?"

"That's what I thought."

"No woman of mine is going to have some jackass fawning all over her to make pictures that bunch of sickos can go on-line and masturbate to them."

"Maybe she can be convinced to design something else?"

"What's the point? Our woman shouldn't have to work. She should be at home taking care of the house and available for our needs."

"Oh, I got to be there when you inform Patton of that." Slade could only just imagine how well that conversation would go.

"She'll adjust." Slade doubted it, but he kept that opinion to himself. In all the years of confrontations, it had always been Chase who had adjusted. "I'm going to catch up on some paperwork in the study. I got a meeting at the bank this morning."

"I've got to go get those parts from John over at Hindle."

"We have a delivery coming into the south field this afternoon. Devin is overseeing it. I'll be out there helping them?"

"Okay." Slade nodded. "Hey, what about the party tonight?"

"What about it?"

"We're expected to be there."

"So? We go."

"And leave Patton home alone?" Slade didn't think much of that idea. From Chase's growing frown, neither did he. "Besides, you think that she wouldn't eventually find out about the part and what happens there?"

"It's not like I planned on doing anything...or anybody while there."

"I know," Slade retorted, disgusted that Chase didn't see the obvious. "You think that will matter to Patton? I think just the fact that we stepped into the room will be grounds for mayhem and slaughter once she finds out."

"What am I supposed to do Slade? We're the Masters of the Festivities. We have to show up for a while to start the different events."

"Not all three of us."

Chase's scowl suddenly turned into a smirk as he shook his head at Slade. "I see where this is going. You're angling for some alone time with Patton."

"I'm just making a point."

"You have to show, Slade. You're the auctioneer."

"Somebody else can do it."

"Let Devin play babysitting duty tonight."

"Why him?"

"Because all he does is get trouble when he's bored. If he's not going to be distracted with the women, he'll just be screwing up everybody else's fun."

"He's not that bad."

"We won't be gone long."

That what Chase said now, but Slade didn't believe it. He could already see how this night would play out. Chase would never be able to pull off a hit and run appearance.

Even if they weren't going to busy introducing new women to their new rules as slaves, there would be plenty enough distraction with the gambling and the games of strength and skill that would be on-going during the festivities. All it would take was one little comment from some drunken trash talker and Chase would be spurred into the action.

That wasn't the only thing he needed to talk to Chase about though. "Hey."

Chase paused at the door. "This matter is closed, Slade."

"You may want to, uh, give Charlotte the rest of the day off."

"Shit." Chase rubbed a hand over his forehead. "Forgot about her."

"Yeah, I'm thinking we should let her go onto the auction block. See if we can find a new master for her."

Chapter 29

Patton stared at her reflection in the mirror. She felt much better after a long shower. While her body was still tired, her mind was wide-awake and focusing on her future. She'd soon be Mrs. Davis, Mrs. Chase Davis.

Her fantasy played out before her eyes. The years that stretched before her filled with love, family, children, big Christmases, birthday parties and Easter egg hunts, and then, one day, even grandchildren. It would be a full life, filled with sex and laughter and love.

There would probably be a good number of arguments as her arrogance clashed with theirs, but she'd survive them. She always had. Even if she was willing and enjoyed their concept of punishment and discipline, that didn't mean she would make it easy for them.

Patton didn't kid herself. The brothers might argue amongst themselves, but when it came to her, they had a long tradition of showing a united front. She would do well to choose her battles wisely.

Two battles were already clearly defined, her bike and her business. Patton already knew what Chase would say about each. The bike was too dangerous. He wasn't willing to let her risk life and limb for such a stupid thing.

Patton would cave on that one. She liked her bike, but she loved her business. Not that she didn't plan to put up a fight over the motorcycle, but it would go better if Chase thought he won one round. It would make it easier for him to accept losing the second round.

No way would she give up her business. Patton could already guess at what Chase would have to say about that. His first response would be macho based, no woman of his would be taking half naked pictures with another man.

Patton already knew how she'd get around that. The idea sent a thrill through her. Devin would love it, too. Slade, well, he'd probably accept it for what it was, meeting them half way. Chase, though, would move onto his second point.

No woman of his was going to work for a living. Patton had no illusions that Chase was anything other than he was, a throw back to age of sexist men. If it was just a matter of pure sexism, it would be almost impossible for her to win, but Patton knew that beneath it was a deeper emotion.

Chase had struggled his whole life to support his family. It was a matter of honor and pride. The fact that his wife didn't work would be the ultimate statement of his success. That meant a lot him. She had to figure out a way around that hurdle.

"Patton," Slade shouted from the bedroom. "You going to be all day in there? I'm hungry."

She had to wonder just what he was hungry for. She hoped it was actual food. Her stomach rolled and grumbled in agreement. No more towels hung from the racks, nothing left to cover up her nakedness.

Even though she'd sauntered into the bathroom without a care for her nudity, it felt different to saunter out the same way. There was nothing for it but to do it with style. Opening the door, she strutted back out into the bedroom.

* * * *

Slade's throat constricted down making it hard to breath as he watched Patton strut back out of the bathroom naked. What with that and all the blood rushing from his head to his suddenly painfully hard cock he felt almost lightheaded. God she was more beautiful than any woman he'd ever seen.

Her breasts were full, so perfectly round and soft looking. They were topped with pink nipples that bled outward toward dusty rose and damn if they didn't harden to tempting little nubs as he stared at them. The sight almost broke his control not to cross the room and take a taste, to enjoy again licking and nibbling on them.

A few stray droplets of water dripped down from the ends of her hair. He watched, hypnotized as they rolled through the shadows her breasts cast over her rib cage and down the soft curves of her stomach before disappearing into the smooth skin of her pussy.

She was long and lean with a slight roundness of her stomach with a waist that dented in before flaring out to beautifully round hips. Hips made to be held onto as he buried himself balls deep in between those curvy legs.

Slade swallowed trying to get some moisture back into his mouth as his gaze settled on her naked cunt. She was the sweetest fruit he'd ever eaten and now he could enjoy her anytime he wanted. The only thing better than eating her pussy was fucking it. So tight, hot and wet, he could live the rest of his life contentedly buried inside her.

Only problem with that idea was starving to death. His stomach, rarely an organ that had much to say, spoke loudly to him today. He could only imagine what Patton's said to her. Part of loving her was taking care of her. He'd be a failure if she starved to death.

"Go on and get dressed, baby." Slade finally managed to speak as he gestured to the clothes he'd laid out for her.

Patton frowned over that fact. The full-length skirt and knit top were something she would have worn to please them a week ago, but now her nose wrinkled at the idea. She reminded herself to pick her fights and this one she did not want to waste the energy on now.

After all, she could change later. She would add a pair of underwear then, too. Patton didn't think they'd forgotten to add the panties that matched the lacy bra.

Without comment, she dressed. Once she'd put on all the articles Slade had selected, she headed off to her room to find her brush.

Slade followed silently in her wake. When she settled down at her vanity table to work through the knots, he stepped behind and took the brush from her hands.

"Don't you have something better to do?" Patton frowned at him in the mirror.

"Nothing is better than being with you." Slade didn't look up when he answered.

"Okay, more important."

"Nothing is more important than you."

"Slade." Patton sighed. "Don't you think this is a little much?"

"What is, sweetheart?"

"Picking out my clothes, brushing my hair, I thought I proved last night that I'm not a little girl."

"No, you're a woman, our woman." Slade met her eyes in the mirror. "I fought hard for you, Patton, let me enjoy my spoils."

His words made her shiver with cool reality and not warm comfort. Her eyes darted to his busted knuckles.

"You didn't really hurt Cole, did you Slade?" Patton asked hesitantly, not sure if she wanted to know the answer.

"Don't you worry about him, Patton. He got what he deserved." Slade's voice took on a hard edge even as his hands continued their gentle strokes as he worked her brush through her tresses.

"But he didn't do anything." Patton knew she should drop the topic, but couldn't seem to stop her mouth from moving.

"He touched you."

"But—"

"No, buts. Devin warned him. Cole knew if he touched you, he was a dead man. He made his choice."

Slade put down the brush. He kept his eyes focused firmly on what he was doing, making sure to keep his expression hard. She'd gone stiff underneath his touch.

"Come on, Patton. Let's get breakfast." He stepped back and held out his bruised hand toward her.

Patton stood and stared at his hand.

"You didn't kill him, did you?"

"That's not your concern, Patton."

"Are you insane? Of course it's my problem."

"Don't worry, Patton. I took care of everything."

"Don't worry? How can I not when you are implying that you killed somebody?"

"I'm not implying anything." Slade latched onto her hand and began tugging her toward the door. "Now let's go eat."

"No!" Patton latched onto the bedpost with her free hand. She used it as an anchor to bring him to a stop. "You tell me now whether or not you killed him."

"Patton. It's my responsibility to handle and I handled it. It does not concern you."

"Doesn't concern me?" Patton shrieked, tightening her grip on the bedpost. "You killed him because of me. Jesus, Slade you can't go around killing every man who..."

"Who what? Who kisses you and touches you?"

"Nothing happened."

"The fact that you were alone in his truck, with your shirt hanging open, tells me something did. Cole knew the score."

"I know, but that—"

"You know?" Slade let her hand go so he could ball his fists on his hips. It wasn't hard to play his role. Slade was truly pissed at the whole game Patton had orchestrated last night. "How do you know?"

"Cole told me and I told him not to worry."

"Well, he shouldn't have listened to you."

"I didn't think you would really hurt him."

"You thought wrong."

"Damnit, Slade." Patton began to shake as the emotions inside began vibrating out of her body. It might have been cruel, but Slade hoped she felt fear, anger, guilt, all the worst that a person could feel.

It would help her learn her lesson about boundaries and taking things too far.

"Don't beat yourself up over it, Patton. How could you know we'd show up?" Slade held his hands out as if he intended to hug her. Patton flinched away.

"I...I...I should have known you'd find out."

"Yeah, well. I don't know if I would have hurt him as bad if I had just found out. But Hailey seemed worried. I guess her fear sort of got me more fired up more than normal. I'm sure having those few beers didn't help. I might have gone too far."

"Oh, God." Patton sank down onto the edge of the bed.

"What is it, sweetheart?" Slade crouched down in front of her. "What's wrong? Aren't you feeling well?"

"It's not that. It's just..."

"Maybe you should lie down, Patton. You look awfully pale."

"I'm so sorry, Slade." Patton looked up at him through the sheen of tears making her eyes appear bigger, more guilty.

"What are you sorry for, sweetheart?" Slade asked softly as he brushed away the first tear that fell.

"It's all my fault."

"No, it isn't, honey." Slade pulled her into his arms. "Cole knew what he was getting into."

"I knew ..."

"What, baby? What did you know?"

"That you'd find out!" Patton shoved him away.

"We're going in circles here." Slade forced her back into his arms. In a real attempt to soothe her, he began to rub her back. "It's not your fault. You had no idea we'd show up there last night. So you had no way of preventing the situation."

"That's just it. I knew you'd show up," Patton cried. "I told Hailey to tell you where we were. I told her to imply that we were...were..."

Patton buried her head in his shoulder and began to sob uncontrollably. The action made Slade feel guilty, but he forced the emotion aside. If he caved now, Patton would just get mad and there would be no lesson learned.

"What are you saying, Patton? You set this up?" Slade pulled back and gave her his best confused look, he hoped. Not that it matter. Patton was so distressed he doubted she'd notice if he grinned.

"Yes." Patton sniffed hard, trying to get control of herself. "I know it's horrible of me, but I couldn't think of any other way to force your hand. I just wanted to be with you and nothing I said changed your mind. I just thought…"

"You thought if you made us so jealous, we'd give in and take you before any other man did."

"Yes," Patton whispered, raising her head to look on him with sad eyes. "But I didn't think you'd really hurt Cole. I just thought you'd hit him once or twice."

"Patton." Slade pulled her back into his arms. "There's no need to cry."

"I don't want to lose you."

"You're not going to lose me."

"You didn't…Did you…kill him?"

"No, sweetheart. Cole's still among the living."

"But he might press charges," Patton whispered.

"Cole wouldn't press any charges," Slade assured her. "Nothing is going to take me from you."

"Are you sure?"

"I'm sure."

"I hope you're right." Patton sagged into his embrace. "I'm still worried though."

"Well, honey, I think you should still be worried." Slade rubbed her back. "Because as far as I can tell, you just confessed to setting this whole thing up. We're going to have to punish you for that."

"It's a small price to pay."

Slade gave Patton a few minutes to collect herself before pulling her off the bed and down toward the kitchen. He couldn't deny the guilt he felt over having pushed her so far, but, he reminded himself, she did deserve it.

If it hadn't been for Chase holding him back at first, Slade would have rushed up to Peter's Point and beaten Cole to a bloody mess. The fact that he hadn't didn't excuse Patton's behavior.

That lesson would continue tonight when she faced the consequences of her actions. He wished he had time now to see to the matter, but all three brothers had a busy day ahead. Her punishment for this misdeed would take some time and attention. They didn't need to be rushed when administering it.

* * * *

"You want some cereal?" Slade let go of her to check the pantry.

"I can get my own breakfast." Patton went toward the refrigerator. Her emotional release moments ago had wiped out the reserves of her energy, leaving her beyond exhausted and in need of substance.

"That's a frightening thought," Slade muttered.

"What was that?"

"Nothing, sweetheart."

"That's what I thought." Patton pulled eggs and cheese out of the refrigerator. Dropping them on the counter, she turned around.

"I'll just have the cereal." Slade dropped the box of raisin brand on the island.

"Where are the pots and pans?"

"What?" Slade's eyes scanned the kitchen before shrugging. "Hell if I know."

"Don't you ever cook?" Patton began opening the lower cabinets.

"That's what women are..." Slade stopped as Patton shot him a dark look. "I think I'll get my milk."

"Go on, Slade. Don't wimp out now. Say what you were going to," Patton demanded hefting a large frying pan out from the cupboard.

"I was just being flippant." Slade eyed the frying pan. "You know that's not why we kept a woman around. We're just too busy to take care of the house."

"What crap. I know why you kept a woman around," Patton snapped. "But that woman is me now."

"Yeah, well. We'll probably still hire a housekeeper."

"I'll hire the housekeeper." Patton clanged the pan onto the stove.

"What?" Slade couldn't help grinning. "Don't you trust me?"

"Listen here, Slade Davis. Let's get one thing straight. If I find out you so much as looked at another woman, even one in a magazine, I will rip your eyes right out of you head."

"Did I ever tell you how sexy you are when you're mad?" Slade stepped up behind her to wrap her in a quick hug.

"I'm not kidding, Slade," Patton warned him even as the heat in her tone changed from anger to arousal as he began to place nibbling little kisses down her neck.

"I know, honey." Slade slid his hand down her thigh, grabbing a fist full of her skirt.

"Slade," Patton breathed out as she felt him pulling her skirt upward.

"Hmm."

"I thought you were hungry."

"I am."

Chapter 30

He turned her, sealing whatever else she might have said behind his kiss. Patton returned the gentle, rubbing kiss. When she nibbled seductively on his lower lip, her tongue asking permission to enter, Slade's heart tripped over itself. Slamming into his ribcage, it began to pump overheated blood through out his body.

His mouth parted, allowing her tongue to lazily slide inside and stroke the fire burning up his body. The taste of her crashed through his control, eclipsing rational thought.

In one beat of the heart, the lust that always shimmered just beneath the surface whenever Patton was around overwhelmed him. Taking full control of the kiss, he aggressively invaded her mouth as his fingers curled over her mound and touched the hot liquid proof of her desire.

Slade stroked his fingers through her slit, slipping first one then two thick fingers into her weeping cunt. His thumb moved upward to press down on her clit. He rubbed her sensitive nub as he relentlessly thrust his fingers into her.

Patton's entire body jerked as the sudden climax ripped through her turning seconds into hours. Slade released Patton's mouth as her body went limp against his. He hadn't planned on taking things that far, but he seemed to have no control where Patton was concerned. Breakfast became a distant thought as his mouth watered for something sweeter than cereal.

With a growl, he went to his knees, lifting one of her legs over her shoulders and leaving her completely exposed to his questing mouth. He stroked his tongue along her swollen, creaming slit with long, slow licks that made her squirm and arch. Slade lapped at her clit and smiled when she cried out, her hands coming to clench his hair and force him closer.

He continued the teasing flicks until she writhed with her need, her pussy flooding with her sweet cream. He knew she was close to coming. Pushing two fingers into her clenching depths, he swirled them and pushed her right over the edge.

Slade knew he had hit her sweet spot when her entire body bowed. Patton screamed and bucked beneath him. Her thighs clenched around his head as her pussy spasmed and the proof of her release flooded his mouth.

Her taste was addictive. Like a drug to his senses, it made him want to shove his face deeper, gorge himself on every single delectable inch of her pink flesh. Without hesitation, he fucked his tongue past her clenching inner muscles with deep greedy strokes.

Above him, Patton sobbed, her hands now trying to pull his head away. Slade was not deterred, and he continued to consume her with greedy, carnal abandon. He forced another climax on her, this one fast and hard.

He lifted his head, his hands going to his pants as he stood. He fought to get his zipper down between his clumsy fingers and his cock pressing outward.

A breathy laugh brought Slade's eyes back to Patton. She watched his struggles. Her grin made him growl again.

"Need some help?"

"You're going to be the one needing help."

"Not if you can't get your pants down."

"You are in trouble now." Slade managed to get his zipper down, but it caught in his boxers and pulled some of his hair with it. "Oooh."

He bent slightly with the pressure, making Patton laughed again.

"Don't hurt anything important now."

Slade eyes narrowed dangerously on her.

"Come here."

Patton shrieked with laughter and tried to duck to the right, hoping to make it to the safety of the other side of the island. Slade caught her by the waist and pinned her in place. Patton continued to struggle halfheartedly.

Slade ignored her attempts to get away and her laughter. Lifting her up along the edge of the counter, he wrapped her legs around his waist. Patton arched into him, rubbing her wet pussy against the thick length of his cock.

He felt her swollen folds divide, allowing his dick slide along the length of her slit, up against her clit. Patton moaned and repeated the motion, becoming more frantic with each pass.

Slade wasn't about to let her get off on her own again. This time he intended to be with her. He shifted, letting his weight sag her down until she was right where he wanted her. Her tight little opening pressed against the head of his rock-hard cock.

With one hard thrust, he embedded himself fully into her wet sheath. Patton cried out as one of her hands knotted in his hair. The other dug beneath the collar of his shirt, biting into the skin around his neck.

The small stinging pain drove him overboard. Slade set up a quick, fast rhythm of deep hard thrusts. Her pussy sucked him in, squeezing him tight. The strong fist of her inner muscles made him growl and pound even harder into her.

Patton turned into a thing of wild need in his arms. Her breathing ragged, her nails scratched him as she clawed at his shoulders. Even her teeth took a stinging nibble on his neck as he felt the beginning contraction of her climax milking him.

"Come for me, Patton," Slade demanded.

Patton screamed out her agreement, throwing her head back as the fierce inferno of ecstasy consumed her. Slade's lips pulled back in carnal triumph as he felt her release trigger his own. It shot through him like the blast from a shotgun, driving him deep into Patton, sealing them together as one.

Slade rested his forehead on hers, willing his heart back to a less dangerous speed. Patton's choppy breath matched his own pants and, for several minutes, they stayed like that.

"Is this the less filling, better tasting diet?"

Patton jerked, startled by Chase's dry comment. Her eyes flew to the doorway where he leaned, a coffee cup dangling from his fingers. He could see the flush in her features change from desire to embarrassment. Why was beyond him.

Earlier she'd starred him down, sharing her pleasure as Slade took her body. Or course that had been in the bedroom. One thing Chase had learned about women, location mattered. What had been acceptable in the privacy of the bedroom was not in the public domain of the kitchen.

Slade sighed when Patton squirmed for freedom. With obvious reluctance, he stepped back, letting Patton's leg slide down to support her own weight. She immediately began fussing over her clothing as he straightened his own.

"You really know how to kill the moment, bro," Slade muttered as Chase prowled pass him toward the coffee pot.

"And you really are running late, *bro*." Chase gave him a pointed look toward the door.

"Yeah, yeah, yeah. You don't have to tell me twice," Slade muttered. He tilted Patton's chin up to drop a quick kiss on her lips. "I'll see you later, sweetheart."

Chase watched as Slade walked away. A moment later, the front door slammed shut. At the sound, Patton exploded into activity. Cracking some eggs into a bowl, she set about whisking them with more enthusiasm than necessary.

Carefully setting the coffee pot back onto its burner, he went around the island to take a seat on a barstool. He sipped from his mug as he watched her flitter about with rapid motions. A slight smile tugged at his lips. Little Miss Patton was nervous and that suited his needs just fine.

Patton busied herself making her omelet. She was keenly aware of Chase. A strange tension slowly filled the room and she knew it came from her. For some unexplainable reason, she suddenly found herself feeling shy.

It was Chase's fault. He watched her the way a predator tracked its next meal, making her nerves fire as her body prepared to flee. This was one of Chase's signature moves.

Whenever he planned to lay down the law and tell her something she didn't want to hear, he started with his intimidating gaze. Normally it made her bristle as she prepared to go toe to toe. Then again, normally all he could do was tell her no and she could scheme her way around him.

Even if she got caught, the most punishment he'd ever doled out was guilt and grounding. Slade and Devin had always helped mitigate whatever wrong she'd done, either working on alleviating Chase's anger or helping her feel better about being stuck at home.

Everything had changed now. He had the upper hand. The range of punishment he could dole out had widened to an impressive field, the variety of which Patton knew she could barely comprehend. The fear of the unknown only added to her anxiety.

So did the knowledge that she no longer had Slade and Devin on her side. It had always been Devin and her pitted against the authoritarian figure, Chase, with Slade playing referee. Now it was the men against the woman, three against one.

Three stronger, more experienced men against her single-minded determination. Patton plated her omelet as she considered the diminishing merits of determination in the face of sexual domination. The things she'd seen them do to other women...Patton shivered, feeling her face flame another notch as her mind superimposed her own image in their place.

Chase's hand shot out as she turned the corner of the island, bringing her to a stop. Her eyes darted up to his smoldering gaze and just as quickly looked away. She could see the knowledge in them, as if he could read her thoughts.

"You're embarrassed." Chase's voice deepened to a sexy growl as he removed the plate from her slightly trembling hands.

"I am not." The retort lost any bite, coming out more mumbled instead of sharp.

"No?" Chase rubbed her cheek with the back of his fingers. "Then why are you blushing?"

"I am not blushing." Patton shifted slightly away from him. "It's just hot working over the stove."

"I see." Chase studied her for a long, silent moment. "Strip."

"What?" That got her eyes up and she looked at him in shocked amazement.

"You heard me. Strip." Chase let go of her arm, allowing her to back further away from him.

"You can't be serious." Patton's hands came up to protectively cover her chest.

"I'm very serious." Chase stood up, crowding her back against the cupboard.

"We're in the kitchen!"

"So?"

"But—"

"I want you naked." Chase hardened his tone. "Now, Patton."

"Why?"

"Because that's what I want." Chase raked his gaze down her body, pleased when he saw her shudder softly. "Now take off your clothes or I'll do it for you."

"Can't we talk about—"

Patton's words ended in a shriek as Chase reached out and tore her shirt in two. Her hands slapped ineffectively at his as he made quick work of tearing the rest of her shirt and skirt into rags.

In less than a minute, she he had her naked except for the little lacy bra. Chase watched her eyes dart around, checking to make sure they nobody saw her. He could have told her that he had dismissed Charlotte and all the hands had been sent out into the fields.

They were completely alone, but he didn't bother to reassure her. It played into his hand to keep her anxious. The more she focused on her situation, the easier the coming conversation would be.

Chase knew Patton was used to getting her way. He'd need all the advantage he could get to win the coming argument. If forcing her to have it naked weakened her confidence then that's how far Chase would sink. Nothing was too low to do to save Patton from killing herself on that damn bike.

God, but he loved her.

* * * *

He hooked a finger between the cups of her bra and raised a brow at her. Patton caved. She didn't want to lose the sexy piece of underwear she had designed and sewn. The bra fell to the floor.

With the loss of that final piece of fabric, Patton felt her nervousness explode into an arousal. It gave her an erotic thrill being completely exposed to Chase's gaze as he towered above her and it couldn't be denied, he looked.

Goose bumps pimpled all down her body as his heated gaze made a slow pass over her. Her breasts puckered, her pussy pulsed and wept, and when he finally reached out to pull her into his arms, she all but melted against him.

His callused hands felt warm and strong as they gripped her waist. She offered no resistance as his hands slid down over waist to massage the bottom. The gentle, tender caress lulled Patton deeper into his embrace.

Instinctively her head tilted back and his mouth greeted hers. His lips whispered over hers like a feather, teasing her. As her mouth opened, his tongue slipped inside, stroking, rubbing, and drawing out her response.

The kiss quickly turned from a sweet, gentle exploration to a rough, hungry devouring. Chase couldn't seem to get enough, wouldn't ever be able to get enough. A desperate part of him needed this, needed the proof that he held Patton in his arms and not a dream.

The smell of her arousal called to him and his hands traced down the seam in her ass to brush against the wet proof of her desire. She moaned into his kiss, her legs separating to make room for his hand. It was an invitation Chase did not have the will power to deny.

Her hips jerked toward his touch as his fingers teased along the edges of her slit, traveling upward to flick her little piercing. He pressed harder on clit, circling and rubbing the nub until she trembled her fingers clenching on his arms as she tried to remain upright.

She lost the battle when he slid his fingers down to thrust them deep into her. She would have fallen to the floor if he hadn't caught her around the waist with his free hand. Pleasure flooded her body, carried on the roaring waves of her own blood supply until she couldn't distinguish one touch from another.

Her hips jerked, keeping pace with the rhythm his hand set as he continued to fuck his fingers into her clenching heat. The thumb he stretched up to tease and torment the sensitive nub at the top of her folds that undid her.

Patton gasped, her eyes rolling back into her head as she gave herself over to the ecstasy tearing through her. Minutes stretched into an eternity as she remained suspended in the fine web of orgasmic pleasure.

Chapter 31

The strings broke and she collapsed back to reality, her body caving in to his for support. She stayed there in the safe haven of his arms as she tried to regain control of the racing beat of her heart. It pumped too fast and forced her lungs to draw in painfully harsh breaths.

The rough feel of his clothes against her tender, exposed skin brought her fully back into the moment. Her brain kicked in, reminding her of what had led up to this moment.

Chase had played her body like a master. She had no defense against him, against any of them. It humbled her to recognize how completely she surrendered when they took command of her body.

They could do anything they wanted to her. Not only was she incapable of resisting, but her body gloried in her submission. That thought more than anything brought her back to Earth.

Pulling in a deep, steadying breath, she finally lifted her head to meet his gaze. She could find no mocking triumphant in his darkened gaze, only unmasked desire. The need she saw in his eyes more than the hands tenderly stroking over her body soothed her.

"You came again without permission," Chase growled softly, making her lax muscles stiffen with renewed tension.

"That's not fair," Patton muttered as she pushed away from him. "You're the one who drove me to it."

"That's my right." As if to prove the point, he reached out with one finger and flicked the little bar piercing making Patton gasp and shiver with pleasure. "It's not your right to come until you receive permission."

"How can I remember that when you are driving me insane?"

"Don't worry, baby. I'll teach you." Chase took her by the arm and led her toward the small dinette table.

"Why am I not assured?"

"You're not supposed to be." Chase pulled out a chair. "Sit."

Patton shot him a mutinous look, but she sat. "You know I'm not a dog to be ordered about the place."

"I know."

"You could try a please every now and again."

"I'll remember that."

Patton doubted that he would, but she imagined over time he would lighten up. She imagined right now he needed to push her, to test her limits to try and make her break. If she broke, then he'd feel justified that all his concerns had been right and they were doomed to disaster.

"Spread those legs. Whenever you're in my presence, I want those legs wide enough that I can put my hand, face or dick between them at my leisure."

Patton clenched her jaw and hesitated. Her contradictory nature urged her to defy him, regardless of the consequences. Her body disagreed. It melted at the ideas his words planted in her head. To be available, vulnerable to his lust, a lust that appeared never ending…Patton shivered.

Slowly, she slid her legs apart.

"Wider."

Gritting her teeth and keeping her head bowed, she did as he commanded, continuing until her ankles wrapped around the chair's legs. That most have pleased him because he moved off, a second later returning with her plate.

"Eat up, baby. You're going to need your strength."

Patton managed to swallow a few bites of the cheese omelet, but it was hard. Her favorite breakfast now tasted like bland mush. Her mind was distracted by its own thoughts.

Chase wasn't just pushing her to test her limits. He wanted something. The jackass thought that by forcing her to bend to his will and eat naked, he'd somehow gained the upper hand for whatever argument he intended to start.

Her motorcycle, her business, Patton didn't know where they were headed. She did know that whenever Chase staged his attack, he was in for a shock. Despite all appearances, Patton wasn't subdued.

* * * *

"We need to talk about a few things, Patton."

Chase finally spoke after watching her try to look like she enjoyed her food. She might have many skills, but acting wasn't one of them. It went against her expressive nature, which made her honest even when she didn't want to be.

"Your motorcycle," Chase began only to come to an abrupt stop when her fork clanged to her plate. Finally, she looked up at him, her eyes narrowing dangerously. For a moment, he reconsidered his plan of attack. As nervous as she obviously was, it was still not enough to dent her normal determination.

"What about it?"

"We're getting rid of it," Chase decreed, keeping his tone hard, his features inflexible.

"Oh, we are, are we?"

"You're getting a car, preferably something made out of metal."

"I don't think so."

"This isn't up for discussion."

"You're right about that." Patton leaned forward, appearing to forget in her annoyance that she completely vulnerable sitting there in the buff.

"Listen very carefully to me, Patton." Chase matched her aggression, leaning into her until their noses almost touched. "If I have to dismantle that machine piece by piece, I will."

"I'll just buy another one."

"I'll crush it with my Dooley."

"Then I'll buy another."

"You can buy as many as you want. I'll destroy every one. While we're playing this game, you'll be completely dependent on Slade, Devin and me to give you a ride."

Checkmate. Chase relaxed back, confident he'd won by the look of astonishment on her face. He couldn't help but smile.

* * * *

Bastard had her with that one. Patton settled back into her seat, eyeing him like the blue jean mobster he was. That was exactly what he was, using threats and intimidation to get what he wanted, making a living off sex and women, and no doubt backed by his fellow blue jean tyrants.

He thought he had her cornered. Not a chance in hell. That smug little smile of his needed to be turned upside down and Patton knew just the trick.

"I guess I'll just have to buy a car then, along with my new bikes."

"Damnit, Patton!" He shot forward and so did she.

"You can't make me—"

"Would you be reasonable—"

"—with your high-handed orders—"

"—stubborn, hard headed—"

"—tell me what—"

"—kill yourself—"

"—pain—"

"—in my—"

"—ass!"

"Ahh!"

Patton fell back into her seat, retracting the finger she'd been leveling at him to fold her arms over her chest. She tucked her chin into her chest to glare mutinously at him. He matched her scowl with his own equally determined one. Instead of screaming out his frustration, he settled back into his chair with a growl.

A heated silence filled the kitchen with no less tension than their shouting match had. It communicated just as much too. Neither of them had bothered to listen as they yelled over each other, knowing that anything the other had to say would not change their own stance.

"Look, Patton," Chase took a deep breath in an obvious attempt to sound reasonable. He just sounded condescending to her. "Motorcycles are dangerous. I'm not going to sit idly by and let you gamble with your life."

"It's my life to gamble with."

"What if you get pregnant?"

"Pregnant?"

"Are you going to put the baby's life in danger, too?"

"Pregnant?"

"Yes, Patton, Pregnant! You know that thing that happens when a sperm meets an egg. It's normally the result of having unprotected sex, like what we did all last night and this morning." Chase paused, but when she continued to stare at him as if he'd grown a second head, he sighed. "Don't tell me you hadn't thought of it."

"Well." Patton shifted slightly. "No."

"Well," Chase mimicked her slightly whiny tone. "Do. It's a reality that's bound to happen at some time."

A baby?

Was it horrible that her first response was abject fear and terror? In a lot of ways, she was still the baby. Pampered and protected, she could be as reckless and irresponsible in her personal life as she wanted. Then she had to consider her professional life.

Things were going well, but they could go better. It took a lot of time to continually keep up with all the paperwork, the clients, find the time to design and create, not to mention handling all the issues with outsourcing the actual production. This trip alone had set her back, leaving her work piling up. What would a baby do?

"Earth to Patton." Chase waved his hand in front of her.

"What?" Patton blinked and then scowled at him. "I don't think we should be talking about children yet when we can't even agree on a motorcycle."

"That's backward logic given you could already be pregnant."

"I'll find out and then I'll go on the pill, until then you can just wear a damn condom."

Chase snorted. "I don't think so."

"Why the hell not?"

"Because I don't like them."

"And here you're calling me the irresponsible one. With that attitude who knows how many little Chases there are running out there already."

"We used condoms with all other women, Patton." Chase barked. "Jesus, how little do you think of us?"

"You would protect them, but you wouldn't protect me?" Patton shot back.

"I'm trying to. Why the hell do you think I want you to get rid of that damn motorcycle?"

She made his head hurt. It never changed. She had a knack at saying all the right things to drive him completely crazy. If her antagonistic response weren't enough, she went in so many directions he couldn't keep up. He became frustrated even trying.

"I say we just put the issue aside for right now." Patton waved her hands, as if trying to physically shove their conversation out of the way.

"Which issue? Pregnancy or the motorcycle?"

"Both. We'll discuss them at a later time."

"You don't grasp the concept of pregnancy, do you?"

"What do you mean by that?"

"Unless you are practicing abstinence, the issue exists whether or not you want talk about it."

"And who says I wouldn't be practicing abstinence in the future?" Patton rolled her head.

"I do."

"Well who says your opinion…"

Wherever that sentence led, Patton wisely stopped before she reached her destination. Chase helped her come to that conclusion by crossing his arms over his chest and narrowing his gaze.

Oh, but she made the palm of his hand itch to tan her delectable backside a beautiful shade of sunburn-red. Hard-headed and obnoxious, he'd known this would never work. So what if she enjoyed the previous night's games…and this morning, that didn't make her a submissive.

Even now he could see her scheming as her eyes lowered and she worried her lip through her teeth. Yeah, Patton was considering her next move and Chase had no doubt it would drive him even further off the cliff of insanity.

Chapter 32

"You know, I think we can reach some sort of agreement." Patton scooted her chair right next to his. She whispered sultrily as she dropped her hand into his lap, "Don't you?"

"Patton," Chase growled in warning as her hand slid up to rub against the hard bulge in his jeans.

So this was it? She was going to try and use sex as a bargaining chip? Chase couldn't believe it. The woman had no idea what she was getting herself into.

"Yes, master?" Patton whispered in his ear before nipping on the bottom of the lobe.

Damnit!

The husky sound of her voice stroked over him much as the hand in his lap did. His body throbbed with barely controlled passion. All his nerve endings screamed with need. His hands itched to burry themselves in her hair, push her head down into his lap, and...

Oh, yeah.

The cool metal of his zipper painfully bit back on his cock as it tried to beat its way free of his jeans. He sucked in a harsh breath as her hands moved up to the waistband of his jeans. The action gave her just enough room to wiggle two fingers under the edge of the denim.

With eyes tightly closed, he endured the gentle searing touch of her fingertips on the tip of his dick. Knowing he could stand no more, he grasped her wrist pulling her hand free.

"You're going to pay for that, babe," Chase warned.

"Just name your price." Patton licked her lips as she pushed her breasts into his side. "I'll be happy to oblige."

"Patton," Chase drew out her name with a groan. "I thought you planned on practicing abstinence."

"I didn't think I got to make that decision."

"It's not. I just expected some amount of resistance."

"Hmm." Patton nuzzled closer to him. "What is the point in arguing?"

"And if you get pregnant?"

"I'll be a hormonal bitch and you'll regret the day you ever met me."

Chase decided to change directions when she slid her hand back into his lap, her fingers wrapping around the large ridge his erection made in his jeans. Patton wanted to play, then he'd play. They'd see just who won control when it came to sex.

He returned her intimate exploration with one of his own. Big difference, he had nothing in the way of his hand as he slid it up her leg and drove his fingers straight into her tight sheath.

Patton moaned against his neck, her lips halting their teasing exploration. Her legs parted more, her ass coming to the edge of the seat. Chase smiled grimly as he fucked his fingers into her.

The little tease had forgotten all about her game of tormenting him. Instead, Patton focused completely on what he was doing to her. Her hips arched toward his hand, trying to take his fingers deeper.

She was wet and ready. The squishy sounds of his fingers driving into her heat filled the kitchen. Chase knew he should pull out, to leave her wanting. It would teach her a valuable lesson about trying to manipulate him with sex.

Then again so would what he had planned. Better yet his plans included him getting some release from the painful ache fisting in his balls. His already painfully engorged cock was now trying to grow its own exoskeleton. His plan to intimidate her by keeping her naked had backfired, but he wouldn't be the one who would pay for his mistake.

She issued a protesting groan when he released her tender flesh. Her glazed eyes went wide when he abruptly stood and lifted her onto the table. With rough motions he laid her out over the wooden top, pushing her onto her stomach and arching her hips so that her ass came up, her legs went wide, leaving her completely open and vulnerable to him.

His raging lust allowed no time for preliminary petting. He barely managed enough time to get his zipper down. Chase wasted precious seconds of sanity to slide his fingers deep into her pussy, checking her readiness.

Hot, wet and willing, all systems were a go and so he went. Chase rammed himself so hard and deep into her she momentarily lifted off the table. He didn't worry that he had hurt her.

Patton's screamed out her passion as her sheath rippled and convulsed around him. Her back arched and her hips quickly matched the fast paced rhythm he set, bucking backward so she could slam herself down his length as he powered forward.

Too soon, her enthusiasm overwhelmed her and she outpaced his thrusts. Chase grunted, winding her hair into his fist to control her exuberance. It made little difference. She was lost in the first waves of rapture constricting her cunt and making her shriek incoherently.

"No," she screamed, fighting his hold when Chase came to a sudden stand still. "You bastard. Don't you dare stop."

"You need some lessons on pillow talk, sweetheart." Chase chuckled unsteadily.

"Damnit, Chase! Ohhh…" she gasped, forgetting her annoyance as his hand slid around her hip to feather over her mound.

His tantalizing touch turned out to be nothing more than a temporary distraction. His hand pulled back, smoothing over her ass until his fingers circled the tight entrance to her rear. Patton tensed immediately from the suggestive caress.

She'd known this would eventually happen, had fantasized about it, but never in the kitchen, spread out like a feast before Chase. The images and dreams that had always played through her mind had been

more romantic or at least matching the energy of sexual frenzy that
had marked the previous night's adventures.

This was a much more calculated experiment. The sterile
environment, the slow repetitive motions of Chase's hand collecting
her own moisture to lubricate her ass all contributed to her anxiety
constricting her muscles which only added to erotic pleasure boiling
out from her lower body.

Chase could see Patton shaking, fearing what was to come. Christ,
he didn't want her scared. He wanted her moaning in pleasure,
begging to be filled. Part of him wanted to step back, call the whole
thing off and then snuggle her close.

None of them had ever been a woman's first anal experience. All
the women they'd ever dealt with had already been taken in that way.
Sure, some of them had never had men as large as them, or two men
at once but they hadn't been innately afraid of the experience.

Chase knew that once Patton adjusted she would love having two
men inside of her. The feeling of being so full of cock, stretched so
tight that she wouldn't be able to tell who was doing what to her as
her body exploded in ways she never would have imagined, most of
his clients couldn't get enough.

Right now, though Patton probably wanted to get away. She was
scared and for the first time he didn't know how to proceed with a
woman. Patton wasn't just any woman and he couldn't treat her that
way. She was the very heart of his soul and he ached to giver her the
pleasure she deserved.

"You want this, don't you, Patton?" Chase needed to know that he
didn't force anything on her.

"Yes." He barely heard Patton's faint reply.

"We'll make it good for you. Just let me get you ready. All right?"

"All right."

Patton bit down on her bottom lip, whimpering as she felt the
cool, slick feel of Chase's fingers as they dipped into her back
entrance. They left a wet trail as he circled around, spreading her

opening wider and wider. Again and again, he pushed further into her with each foray.

Patton began to relax, accepting the feel of his fingers. The feeling wasn't completely unpleasant. Memories of the past night and how it had felt to have her dildo packed tightly in her rear eased her fears even more. She'd enjoyed the experience. It had been shamefully erotic and amazingly stimulating. All those good thoughts fled though when she felt the engorged head of his cock pressed against her entrance.

Oh, God, he was much thicker, wider than the little toy had been. She felt as if she would rip open as he pushed through the tight ring of muscles at her entrance.

Her hands curled into fists and she could feel the hot splash of her tears falling onto the table. Chase's hands smoothed over the tense muscles in her back, trying to soother her even as forged deeper. If she could relax, it would be easier for her.

"It's going to be all right, sweetheart." Chase's harsh, choppy tone matched his ragged breathing.

"Hurts," Patton mumbled into the table.

"I know, sweetheart, but it won't last long. Just relax, take a deep breath."

Patton did as he ordered and Chase could feel her muscles loosen for a second, allowing him to slide past her entrance before her untried channel clamped back down on him. The walls of her back passage spasmed around him and he groaned fighting the urge to come right then.

"Too big," Patton complained, squirming to get away and inadvertently taking more of him into her.

"It's all right sweetheart," Chase whispered, trying to calm her. "The hard part is over now."

"I can't do this," Patton whimpered.

"Yes, you can," Chase assured her, sliding his hand around to her pussy.

"No," Patton sniffed. "I'm not ready."

"Yes, you are." Chase began to tease her clit. "I can feel how wet you are. Your pussy is already so tight. Can you imagine how much tighter it's going to be when two of us are fucking you together? We're going to drown you with pleasure. Just think of it, two cocks pushing in and out of your body at the same time. You're going to climax like you never had before. Don't you want that, Patton? Haven't you dreamed of it? Fantasized about it?"

"Yes," Patton gasped, barely comprehending what he said thanks to the shivers of pleasure tingling out from where he manipulated her clit.

"I'm in, baby." Chase leaned down to nibble and kiss the back of her neck.

The motion made his cock jerk, forcing her to realize that he had buried himself all the way inside of her. The sensation of being so filled, of having her ass completely stretched hit her, sending cascade of amazing pleasure flowing through her. Patton shivered, but this time in pleasure instead of fear.

"God, sweetheart," Chase groaned. "If you do that, I won't be able to give you the time you need to adjust. You have the tightest, sweetest ass. It's heaven feeling you clamping down on me, but if you don't relax for a moment, I'm not going to be able to control myself."

Patton took a panting breath trying to force her muscles to do as he asked, relax. There was no point. Her body had a mind of its own. The stinging pain of being stretched rippled into a searing pleasure that grew in intensity with every spasm of her muscles. She couldn't stop from wiggling slightly, increasing the pressure until the pain blurred into rapture.

"Patton," Chase groaned. "Don't."

"Can't stop," Patton panted and wiggled again.

"Does it still hurt, sweetheart?"

"Feels good," Patton moaned, tilting her hips backward to try and take more of him, but he had no more to give.

"Ah, hell." Chase couldn't take the little motions and his control snapped.

He tried to be gentle, to go slow and easy. Patton wouldn't let him. Her little mewing sounds grew louder, sharper as her hips began to move in rhythm to his thrust and counterthrust. Their movements increased, his thrusts growing stronger, harder, leaving her gasping for breath.

Chase gripped her hips, trying to keep up with the rhythm Patton set. Searing heat built up in his balls and it became painful holding back. Sweat poured down his face as his heart thundered, trying to beat its way through his chest, but still he managed to hold onto his control by the barest of threads. He would not come before she found her pleasure.

Patton slammed harder against him as the first quakes of her climax began to spread cracks through her body. Behind her Chase growled and began working her hips in a fast rhythm. Back and forth, he impaled his full length into her as hard as he could.

It undid her. Her eyes rolled upward as her body shattered under the most explosive climax she'd had yet. As they flicked across the doorway, she caught sight of Charlotte standing there. She couldn't focus on the other woman, but the knowledge that somebody watched Chase fuck her in the ass on the kitchen table only added to the thrill of the moment.

Patton's back arched, her hair falling in beautiful, perfect waves as she screamed out her release. She went wild with her release, triggering his own animalistic response. Chase covered her, biting down on her shoulder as he forced her to take his full length one last time. He held her tightly as he spilled his seed into her contracting body.

Several minutes past before he had the energy to recognize reality. Immediately he tensed, lifting himself off of Patton who had been squashed to the table beneath him.

Ah, damn.

Had he hurt her? He'd completely lost it there at the end. Without a doubt, he had never had a sexual experience that came close to taking Patton's virgin ass. Nothing compared to the amazing release she had given him. Chase hadn't realized he could feel so much pleasure, but even that wasn't worth hurting her.

"Patton?" Chase tucked her perspiration-slick hair behind her ear so he could see her face.

She didn't respond to his prodding. From the deep even breaths going in out of her parted lips, he knew she had passed out. He smiled slightly at the picture she made. The woman who had moments ago burned him alive with her untamed passion had gone back to looking like an innocent.

A worn out innocent from the flush in her cheek and the sweat rolling down from her forehead. Chase felt something else he had never experienced with a woman move through him, tenderness, peace, contentment, the urge to roll her into his arms and snuggle her close while she slept.

It had been that way last night. She'd passed out then, too. Chase's smile took on a cocky twist. Whatever other accusations Patton may lobby at him over their lifetime, she'd never be able to say he didn't satisfy her, please her to the point of exhaustion.

Grimacing, he tried to pull his cock gently out of her clinging sheath. Her ass didn't seem to want to let him go, clamping tightly down around him, making him struggle slightly for release. Despite her body's enthusiasm, Patton eyelashes didn't flutter. Only when he lifted her into his arms, that she showed any signs of life.

"Come on, sweetheart. We have to get you cleaned and dressed." Chase kissed her on the forehead as he carried her out of the kitchen. Her only response was a muted murmur, expressing her displeasure at being disturbed.

Chase grinned as he mounted the stairs. He may not have won the argument about her motorcycle or gotten a chance to start the one about her photos in the catalog, but he had just discovered the perfect way to end an argument with Patton. That knowledge would definitely come in handy in the near future.

Chapter 33

Hailey frowned at Patton who smiled back at her friend. With a turn, Patton waved at Chase who beeped his horn at her before taking off down the street. Patton had an hour to get her bags packed.

Chase's goodbye was a good deal friendlier than Hailey's hello. Not bothering to speak to Patton, Hailey turned and stormed off into the kitchen. Patton followed her, pausing only to close the door.

"Rough night?" Patton asked as Hailey glared at her over the rim of a coffee cup.

"Worse day."

"I hesitate to ask." Patton poured herself a cup of the black brew that Hailey called coffee.

"I can understand why, considering it's all your fault."

"My fault?" Patton gave Hailey an inquisitive look. "How so?"

"I ran into Cole down at the bakery this morning."

"Oh." Patton cringed. "How was he?"

"How was he?" Hailey slammed her cut down.

"Was it bad?"

"Bad?"

"Look, Hailey. I can tell you're upset." Patton tried to calm her down. "Just tell me how bad he was hurt."

"He wasn't hurt at all, Patton. That's not the problem."

"What do you mean he wasn't hurt?"

"Did I stutter?"

"But...I...are you sure?"

"Am I sure of what?" Hailey scowled.

"That he wasn't hurt. Maybe Slade spared his face."

"Please, there wasn't a scratch on that boy."

"That doesn't make any sense. I saw Slade hit him."

"Are you sure?"

No, Patton wasn't sure. She actually hadn't seen Slade hit Cole. She'd just seen his arm flexing and pounding into something. His knuckles had been all torn up.

"He hit him." Patton nodded with her conclusion. "Maybe he hit him in the stomach, but he ripped him from the truck screaming he was going to kill Cole."

"Why would he do that?"

"Because he was jealous." Patton snorted. "That was the plan."

"He knew it."

"You don't know—"

"Chase figured it out at the bonfire and called me on it."

"What?" Patton blinked.

"They knew, Patton." Hailey waved her hands in the air. "The jig was up."

They knew. They'd played her. Chase and Slade had set the whole thing up last night. They had just been acting at being enraged. Then Slade manipulated her into not only feeling bad, but confessing to her own plans.

"That sneaky son-of-a-bitch," Patton whispered. She wasn't about to let him get away with that.

"Are you listening to me?" Hailey's cup hit the table hard.

"I heard you." Patton sat down at the kitchen table, across from Hailey. "They played me."

"Not before you and I played them."

"Oh, I see." Patton reached across the table to give Hailey's hand a comforting squeeze. "Don't worry, honey. I'm not mad at you. You can't help it if you're not a good liar."

"Mad at me?" Hailey snatched her hand back. "No. You're not the one who gets to be mad. I'm the one who is mad at you."

"Me?" Patton bit back a laugh. "Whatever for?"

"You dragged me into this stupid ass game and now I've got the hounds of hell on my heels."

"Are you worried about Chase and Slade?" Patton scowled. "Don't be. I can control them."

"Such ill placed confidence, but no. They're not my problem."

"Hailey will you just tell me what is going on?"

"Cole." Hailey spit his name out as if it was a sour taste in her mouth. "Cole Jackson and his two sidekicks, Beevis and Butthead. That is what is going on."

"Cole? He's what's got you all concerned?"

"He walked up to me at the bakery and said 'game on' with those two twits snickering at his side."

"What two twits?"

"Jake and Aaron."

"Doesn't ring a bell." Patton shook her head.

"They were two grades ahead of us. Remember Aaron drove the black Malibu SS."

"Malibu what?"

"It's a muscle car."

Patton shrugged. "Sorry."

"Jake had the beat up Chevelle they worked on in shop class."

"The Chev…what? Isn't that a rock band?"

"It's an old Chevy."

"Don't give me that look, Hailey. I didn't take shop."

"Well, I did and those two Neanderthals made my life hell," Hailey snapped. "They're Cole's cousins. They work with him down at his shop and they're just as bad as Cole."

Patton snorted. "Cole isn't that bad. I wouldn't sweat him."

Hailey's mouth fell open. "Don't sweat him?"

"Yeah. So what if Cole has taken an interest in you. A woman could do worse. He's a hottie."

"He's a walking advertisement for the convent. A woman could make him wear four rubbers and still not be sure she wouldn't get infected," Hailey snapped. "Besides he hasn't taken an interest in me, he's declared war."

"Just because of what happened the other night?"

"He's been ticked at me since I turned him down a year ago."

"He asked you out and you turned him down?" Patton's mouth fell open. "Why am I just hearing about this now?"

"He didn't ask me out. The sleazy, arrogant, bastard just wanted to get his hands—"

"—on your hot little body." Patton grinned.

"On my car." Hailey waved her hands in agitation. "Hello? Remember our conversation?"

"Your car?"

"You never listen to me." Hailey sighed. "I'll make this short. Cole has been lusting after it since I bought it. Thinks he's God's gift to wrenches and been insulted ever since I told him where he could stick his ratchet. I take care of my own car."

"Sounds like the beginning of a beautiful relationship."

"There is no relationship!" Hailey shouted. "I'm telling you he's been lusting after my Commander for a year now. Oh, I've seen his eyes all over my baby, checking her out when my back is turned. I don't trust that man and I know full well what the double dorks are capable of."

"Don't you think you're blowing this out of portion?"

"No, I don't." Hailey crossed her arms over her chest. "You remember when somebody super glued my books to the shop table?"

"Oh, yeah, that was funny."

Hailey's eyes narrowed on Patton. Obviously she hadn't found any humor in the joke. "That was Jake and Aaron led by their then leader Kyle."

"Kyle? Kyle Harding?" Patton grinned. "He's hot, too."

"He's an ass."

"Oh, yeah, he certainly has one of the best."

"Patton, the man rivals Cole for the title of jerk of the century."

"Don't you think you're exaggerating?"

"No."

"I talked to him last night and he was nothing but a gentleman." Patton pursed her lips and wiggled her eyes brows. "Much to my disappointment. Cole and him appeared to be good friends."

"They're partners in the restoration shop in town."

"I wonder if they partner in anything else?"

"Patton!" Hailey's mouth fell open. "You have three men at home. Now you want two more on the side. What do you want, to die with your legs spread?"

"I wasn't thinking for me, sweetheart."

"Oh, no." Hailey shook her head at Patton's look. "That's your sick dream, leave me out of it."

"Just think, Hailey—"

"Never going to happen."

"But—"

"I talked to Kyle, too, last night and he was the same dickhead he'd always been."

"Were you a bitch first?"

"If I was, I was justified. Remember the time when somebody rigged the exploding stink bombs to my locker door?"

"Kyle?"

"Or the time when somebody wired my toolbox to deliver an electric shock when I touched it?"

"Oh, yeah." Patton laughed. "Your pinky twitched for almost the whole day."

"Yeah, that was a great laugh. It was even funnier when somebody vaselined the path to the liquid recycling bin and I busted my ass, knocking over a drum and got covered in used motor oil. I almost shit myself I laughed so hard."

"Okay, okay." Patton held up her hands. "I give in. But if you knew Kyle did all these things, why didn't you say anything in high school?"

"Because I didn't find out until years later when Kyle broke up with Mary Katherine and she ratted him and his friends out. Besides, what would I have done? You're the master at these juvenile games. Me, I'm too mature to pull off those kinds of pranks."

"Oh, come on. Don't underestimate yourself." Patton smiled. "I'm sure you can do juvenile and if you need help, I'll be there for you."

"You're the reason I'm in this mess."

"And I'll get you out of it."

"Aren't you going to be a little busy? Or am I mistaking that big, I-got-laid grin on your face?"

"Nope. No mistake." Patton settled back in her chair. "The Davis boys are officially mine."

"Congratulations," Hailey offered begrudgingly.

"Now the fun really begins."

"Whoopee."

"First on the list is Mr. Slade and punishment for scaring the hell out of me."

"I don't understand you," Hailey stated with a shake of her head. "You got your way. You played your games and won. Why not celebrate? Be happy and forgive Slade for whatever he did."

"Where's the fun in that?"

"Where's the fun in tormenting him?"

"It's double fun, actually. I get to enjoy tormenting him first. Then I get to enjoy his revenge." Patton couldn't help but grin just imagining what kind of revenge Slade would take. It would be a very good night.

"Then what?" Hailey's sour tone dimmed Patton's enthusiasm for a moment. "You have to get even? Where does it stop?"

In bed, sweaty and exhausted with a big smile on her face. "Hopefully never."

"Whatever."

Hailey's dour mood annoyed Patton. "Don't whatever me, Hailey. You could do with lightening up a bit. Have you ever thought about getting even with Kyle for all the crap he pulled in high school?"

"No."

"It would be more satisfying than being bitter and cussing him."

"I enjoy bitterness. Besides, there are consequences to these little games you like to play. I'm sure Chase isn't going to be thrilled to dance to the tune you set for the rest of your lives."

"Oh, him." Hailey would have to mention Chase. "He already tried to take away my motorcycle."

"I take it you won that round."

Won? Patton shivered with remembering just how the argument had ended. "Not exactly. I'd say it was a draw."

"Hmmm."

"Besides that's not the real battle. The big fight will come over my business."

"Your business? You really think he'll try to make you give it up?"

"Oh, yeah, but he's not going to win that argument. I'm not about to give up my career for anything, not even the Davis brothers. Which actually brings me to the favor I need."

"Oh, no. No more favors. I'm in deep enough trouble thanks to you."

"Come on Hailey. It's just a little favor."

"No."

"I swear there is no way it will backfire on you."

"No."

"What if I helped you with Cole?"

"Hell no."

"I could promise he wouldn't be any kind of problem for you."

That tempted her. Patton could see it in the narrowing of Hailey's eyes. "No, you couldn't."

"I swear it. Cole Jackson will never look your way again."

"How will you do that?"

"I have my ways." Patton grinned. She knew just what to do to assure Cole never bothered Hailey again. "So, will you help me?"

"I'm going to regret this. I just know it."

Chapter 34

Slade leaned back in his chair and flicked his pen across the desk. Chase and Devin had just pounded up the stairs to clean up after their day working in the field. It would be an hour or so before Chase dragged him out the door and off to a party he should have been looking forward to.

They were running late, which was just fine by Slade. He didn't want to go out tonight, not even for the biggest orgy of the year. A turn of events that would be looked on as tragic by his fellow Cattlemen, but Slade didn't care what they thought. None of them had Patton waiting at home.

That fact changed everything. It made the day seem longer. After years of enjoying the hard days and sometimes even harder nights, knowing Patton waited for him at the end of the day made him anxious to be done with his work. Hell, it made him slow to leave in the morning, too.

Slade closed his eyes and rested his head on the back of the chair. He wondered what Patton was up to. Chase had lugged all her stuff upstairs hours ago. It hadn't been ten minutes after he left though that Hailey appeared with another set of boxes that neither woman had let him help carry.

It had been difficult for him to watch the women struggle and sweat to lug whatever Hailey had brought over up the steps. Every time he'd tried to pick up a box though, Patton had been there ordering him to put it down. She'd nagged him right into the study where he had stayed cooped up for the rest of the day.

Well, he had ventured out after Hailey had left. When he'd knocked on Patton's door, she'd barely cracked it open. Peering out with one eye, she'd told him she was busy and then slammed the door in his face.

If that wasn't enough to warn him that she was up to no good, the click of the lock turning had sealed his suspicions. Normally he'd have shredded the door over such an outrageous move, but Slade had gut feeling he knew just what Patton was up to.

Chase was going to shit bricks if Slade was right. It would be better if Slade had no knowledge beforehand. That way he could stay clear of the explosion when it occurred. For that reason alone, Slade had sauntered back to the boring piles of paperwork waiting for him in the study.

Now that everything had been handled, he sat there idly wondering what Patton was doing. Slade now had a little time for some mischief. He probably shouldn't. She was no doubt sore from all the activity last night and this morning.

Devin would no doubt be pissed if Slade wore her out before he got his alone time with her. Not that his younger brother would show Chase and Slade the same consideration while they were out at the party. No, he should probably get while the getting was good.

* * * *

Patton peered out into the hallway, making sure the coast was clear before she tiptoed down to the big master bedroom at the end of the long passage. She could hear the shower running in the bathroom that sat between Chase and Devin's room.

From what she'd heard a minute ago, they'd be busy for a while. That played perfectly into her plans. Chase commenting to Devin he needed to shower first because Slade and him had a party to go to, did not.

Patton knew just what Chase had been referring to. Cole had let it slip about the wild party that would take place at the lodge tonight. She didn't need details to add what a bunch of dominant men and a lot of sex slaves equaled to. No way in hell were any of her men going to that party.

Asking them not to, begging, trying to guilt them, none of the normal options sounded like the answer she needed to keep her men at home. No, this situation called for extreme measures. Patton knew just what she needed to do to keep her men too busy at home to be worrying about being late to a party.

What she needed waited for her in her new bedroom. She hadn't said a word to Chase when he'd lugged up her suitcases of clothes to her old bedroom. There was no point, just as there had been no point in making an issue out of all the stuff he'd left behind at Hailey's.

Patton had known Chase wouldn't bring over any of her work stuff. It had been a silent statement—a call to arms that she had anticipated and planned around. Hailey had been relieved to learn all her favor would consist of was moving the rest of Patton's stuff to the ranch.

Patton had asked her to help move her real luggage to her new master bedroom and rearrange some furniture in her old room before letting Hailey off with a heartfelt thanks. Then she'd spent most of her day setting up her new home office. It had been easy to accomplish without any interruption from her men.

Well, Slade had made an appearance, but he hadn't pushed to get into the room. Little did he know what she was up to, Patton grinned. Not that she expected Slade to shit bricks over what she'd done, but he'd rat her out to Chase. That wasn't the way it was going work. Patton would be the one to reveal what she'd done to Chase, in her own time and her own way.

Right now she had a different game to play with her men. She just needed one little thing from the cupboard of toys they'd stocked her master bedroom with. Earlier, when she'd been unpacking her clothes into the unused closet, Patton had snooped around and discovered her new room came with an interesting assortment of gadgets.

Many she had no idea what they did with them. She could make a few guesses though thanks to the way everything had been meticulously organized. Slade's handiwork, no doubt. Everything had been grouped together perfectly, harnesses here, dildos there, floggers all hanging from the door, and whatever those things were…Patton nose wrinkled and she turned toward the shelf of binds.

They had a great selection from velvet ties to leather straps, twist-cuffs to real handcuffs. Ideal for her purposes were the individual locking rings. Made of metal and in various sizes, Patton picked up the largest set of rings and undid them with the key.

After hanging them from the waistband of her skirt, she dropped the key back on the shelf and headed down the stairs, grinning with anticipation.

* * * *

Slade had just talked himself into not being so considerate of Devin's good time when he heard the door open. Patton must have felt his mental thoughts, because there she stood, smiling at him. Slade smiled back, shifting in his seat to accommodate his rapidly hardening cock.

"Whatcha you doing?" Patton crossed the room toward him, her hips swinging proactively.

"Finishing up some paperwork," Slade responded absentmindedly, too focused on the delicious body coming closer.

"Hmm." Patton settled down on the edge of his desk. He let her push his chair back so she could sit right in front of him. "Did you get it fixed?"

Slade didn't hear her question. He was too distracted by the way her dress had ridden up to the tops of her thighs. His hands itched to push that little floral skirt up the rest of the way and expose the bare pussy he knew waited for him under its folds.

"Slade?" Patton laughed and nudged his leg with her foot.

"Hmm?" Slade looked up.

"Something wrong?"

"No. Why?"

"Because I asked you a question and you didn't answer."

"Just lost in thought."

"Really?" Patton raised an eyebrow. "Let me take a guess. You were thinking about my pussy. Probably thinking you were ready for a before dinner snack."

"Of course not." Slade slid his chair closer, letting his hands come to rest on her knees. "Why would you say that?"

"Because you appear to have a pussy eating addiction."

"I resent that." Slade kept his face straight as he wheeled himself closer. "I happen to be a connoisseur."

"A connoisseur?" Patton laughed. "What? Do you travel all over the world, sampling the local variations?"

"No, sweetheart. They come here for the taste testing." He slid his hands up a little, catching the edge of her skirt and raising it very slowly.

"Well then, I guess I should be honored that you find mine so delectable."

"Best I ever had."

"And what if I told you I was a slightly different type of connoisseur?" Patton leaned down to drop a quick kiss on his hard lips.

"You better not be," Slade warned her.

"Perhaps connoisseur is the wrong word." Patton nibbled on his bottom lip. "But I am hungry."

"Patton…"

"Come on, Slade." Patton slid off the desk and into his lap. "Let me have a little taste."

Pressing him back into the chair, she began kissing her way down his neck. Her hands had already gotten busy on the buttons of his shirt. Slade knew he should stop her. Patton was doing it again, trying to take control.

The temptation though was too much. Just the idea of her full lips spread wide as her hot little tongue licked down his cocks had his balls drawing up painfully tight. That mischievous little mouth had already made its way to his chest. Slade gave in and relaxed back into the chair.

"That's it, sweetheart," Patton whispered huskily as she slid off his lap and onto the floor between his legs. "Just close your eyes and let me take care of you."

Slade's eyes closed in bliss as he felt her hands begin to go to work on his zipper. Her mouth went in hot pursuit of her fingers, trailing kisses, nibbling bites and heated licks across his stomach.

Then her soft, gentle fingers touched his hot flesh. She pulled him free of his jeans, letting her hands runs run down the length of his cock until she could fondle and squeeze his balls.

Slade groaned, enjoying the sizzling spikes of pleasure vibrating up his spine. Her wet, curious tongue came out to lick his head and he jerked under the teasing caress.

"Like that?" Her hot breath tickled his cock and Slade snarled.

"Don't tease, Patton. Suck…ah, yeah."

His command ended in a growl as she sucked his whole length deep into her throat. He felt his cock head hit the back of mouth, her tongue flicking all over his sensitized shaft. Then she swallowed and Slade gasped as a little more of his length settled into her mouth.

His hands bit into the arms of the chair, fighting the need to bury in her hair and force her to fuck him with the rhythm he set. That would come soon enough. For right now, he wanted to be driven insane by her teasing.

That hope shattered when she pulled back off his cock. He opened his eyes to watch her sit back and smile at his hardened length, now glistening with moisture.

"Suck it, Patton."

"Hmm." Patton pursed her lips and looked up at him. "I don't think you get to make those demands this time, Slade."

Slade growled and tried to grab her. Cold metal bit into his wrist, locking his arms in place on the chair.

"What the..."

He stared in amazed confusion at the locking rings binding him to the chair's arms. He knew what they were and exactly where they came from, but his mind just went blank at the realization that Patton had bound him with them.

"You see," Patton stated conversationally as if she didn't have a large man boiling to a rage in front of her. "I had an interesting little talk with Hailey this morning."

"Take these off."

Patton ignored his demand. "It seems to me that I'm not the only one who played a little trick last night."

"Now, Patton!"

"Tell me, Slade, did you pound your fist into the ground just to bruise your knuckles?"

"Sweetheart, this is going to go very badly for you in the end." Slade tried to sound reasonable, but his heart pounded at a furiously beat and not in a good way. Already his dick began to soften and curl back in on itself.

"Oh, yes. I'm going to be punished for manipulating you last night." Patton sat back down on the edge of the desk, crossing her legs. "But you manipulated me last night and this morning. It only seems fair that you be punished, too. Right?"

"What?"

"Yes." Patton smiled at his fierce frown. "I'd be worried if I were you."

"Patton." Slade took a deep breath, his fingers curling into fists. "Think about this. You know at some point I'm going to be freed."

"Yep." Patton nodded. "At some point."

"Chase and Devin are upstairs."

"I know."

The way she purred those words made Slade's jaw clench. "They'll come down soon."

"Not for a while yet."

"Then it will be our turn and you know we're better at this particular game than you are."

"More experienced, that's for sure, but that just means I need to make my punishment count." Patton tapped her finger on her chin as she contemplated her options.

"Whatever you come up with will be returned to you in triple numbers," Slade growled.

"I got it." Patton snapped her fingers.

"Got what?"

"Don't you worry, baby." Patton slid back off the desk, going down on her knees between his spread legs. "Now just relax, Slade, and let your mistress take care of everything."

"My mistress," Slade's grumble turned into a groan as she swallowed his cock whole.

There were no teasing licks or playful tasting this time around. She immediately set up a fast pace that had his cock hitting a growth spurt. In seconds, she had him back to full mast. In minutes, white-hot bolts of ecstasy began to tear through his body and he ground his teeth together to hold back the sounds of passion burning in his throat.

Right then the devil stopped, leaning back on her heels to give him a triumphant smile. Slade couldn't hold back the litany of violent curses that poured from him as he realized just what kind of hell Patton planned to put him through.

He watched her with narrowed eyes, his mind too fogged with lust to come up with any ideas of an appropriate retribution, but he would.

He vowed it as her hands came up to stroke his dick, tugging and squeezing him, sliding down to tease his balls and keep him in a heightened state of arousal.

Over the next half hour she tormented him, using her mouth and hands to bring him consistently to the edge of climax only to leave him in a painful agony that had every muscle tensing, his arms flexing as he tried to break the molded plastic arms of the chair.

* * * *

So intent was she on her task that she didn't hear the footsteps coming down the hall or notice when Chase opened the door to the study. Slade bit his lip holding back the pleas he refused to give her the satisfaction of hearing, but Chase could easily read the anguish in his younger brother's eyes.

His gaze dropped to the metal binds holding Slade to the chair and he snickered silently to himself. Little Patton wanted to play. Too bad for her, the cards were stacked against her.

With a finger to his lips, he motioned Devin to be silent as he appeared in the hall behind him. With a nod of his head, he signaled Devin to come close. Devin peeked through the door and smirked before heading up the stairs. Chase didn't need to tell him what had to be done. It was obvious.

Chapter 35

Patton's eyes popped wide open when she felt her hair pulled painfully tight around a large fist. She wasn't given time to wonder or question as the hand forced her all the way down Slade's length. Unrelentingly, her capturer set a fast pace that had Slade groaning out his release in minutes.

Patton swallowed, struggling not to spill any of the hot jets of seed that flooded her mouth. It was difficult, but she managed. With a load like that, she wouldn't have to worry about one brother. At least not for a while.

That left two others, the biggest of which dragged her to her feet. Chase didn't appear to be particularly upset, but neither did he look to be pleased. Patton wanted to grin, right on time. Now it was time for part two of her plan to keep him and Slade away from their little party tonight.

Going with her plan, Patton tried to fake an air of docility. She bowed her head low, clasped her hands in front of her, and silently reminded herself of the rules. Her submissive façade wavered when she heard the den door open. Instinctively she turned to see who had entered.

She saw enough of Devin to know two things. He was amused and he had retrieved the key for Slade. She caught a flash of some other stuff in his hand, but didn't get a good enough look. Chase's hand on her chin turned her head and her attention back toward him.

"What are you wearing?"

She had not been expecting that question. His calm, curious tone threw her off. It was too bland when she had planned for angry. A calm Chase meant an in control Chase. That did not bode well for Patton.

"Uh…" Patton tried to think of the correct response. It eluded her.

"Not what you were told to wear this morning."

Uh-oh.

Her list of things to worry about grew. She could see in the corner of her vision that Slade had gotten free. For a man who had just orgasmed, he didn't look happy. Perhaps this hadn't been the best idea she'd ever had.

Chase took center stage in her concern department as he reached out to finger the edge of her dress. Patton tried not to flinch away, but his raised eyebrow told her she'd failed to conceal her apprehension.

A second later, he proved that her concern was well placed. His fingers curling around her collar preceded the loud ripping sound that left her dress in a puddle at her feet and her standing there in nothing more than a skimpy pair of panties.

"Hey." Patton jumped back, forgetting her plan of appeasement and falling back into her normal mode of irritation. "That was a great dress!"

"Then you should obey the rules."

"You can't just go around destroying all my clothes because you're feeling pissy." She crossed her arms over her bare breasts.

"Pissy?"

"All you're doing is wasting money. Now I have to buy a new dress."

"Really?"

"Yes, really," Patton snapped. "It's not as if you can keep me naked all the time."

"Wanna bet?"

"You wouldn't—"

"What are those?" Chase stared at her panties.

"Oh, no you don't." Patton knew exactly what thought circulated through his perverted mind.

"I think that's against the rules, too."

"No." Patton backed away from him. "Don't even think about it."

"Are you going to run?"

The idea obviously amused him. It was no doubt a fruitless option, but what else could she do?

She made it to the door, even got it halfway open before Chase's heavy weight slammed into her from behind, snapping the door closed and squishing her against the hard surface. Patton squirmed, shrieking as he tore the last scrap of clothing she had on away.

"Damnit, Chase! That was one of my favorite pair of panties!"

"I prefer you better this way," he growled back before forcing her away from the door.

With his arms locked around her waist, he kept her plastered to his front as he walked her back toward the desk. Patton fought his hold until she noticed Slade and Devin had moved. They'd settled down on the leather couch, watching the show with avid interest.

They had this thing planned already. That thought sobered her up. The three brothers had the edge on her not just with numbers, but also with experience of working together. Another fact she'd not anticipated when concocting her scheme.

Worse news came in the form of the objects that had miraculously appeared on the coffee table. Patton's stomach clenched as her eyes skipped over the velvet ties and the tube of lubricant to settle on the ominous black straps of the flogger.

They wouldn't really whip her, would they? The idea had a paralyzing effect on her body. Even as her heart began to pound with fear, the traitorous bitch that was her pussy quivered and pulsed with excitement at the idea that had her mind screaming at her to flee.

Escape was not an option with the steel bands Chase used as arms locking her firmly into position on his lap as he settled onto the edge of the desk. The position felt familiar.

He used his own enormous thighs to splay her legs, but this time instead of a mirror, Chase planned a live act complete with two intensely interested audience members. He added one new addition to the play today.

Patton started when she felt smooth fabric wrapping around her face. Chase leaned in from behind her nuzzling her neck before pulling the blindfold tight across her eyes. She trembled against him as the world went black, her breath picking up to panting speed. The strong sent of her own arousal betrayed her body's excitement.

Patton couldn't stop the moan that came as she felt his hands sliding around her body. One went to her breast, the other slid down over her abdomen to her mound. Chase feathered soothing kisses along the top of her shoulder as he began to tease the tip of first one and then the other breast. He squeezed, plucking and rolling her pink nipples till she squirmed in his embrace, thrusting her breast forward in silent demand for more.

Patton shivered, anxious and aroused. Though she couldn't see them, she knew that Slade and Devin watched as Chase put her body on display for their pleasure. This new game sent dark tendrils of erotic fear twining over her escalating lust, spicing it with a rich texture that intensified even the small sensation.

When his second hand moved, slipping into her wet folds to toy with her clit, Patton cried out, bucking into his hand as bolts of pure energy shot through her.

"You're so wet, so hot and slick with desire." Chase murmured roughly against her neck. "Widen your stance, sweetheart. Let Slade and Devin see everything I'm about to do to you."

Patton whimpered, doing as he commanded. She felt his other hand leave her breast to slide down and join its mate. With the fingers of one hand, he held open her swollen outer lips, allowing his brothers a perfect view as the fingers from his other hand stroked down and around her opening before sliding in.

Slowly he began to thrust into her clenching heat, occasionally allowing a stray finger to rub and flick against her clit. His touch became less teasing and more insistent, devastating her with pleasure.

Patton began to whimper and sob as he drove her to the desperate edge of climax. He stopped, leaving her there and she cried out in denial.

"Play with your breasts, sweetheart," Chase instructed as he bit down on the sensitive spot where her neck met her shoulder. "You know you want to. We can all see how hard your poor little nipples are. They want attention."

As he spoke, he began again with the slow teasing touches between her legs. Patton had no will left to defy him, no mind left to hesitate. Her hands eagerly came up to pleasure herself, to lift her breasts up so that her tongue could lick and her teeth nibble at their pointed tips.

Again and again, he drove her to the razors edge of ecstasy only to stop short. Patton growled, snarling out demands for him to continue. They fell on deaf ears. She could feel his hardened length prodding against her backside and rubbed against it, trying to entice him to remove his clothing and give her what they both wanted, needed.

She thought she'd succeeded when Chase lifted her away from him. The sound of his zipper lowering gave her hope. Then he shoved her onto her knees and Patton realized he had altogether different intentions.

As a perfect repeat of the scene with Devin, Chase's hard, hot cock bumped against her lips, teasing her to take a taste. With Chase, he didn't need to order her to suck him and not to tease him. The hand he buried in her hair assured her silent obedience.

Chase closed his eyes as the blistering heat of her mouth consumed him. The searing caress of her tongue dancing down his length made his jaw clench as he fought to hold back the seed boiling in his balls and threatening an early release.

Not yet. He wanted to enjoy the riches of having the most talented mouth he'd ever experienced suckling on his needy shaft. Through narrowed eyes, he watched as inch by inch his cock stretched her full, pink lips wide.

He slid smoothly into the moist recesses of her mouth until he hit the back of her throat. She swallowed, trying to make more room for his thick cock and squeezed him tighter in the process. Chase groaned, yanking her head back up before the pressure became too much to resist.

They had too many stages left in this game for him to be losing it now. He fought to remember that fact as he set a pace that brought him to the edge of ecstasy in the confines of her suckling mouth. That wasn't what he wanted milking him into release.

Patton's body offered a hotter, tighter treat just waiting for him to fuck and fill. The temptation of that promise gave him the strength to pull out. With rough, hurried motions he turned her, positioning her on all fours.

In less than thirty seconds, he slammed his full length into the sweetest cunt he'd ever had the privilege of fucking. Sinking into her tight, hot depth was rapture, pure white-hot rapture. He didn't last, couldn't. Six strokes later, he crushed her hips in his grip as he held her as tightly to him as humanly possible.

* * * *

Devin scowled. That had been short. He'd been expecting a much better show. It had been good, for the moment it had lasted. Her skin all flushed with her excitement, mouth wide issuing those sexy little moans and grunts that would drive any red-blooded man into heat, and the sight of her full breasts bouncing with each hard thrust as Chase embedded himself deep into her...

Devin's hand curled around his own throbbing erection. Soon, really soon it would be his turn to mount her and ride her to completion. Much more of that sight and he'd have found his release before his jeans came off. So perhaps it was a good thing Chase was a short stroker this evening. Patton obviously disagreed.

"No! You bastard!"

She screamed, her hands immediately reaching for her blindfold. Slade was on her in a second, locking both her wrists into one hand. He pulled her arms out from under her and she fell flat onto the floor. That didn't deter her from fighting.

Devin quickly prepared the coffee table as she thrashed about, hurling obscenities and threats at all three brothers. She might be small, but she was in a full, unrestrained rage now and it took both Slade and him to move her from the floor to the table.

Devin held her down as Slade tied each arm and leg to a different post. Only when they had her securely bound did Devin ease his weight off her stomach. She still hadn't settled down and fought the binds with all her energy, but they held.

Nothing, though, gagged the curses she slung at her unseen capturers. It would have given Devin pause, but she didn't scream for freedom. She demanded to be fucked and she wanted it now.

That wouldn't happen now. Patton seemed to realize that the moment Slade tickled her neck with the end of the flogger. Abruptly she fell silent, her body tensing as Slade danced the tips down her body.

Patton swallowed as her entire body tuned into the sensual slide of the bunched suede straps. The light touch almost tickled as it feathered back up over her thighs. It definitely provoked a delightful shower of pleasure when it paused to slap ever so lightly against her spread pussy lips.

The next stop, her breasts. The soft suede almost tickled as it circled first one and then the other tip. The slow motion had the desired effect of brining her excitement back to a boil. It did not however lull her into believing this was all he intended. Even as the gentle touch of the flogger sent shivers rattling across her skin, she tensed, anticipating the next step.

"Do you know why you're being punished?" The flogger slid down toward her cunt and she swallowed hard. Surely, he wouldn't hit her there.

"Patton?" Slade pressed.

"Yes," she managed to squeak out.

"Why?"

"Because…because I…chained you to the chair and tormented you."

"You were not concerned about punishment then, were you?"

"No."

"But you are now."

Patton wanted to lie, to say no. She wanted them to know that no matter what they had not broken her spirit. The flogger lifting off her skin changed her response.

"A little."

"Let's see if we can make that a lot."

Chapter 36

The first lash fell directly across her breasts and Patton let out a deep sigh. That hadn't hurt. Just the opposite. Sparkles of heat and pleasure blossomed out of her breasts, quickly spreading the good feeling through the rest of her body.

The soft, teasing slaps continued across her body and inflaming her desire until she mewled and arched into the blows. She was so wet now she could feel the moisture dribbling down her thighs. She was primed and ready, but frustratingly nowhere near a climax.

With each blow, Slade drove her arousal higher and higher, but maddeningly never near the edge of ecstasy. She needed something more, something harder. The thought echoed through her a moment before pure fire shot out from her tits in a searing rush.

Damn, that hurt! He'd hit her a lot harder that time. Tears stung the back of her eyes as the burn rolled into a wave of scorching pleasure. No sooner had the inferno morphed into pleasure than he struck her again. This time her pussy exploded into a flaming ball of heat. She screamed under the assault, but received no reprieve.

In rapid succession, he cracked the flogger over her body, working from her pussy to her breasts and back again. Gone were the gentle love taps. He struck her with a force that had her whole body feeling the sting.

Each time he hit in a slightly different location until no spot between her shoulder and thighs didn't burn, didn't send out tendrils of pained pleasure. She felt like a confused mass of aching lust, barely realizing when he stopped.

Her body still shook with aftershocks when a set of soft, warm lips settled over her knee and jarred her out of her stupor. The gentle lips kissed their way up her thigh, pausing as his inquisitive tongue snaked out to taste the liquid proof of her desire. Patton flexed slightly, silently asking that the tongue move higher to where she needed a kiss most.

The mouth intentionally skipped over her mound to lick its way across her stomach. Patton didn't object. Like a gentle breeze, the kisses soothed her overheated skin. She moaned softly as a second set of lips joined the first.

Nothing prepared her for the decadent feeling of having two men working their mouths in union across her inflamed flesh. Not knowing who touched her heightened the sense of sensuality to the moment. All too soon, they stopped and Patton murmured a protest.

"We're going to release your wrists now," Devin informed her. "You're to remain still. No trying anything."

"I'll behave."

She'd have promised them anything to speed things up. Surely, they had finished with the punishment phase and planned to move into the fulfillment phase. Patton hoped so. Otherwise she would end up driven completely insane.

Two sets of hands undid the binds around her wrists. As her arms lowered, she groaned. Sharp shards of pain followed in the wake of her blood as it rushed into her limbs. They massaged her from wrist to her shoulders, following their hands with their lips. Patton stretched, enjoying the tender, gentle attention.

Next they freed her ankles, repeating the magical caresses of hands and lips. This time though a hard, naked male body followed in their wake, settling on top of her in a position that promised to lead to more.

Devin could feel the fast pounding of his heart echoed in the throbbing pulse of his cock. As he kissed his way up her body, he had to fight to only teasingly lick at her breasts instead of devouring as his mouth watered to do. Finally, he settled against her, his cock brushing against the moist heat of entrance.

"Devin," she whispered causing his heart to clench as she rubbed against his erection.

"How did you know it was me, sweetheart?" It pleased him inordinately that she had. It made him feel special, loved, but wondering she'd just made a lucky guess.

"I know your scent, your feel." Patton arched her back, forcing her wet heat more firmly against his cock.

His dick jerked, hungry for the feel of her tight little channel squeezing around him, bathing him in the hot wash of her liquid desire. It remembered her feel too and demanded to know it again. Soon, Devin promised himself, real soon.

Until then, he had to be content with a kiss. His tongue plunged into her mouth, stroking into the sweet moist recesses as his body ached to do. Her tongue tangled with his, fighting him for the right of possession. When he tried to pull back, her lips closed around his tongue, sucking it back into her mouth with a strength that left him trembling.

Of its own volition, his cock jerked forward, embedding itself an inch into her. The tight ring of muscles at the opening of her hot little cunt squeezed his head. Devin groaned and pushed, popping the head past the tempting vice and into the snug heat of her passage.

"Please, more," Patton moaned lifting her hips to try and force him deeper into her body.

"Patton," Devin warned. "Remember the rules."

"I'll be still. I just need more. Please, Dev, I just need more," Patton begged, unconcerned about dignity or pride. Those things didn't matter. Not here, not with her men.

Despite her plea, she settled back down onto the table. The last thing she wanted was for them to leave. Devin was already naked and pressed between her legs. She could hear another brother shedding his clothing off to the side. They had to be planning on fucking her. She was so close to having what she needed, but she had to remember the rules.

"You'll get it when I give it to you."

Devin pulled back popping out of her body. Patton didn't have a chance to worry over the loss, even when his warm weight lifted off her.

"What…" Patton started when she felt two large hands lifting her up by the waist.

"Relax, Patton," Slade soothed her.

"I'm going to put you on Devin," Slade explained as he lowered her down on top of his brother. "You're going to take his cock inside of you but you're not to move. If I see you fucking yourself on to his cock, I'm going to lift you off and we'll tie you back up and leave you here. Understand?"

"Yes, Slade."

Without a word, Slade lowered her down over Devin's thick shaft, letting the fullness slide all the way into her aching pussy. The stretch, the slight burn of fullness elicited a sigh from her that was echoed by the man beneath her.

She whimpered softly as Slade pressed her down against Devin's chest with a hand to her back. Inadvertently he pushed her tender breast against Devin's lips. Sizzling heat speared through her as his rough tongue flicked over her nipple before sucking it past the hard scrape of his teeth and into the hot confines of his mouth. Patton moaned as he suckled first one and then the other tip.

Electricity shot out from her breasts, lighting every nerve ending in her spine before exploding in her pussy. She felt herself tighten around his cock. The full feeling intensified and she couldn't stop her hips from rotating, enjoying the electrifying spasms her motions caused.

"Patton." Slade's smack burned across her ass. "You've been warned."

Patton whimpered, stilling at the harsh reminder of what her fate could be. Devin released her breast with an audible pop and pulled her tightly into his chest. She let him tuck her knees along his side.

A moment later he slid his hands down over the cheeks of her ass, spreading them and leaving her no doubt what came next. Fingers of fear trickled like ice cubes down her spine, it had only been that morning when Chase had taken her that way.

Even as the memory made her shiver, the anxiety still lingered. Chase had filled her to the point of pain. What would it be like to take Slade that way when Devin already pushed the limits of pussy?

She didn't have long to wonder. Slade made short work of lubing up her ass with Devin's help. Barely a breath later, the smooth head of his cock brushed against her back entrance.

Patton bit her lower lip, fighting to hold back the grimace of pain as he forced the tender ring of muscles at her entrance wide. For several seconds, she feared he would rip her trying to force himself in. Just when she was sure that he wouldn't succeed, he popped through.

"Take a deep breath for me, Patton."

That did it. Her muscles relaxed for just a moment, letting him slide another inch deeper in before snapping back and tightening around his cock like an angry vise.

"It burns."

"I know, baby. I know." Slade brushed her hair off her shoulder so he could place soothing kisses along her neck. Devin helped, nibbling along her jaw as his hands went to work on her breasts.

"It'll get better, I promise. Now keep taking deep breaths and try to relax."

She tried, but it was hard. She could feel her muscles tightening, instinctively fighting his invasion. The two cocks filling her dueled for space, warring over what little territory her tight channels offered. The internal struggled sent a riot of confusing sensations spreading throughout her.

"I'm in."

Slade's groan came as a welcomed relief. He'd managed to seat himself deep inside without causing her to tear in two. Now as long as neither brother moved, she might survive this new experience.

That thought was forgotten when Slade slid his hand around her waist. He found her piercing and immediately began to tease her back into a state of shivering excitement. He took her straight to the edge of a climax before he began to gently ease out of her body.

Slowly at first, the brothers slid in and out of her in alternating strokes that left her constantly filled and empty. Patton forgot about the pain. The pressure remained underneath the layers of rapture tightening her body to the point of shattering, but instead of diminishing her pleasure the pain only heightened it.

The sharp spikes of pleasure ripped away her humanity, reverting her back to a lust-filled animal intent on finding her fulfillment. She bucked between the two hard male bodies holding her captive, trying to force them to increase their speed, strength their thrusts.

Devin bit her shoulder, thrusting hard upward at the same time Slade buried himself to the hilt inside her tight ass. The brothers moved in union now, riding her hard and rough as they drove her toward release.

"Oh, God," Patton screamed. "Yes! Yes! Harder! Fuck me harder!"

Her cries of pleasure drowned out the slap of sweaty flesh against flesh. Her body ignited in a series of violent fireworks, burning her from the inside out until she thought she'd die from the intense flames. Everything inside of her tightened and she felt both her passageways clamp down, heightening the intense feeling of their cocks pumping into her. Buffeted by waves of ecstasy, she lost track of time and it felt like forever before her body collapsed.

It was too much. As Patton slingshot over the edge of ecstasy, her channels milked the brothers' cocks, forcing them into their own climaxes. Slade's roar echoed Devin's as his balls tightened, firing out their massive loads of cum deep into the sweet depths of Patton's body.

Slade collapsed on top of Patton and Devin groaned under their heavy weight. He didn't know how long they stayed like that, it felt like hours, but surely it had only minutes before his heart rate returned to normal and his brain began to function enough for him to roll to the side.

As he did, his cock slid out, pausing for a second at the resisting muscles of the entrance to Patton's sweet little rosebud. She murmured something that sounded like a complaint as he popped out of her body.

"You all right, sweetheart?" Slade asked as his wits came back to him. Concern sounded in his voice as he began to worry that they'd been too hard, too rough with her.

"Sleep now," Patton mumbled and she appeared to be headed toward just that.

Slade laughed at her comment. His body was exhausted but his mind and heart raced. In all the years, he'd never had such an amazing release or felt so whole and happy afterward.

"It's not time to go sleep, silly," Devin admonished her

Patton groaned as she felt herself being lifted off Devin. Damn men, they kept doing this to her, making her stand when her legs only wanted to fold beneath her. If she had enough energy and hadn't already been completely worn out, she'd have objected.

Chapter 37

Chase looked down at Patton and couldn't have been more pleased. They'd trained a lot of women in their time, but never had he felt such personal satisfaction in having one trust him so completely. He'd never really considered it before.

The women they had worked with over the years had sought him out. While he'd long ago learned to watch a woman for the signs that they pushed her too hard or too fast, he'd never worried about them trusting him. They'd always been free to call a halt to the program and walk away, no questions asked.

Patton didn't have the luxury. Neither did he. That harsh reality had bound him in layers of caution and concern over the years when it came to his interest in her. For the first time in a long time, he finally felt relaxed.

Things would work out. They had pushed her this evening and she'd responded with heated passion. She deserved a reward for pleasing him. That would take more time than he had to give. He still had that damn party they had to make an appearance at.

It did create the perfect window to get in an early evening training session. She'd earned so many punishments from her inability to control her orgasms to the stunt she'd pulled this afternoon. Patton needed discipline. Her reward would have to wait until later tonight. Then he would do something special for her.

Despite the temptation, Chase gathered the strength to resist the siren's call of Patton's nude body. Time to move this party to the next stage before he cracked and threw their schedule into complete chaos. This interlude alone cost them time.

Devin helped hold Patton up as she docilely leaned against him for support. She played the good girl — for now, given a chance she'd chain anyone of them up and torment them in revenge. Nothing they could do to break her inner spirit and for that Devin was thankful.

He liked having a woman at his mercy. It aroused him, but at the same time, blind obedience could easily become boring. For now, though, it excited him as she stood following the gentle command of his hands on her hips. The sight of the red lines across her body where Slade had flogged her did not.

Devin reasoned a responsible master to rub away any discomforts she had. Her skin was so soft. It caressed his hands back as he tenderly cupped her breasts. She arched slightly, offering herself to his petting.

* * * *

Patton felt Chase step up close to her, knew him by his scent. It made her feel so fragile to be pinned between two such large, strong men. Devin had dressed and the rough feel of their clothing against her naked flesh reminded her that she was vulnerable in ways they were not. It sent a thrill through her already satiated body.

"Do you remember what I said about training this morning?" Chase whispered kisses down her neck. His hands slid down her waist, his fingers rubbing against the smooth skin of her mound.

"Training?" Patton barely had the breath to repeat the word.

"You've been coming without permission at every turn, Patton." Devin's thumbs extended out to tease her nipples.

"I know," Patton gasped at the feel of thick, hard fingers sliding back into her pussy. "I'm sorry."

"Sorry isn't the answer, baby." Chase bit down on the tender skin where her neck met her shoulder.

"What do you want me to do?" Patton whined, not knowing which way to move. Her hips wanted to chase the fingers teasing her pussy while her breasts wanted to go in the opposite direction to increase the pressure of Devin's touch on her swollen globes.

"You said you couldn't help it, that you couldn't control your orgasms."

"It's hard, but I'll try."

"We're going to make it easier for you."

"Chase, please."

"What do you want?"

"I want to come."

"And how do you want to come? Would you like to be stroked into it?" He slid his fingers deep into her.

"Perhaps licked instead?" Devin took a quick taste of her nipple.

"Or would you rather be fucked into oblivion?" Chase pressed his hard bulge into her back.

"I don't care," Patton whimpered. "Just do it."

"See that's the other problem. You don't give the orders." Chase stepped back.

Patton shrieked as she felt herself lifted off the ground. Her arms fastened tightly around Devin's neck. She curled into him as she felt him moving through the house. It disoriented her to be carried around naked and blindfolded. Not to mention highly embarrassing not knowing if anybody else caught the show the brothers put on.

"Devin," she gasped when she heard a door close and felt the warmth of the fading sun on her skin.

As she felt him moving down the steps, she tried desperately to turn in his embrace and hide as much of herself as she could against his chest. Arrogant man, he laughed at her obvious embarrassment and tightened his grip to hold her steady.

He had fun at her expense and she couldn't do a damn thing about it. That fact annoyed her, but her annoyance quickly turned by the cool air that suddenly drifted over her skin as the warmth of the sunlight blinked out in an instant.

The barn.

Her stomach tightened with nervousness as she realized that was the only place he could be taking her. The creaking sounds of the old wood door opening to the backroom confirmed her suspicions. Despite what had just transpired in the den, the realization that he had taken her to the training room filled her with erotic fear.

What went on here could not to be dismissed. They meant business this time. A second later he laid her down on the bed. Her fears grew when she felt her hands being lifted, rope wrapped around her wrists.

As nervous as she felt Patton didn't resist as they tied her spread eagle to the small, hard mattress. To do so would bring about more punishment. Besides, everything they'd done to her so far had brought her pleasure beyond her imaginings.

She felt the bed sag and the rough feel of jeans against the inside of her legs. Her breath caught as hope flared that they'd be touching her again soon.

Devin looked at Patton laid out as if in offering before him and had to bite back a groan. She was so beautiful. It went beyond the matter of physical perfection. If that was all that attracted them, they'd be quickly satisfied and just as quickly moving on.

Devin didn't think he'd ever get enough of Patton. More than anything, her personality held him transfixed. With her mix of sweet and spicy, strong but vulnerable, funny and smart, all the contrasts that made up who she was made her the perfect woman for all three of them.

Now here she was nervous but trusting. The sight was a powerful aphrodisiac and he couldn't resist teasing her just a little. He leaned over and ran his tongue along the edges of her pussy. She whimpered, her hips lifting to follow his tongue as it left her body. He rewarded her with another little lick that seemed to go on and on as he quickly became lost in her essence.

Chase smacked him on the shoulder in an unsubtle reminder that now was not the time. Devin growled but sat up. He clenched his jaw, fighting the urge to return to the delectable heaven between Patton's thighs as she writhed and panted before him.

Taking the vibrating egg from Chase, he reached down to insert it into her cunt. The little toy slid easily into her thanks to all the liquid leaking out of her body. After making sure the egg was placed securely into her channel, Devin gave her a little suckling kiss on her clit before withdrawing from the bed. With one last look at his beauty, he turned and left.

* * * *

"Chase?" The panic in Patton's voice was obvious as the door shut behind Devin.

"How did you know it was me who was still here?" Chase sat down next to her on the bed.

"I just knew," Patton whispered, not realizing how much her words pleased him. "Why did Devin leave?"

"Does it make you nervous to be alone with me?" Chase leaned down to feather kisses across her cheeks.

"No," Patton sighed, soothed by his kisses. "I'm just confused. What are you going to do?"

"You'll see." Chase kissed her tenderly on the lips. "You trust me, Patton?"

"You know I do."

"Then trust that you'll be safe here."

"You're going to leave me." The sadness in that statement made Chase's heart clenched.

He wanted to say never, but he couldn't stay and watch her desire build and do nothing about it. Patton needed to learn this lesson on her own. "Just for a while."

"You're going to go to the party at the lodge and leave me here, aren't you?"

Chase grimaced. She already knew about that. He wanted to assure her that she had nothing to worry about. She didn't. He would never stray, never desire another woman the way he did Patton.

He couldn't bring himself to give her the words though. Some part of him worried that it would give her all the power. Patton empowered was a dangerous Patton and too many issues still existed between them for him to risk a show weakness.

"Chase?"

"Shhh, baby." Chase stroked her cheek, touched when she turned toward the sooth caress. "You have nothing to worry about. Everything is going to be all right. You'll be safe here and very soon back in my arms."

With a final kiss, he reached down to pull the blanket up over her. He flicked the on button on the little remote he had. Patton's response was instantaneous. With a muffled shriek, her body jerked.

Chase watched her tremble and writhe with the pleasure the toy gave her. When he knew she was lost in the sensation, he silently retreated from the room. Devin waited outside. He made no comment as Chase locked the door from the outside.

Rarely did anybody go into the barn without permission, but that didn't make it completely unheard of. If one of the guys from the club stopped by to grab an instrument or two and nobody was around, they'd just leave a note. Chase wouldn't take the chance of anybody walking in on Patton.

"How long are we going to leave her in there?" Devin fell into step with Chase as he emerged from the barn.

"No more than two hours." Chase flicked the button on the remote back to off. "Slade and I should be back from the party by hen."

"You don't think this is kind of like jumping into the deep end?" Devin glanced back at the barn. "Leaving her alone all tied up I mean?"

"What would you rather do? Pansy around at first and then shock her into heart failure later?" Chase paused at the bottom of the porch steps. "Besides she's handled everything else well."

"Yeah, I guess." Devin frowned as he looked back over at the barn. "I just hate to think of her worrying."

"She's not going to be worrying. She's going to be too busy learning not to climax." Chase handed him the remote. "Here, keep an eye on the barn. Slade and I have to get moving so we can get back sooner rather than later."

* * * *

Devin checked his watch before looking back down at the row of numbers on the laptop. With a groan, he rubbed his eyes, trying to fight off the headache he could feel coming on. It had been an hour and a half, but it felt like twice that time.

It always felt like that when Chase forced him to work on anything technical. He could deal with most of the paperwork, but when it came to the computer, they made his head swim, his eyes go dry, and his body beg for release from the tension gripping it.

That was probably why Chase had asked him to update the website. He was being punished for some former misdeed, or perhaps for some future one. Just like Patton. Devin looked over at the remote and hit the switch again before checking his watch.

Twenty-eight minutes before he went to her rescue. By then, she would be primed and ready to work off all the stiffness right out of his muscles. Devin smiled at that though as a new body part hardened with anticipation. Hopefully, Slade and Chase would be late getting home and he'd get some precious alone time with Patton.

He greeted the sound of the phone ringing in the background with unusual enthusiasm, any excuse to get away from the laptop. Dropping the small machine in the rocking chair beside him, he hit the remote switch a second time. With a quick glance around the empty yard, he went to answer the phone.

* * * *

Patton couldn't tell how long she'd been tied up. Time became defined only by pleasure or the absence of it. Again and again, that little egg vibrated her to the edge of orgasm. Every time she though she could take no more, the toy would stop, leaving her panting with need.

This was true punishment. Compared to the other times they'd disciplined her, this was a hundred times worse. Tears of frustration seeped from her eyes as the pleasure became so painful it threatened to rip her body apart at any moment.

After a while, she'd fought her binds, desperate to get free and end this torture. It had been pointless. She didn't have the strength to carry on with her struggles when the egg again lit up her cunt with spasms that echoed through out her body. All too soon, it stopped and she was left on the brink.

As the pattern repeated itself, Patton began to learn how to breathe through the pleasure, learning by degrees how to stave off the more extreme sensation. What hours ago she had thought impossible, she finally began to learn to do. She could not deny the pleasure, but she did begin to learn how to control it.

Just when she knew she could stand it no more, that no amount of breathing would help her last another attack if the egg should start to vibrate, she heard a sound along the barn wall. A thumping noise that echoed in the stillness. She couldn't tell if it had come from inside or outside, but it sent shivers of fear through her.

"Wh…who's there?" Patton stuttered, promising that if it was one of the brothers she would get him for scaring her so bad.

Nobody answered as the noise continued for a few more seconds. It sounded like something hitting against the wall at erratic intervals.

Patton held her breath, waiting for another clue as to the person's intentions. The silence that thickened the air became so oppressive Patton once again spoke, attempting to break the fear that became the source of her beating heart.

"Chase...Slade...Devin, are any of you there?"

No response came through the darkness. No shuffling sound of footsteps, whisper of clothing or the slightest sigh of a breath. Patton swallowed, telling herself it had been nothing. Perhaps a bird had flown into the outer wall or maybe a pinecone had fallen against it.

Whatever, nobody was here. She was still alone and nothing bad would to happen. Chase had asked her to trust him. He'd promised her she would be safe. This was probably just another test. That's all it was.

Patton repeated that idea to herself as she took deep, even breaths. Her muscles began to ache from the tension gripping her body and she forced herself to slowly relax. It worked until a new sound came.

A strange crackling noise whispered through the night noise. She strained to hear it, trying to identify where she had heard the familiar noise. When the smell of smoke and burning wood wafted over her recognition hit.

Fire.

"Chase! Slade! Devin!" Patton screamed as she began to fight her binds with energy renewed by adrenaline.

Chapter 38

"That sounds like a lot of fun." Devin pinned the cordless phone between his ear and his shoulder as he listened to Bryant. With his hands free, he ripped into the bag of peanut M&M's he'd found stashed in Chase's desk.

"Yeah? I didn't realize Jerry knew how to fish. I thought he went out on the water to drink without Shelia nagging him." Devin snickered as he propped his feet up on the coffee table.

He sprawled out on the couch, watching the driveway through the front windows. He'd thought he'd heard the sound of an engine a minute ago, but when he'd come into the living room to check, nobody was there.

Anybody who approached the house would have to come up the drive. He could watch the front just as easy as he could the back to make sure nobody accidentally walked in on Patton. Talking to Bryant beat the hell out of working on the website.

"Three feet, yeah right. Try more like three inches. You can't believe anything that boy says when it comes to fish." Devin snorted before chugging back a handful of the chocolate candies.

"Oh, yeah, yeah. I remember her. Blonde, big boobs, with that lizard tattoo." Devin nodded instinctively, almost dropping the phone as he poured out another handful of M&M's. Devin tossed one of the M&M's into the air, trying to catch it with his open mouth as Bryant invited him to a little festivity with the blonde on Jerry's boat.

"Ah, no, man. I'm off the market." Devin tried again unsuccessfully to catch another M&M.

"Nah, it's a permanent condition." He gave up attempting the trick that only Slade had ever pulled off and shoved the rest of the little round chocolates into his mouth before they melted in his hand.

"Yeah, well, Chase and Slade are in my boat on this one. You're going to have to count us all out."

His nose tickled and he rubbed it as he listened to Bryant come close to whining. Bryant was an old high school friend who had moved out toward Pensacola. Whenever he came to town the guys treated him to a night at the lodge.

"I don't know man. Whatever happens with the club, happens."

Devin's hand froze as he poured out another mouthful of candy. He sniffed the air, smelling an odd odor.

"It isn't a shame, Bryant. It's good news," Devin corrected as his feet came off the table.

"Hold on a second. I think I smell smoke…no, I'm not trying to cook anything," Devin retorted in exasperation. The smell smoke grew alarmingly strong as he moved toward the kitchen.

"Oh, shit."

Devin dropped the phone as he his eyes focused on the barn outside the window. Massive flames licked over the structure, devouring the dry wood with menacing speed. He stood paralyzed, his mind trying to compute what his eyes saw

Patton!

* * * *

Chase fought down the tremors of fear still racing through his body as he stared at the smoldering debris. His hands clenched into fists as he struggled to contain the violent emotions fighting to take control of him. Rage, fear, anguish, they all fed off the pool of helplessness calcifying his stomach.

"The barn is on fire."

With those simple words from Devin, everything inside Chase had frozen. His heart had seized painfully, stopping all blood flow through Chase's body, leaving him lightheaded with a ringing in his ears as his mind struggled to put the pieces together. His thoughts had shattered around one word. Patton.

He couldn't lose her.

"Chase. Chase! Are you listening to me?" Devin yelled into the cell phone, but Chase had already dropped the damn thing. His brain no longer in controlled his body. Instinct had taken over, driving him toward the woman that was the essence of his very soul.

"I hear you." Slade had snatched up the phone as he rushed to keep up with Chase. He barely made it out of the club and into the bed of the truck before Chase kicked up a wave of dirt and dust as he tore off down through the field, taking a short cut straight through the plains to get home.

"Patton is all right. Tell him that."

"Um," Slade glanced through the back window, doubting Chase would hear anything he tried to tell him. "It's little late for that. Why don't you tell me what is going on?"

"The barn caught fire."

"Shit." Slade hadn't fared much better with that news than Chase had, but knowing that Patton was fine went a long way to helping him keep his sanity. "How the hell did that happen?"

"I don't know."

"What do you mean you don't know?"

"I went in the house to get the phone and the next thing I knew the building went up in flames."

"With Patton in it?" Slade gripped the phone so hard that it amazed him the plastic casing didn't crack.

"I got her out." Something about Devin's answer didn't fully reassure Slade.

"But she is all right?"

"She's fine."

"Define fine."

"Some smoke inhalation…"

"And?"

"A few small burns."

"She was burned?"

Devin rushed to reassure him. "It's not serious."

"Not serious. How not serious is it?"

Whatever Devin's response, it had been lost when Chase had slammed on the brakes, sending Slade crashing into the bottom of the truck bed and sliding across the liner. The phone had been knocked out of his hand and clattered across the hard plastic.

Slade hadn't bothered to reach for the thing. Devin already rushed down the porch steps and yelling for Chase who had bounded out of the truck and went running through the maze of fire trucks and first responder vehicles for the barn.

Chase had almost plowed over Devin who had thrown himself into his older brother's path. He had still been lost in the sea of agonized focus when Devin had grabbed him and forcibly turned him toward the house.

"She's in there."

With those three words, Chase's hearing had finally snapped back into focus. The reality of the situation began to solidify around him. If he had been capable of rational thought, he might have wondered how he had gotten there. Everything between the word fire and that moment had been lost in overwhelming fear that had gripped him.

Without a word to Devin, he had changed directions. While the world around him began to drip back into cohesive scenes, nothing would penetrate the final layer of his fear until he saw Patton with his own eyes.

Devin nipped at his heels, talking rapid fire. Chase still didn't comprehend any of the words Devin said. He bounded up the steps, rushed across the porch and came to a stop so sudden Devin crashed into his back.

There she sat on the couch. His eyes traveled over her, assuring himself that she was alive. She was and for the first time in five minutes, his heart beat. In that second, fear had transformed to rage.

She looked pale, the loss of color accentuated by the blacken smudges of soot stretching ominously over the edges of her body. The two large white bandages wrapped around her right arm stuck out like red beacons to the bull raging inside him.

Instantly he was beside her, growling at the paramedic who got in his way. He knew that the man only tried to do his job, but the sight of his love looking so frail and sickly overwhelmed any consideration for the others in the room.

Her face was mostly obscured by an oxygen mask and she pushed it out of the way probably to assure him that she was all right. He didn't give her a chance to speak before he shoved the mask back down. If the paramedics had put it on her, then they had done so for a reason.

"How is she?" he barked that demand at Jimmy Mathews, the paramedic he'd almost trampled. Chase put his arm around Patton and all but dragged her into his lap.

"She'll be fine, Chase," Jimmy quickly assured him. "It just a little smoke inhalation and a few minor burns."

"What are minor burns?"

Patton tried to answer, but the mask muffled her words. Not that Chase listened to her anyway. He knew Patton well enough to know that she would downplay her injuries. He wanted to hear it from Jimmy.

"Second degree, but they're small burns," Jimmy hastened to add when Chase tensed.

"They're big bandages," Chase shot back. "Are you going to take her to the hospital?"

Now it was Jimmy who tensed and Patton who began to squirm in Chase's lap. She tried to shove the mask off again, but he held it in place. He knew her answer to that question. It was always the same with her. Patton hated the hospital.

"Jimmy?" Slade pressed.

"I advised it. We could clean her burns better. They tend to leak a lot, so it would be nice to give her some fluids. Plus we could monitor her lungs, though I don't think she inhaled too much smoke."

"So what the hell are you waiting for?" Chase demanded.

"She signed the papers saying she didn't want to go."

"Fuck that."

Chase stood, lifting Patton straight into his arms. Her mask got pulled off by the motion and she was finally able to speak. Not that Chase listened to her. All he could hear was the hoarse sound of her tone and the slight wheezing of her breath.

He carried her straight out to the ambulance and climbed into to dump her unceremoniously onto the stretcher. Immediately she began to try to get up, her hands clinging tightly to the blanket somebody, probably Devin, had wrapped around her. The faded brown throw was the only thing she wore and she struggled to sit without revealing anything to the men trailing in Chase's wake.

Chase didn't intend on wasting time fighting with her. He stilled her motions with the grim warning that he would chain her to the bed if she didn't settle down. He had seen the annoyance in her eyes as she obeyed him and knew she was not happy with his highhanded tactics.

Chase didn't care. She could be as annoyed as she wanted. Nothing would stop her from getting the medical attention she needed. He had wanted to be there to make sure that had happened, but somebody needed to stay and handle the firemen.

He had sent Devin in his stead. He'd received a burn as well and would benefit from the trip to the hospital. Not that Chase was as concerned about Devin's injuries. Then again, his brother hadn't been wheezing when he breathed and his color looked a hell of a lot better.

"Chase." Danny Ritter stepped up alongside him bringing him back to the present.

"Danny." Chase nodded his head to the large, sweaty fireman.

"Hey, man. Sorry about your barn." Danny tucked his helmet under his arm and looked around at the wreckage. "It was a historical spot in this town. The men at the club will be sad to hear it's gone."

"It's just a barn."

"Yeah." But Danny still sounded forlorn. "I guess you can always rebuild."

Chase didn't respond to that. What would be the point in rebuilding? They had no use for the barn anymore. There were no women left to train except one. If they needed a special room for Patton, they'd build one for her, but it would be her room. She deserved that kind of consideration.

"So, how's your brother doing?" Danny inquired.

"He went to the hospital with Patton."

"Patton?" Danny turned startled eyes on him. "Don't tell me she's the woman Devin pulled out of there?"

"What of it?" Chase demanded, feeling his neck hairs stand up at the shock in Danny tone.

"Nothing." Danny held a hand up. "I just thought…well, that the woman was…you know…in the training room."

Chase didn't respond to that. Danny knew Patton as his sister, not his lover. When she became his wife in the near future, Chase knew it would shock a lot of people in town. They'd get over it or they could go to hell, as far as Chase was concerned. After all, Patton wasn't his sister.

"Chase." Billy Glover strutted up, his face set in hard lines. "I gotta talk to you."

"What's up?"

"Chase." Before Billy could respond, Slade came jogging up. "Charlotte's gone."

"So?"

"So, she said she didn't wan to come to the party. She'd rather just leave and head back home. I told her I'd give her a lift to the bus station in the morning. I went to check on her, she and her stuff was gone and so is the blue Ford."

"Ah, shit." Billy scrubbed an aggravated hand over his face before Chase could respond to Slade.

"What's up, Billy?" Chase narrowed his eyes on the haggard looking man.

"The fire was intentionally set."

"What?" Slade stared at him as if he had just announced he was an alien.

"We'll have to investigate more thoroughly, but the fire appears to have been set along the back wall of the barn using an accelerant of some kind."

"An accelerant?"

"Probably gas." Billy scratched his neck. "It's the most common and readily available thing to use, but, like I said, we gotta investigate the matter before we can give any firm conclusions."

"Who the hell would want to burn down your barn?" Danny scowled. "You piss anybody off lately?"

"Anybody around at the time?" Billy asked at the same time.

Chase cut a hard look at Slade. The place had been cleared out during the evening as the hands made their way to the party. Only people around were Devin, Patton and Charlotte. Only one of those three had a reason to be mad, a reason for setting the building on fire with Patton in it and only one had gone missing.

Without a word, Chase turned on his heel and stormed toward the main house.

"Hey, Chase," Billy hollered. "Where you going?"

"I gotta make some calls."

The first person he'd intended to call, the sheriff. He wanted his truck found and, more importantly, he wanted Charlotte found.

Chapter 39

Patton sighed and rested her cheek on her crossed arms. The morning had already started to warm, promising a hotter afternoon. The guys had already started to sweat, some had taken their shirts off to alleviate the heat. Later they'd douse themselves with water.

Some would dunk their heads in buckets, others would wrap soaked shirts or bandanas under their hats, all in an attempt to stay cool. A well known fact to those who had to work under the sauna of the sun, keeping your head cool kept your body cool, somewhat.

They might do it for practical reasons, but the effect would be spectacular. Water droplets would glisten in the sun, twinkling as they dripped down over well muscled pecs, dribbling between the hard ridges of ripped abs, drawing a woman's eyes right down to leather belts and denim waistbands.

Now that was a happy trail and no man's body offered a better path than hers. They were out there, somewhere in the mix of cowboys moving a herd into the feed yard, but with so much hardened, tanned flesh moving about the place she couldn't keep track of them.

Patton didn't even try. She might love Chase, Slade and Devin, but that didn't mean she didn't have eyes or a great appreciation for the male form. The smile pulling across her lips faded as she realized this sort of behavior was a punishable offense.

That is it would be that is if her men were still into that kind of thing. It had been three long weeks since the fire. Three weeks of nothing but sweet, tender attention. Not once had any of her men touched her with anything but a gentle hand.

No more arrogant demands. No more warped rules that she had any hope of not breaking. No more sex in the kitchen, the study or even the shower. No more being tied up, blindfolded or flogged. No more toys. No more punishments. Just plain vanilla sex all the way.

The only thing kinky left going on in her new bedroom was the fact that she had three hunks revolving out of it. The situation was getting on her last nerve. Her men treated her like she was a porcelain doll that would shatter if they didn't treat her delicately.

Patton wasn't some dainty flower. She had needs, perverse, dark, erotic needs they had awakened in her and now ignored. It was cruel and inhumane. At least, she got laid, Patton consoled herself.

They were still capable of sex. Not so capable of standing up to her. Before her very eyes all three brothers had wilted into pansies. The worse had to have been when Chase discovered what she'd done to her old bedroom. Patton had revealed her masterpiece confident it would spark him back into his old routine. It hadn't worked.

Chase had looked at her new workspace and just nodded before walking away. That was when Patton realized how dire the situation had gotten. She had seen it then in his eyes. Chase hadn't just acted defeated, he was.

That wouldn't do. Patton wanted to get things her way, yes, but she didn't want to change Chase. She loved him for being the macho, sexist jerk he'd always been. She loved knowing he'd always push back. It made it more exciting to try and scheme around him, knowing that when she got caught, she'd be in trouble. He had made her strong, smarter, tougher, because he had always been those things. Not anymore.

Patton sighed and pushed off the fence. The sad, sick truth was she liked being in trouble. Especially when it resulted in her naked and begging, Patton shivered even in the heat of memories of the last time she'd gotten into trouble replayed through her mind.

Then the fire had ruined everything. Patton had healed for the most part. The spots where she had been burned were still marred by tender new skin. Those were her only scars. She didn't have nightmares or anything like that. It had happened and she had survived, end of story.

Well, for her, not for the brothers. They were obsessing over the fire. It was the only time Chase's temper showed itself. He'd exploded all over the sheriff when he'd come out to tell them they'd tracked the old truck to the bus station and had followed up to find that Charlotte had an air-tight alibi. She'd been on a bus home to Louisiana when the fire took place and had witnesses to prove it.

Chase had gone on a mini-rampage after that. Patton understood, he wanted to protect her, but not knowing who to protect her from drove him insane. He'd settled on protecting her from the whole world and had issued his only king like edict since the fire. Patton could not leave the ranch without a proper escort.

That hadn't been worth fighting over, but it had given Patton hope that hidden within the beast still lived in the man. All she had to do was figure out a way of antagonizing it back to the surface.

Patton thought she might have figured out the answer. All she had to do was set the stage. Soon enough her men would come in for lunch and if everything went well, they'd stay home the rest of the day, teaching her a well earned lesson.

* * * *

Chase stomped into the kitchen with Slade and Devin on his heels. It used to be that lunch meant very little. A quick bite, normally a sandwich and a glass of sweet tea, and back to work in under thirty minutes. They'd almost never actually come in the house for lunch, but used to eat with the hands.

Sitting around joking and relaxing, that was what lunch had always been about until Patton had moved back in. Now like robots when break hit, they came looking for her, just to make sure she was safe and happy.

The latter she hadn't appeared to be much of over the last week and it worried him. Was she already regretting her decision? Chase didn't know how he'd survive if that were the answer. It couldn't happen. He'd do anything to make her happy.

He'd tried, really tried over the past few weeks to live up to that. They'd called a halt to all the games they enjoyed, bending their desires to match what a woman like Patton deserved. It had to be done.

They'd broken the line of trust that needed to exist between master and slave. They'd left her alone. After promising Patton she'd be safe, he'd left the ranch to go to some damned party and what had happened? She'd almost died.

Chase's jaw clenched as that day replayed in fast forward mode through his mind. He'd lied to her. She hadn't been safe and he hadn't been there to save her. He did not deserve the title of master and would not force Patton to recognize it.

All he could hope was that in time she would forgive him. Not that Patton had said anything, but every time he looked at the ugly pink skin of her still healing flesh, he felt the condemnation coming down on him. It ate at his soul like acid did at a metal barrel.

He'd never be able to make it up to her, but he would try. He would become the man of her dreams, warm, considerate, tolerant, anything, no matter how it hurt. It did hurt.

Over the past week she'd really been pushing him, becoming disagreeable and almost a downright brat. Too many times to count he'd been left flexing his hands in an attempt to chase away the ache in them to smack that ass until it was red and ready to be fucked.

The worst had come when he'd seen what she'd done to her old room, he'd wanted to charge in and rip it all down. He wanted to roar at her and tell her no woman of his was going to prance around in her underwear in front of a photographer while some male model drooled over her. No, not his woman.

He'd seen the whole catalog. The thing was borderline pornographic, barely a step above. Patton was better than making little lacy things that were designed to send men into a heat that them ripping off the barely there underwear.

She shouldn't even be working. He made more than enough to keep her happy and comfortable. What did it say about him as a man that his woman worked? It told the whole world he wasn't enough. His woman needed more than he could give her.

It scared him and enraged him, but when he'd looked into her eyes and seen the happiness shining back at him, Chase would have suffered through hell than destroy that. Without a word, not trusting what would come out of his mouth, Chase had backed out of the room and fled.

Yes, he, Chase Davis, had turned tail and run from a woman. Chase sighed and shook the water from his hands before stepping away to give the sink to one of his brothers. Toeing off his boots, he looked around, but didn't see Patton.

Odd. She normally appeared in a matter of minutes when they came in for lunch. Chase called her name as he moved out of the kitchen. When he got no response, his heart seized. She should have been safe here.

Chase stormed up the stairs roaring her name, but no response came. The bedrooms where empty, the bathrooms silent. As Chase came pounding back down the steps, Slade came into the hall.

"What's going on?"

"Patton. I can't find her." Chase pushed in the door to the study, the first in the hall, and came to a sudden stop. "Damnit, Patton! Why didn't you answer my call?"

Patton looked up from the stack of papers she held in her hands and glared at him over the edge. "What am I, some kind of dog that harkens to your command?"

Chase clenched his jaw at the sharpness of her tone. Oh, but she tempted him. "No, of course not," he ground out. "I just like an answer when I—"

"When you ask a question? I like them too, but sometimes we just have to find our own answers because nobody will tell us what the hell is really going on."

Something in her tone brought him up short. He finally took in the whole image of Patton sitting behind his desk. Papers were littered everywhere. The printer behind her whined away, churning out more pages. From the angle of the monitor he could see that she had the computer on.

"What are you doing?"

"Getting my answers."

Chase closed his eyes, took a deep breath and counted to ten, then to twenty. It didn't help. "Answers to what, Patton."

"I've been asking you for the past I don't know how many weeks about this little club you have going on and nothing. So I went looking on my own."

"Excuse me?"

"You should ask more than that of me. Shame on you, Chase. You have married men in this damn thing." Patton waved the papers at him and it dawned on Chase just what they were.

"You looked at the membership files?" *Oh, shit.*

"Oh, I looked all right. I looked at everything. You have yourself a very profitable little prostitution ring going on, don't you?"

"It is not a prostitution ring," Chase bit out.

"Men pay to have sex with women, what do you call that?"

"The women pay, too." It took all his will power not to storm across the room and give Patton what her actions so grossly called for. The punishment of a lifetime. "It's perfectly legal."

"Of course it is. Who is going to say otherwise when you have more than half the police department, both judges and the damn mayor as members. I'm sure the feds would love to find out about this."

"It is a sex club, there is a difference."

"I can see it on the national news already. Kinky sex in lower Alabama. The Cattleman's Club, wanna play? The anchors are going to have a hard time keeping a straight face when they report this one."

"Nobody is going to report anything. All the legal documents are in order. Everything this above board."

"I swear I would have thought about this twice if I had known I was going to be marrying a pimp."

"I am not a pimp!"

"Damned denim clad mobsters," Patton was mumbling to herself now, but Chase heard every word. He could feel the heat flushing his body as his muscles started to shake. "You're going to drag my business down with yours. It will never survive this scandal. My reputation will be ruined. No respectable woman will buy one of my outfits. I'll end up making outfits for damn porno stars the rest of my life."

"We're not going to take you anywhere," Chase snapped. "Nothing bad is going to happen."

"What do you think the media is going to do with this?" Patton picked up a new stack of papers to wave at him. "I got your charter right here. Let's see, you have three types of memberships for men.

"Apprentice woman whipper, oh, excuse me, I mean associate member. They have to prove that they can put a woman in her place before they rank enough to be a regular member. When they reach that esteemed status they get their own women to turn into lap dogs for all their perverted desires."

"Patton." Chase felt himself take a step forward. This was the worst. He hadn't ever wanted her to find out the details of the club.

"Oh, no, the Master is mad," Patton cried in an overly theatrical tone. "That is your title. The one you earned at the club after demonstrating publicly on one of your little pets your mastery of…let's see." Patton's finger moved down the page as she began to read aloud, "Binding, utilizing at least three different tying techniques. Flogging, demonstrating a skill at bringing a woman to no less than five orgasms using no less than three different forms of whipping equipment."

She looked up and pinned him with a hard look. "Special points allotted for attaining your pets orgasm using less than seven hits to the pussy. Classy, Chase, very upper crust. Then there are the toys, dildos, butt plugs, nipple clamps…clit clamps."

Patton looked up again. "I guess I know where you got your skill with my piercing, don't I?"

"Patton—"

"I'm not done. Let's see, there is the harness—"

"I know what is in the damn charter! I wrote the fucking thing." The minute the words were out of his mouth, Chase knew he'd snapped and gone too far.

"Oh, you did, did you?" The look she gave him chilled Chase to the bone. "So you're the one who came up with the two possible memberships a woman was forced into choosing from, plaything and slave. Oh, excuse me, did I say choose?"

"It's not like it sounds. Those women are willing. Nobody forces them into the club."

Patton stared at him for a moment before turning her attention back to the charter. "Let's see here, the duties of a master. An associate member must have a master present at all times during any training session with a slave. Associate members are not eligible to train a plaything, but may assist a master in his training.

"Masters are to conduct random audits of all regular members sessions with their playthings and/or slaves to assure the females are enjoying their experiences. This can and will include the masters participating in both training and intercourse with the regular member's plaything and/or slaves."

"Patton—"

"Oh, no wait. This is my favorite part. All playthings must past the appropriate test conducted only by a master in order to earn the ranking of slave." Patton slammed the papers down onto the table.

"It is not what you think."

"It is exactly what I think." Patton shot out of the chair. "You think I wouldn't want to know that the man I'm going to be marrying is going around fucking a bunch of doe eyed whores!"

"Stop it," Chase yelled back. "We're not—"

"That's right." Patton marched around the desk, that finger Chase loathed pointed right at him. "It stops now. The club is closed. No more, Chase. I wouldn't tolerate it."

Chase flexed his jaw. It irritated every single part of his being to be talked to that way, by his woman no less. Not that he'd planned to continue his duties as a master. Ah, what the hell did it matter then? He didn't need the club. He had Patton. If this was what she wanted, needed from him, then he'd do it. For her. Despite the fact that it about killed him inside.

"Fine," he managed to get the word out. "We'll close the club."

"Good." Patton smiled. She gave him a quick kiss on his cheek, apparently ignoring the muscle he could feel ticking in it. "I'll go make lunch."

She all but danced past him and down the hall. At least he had made her happy. He certainly hadn't made Slade that.

Chapter 40

"Have you completely lost your mind?" Slade couldn't believe what he'd just seen, heard. It was all too much. He grabbed Chase by the arm, forcing his brother back into the study when he turned to walk away.

Chase shook him off, but not before Slade got him clear of the door. He heard it slam behind him, knew that Devin had done it. At least he had one brother on his side. Too bad it wasn't the one he needed right now.

"Well?"

"What?" Chase crossed his arms over his chest and glared back at Slade. He could read the signs. He'd lived in this house long enough to know when Chase was spoiling for a fight. His older brother might be mad at Patton, but he'd have no qualms about taking out his anger on Slade. That was fine by Slade. This issue was worth fighting for.

"You can't shut down the club."

"Why not? We don't need it anymore."

"Maybe not for that, but losing the money it generates will make a difference."

"So? It's just money. Besides," Chase's cheek ticked, "Patton has her own business that will bring in money."

"Oh, my God," Devin whispered. "He didn't really just say that."

"Yes, I did. Whatever makes her happy."

"What about the town?" Devin shot back.

"What about it?"

"Come on, Chase. That club generates a lot of money for this town. It's the only tourist attraction we got."

Chase shrugged. "I can't be responsible for a whole town. I don't really care about the town as long as Patton is happy."

"You think she's happy?"

"She was smiling, wasn't she?"

"Ahhh," Slade yelled. He had to relieve his tension somehow before he put his fist through he wall. "God, you can be so damn dense sometimes."

"Don't push me." Chase took a threatening step forward. "You might not make it out of this room alive."

"Patton is not happy, Chase."

"Why the hell not? She got what she wanted. I said I'd close the club just like she asked."

"That's not what she wanted."

"It's what she said she wanted."

"She lied."

"Why would she lie?"

"Don't you see, Chase? She intentionally pushed all of your buttons. She baited you into responding and you didn't."

"Are you saying she tried to piss me off? That is what she wanted?"

"Yeah, I think it is."

"Why?"

"I don't know." Slade honestly didn't. "But I'm going to find out."

He heard Chase and Devin follow him out of the room. When he got to the entryway to the kitchen, he put up his hand, signaling them to wait in the hall. This would go better with him alone.

Patton stood at the counter, shredding carrots with vicious motions that didn't express joy. Just the opposite. Her lips were pursed, her face drawn and from the way her head shifted in tight, little jerks, Slade guessed she was silently ranting to herself about something. He wanted to know what.

"Hey, baby." Slade slouched against the doorway, going for a relaxed pose. Patton's head snapped up. A second later a big, fake smile spread across her face. For barely a moment, he'd gotten a glimpse at the rage in her. No, Patton wasn't happy. She had not gotten what she wanted out of Chase.

"Hey, Slade," she responded in an overly cheery tone. "Lunch will just be a few minutes."

"Hmm," Slade let the sound rumble out of his chest as he pushed off the jam. Patton went back to work, ignoring him as he ambled toward the island. He straddled a stool, letting his chin come to rest in his palm as he studied her.

"Congratulations."

"Pardon me?" Patton cast him a quick look over her shoulder.

"You played Chase perfectly and got exactly what you wanted.

"Did I?"

"Oh, come on Patton. It's just you and me now. You can admit it. That scene in the study was nothing more than a well staged act."

"I am truly appalled at what you are suggesting." She didn't sound insulted, didn't even look up.

"I know, Patton."

"Really?" There was a touch of sarcasm in her tone now. "What do you know Slade?"

"I know Chase keeps all his passwords on a post-it note and he always keeps that under his journal, on top of the ledge where it wasn't the other day."

He bluffed, but it worked. Patton's hands stilled and he could well imagine she was trying to remember exactly where the post-it had been and where she'd put it back. Slade didn't give her time to think and discover his lie. Instead he pushed, using what little leverage he'd gained.

"You'd already checked everything out before this morning."

"You can't prove that."

"You stopped asking questions about the club five days ago."

"So?"

"So why ask a question when you already know the answer?"

"I don't know. You do it all the time."

"You don't. You pester and nag until you know what you want to know."

"What is your point, Slade?"

"You don't get over being pissed quickly either."

"So now you're a shrink. Okay, Dr. Slade, what do you want to know?"

"I want to know what the point of that act was?"

"I wanted the club closed and I expected more resistance from Chase, so I stacked the deck in my favor and ambushed him. Happy?"

"You're lying."

"Now a mind reader."

"You're not happy Patton. You didn't get what you wanted. Your plan failed."

"Damnit, Slade!" The shredder smacked onto the counter as Patton turned on him. "What in the hell do you want?"

"Just tell me what you hoped to gain from the little scene you just staged."

"I got what I wanted."

"Then why aren't you happy?"

"Because you're irritating the shit out of me with all these questions. You're becoming a nag, Slade."

"You're pissed about something all right, but it's not me and it's not the club. I want to know what it is."

"Don't make any mistake about it Slade, I'm totally repulsed that you have married members in your little sex club."

"So? Those men's spouses know. They either don't care or are members themselves. Amazingly some women like to be shared and like to share."

That did it. His words had her advancing on him, her own coming out soft and threatening. "Understand this now, Slade. If you look at another woman, I'll rip your eyes out. Touch one and I'll cut off your hands. Kiss her and I'll sever your tongue from your mouth.

"You don't want to know what I'll do if I find out your dick got anywhere near another woman. So the choice is yours, you can live life as a blind, mute eunuch with stubs at the end of your arms or you can close the club."

"We're not closing the club." Slade raised his tone when Patton started to respond and continued talking over her objection. "Unless you shut down your lingerie business."

"Excuse me? Are you insane?"

"Choice is yours," Slade retorted. "Or we can compromise."

That got her attention. She studied him through narrowed eyes for a full minute before taking the bait. "What are you thinking?"

"We have a lot of female members, members who would be a good client base for your business."

"You're going to let me market in the club. What do you want?"

"A new catalog, both print and website, with a model who is not you."

"I happen to be a fan favorite."

"Your fans will have to find a new favorite."

"What about your image up on Cattleman's Club website. Don't look at me like that. I saw you and Devin posing with your jeans unbuttoned and your shirts off. After all the grief you gave me, I didn't pose half naked with the motto, 'wanna play' typed next to me."

"Nobody can see our faces."

"I knew it was you."

That fact impressed him. It pleased him for some odd reason. The way Patton seemed to be able to recognize them no matter what, even blindfolded, warmed some part of Slade that only she could ever touch.

"Fine. We'll get some other guys to take the picture and have a new banner made."

"Fine. I'll stop doing private showings, if—"

"You do private showings?" Slade felt his stomach open up and let his heart drop right through. He hadn't known that. The very idea made him want to—

"If," Patton yelled, forcing his attention back to her. "You completely disassociate yourself from any of the tasks of a master up to and including telling *your* list of private clients they'll have to settle for somebody else."

"If you ever do another... private," he could barely get the word out without chocking, "showing, I swear to God, Patton, I'll..."

"You'll what?"

"You don't want to find out."

"Hmm," she tilted her head. "Tell me did you like the little red, leather outfit Gina wore the last time she came to the club?"

"Gina?"

It took Slade a moment, but the mention of the red, leather outfit sparked his memory more than the name. He remembered Gina. She had been the one who had mentioned she knew Patton when Chase's wallet had fallen open onto the floor. Gina had cheerfully pointed them in the direction of the Barely There website.

"Oh, shit." He added the facts up quickly.

"At least my private clients don't write you thank-you notes and brag about what a wonderful fuckfest they had with me over holiday vacation. Which explains why you were too busy over Easter for me to come home for a visit."

Slade cringed under that accusation. Yeah, he remembered Easter, Gina and her sexy lingerie. It had been fun. Knowing that Patton knew about that, that Gina had bragged to her, made the memory almost painful. He felt about two inches tall now.

Damn, but she had turned the tables on him. He hadn't come in here for this, but somehow Patton had gotten him so far off track, Slade didn't know if he could recover. He would try though.

"That was the past," Slade stated with authority despite the way her icy gaze made him itch to squirm. "We're discussing the future. No more private clients for anybody."

"Fine. You're not allowed to go to the Cattleman's Club without a proper escort."

"A what?"

"An escort."

Slade didn't even know what to say to that. She had completely caught him off guard with that suggestion. "What escort?"

"Me."

"No."

"I'm the only one who has a vested interest in making sure you boys stay in line."

"You don't trust us?"

"Every man has his breaking point, right?"

"We would never cheat on you, Patton."

"What about when I'm pregnant and barely fit through the door? When I'm a hormonal bitch and you can't touch me?"

"You're being a bitch now," Slade muttered to himself.

"Excuse me?"

"You have nothing to worry about." He managed to force the words past teeth grinding together so tightly they might end up as one.

"Okay, you can go to the club unescorted and I can go anywhere I want unescorted."

That gave him pause. She'd folded too easily and he had to wonder why. "What do you mean anywhere?"

"I mean anywhere, including…oh, a male strip club."

Slade opened his mouth to tell her that would never happen, but stopped himself. She'd baited the hook and he wouldn't let her reel him in. She was bluffing. There were no clubs like that around here.

"Fine, anywhere you want."

"Great, I'll call Hailey after lunch."

"Hailey? What does she have to do with anything?"

"I'm taking her with me when I go back to Atlanta next week. She wanted to go to some clubs that I told her about, but I said no, you wouldn't let me do that. Now…" Patton shrugged.

"You're not going to male strip club."

"Why not? Dick is dick, right?"

Dick is dick? Slade shot right to his feet, his stool shooting back across the floor on a wobble before it crashed to the ground. "You're not going and that is that."

"Don't you trust me?"

"Oh, don't even play that game with me, Patton. I said no and I mean it."

"Yes, dear."

"Don't fucking 'yes, dear' me. If I find out you went to a strip club I will paddle your ass so hard you wouldn't even be able to lie on it for a month!"

"Are you sure you're up to that?" Patton tilted her head and studied him. "I mean, that could be a stretch for you these days, don't you think?"

"What did you just say?"

"Perhaps you should start with something easier."

He had just about been ready to launch himself over the counter and show her 'something easier' when it hit him, what she was doing. Patton had intentionally taunted him into a rage, just like she had tried to do to Chase not minutes before.

There could only be one explanation for why. The answer almost made him smirk. So obvious and it had taken him this long to figure out. Well, if that was what Patton wanted, she'd get it. He'd be glad to give it to her, but first he wanted her to ask for it. That would be her first punishment for putting him through this argument.

"Fine." Slade relaxed back and watched as the anticipation in her gaze fizzled into annoyance. With intentionally slow moves, he righted his chair and sat back down. "I trust you. You can go anywhere you want without an escort."

Patton inhaled an audible breath right through her nose, her shoulders straightened and her whole body tensed for a moment. Then like magic she released the breath and apparently all her tension with it. That fake smile came back to pull at her lips.

"Well, then I guess that settles everything. I have to make lunch."

Chapter 41

He'd been close, so close. Patton had seen the feral aggression break free of Slade's control. For a minute the unleashed beast had set its sight on her, building its momentum to leap across the counter and bring her down. A second later the primitive man had been caged by the civilized one sitting behind her.

She'd plotted, planned, bluffed and outright taunted him and what had it gotten her? An agreement that she could go to a strip bar on her own. Well, ya-dee-da. That was worth about as much as spit in a puddle to Patton.

She didn't want to go see a bunch of over oiled studs gyrating on some dance floor while screaming women pierced her eardrums. That didn't sound like a good time to her.

Taunting her men until one of them snapped and reverted back to the barbaric cavemen she knew they all were at heart, that sounded like a good time. Only problem with the plan was that none of them had caved yet.

She'd totally underestimated their control, particularly Chase's. She'd been sure that demanding he close the club would be the flare to the short fuse of his explosive temper. Yeah, right. Slade had more easily risen to her bait and even that stupid, jackass had managed to hold out on her.

A new plan was needed. A better one. One that made sure that she ended up bound and begging, but what good would that do? She'd pulled out her big guns to no avail. There had to be something that would get them over the hurdle and send them spiraling back to their old behaviors.

Patton finished mangling the last of the carrots. Her attention turned to chopping up the cucumbers. That felt good, having a knife in her hand, the slick of metal cutting right through the meat of the long, green shaft. Unconsciously her grip tightened on the handle and her arm picked up speed.

"I get it now, Patton."

She swallowed and about broke a vocal chord trying to force a nonchalant tone. "Get what, Slade?"

"The point of all this. What you hoped to accomplish with your little act in the study and here in the kitchen, I get it."

Back to that. The dip-shit didn't get anything or she wouldn't be standing here having to pretend to have a normal conversation. She'd already be naked and on her knees.

"I know why you're not happy."

"I'm happy."

That got a laugh from the bastard before he contradicted her. "No you're not, but I know how to make you happy. There is a catch though."

He sounded smug, irritatingly so. All she wanted to do was snap back, but she instead she managed to respond with polite words, if not tone. "Okay, I'll play along. What catch?"

"You're going to have to ask for it."

That figured.

"If I have to ask, then you don't know me at all."

There, that bit of old female logic should return his annoying behavior with interest. It should have, it didn't. He just laughed again and Patton almost cut off her own damn finger in her exuberance to chop the cucumber into little pieces.

"I guess we'll just have to have a nice, relaxed lunch then."

There was something telling in the way he spoke. That bastard did know. He'd somehow figured it all out. Instead of being a man and taking care of his woman's needs, he had decided to play games.

"Yep, these past few weeks have been so peaceful, almost too much so, wouldn't you say?"

Patton chunked the hacked up remains of the cucumber into the salad bowl and turned to yank the dressing out of the fridge. On her way she caught Slade's smirk and shot him her best 'eat shit and die' look. That just widened his grin.

"Yep, you in particular are on a roll, aren't you?"

Slade babbled happily away, ignoring her not so silent response when she slammed the refrigerator door and cracked the salad dressing bottle on the counter. Patton refused to respond, knowing her control hung by a thread. He wouldn't taunt her into breaking. She could hold up just as well as he had.

"Yes, sir. You've gotten your way at every turn lately."

Patton yanked open the oven door and almost reached in to grab the casserole dish with her bare hands. Stupid, she growled annoyed with herself, but blaming Slade for distracting her. Another burn would not help her cause. They'd only freak out even worse.

"Our precious, little Patton. We do love spoiling you."

His precious, little Patton was about to kick his precious, little ass if he didn't shut up soon. She yanked on the oven mitts and didn't bother to check the casserole to see if it were done before she dragged it across the rack and kicked the oven door closed.

"How could we not spoil our dainty, flower of womanhood?"

That did it. "Screw you, Slade."

She dropped the glass dish on the stove with enough force to send a spider web break through the thick wall. She didn't care. She focused completely on the man driving her insane.

The way his mouth fell open in an overly dramatic look of astonishment would have been comical, but she couldn't see any humor in this situation. The look matched his indignant tone and added more fuel to Patton's fire.

"What did I say?"

"I'm not dainty and I'm sure as hell not a flower of womanhood."

"I meant that as a compliment."

"Yeah, right. Do I look dumb enough to believe that? Or are you dumb enough to actually believe it?"

"Of course I believe that. You're my delicate little flower."

"I'm not delicate!"

She'd had it. Things had gotten way out of hand. She'd tried to fix them, but nothing worked. Well now she was done trying to be subtle. If Slade wanted to hear it said, she'd give him a whole bunch of choice words. She'd show Slade what a dainty, delicate flower looked like on a rampage.

"Sweetness, what's wrong?"

* * * *

Slade had to struggle not to laugh as Patton's ears went red. He'd gotten her, gotten her good. He could almost hear the snaps of Patton's brittle control shredding under the weight of her anger. They echoed under the sound of her voice screaming at him.

"Stop it! God, just stop. I am not sweet. I'm not a fucking flower and I am sure as hell not delicate. I am so tired of this shit."

"I didn't meant to upset you, baby. I—"

"Shut up. Just shut the fuck up. I'm so sick of this."

Slade knew what she meant, but prodded her anyway. "This? I don't—"

"Yes, this. How many cuss words did I just use? Isn't that an infraction punishable by extreme sexual torment? Oh, but it's okay." Patton waved away the concern in an agitated motion. "I'm just a darling, fragile doll. I've been traumatized by the horrible ordeal that I suffered. You have to make allowances for my acting out."

Patton was on a roll and Slade couldn't have been happier about that. When she finally crashed back into reality, everything would be set to right. After three weeks of playing the good guy, the concerned, considerate lover and boyfriend, he was worn out.

Despite all the obnoxiousness she spewed forth, she still hadn't said what he wanted to hear. Slade needed to hear it, to know she wanted exactly what they did.

"I know it's been hard on you, baby, but—"

"Hard on me," Patton parroted back with a sneer. "You want to know what is hard on me, Slade? Having to put up with you dick wilted wimps and the tip toeing you've been doing around here for the past three weeks."

That insult ruined some of his good mood. "Excuse me?"

"I swear somebody would think it had been you guys trapped in the damn fire for all the pussy whimpering ways you've taken up. You know if I wanted to get involved with a bunch of pencil-dick dweebs I would've stayed in Atlanta and had my pick of the pocket-protector pansies."

"Are you trying to tell me you regret becoming involved with us?"

"With what you've become? Yes." Patton leaned over the counter. Her dress billowed out slightly to rest on the casserole. "I never thought I would say this, but I've lost respect for you."

Slade told himself that he wanted to hear this. She needed to say it. This explosion was healthy, needed to wipe away the tension. Still that got him. He felt his anger stir. "You've lost respect for me?"

She snapped back up. Though he could still see the rage flashing in her amazing eyes, her tone dropped to a more conversational level. "You know what happened yesterday?"

"No."

"I put Devin's prized January 1996 Playboy, autographed by Pam Anderson herself, in the trash compactor and crushed it." Her hands smacked together, fingers entwining into one large fist. Her grin was pure evil. "Twice. Then I pulled it out and took it to Devin. I told him," her voice became soft and sad, "I was really sorry, but I accidentally picked it up when I cleaned his room and, well…

"You know what he said?" Patton's tone changed again, going back to the aggressive snap. "He said it was all right. I'm not to worry. He's not mad at me. He knows it was an accident."

Slade winced at the bark of hysterical laughter escaped Patton. It sounded slightly insane. A fact she must have been aware of, because her hand came up to cover her mouth and trap the sound inside.

A good thing given that Devin stood just out in the hall. As unnerved and annoyed as Slade was, he could only imagine what Devin felt. Patton would pay for that confession, pay dearly.

"God, what planet does he live on?" She had her voice back in control, soft and snarly. "Have you ever known me to clean one of your rooms? To believe that I would accidentally destroy a playboy…can you spell stupid with a capital S?"

No, but he could spell capital offense with a c and o. Poor Patton, Slade almost felt bad for taunting her into digging this grave. Almost, but not enough to stop her as her lips pursed, rolled and opened to continue with her tirade.

"Did you notice Chase's boxers?" He watched her cheek twitch, her lips kicking up as the sides until she swallowed and tightened her jaw. Another laugh, this one suppressed. "Notice how he had to rush into Dothan the other day to go shopping?"

Actually, he had, but when he'd questioned Chase about the impromptu trip, he'd got nothing but an abrupt response. Slade hadn't wondered or worried over it, but now he had a feeling Patton was about to sink her own battleship.

"It was a shame about his boxers and shirts. They all bloomed pink. Just an unfortunate accident when silly, little me added a new red shirt to his load of whites."

Patton's features changed again, her eyes going wide and lower lip pouting out. The thing that most impressed Slade though was her ability to call forth that little girl voice that worked magic on him and his brothers. Who knew that all these years it had been nothing more than an act?

"I was just so upset when I ruined all his clothes. I knew he'd be upset and I'd never want to do be a bother. That's all right. Chase could never be upset with his baby girl. I've just been through a lot."

Patton rolled her eyes and snickered. Now would be a good time to shut her up. He'd lost control over the conversation. In an attempt to get her to confess her desires, he'd gotten her off track and confessing to mortal sins.

It didn't surprise Slade to learn that Patton had been running lose, creating havoc. What surprised Slade was that neither Chase nor Devin had come storming into the kitchen. If he didn't shut her up, that wouldn't last and then he wouldn't get his revenge of hearing her say aloud that she wanted to be dominated.

"Patton, I don't think—"

"Yeah, that's right. None of you are doing much with that muscle lately. I swear, how dumber than dumb do you have to be to think that a designer would make the idiotic mistake of dropping something red into a load of whites? You want to know why I did it?"

"No, I—"

"Because pussies wear pink."

Slade closed his eyes at that. She'd done it now. He wasn't the least bit surprised to hear Chase roar from the doorway.

"Did you just call me a pussy?"

Chapter 42

Patton shrieked at the sound of Chase's voice. Like a hammer to glass, it shattered the web of insanity that had wrapped itself around her over the past few minutes. Reality was a very nasty thing to wake up to when there was a six-foot beast filling the door with rage in his feral eyes and steam billowing out his flaring nose.

She was in trouble now. Serious trouble and part of her reveled in it. That part already started to go soft and wet with anticipation of finally getting what it so greatly desired, a rough ride.

The rest of her though had a little more sense. Even if her pussy couldn't recognize that there was punishment and then there was true torment, her mind could see the difference. The difference was in the white knuckles of Chase's fist, in the slow advancing steps that brought the devil closer and closer.

Patton wisely began to back up, curving with the counter and unashamed to admit that its bulk might save her if she could just get enough distance between them.

"I asked you a question, Patton. Did you not just say you dyed my boxers pink because I'm a pussy?"

She didn't think answering that would get her anywhere. The truth might just make him snap, so could a lie. Silence probably wouldn't do her any good, but of the three options, it would be the best. A little prayer wouldn't hurt.

Since she'd already lost this point, Patton prayed that he hadn't heard the whole conversation between Slade and her. The beast that stalked her seedily around the counter did not need anymore white-hot pokers spurring it onto greater heights of rage.

"All these so-called accidents these past couple of weeks haven't been absentminded mistakes because you're still distraught over the fire, have they, Patton? Devin's Playboy, Slade's hat, the scratch from the fence you knocked down with my truck, even pitching a fit over the club and demanding I close it down, all of it has been nothing more than staged performances so you could see how far you could push us."

Patton cut her eyes to Slade, realizing now he'd played her. Chase hadn't just been in the hall listening, Slade had known he had been there. He'd figured her out and instead of just giving her what she wanted, he'd returned the favor.

She probably didn't have any right to be mad at him, but that didn't stop her. Not that he seemed concerned with the annoyance she tried to convey in her gaze.

Slade just shrugged. His lips folded in, he watched her with the same expression a priest might look at a man as he took his long walk to the electric chair. Bastard.

He didn't appear nearly as upset as Chase did, neither did Devin for that fact as he stood in the doorway watching the scene in the kitchen unfold. That jerk actually smiled at her, as if the whole thing was funny. With his twisted sense of humor, it probably was to him.

Despite their appearances, Patton fanned out far away from their reach as she continued to back away from Chase. They might not look upset, but she knew where their loyalty lay.

"It stops now, Patton," Chase growled, drawing her eyes back to the true predator in the room. "You've pushed too far and now you have to pay."

Patton screamed when he lunged for her and took off. Despite the fact that she had pushed for this, that she had wanted things this way, her response was one of pure defense. Like prey fleeing for it's life, she charged Devin, expecting him to try and block her exit.

He didn't and she didn't have time to be shocked that he stepped out of her way and let her run screaming from the kitchen. She flew up the stairs, hearing the pounding of heavy male footsteps echoing in the thunder of her own heartbeat.

By whatever miracle, she made it into her bedroom, clicking the lock even as a large object slammed into it on the other side. Silence followed and Patton back away from the door with eye glued to it. She half expected to hear the demon on the other side howl, but nothing.

She made it to the middle of the room before the door began to splinter as something in the hall began to rip into it. Patton screamed and ran for the only exit, the window.

The next few seconds blurred together for her in a rush of wood cracking and her own panting breaths as she levered herself over the window sill. The ground looked far away today and she stretched out, hanging in uncertainty with both hands gripping the edge.

The pound of footsteps vibrating straight through the wall made her decision for her and she let go. She didn't fall. Two bands of unbreakable bone and muscle locked around her wrists and began to pull her unceremoniously back through the window.

Patton didn't go willingly. Despite the hard landing waiting her at the other end, she kicked and screamed, fighting every inch of the way as Chase dragged her straight through the window and back into the bedroom. Even there he didn't release her, but kept her arms held over her head as she jerked and cussed, demanding her freedom.

Her fit got no direct response from Chase, who transferred both wrists into one hand so he could take the stretch of leather Devin held out to him in his now free hand. The motion drew her attention to the fact that Slade and Devin had made their way into the room. The wardrobe was open and Slade had already begun to pull things down. He handed off items to Devin who sauntered back to Chase.

Uh, oh.

That was all her mind could come up with to accurately describe the open pit sensation that she could feel herself falling into as Chase deftly bound her wrists together. They were way too calm, way too methodical and she was in serious trouble now. Like déjà vu, the brothers worked in perfect flow with each other. Silently, they seemed to know exactly what the other thought without the need for any communication that might reveal to her what they had planned.

Patton's eyes widened as Devin handed Chase another bind, this one for her mouth. They weren't going to muzzle her, not if she could help it. Clamping her lips tight, she raised her chin. They weren't the only ones who could communicate without a word.

From the smirk Devin gave her, she knew the message had been received. Received and responded to with a hard pinch and twist to her nipple. That got her mouth opening on a shriek. The sound got cut off by the gag Chase expertly inserted. Even as she tried to spit the offensive thing out, he had it tied and latched into place.

That task completed, he finally released her. Patton glared at him as she lowered her arms and allowed blood back into her limbs. Either her condition or her obvious anger amused him, because he returned her look with a smile.

Somewhere between the door and the window, he seemed to have lost his rage, because he appeared to be way too relaxed and calm given what had led up to this moment. Patton envied him those emotions. She had a feeling it would be a long time before she got to enjoy them again.

"Do you know what the greatest insult you can give a master is, my pet?"

He reached out to stroke her cheek with that endearment. Patton flinched away from the touch. Not out of disgust or fear, but distrust of what came next.

Chase smirked. No doubt assured he knew the reason behind her rejection. He knew all the stages of this game, all the steps his opponent could make. In this, he was the master.

"It's for a woman to tell him she has no respect for him."

Uh, oh. He'd heard it all. Patton had no delusions of how a man like Chase would take that comment. That's why she hadn't used it on him at any point. She might have been desperate, but she hadn't been insane enough to go with the nuclear option. Now she'd unwittingly detonated the big bomb and the repercussions would probably last a lifetime.

Slade stretching up onto his tiptoes in the middle of the room drew her momentarily away from that worry. Her attention refocused on a new one as she watched him thread a large hook into a hole in the ceiling. Funny, she'd never noticed that detail before.

Patton didn't get a chance to wonder what other hidden features she'd failed to discover in her new bedroom. Devin crossed the room and her eyes shifted to the blindfold in his hands.

Memories of the last time they'd blinded her seared through her starting a fire in her gut that quickly warmed her entire body. That had been the last time they'd played these games, three long weeks ago. She'd thought she was ready to play again, but the tension inside warred with the desire, making her wonder if she shouldn't have left the beehive in the tree as Chase took the blindfold from Devin.

It looked so ominous in his hand, his big hand. God, he was big all over. Big and strong, he seemed so even more today as her gaze traveled over his body. Only when her eyes finally lifted to meet his did he speak again.

"You see, Patton, more than being called a pussy, or a pencil-dick dweeb, or stupid or compared to a pocket-protector pansy, being told you lost respect for us is an insult that can not be ignored."

As he spoke, he circled her until he stood behind her. Patton knew better than to move. God they were already driving her crazy. The more they drew things out, the more it heightened her desperation, feeding both her desire and apprehension.

"We are your masters, my pet. If you need us to prove it then we will gladly take the test. You remember reading about the test, don't you, Patton?"

She should. She'd read it twice. The words had turned her on and made her envious of the women who got to participate. Now though, bound and gagged, hot and in heat, her memory failed her. All that came through the static of her desire were snippets that drove her lust to even greater heights.

"I asked you a question, pet." Chase accentuated his point with a sharp smack to her ass that made her jump with a strangled shriek. "Answer me. Do you remember reading about that?"

Answer him? He'd gagged her. That only left a headshake, which she gave him before he could add not answering to already long list of offenses.

"Well, let me remind you of the first rule. The test must be administered publicly."

Oh, God.

"So we'll leave the window open and blinds up."

Patton's eyes cut to the view outside. The room faced the back yard where the hands gathered. They should have been working the cattle. They weren't. To a man, they were all staring up at the house. If she could see them…Patton swallowed feeling her pussy pulse and clench.

"Now," Chase words caressed her ear. "Let's see if we can earn your respect."

A second later the world went dark.

* * * *

Chase watched Patton's breathing become shallow in the mirrored doors of the armoire. The room had been artfully staged so, while it didn't have wall-to-wall mirrors, the mirrors that had been angled to assure they could see a woman at any point in the room, from almost all sides as her reflection bounced from one mirror to the next.

It had been an ingenious idea. One that allowed Chase to watch as Patton's tongue tried to reach her lips. The ball gag got in her way. He'd never been a fan of gags. He preferred to have the screams of the woman he pleasured echoing in full volume in his ears.

The restraint served a purpose though. Once gagged a woman knew nobody could hear her. She began to realize she was completely at his mercy. That had been the point he'd wanted to impress on little Miss Patton, mistress of manipulation. She'd played her games and now the time had come to show her how they played theirs.

Soon enough she'd be crying, begging for them to stop, to continue, to do whatever they wanted as long as they fulfilled the promises their torture would make on her body. And it would be torture.

Normally the tests of masters would be conducted using several women. The test were long, requiring the man to bring a woman to pleasure so many times that it would become painful for one woman to experience that many climaxes.

It would also be difficult for her. There came a point when a woman's body was so saturated with pleasure it would be almost impossible for her body to break through the orgasmic wall to experience a true rapture. Instead her body would be so sensitive that every nerve would radiate spike of pleasure so strong it became pain.

While that knowledge served a master well when disciplining his pet, it did not aid in administering the test the club required for a man to take up the mantle of master. This situation was different.

They were not proving to other men that they could master a woman's desires, but proving to Patton that they were the masters of her desire. That changed the rules.

Devin moved toward the windows, silently lowering the blinds. The first true test of a master, one Patton would not knowingly appreciate. The ability to operate in complete silence, giving nothing away to Patton would add to her apprehension, her arousal.

While most tests were held in the great hall, where the sounds of the other Cattlemen would mask what little noises the test taker made, here in this room, bound and blindfolded as she was, Chase knew Patton's hearing would be amplified. She'd be straining to listen for any clues about what was about to be done to her.

It wouldn't do for her to know that they had not carried through with their threat to allow the ranch hands to watch her submission. Not that in a few moments she would care, but later she would. Later she would remember and blush, perhaps even hesitate before she started on a new scheme.

A lesson in humility it would serve its purpose, but Chase didn't have it in him to carry through with the threat. Never before had he been jealous, but Patton was different. Her pleasure, even just the sight of it, was for him and his brothers alone. He would not tempt fates and flaunt the treasure they had found before others.

That task done, it was time to begin.

Chapter 43

Patton jumped at the sudden feel of cold metal sliding along her shoulder. This was the first sign that something had changed. She'd been straining to hear, to catch any little clue as to what they were up to. Only silence had greeted her ears, feeding her imagination and ratcheting up her apprehension, her growing desire.

What was it? What did it mean? Patton tried to guess as she focused on the slender length of metal, too thick to be a knife. The answer came a second later when, with a *sh-click* sound, the strap of her sundress fell down with a sigh.

Scissors, and they moved to her other shoulder. With another whisper of a sound, the second strap was cut. The folds of her dress teased the heated skin of her body as it slipped over her in a gentle caress to pile over her feet. Patton didn't need her eyes to know what the brothers saw.

For the second time, she stood before them in nothing more than a skimpy pair of panties as the cold breeze from the air-condition vent overhead wafted down and puckered her nipples. Another dress had been turned into rags and another pair of hand-sewn panties was about to join the pile.

She didn't flinch this time when she felt the brush of metal over her hips. This was what she'd dreamed of, what she'd gone to great lengths to taunt them into doing. She didn't regret a thing. When the snip came on her opposite hip, Patton dutifully widened her stance to allow the skimpy undergarment to fall to the floor, feeling it catch and slide the cream weeping out of her pussy down her things, knowing the brothers could now see as well as smell the evidence of her arousal.

Shivering she imagined what would come next. Rough manhandling, mauling, being bent over and fucked, toys and whipping, all the possibilities swirled through her mind, heightening her excitement and leaving her prepared for anything they would do next.

Anything, but what they did. Large, callus roughened hands smoothed over her back. Chase, he still stood behind her and now he slowly kneaded the tension out of her muscles. As he worked his way down, Patton sighed and involuntarily relaxed back into his strength.

The teasing, soothing circles he worked into her sensitive lower back had her moaning, arching slightly as her hips went limp and opened even more. Warm breath heated the slick skin of her inner thighs and even hotter hands forced them wider apart.

They artfully manipulated her body into the position they wanted, her weight resting now against Chase's chest, his hands holding her still by the hips while a mischievous tongue came to sample the texture and taste of her cunt.

Little laps soon turned to full licks, gentle tugs grew to mind numbing sucks, all too soon they reduced her back to the wild thing of need she became in their arms. Writhing, bucking, trying to chew straight through her gag, the orgasm hit her so hard she almost managed to jerk free of their hold.

They held her steady, keeping her in place for the mouth that continued to torment her already quivering flesh. Up, down, in, out, whoever feasted on her pussy drove her insane, straight to the point where her second climax exploded over the receding edges of her first.

Still they didn't cease their torment. Her body tried to match pace with the sensations twisting her insides into knots, but it couldn't. The euphoria flooding her veins became a nightmare as it held off next explosion, making her sensitive to even the slightest of touches.

She needed something, just a little more to break the damn holding back the rapture. Her tits ached, whispering that just a little touch, a quick pinch and pull would snap the binds and release her from this agony. Bound as her wrists were, her hands could still aide in the battle.

She reached for her own flesh only to have her bent elbows trapped at her sides as the arms at her hips lifted to bind her limbs against her stomach. Struggling against the hold of the man behind her turned out to be a futile effort. An unnecessary one as her third, most violent climax crashed through her.

A category five it wiped out every bit of strength left in her body. Brilliant streaks of fire lit up the darkness behind her blindfold and for a second that stretched into eternity, he pulsed in perfect harmony with the living flame. As the embers sizzled back to nothing more than crackling ashes, Patton went limp and collapsed into the embrace of the hard body behind her.

She felt herself being moved, settled onto a jean-covered lap. A thick cock pressed into her backside and Patton murmured, unsure if she could stand what would come next. Despite her delirium, she thought she knew exactly what the next step would be when strong, masculine thighs split her legs wide.

The time had come for the fucking and nothing got her hotter than be restrained by one brother while another one pumped himself deep into her body. Her pussy clenched painfully in anticipation. Despite her body's objection to being forced to endure another round, her cunt felt empty, painfully so.

The decision wasn't left to Patton, but made for her by the unbreakable hold of the arms wrapped around her, lowering her backward into a position that left her completely vulnerable. The thrill of the moment was short lived when she felt another mouth lower itself to trail heated kisses up her inner thigh.

No! She couldn't do this. Not again. What little energy remained in her body mobilized, helping to struggle against this continued torment, but even her will could not overcome the true strength of the men holding her captive.

A moment later, even her will failed her. This had to be Slade with talented tongue swirling around her clit, sucking the little piercing over the sharp edge of his teeth. He overwhelmed her body's resistance simply by bringing his fingers into play. Thrusting them deep into her cunt, he gave her what she do desperately needed, something to clamp down on.

For a moment she thought her orgasm had given her the strength of the gods and she'd somehow managed to chew through her gag as her own scream of fulfillment drowned out the sloppy sounds of the mouth feasting on her pussy.

Only when strong finger turned her chin, pressing her lips against harder ones, that Patton realized it must have been Chase who removed her gag. His reason became obvious as he attacked her mouth in ways she'd never experienced before becoming the Davis brothers' woman.

Warm lips sealed the sounds of her desire as he angled his head perfectly to allow for the deepest penetration of his foraging tongue. He tasted of the cinnamon gum he liked to chew and of hot, lusty male, a delicious combination that she'd already grown addicted to.

The kiss distracted her from the bone crushing tension being wound through her by the more intimate kiss she received lower. Her shifted focus allowed her next release to come easily, even as it detonated a nuclear attack that guaranteed to leave her completely altered if not dead in its wake.

She ripped her mouth free, giving voice to the agonized pleasure shredding her very being into rags. Incoherent bits and pieces of sentences babbled out of their own free will. The incomplete thoughts still conveyed the desperation in her for a moment, just a minute of peace to recover.

Her demands that they cease were not understood or went ignored as the mouth below continued to feast on her weeping, quivering flesh. Deprived of her lips, the other mouth settled for ravaging the sensitive stretch of skin between her ear and her shoulder. Licking, nipping and sucking it mimicked the motions of the lips buried in her pussy.

This had to stop or her heart would explode. Her fingers found the silky tresses of the head nestled between her thighs and she pulled, hard. Bucking and rolling she fought to escape this torment with the strength of a wild animal putting up the last fight for its life.

For a moment she thought she'd broke free. Soul deep satisfaction flooded her as everything stopped, leaving her trapped only in the whirlwind of sensations still vibrating through her body. It turned out to be nothing more than an illusion as strong hands came to lift her, turn her, tuck her legs beneath her thighs.

She had no ability to maintain the position and her face fell forward into the softness of the mattress. Her eyes fluttered closed and her body prepared to relax into the oblivion of sleep. With a sigh, she welcomed the on-coming darkness. With a whimper, she said goodbye to that dream. Strong fingers cut into the resilient flesh of her hips and pulled her down toward the waiting mouth.

Oh, God. They weren't done with her.

She couldn't do this, couldn't take anymore. Every breath had become a struggle, every contraction of her muscles a searing pain, every limb trembled as her bones threatened to liquefy under the pressure of being forced through another climax.

"Please!"

Patton didn't know if she screamed at them to stop or at herself to just give over, to unleash the climax the talented mouth beneath drove her toward. The tension gripping her insides was almost too painful to bear.

Bear it she did, because neither party listened to her shouts and soon her voice became hoarse from trying to make somebody listen to her needs. She gave over to the sobs, great racking cries poured out of her, expressing the agony of being dragged across the razor's edge of ecstasy.

Only one sensation broke through the fury of the storm holding her in its grip. The hard bite of fingers cutting into the thick flesh of her ass, the cool air wafting across her heated crevice as her cheeks were split open, spoke of their intent louder than any tone of voice could.

They couldn't be planning on doing that. They were. There could be no denying that fact as slick fingers, cold with lubricant, began to stroke into her hidden entrance.

Patton whimpered and, despite the futileness of the effort, she tried desperately to crawl forward and away from the hand preparing her for further torment.

Hands, two sets, held her in place. Growls, three echoed, voiced their displeasure. All three punished.

The first with a sharp scrape of teeth along her clit, a flickering tongue over her piercing. The other brought the thick head of his cock to the entrance of her ass. The third wound a thick fist through her hair, lifting her head until his dick brushed against her lips, wetting them with the evidence of his own desire.

With stomach muscles trembling, she anticipated their invasion. It didn't come. They stilled for what felt like an eternity of anticipation and was probably no more than a second as all three waited for some inaudible signal to begin.

The battle cry came from her own throat. Another whimper brought on by the realization of what they planned. At that small sign of weakness, they attacked.

With a savage thrust, the brother behind her embedded his full length deep into her body, forcing her downward to the mouth waiting to feast on her pussy. Her lips opened on a scream that was muffled as a second thick shaft filled her.

In a mind-numbing symphony of rapture they moved, stroking in and out, pushing and pulling her for harder, lighter licks and nips to her clit. The hand on her head kept perfect beat to the sensual song as it kept her mouth fucking the engorged length of cock before her.

She didn't know who was where, what brother did what to her and didn't care. The orgasm that moments ago had seemed a lifetime away broke over with angry vengeance. Her body trembled under the force, shattering and went wild as the pieces of her former self dissolved.

She'd have collapsed and smothered the man beneath her with her cunt if it hadn't been for the strong arm of the brother behind her wrapping around her stomach, curving her into his body and directing her fall to the right.

It felt like she'd died. She saw the white light, felt the brilliant warmth of utopia, every worry and concern bled out of her in a series of ragged, panting breaths. Too bad for her men, they hadn't come and it was time to pass out.

"That wasn't part of the test," Devin breathed softly into her ear. "That was just for the fun of it. Time to get back to work."

Those words, the husky threat imbedded in them, had her eyes popping back open.

Chapter 44

Chase lay with one arm wrapped around Patton, keeping her snuggled tightly into his side. The even flow of her breath tickled the hair on his chest, but it was not much of a distraction.

She'd passed out almost four hours ago, only two hours into their testing. They'd barely gotten through the first two rounds, the easiest two in Chase's opinion. There were still nine more to go. Then there were the tests for the women, the ones they had to pass to be promoted from pet to slave.

Chase smiled just thinking of what Patton's reaction would be when he told her that she'd have to prove herself, just as they did. It was the new world order, equality. She'd read the charter. She'd know what they had planned for her. She'd be rethinking the merits of equality, no doubt.

Maybe not, Chase sighed. He'd been wrong in so many ways about what Patton wanted. The fact that she refused to just say it half the time didn't help. He wasn't a mind reader after all and it would help if she practiced more honesty and a little less manipulation.

Not that he could complain really. Sure Patton had gotten things her way, but that also happened to be his way. How he'd gotten so lucky, Chase didn't know and certainly wasn't going to question.

It felt too good to smile, truly smile with the happiness warming him from the inside out. How many years had it been since he felt this good? Too many to let that depressing answer ruin his good mood.

Patton sighed and he felt the fine brush of her long lashes tickling his side as her eyes blinked open. He tilted his head to watch as her beautiful violet eyes took in the world around her. She looked so cute with her cheeks sleep reddened and her hair a frizzy halo around her face.

After she'd blacked out, he'd carried her to the shower and held her limp body while Slade had cleaned her. Going to bed with a wet head had made a mess of her normally smooth, silken locks. A fact that he knew she normally would bemoan.

Not this evening. Right now, Patton was too busy remembering and he could tell the exact moment the images in her mind formed a detailed image. Her eyes cut to where the rope still hung from the hook in the center of the room and he knew exactly what she was thinking.

She'd never known a woman could orgasm from just having ropes tied around her body. Chase smiled, knew she'd have called it a smirk if she weren't so busy staring off into the past. There were many things Patton didn't know, many things he would be delighted to show her.

The ropes had just been the beginning. It all had to do with placement of the specialized ropes over a woman's sensitive spots. There were several techniques after that could be used to send a woman from aroused to release though they all relied on constriction and movement.

Each brother worked the ropes in a slightly different way. Devin enjoyed the tease. Binding a woman with the least amount of constriction, he tied feathers in the mix, placing them just so that the woman was tickled into moving.

Slade worked a similar angle, but true to his nature, he went for something less comfortable, more binding. He'd work the ropes just so they were uncomfortable. Eventually the woman would shift and twist, trying to find a better position.

The theory, the more the woman moved the more the ropes pressed and rubbed against her body. Becoming a caress and with enough movement they could work her body right up the mountain and over the edge into ecstasy. It worked, if a man knew what he was doing.

To Chase though, that was a lower skill. The true master of the ropes knew how to make a woman come just from being bound, like he did. He tied his ropes so tight that just breathing made the ropes push against her skin.

Sometimes he helped things a long with a kiss. A little oxygen deprivation forced the woman to take deep breaths and heighten the whole experience. Whatever worked. It certainly had on Patton, but he'd known it would.

She had a very sensitive body. Hell, just rubbing the right spot on her lower back could have her moaning and twisting. A fact he loved. Then again there wasn't much he didn't love about Patton, even when she made him mad and drove him crazy.

"Hey," her sleepy whisper held a note of shyness in it. He glanced down to see that it wasn't just her voice, but her cheeks had also pinked with a beautiful shade of embarrassment.

"Hey," he responded just as softly.

"Where are Slade and Devin?"

"They had to go back to work." In fact, he should have joined them. As the oldest, he had the ability to just shift his chores onto his younger brothers. A benefit he'd never before taken advantage of, but could foresee a change in that tradition for the future.

"Oh." Her eyes shifted away from his, actively avoiding not only his gaze, but most of the rest of the room.

"Rested?"

"Depends." Patton lowered her head to snuggled back into his side. Her arm crept around his chest to hold him close.

"Depends?" Chase repeated with a smile. "On what?"

"On what you're planning to do if I say yes."

He laughed outright at that and gave her a quick squeeze. "I was thinking of food."

"In that case," Patton spoke through her yawn, "I could manage to move to the kitchen."

"And conversation."

"Oh," she didn't sound excited at that prospect. "I guess you're going to lecture me now."

"No. I just wanted to know why you felt the need to try and manipulate me into losing my tempter instead of just telling me what you wanted."

She didn't answer straight away, but tensed slightly before shrugging. "I don't know."

Chase knew she lied and he'd had enough. If she wanted to play games that was fine as long as they weren't intended to disguise her true feelings. There needed to be some level of honesty in their relationship.

Rolling, he pinned her beneath him, making a clear statement about his determination. "Why, Patton?"

"I don't know."

"The truth. I'm not moving until you tell me."

She scowled up at him, clearly annoyed. Beneath though, Chase could sense the worry she tried to hide. "It's not easy, okay?"

"Not easy? I don't get that. You've always been blunt and straightforward about what you want. Why not this time? What made this different?"

"I love you, Chase."

That declaration caught him off guard. Not because she hadn't already said it a million times in the past three weeks, but because it didn't have any bearing on their conversation. He opened his mouth to question her, but she continued in a surprising, annoying, direction.

"But you can be a real jackass sometimes."

"Excuse me?"

"What would you have done if I'd come to you and said the tender, gently loving was nice, but where's the heat? Where's my aggressive, dominant man?"

"I don't know what I would have said, but I would have given you what you wanted."

"And then some," Patton muttered.

"You're getting your 'then some' your way, too, getting more of it than you bargained."

"I'm not talking about sex."

She wasn't? Ah, damn there was that headache she gave him when she did this. As usual he'd lost track of the conversation thanks to Patton's inability to stay on topic.

"Then what the hell are we talking about?"

"If I had come to you and said I wanted my old Chase back, the first thing you would have done is moved all my business equipment out of my room and tried to stop me from perusing it anymore."

"That's what this is about? Your business?"

"Don't deny that you would do all in your power to see me fail."

When she put it like that, it made him feel bad. He didn't want Patton to fail. He just didn't want her to work. There was a difference.

"Well, are you going to deny it?"

"I want you to give up the business," Chase stated carefully.

"And do what?"

"Do whatever you want."

"What I want to do is work on my business."

"That's not what I meant. You don't have to work, Patton. You can enjoy life. We make enough money for you to indulge in whatever hobby you fancy at the moment."

"Is that what you think of me?" Her head tilted backward on the pillow, drawing away from him as much as their position would allow. "That I'm the type of flighty person who is just indulging a fantasy?"

"No. You're twisting my words again."

"Do you know why your father killed mine?"

The abrupt change in topics had Chase growling. This was the third time in under a minute she'd changed topics midstream and he really hated it. Hated it even more when she brought up a topic he didn't ever discuss. What had happened between their fathers had been a tragedy. He'd never forgiven his dad for what had happened.

"I don't know and I don't care."

"Your mother cheated on him."

That grim declaration had Chase stilling. His mother? God's honest truth, he'd never been particularly close to his own mother. As the oldest, he'd received the least of her attention. Not that he'd been jealous. He'd been to busy as a child basking in his father's praise to notice his mother had little to say to him but to wash up and not put his elbows on the dinner table.

Despite that, he'd loved her. When their dad had been taken to jail, he'd tried everything to help her heal, to keep her in the lifestyle she had grown accustomed to. She was his mother and he saw her as the paragon of virtue. That Patton had dared to slander that image chilled him inside.

"You don't know what you're talking about. You were what, twelve, when she died?"

"Remember the letter she left me? The one that you saved for me so I could open and read it when I turned eighteen?"

He remembered and now he didn't want to hear anymore. That didn't stop Patton from talking.

"She wanted me to know why my father died. She thought I deserved the truth. That you deserved it, too, but she couldn't confess her sins to her sons. I think she was afraid you would love her less because of them."

"I don't want to hear this." Chase rolled off Patton and out of the bed.

"She and my father were in love," Patton yelled after him.

"Stop it!" Chase turned halfway across the room. Patton had scrambled up to kneel in the middle of the bed, clutching the sheet to her breasts. "It's history. It doesn't matter anymore."

"But it does. She turned to him because of your father locked her in this house and treated her the same way you are trying to treat me."

"What are you saying, Patton? That you'd cheat on us?" Chase snarled the words. Just saying them made him want to kill something. No. No way in hell.

The jealousy that had shimmered beneath his surface for years exploded with violent intensity. He lunged at her, tackling her to the bed. Patton fought back, kicking, pushing and cursing at him to no avail. Chase barely felt the blows she landed, couldn't hear the insults she hurled at him over the roar of his own anger.

With torrid intent, he shoved his leg between hers and spread her thighs wide. In less than a second, he had his cock nestled intimately between the lips of her pussy. Despite her aggressive objections, she was wet and that was all the invitation he needed to press forward.

"Damnit, Chase. You are such a jackass." Patton panted, still rejecting him with insults even has her back bowed and her sheath pulsed in welcome.

"No man touches what is mine," Chase growled. He could feel the sweat beading along his hairline and down his back as he continued his invasion. "This pussy is mine. Mine, Patton. If any other comes near it, I'll rip his arms off and beat him with them. Do you hear me?"

"I hear you, you jerk." Her response ended in a scream as he plunged his full length into her.

Chase didn't have the mind or the thought for seduction, much less worrying about whether he pleased or hurt Patton. He had her at his mercy and he had none of that precious commodity. No less than the emotions that seared through him and drove him to claim, fuck, possess and never, ever let go.

His anger, his vengeance was completely unleashed and he rode her with the savageness of a beast feeling the whip of betrayal lashing him to go faster, thrust harder. The bite of her fingernails in his back, the howls of her screams echoing in his ears, the sharp scrape of her teeth on his shoulder, all drove him to push harder toward the moment of sweet oblivion.

Then it hit him with more force than any climax ever had. He roared with his pleasure, with his anguish, as his very soul was ripped from his body. With a final grunt of exhaustion, he collapsed.

* * * *

Patton tried to gather the pieces of her shattered body. Her leg muscles spasmed, her arms trembled and deep inside, she glowed. For the first time, Chase had lost complete control and it had been wonderful.

He'd rutted on her like an untamed beast in heat and she'd matched his need with her own feral passion. Nothing yet compared to this experience. It had even been better than when he dominated her. Definitely worth pricking his anger again.

That thought echoed through her, bringing a solemn tone to her joy. Was it truly worth it? Underneath the wild lust had been the rage fueling his actions, a rage born of pain, an emotion that she completely understood the depths of.

Over the years it had been hard enough knowing what he did with those other women. Seeing all the names of the women who had selected her men to be their sex masters had hurt. Just the idea of one of those skanks seducing one of her men made her normally anti-violence attitude do a one-eighty into a murderous rage.

That was what she had done to Chase, insinuated that he had something to worry about. The last thing she ever wanted to do was hurt him. Not even for her own gain would she ever intentionally go that far.

Rolling her head so her cheek brushed against his where he'd buried it in her neck, she whispered, "I love you, Chase. I would never betray you. I wasn't trying to imply that I would."

His head lifted to regard her with his sullen expression. If it wasn't for the look of hurt in his eyes, she'd have told him just how sexy he looked with his hair tousled, clumped into sex sweaty chunks.

"That is what you implied."

"But I didn't mean to," Patton rushed out, desperately wanting to put the situation back to right. "I was just trying to say what your dad did to your mom is what you want to do to me. I'm not a doll you can come home to play house with, Chase.

"I'm smart and capable and talented at what I do. I need to have something else in my life beyond just you. I need to work, to follow my dream."

"And what if that dream takes you away?"

"Away?"

"I may be some dumb rancher, but I know that New York is the capital of fashion. Or is it Paris? Wherever, it's not Pittsview, Alabama or even Atlanta."

"I'm not going to go to New York or Paris. I mean I might travel there for a trip, but I'm not going to move there. This is my home. This is where I want to be."

"That's what you say now," Chase muttered and flopped over onto his back.

Patton scowled up at her image in the mirror over the bed. This was it? The real reason behind Chase's objection to her business. She'd been expecting his normal sexist bullshit about the strong man providing for the little woman, not this.

It made sense though. Chase had lost a lot in his life, both his parents, his freedom of choice, even her for a period of time. It stood to reason he'd be afraid of losing again, just as it made sense that he would have difficulty voicing, much less recognizing, a fear.

Patton rolled to her side so she could stare directly into his sulky gaze. Despite the six plus feet of muscle stretched out beside her, he still managed to look like a little boy who had just heard 'no' from his mother when asking for his favorite treat.

"Chase," Patton sighed. "I'm not going anywhere."

"You don't know what the future will bring."

"You're right, but neither do you. All we know is what we want it to be filled with." Patton snuggled up to his side and rested her head against his chest. "I want it to be filled with long, slow summer days of watching you take your shirt off while you work and drooling as the sweat drips down this sexy body."

She matched her words with a finger sliding over the toned ridges of his stomach toward his hardening dick. "Of nights filled with passion. Sunday bar-b-ques and listening to Slade and Devin brag over who is better at horseshoes. Of Christmases with piles of gifts under the tree and listening to you tell Devin, 'not in the house', after he unwraps whatever new gadget he gave himself."

"What about children?"

Patton hesitated. "I wouldn't mind having kids, just not right away."

"Four?"

"Four?" Patton's mouth fell open and it took her a moment to digest that question. "You know I have to give birth to these things, right?"

"Three then."

"Fine, but I get to choose the sexes."

That got her a laugh. "Okay, but we're going to keep going until I have at least two sons, so keep that in mind when you're making your decisions."

"Sons? What? Don't you want daughters, too?"

"If they're like you…"

"Hey!" Patton slapped him on the stomach in retaliation for his forlorn tone.

"Seriously, I need sons to inherit the ranch."

"Why couldn't a daughter inherit the ranch?"

"A female? Running this ranch? I guess it could happen." Not really, his tone clearly contradicted his words.

"Just for that I'm going to give you all daughters."

"Any other woman and I'd say, 'yeah, right', but you…"

"That's right buddy and don't you forget it." Patton grin faded as her thoughts turned serious. "We're agreed then?"

"About your business?" She nodded and knew he saw the motion in the mirror overhead. "I wouldn't complicate your life with objections on three conditions."

"This should be good."

"One," Chase tone rose over her muttering, "you have nothing to do with the Cattleman's Club. We built the club and we've done a damn good job with it. I'm not going to have any feminist views coming in and screwing it up."

"You can run it as long as it's in big bold letters on the welcome mat that you are not touching or to be touched by any of the sluts that cross through those doors."

"I would never do that to you." He repeated her words of earlier.

"Fine then, I'll stay out of your precious sex club."

"Two, you're to be in this house and sleeping in this bed for at least fifty weeks out of every year."

"Forty."

"Forty five and you have to take an escort with you whenever you travel."

"An escort?"

"Slade, Devin or me."

"Fine, but if none of you can go because of ranch business, I'm still going on my trip."

"If you go alone, you have to be back to wherever you are staying no later than eight in the evening."

"For God's sake, Chase—"

"Promise me."

"Fine, but when I'm out of town you're not allowed to go to the club."

"Agreed. That just leaves your catalog and website."

"I know," Patton groaned. "I'll get a model and re-shoot the pictures."

"Good. Then that settles that."

"You know though, I did have an idea for the catalog." Patton crawled over him, straddling his hips with her legs. "A compromise, if you will."

"I'm not sure I want to know."

"I was just thinking. If your objection is the idea of the male models, why don't you take the pictures with me?"

"Me?" He sounded on the verge of laughing.

"Yeah. Wouldn't you like to lick whip cream off my stomach?"

"That idea gets you hot." His hands trailed up her thighs to rub teasing circles on her ass that made her wiggle and grind against his erection. "You like the idea of being photographed while I play with you?"

"Mmmm," Patton closed her eyes. "It doesn't leave me cold. That's for sure."

Chapter 45

In almost a repeat of the morning that would forever live in her chest of found memories, Patton crossed her arms over the side of the fence and sighed. Unlike that morning three weeks ago, it was late afternoon and everything was perfect.

Today the men were working to corral the cattle that needed branding. The cows weren't dumb, they didn't line up for their turn under the hot iron. Like any intelligent being they ran for their lives. Chase sat on top a horse and chased after them, bringing them down with the lasso.

Patton loved watching him ride. All muscles and intense concentration, he didn't just master her, he mastered the horse, too. She grinned thinking she got a better deal than the horse.

Of course, the horse got to wear more than she had over the past three weeks. Her trip to Atlanta had been postponed thanks to the bossy demands of her three men. There hadn't been a thing she could have done about it.

It had taken them four days to complete all the tests to prove that they were the masters, but prove it they had. Then they had demanded she prove she could earn the title of slave over pet. Those tests had stemmed over two weeks and during that time she'd been kept naked almost twenty four hours a day. Not so bad when she'd also been kept smiling.

Things though had started to return to normal these past few days. They bossed her around in the bedroom and she tried to boss them around everywhere else. The only time they'd actually fought was two days ago when Chase had lived up to his promise and accidentally run over her bike with his truck not minutes after Hailey had delivered it.

They'd argued it out, but Patton hadn't really planned on replacing the thing. It had just been the principle of the matter. She couldn't just let him get away with that kind of barbaric action and say nothing.

Chase had ended the argument in his newly developed habit of stripping her naked and making her submit to every base desire and kinky need that entered his twisted brain. It had been wonderful.

He had driven her through the minefield of ecstasy to come out the other side shattered and exhausted. Then he had collected the wreckage that had been her trembling body and carried her up to the tub.

He'd bathed her, soothed her, curled up in the bed with her and whispered not only his love, but how he couldn't live without her. He'd die if anything took her away from him. That's all she needed to hear to slip into a peaceful slumber.

She knew the feeling. She loved them that much, too.

That warm sentiment dissolved under a shot of pure heat that fired through her body when a large hand smacked her squarely across the ass. Jerking up, she turned to glare at Devin who just grinned back at her.

"You're not drooling, are you?"

"I was just enjoying a little sun," Patton retorted haughtily.

"Yeah, some sun and male flesh." Devin pursed his lips. "What is it you said to Slade? Something about, if I catch you looking at other women I'm going to rip your eyes right out of the sockets."

"That's why she wants to live here," Chase stated, drawing her eyes back over the wooden fence to him. He did it again, crossing his arms over the massive wall of his chest and giving her a look that made her so hot, she just might pass out from heat stroke.

"She's got roving eyes." Slade stepped up alongside Chase. "Maybe we should put some blinders on her."

"I wasn't looking at anything." *Blinders, really.* "Just standing here thinking."

"About?" Slade inquired politely.

Patton could feel the heat in her cheeks warm up several degrees. What should she say to that? That she had been dreaming about the mini-orgy they'd had in the study last night. They knew how hot it had made her to have to masturbate for their pleasure and how it had driven her insane when Slade had forced her to feed him her pussy while Devin rode her ass.

She didn't need to admit to it. Doing so would make their over-inflated egos grow dangerously larger. Besides, it was one thing to talk dirty to them when they had her naked and moaning. It still embarrassed her when they were just having a normal conversation.

"Well, Patton?" Chase raised a brow at her silence. She could tell from his smirk he'd accurately guessed the direction of her thoughts.

"I was considering the merits of native pastures versus tamed ones," Patton retorted. A lame excuse if ever there had been one, but they had her all flustered and her mind couldn't come up with anything better at the spur of the moment.

"You wouldn't be lying, Patton, would you?" Devin growled in her ear.

His arms wrapped around from behind her as his hand settled possessively over her mound. Even through the denim of her jeans, she could feel the heat of his hand. He shouldn't be touching her like this with all the ranch hands around to see, but that concern faded quickly as he pressed his fingers inward and rubbed.

"You know what happens when you lie," Devin warned her.

"Yes," Patton gasped as her hips arched into his palm. Oh, that felt good. He'd managed to force her folds apart and used her own underwear to tease her clit.

"So were you really thinking about pastures?"

"Mmm-hmm." Patton's eyes closed. "But I'm thinking about something else now."

"I think it's time we showed Patton the new barn." That pearl came from Chase.

Her eyes opened at the mention of big metal barn they'd built over the ashes of the old one. Over the past three weeks, they had been very secretive about what they were up to. Not that she had pressed. Her only interest had been annoyance that they had taken over the area she had been considering building on.

She needed a studio, a true work space and little bedroom she used now wasn't cutting it. Still they had enough land for her plop down her own building elsewhere. So she'd said little, but to comment how quickly they accomplished building the whole structure.

Chase and Slade made quick work of jumping the fence. Before she could object, Chase had her by the hand and started dragging her across the yard.

"This is your wedding present," Chase explained as they approached the large metal door along the side.

"Are you sure it's not yours?" Patton muttered, almost positive that whatever they were so keen to show her had been designed more for their purposes than hers.

Devin snorted from her other side as Slade reached for the doorknob. "You're going to feel bad about saying that."

He was right. She stood there in the doorway, paralyzed with shock. The large main room was brightly lit with skylights and windows. Long tables, sewing machines, racks for hanging clothes, an organized wall unit for storing material, even spinning bars for long spools of fabric to hang from, the room was completely outfitted. There were even model forms and in the back corner an entire desk already outfitted with a computer.

"It's your shop," Devin stated the obvious.

"You can work from here," Slade added, as if she hadn't already figured that out.

"You did this for me?" Patton blinked.

She didn't give them time to answer before she thanked them between hugs and kisses. Before any of them could take advantage of her gratitude, she took off around the room, excitedly examining everything that the room had to offer. Talking a mile a second, she began to lay out how where she would put everything as her three men watched her indulgently.

"How did you know what to get?" Patton finally asked as she examined the sewing machines. "Or how to lay it all out?"

"Your partner, Cassie, helped with that," Slade explained as the brothers moved in on her.

"Cassie?" Patton didn't bother to look up and didn't realize that they had started determinedly moving toward her. "What's through this door?"

Patton opened the door at the back and found herself in a large, strangely elegant bathroom. The room amazed her, but a little out of place for a workshop. Her eyes skimmed over the enormous Jacuzzi tub and massive shower before settling on a second door.

"Why did you put a tub in here?" The question answered itself as she opened the second door.

"This is where we'll be honeymooning," Chase explained.

Patton barely heard him. Her eyes had gone wide as she took in the large playroom. So, they had included a present for themselves. Her eyes roved over the updated sex room, taking in several new toys that she had never seen.

Her eyes locked and bulged on one particular device. It was a perverted, strange kind of saddle seat. A bar just past the saddle's horn told which way she'd be facing. On the back end was some kind of motorized contraption with a head that looked as if it awaited an attachment.

Patton didn't need to wonder what kind of attachment as her mind leapt to the obvious conclusion. They intended to strap her into that thing and torment the hell out of her. With their new room, her men had upped the stakes on their kinky little sex games.

Patton shivered and felt her pussy pulse as her eyes moved onto to the other new contraptions they'd decorated the playroom with. Everything had been upgraded. No longer would Devin going to have to pull a chair in front of a double set of full lengths mirrors. Now they had an entire corner of mirrors, almost a box with the walls that came out to surround the stirrup chair in the center.

"It's all made out of metal and cement." Chase's words drew her eyes away from the instruments and to the walls and floors. At least, they had laid down rugs and stained the cement.

"Even if it catches fire, there is a sprinkler system." Slade pointed up and Patton's eyes followed his hand. "And a state-of-the-art security system."

Patton saw what he meant about the security system. Cameras hung from all angles around the room, too many of them to just be for protection. They hung at angles that allowed their unblinking eyes to take in every inch of the room. She did not believe that was all just to catch some intruder.

"Lot of cameras," Patton commented.

"We just want to make sure we can see you at all times," Slade explained smoothly.

"And in all positions," Patton snickered. Slade didn't respond to that but he didn't have to. His small smirk said it all.

"Well," Devin again wrapped his arms around her and tucked her back along his chest, "what do you think?"

"I think you've taken your perversion to a new level."

"Yeah." Devin sounded thrilled at the idea. This time when his hand slid over her mound, it did so from under the waistband of her jeans. "You're hot and wet, Patton. I do think you are ready to go for us on this ride."

Patton didn't answer. She couldn't. Devin's hand had slipped beneath her panties and began to drive her insane as he slowly rolled her little piercing. The door behind them clicked shut and she sighed. Yes, this would be the perfect honeymoon spot.

Epilogue

Across town, Cole scratched his chest and considered the Studebaker parked at the deli across the street. It had been a long day, his hard work showing on him in a fine speckling of grease and few extra nicks on his hands. He should head home to a shower and a change. Two big-breasted beauties awaited him at the lodge for their next round of training.

Normally that would have him high tailing it out of the shop and pushing the speed limit to get through his front door in record time. He'd been on his way to his truck when he'd caught sight of the classic parked in front of Harry's.

"Hey, man." Jake poked him in the side with a cold beer. "I thought you were headed home. Big plans for the night and all that."

"He got plans all right." Aaron snickered as he popped open his own can. "Too bad the woman he's thinking about would dig a fifty foot hole and drop him in it given the chance."

"You don't know nothing about women," Cole retorted.

"I know enough to know that woman ain't interested in you."

"You think?"

"I know."

"What do you know?" Kyle asked as he sauntered down the drive of the shop. Behind him the old, metal garage door whined and creaked slowly downward toward the cement floor.

"That Hailey Mathews would sooner spit on Cole than smile at him," Aaron drawled out with a smirk.

"Hailey." Kyle looked over at Cole. "I didn't know you were interested in her."

Cole shrugged. "I'm not interested in the woman. I want to fuck her. There's a difference."

"Hailey ain't the type of woman you just fuck, Cole," Kyle shot back and if Cole didn't know better, he could have sworn that anger tensed Kyle's body.

"You would know?"

"Kyle doesn't know more than a dog when it comes to Hailey," Jake responded.

"Hailey would sooner kick a dog like Kyle than she would smile at him."

Cole didn't pay any mind to his cousins' babble. He studied Kyle and knew he was right. The man was pissed, which could only mean he was also interested. Too damn bad for Kyle, he'd have to wait his turn. Hailey Mathews owed him and he intended to collect that debt.

That fiery red-head needed to be tamed. Only one Cattleman who was up to that job and it wasn't Kyle. Cole grinned. Bringing down a hard case like Hailey was enough of a prize to a man like him. Being pitted against his best friend and partner only made his ultimate victory smell sweeter.

"Stay away from Hailey, Cole."

"You her man or something?"

"You know I ain't."

"Then you don't have the right to tell me what to do."

"She deserves better than you."

"There ain't nobody better than me."

"There's me."

"So that's the way it is, huh?"

"Yeah. That's the way it is."

"Don't you think it should be up to the little woman to decide who is man enough to make her a real woman?"

"She'd never choose you."

"Well, then." Cole grinned. "Let the games begin."

Before Kyle could come back to that taunt, Cole turned and strutted across the street. Time to let the little filly know her days of running free on the range were numbered.

PATTON'S WAY

Cattleman's Club 1

THE END

WWW.JENNYPENN.COM

ABOUT THE AUTHOR

I live near Charleston, SC with my two biggies (my dogs). I have had a slightly unconventional life. Moving almost every three years, I've had a range of day jobs that included everything from working for one of the worlds largest banks as an auditor to turning wrenches as an outboard repair mechanic. I've always regretted that we only get one life and have tried to cram as much as I can into this one.

Throughout it all, I've always read books, feeding my need to dream and fantasize about what could be. An avid reader since childhood, as a latchkey kid I'd spend hours at the library earning those shiny stars the librarian would paste up on the board after my name.

I credit my grandmother's yearly visits as the beginning of my obsession with romances. When she'd come, she'd bring stacks of romance books, the old fashion kind that didn't have sex in them. Imagine my shock when I went to the used bookstore and found out what really could be in a romance novel.

I've working on my own stories for years and have found a particular love of erotic romances. In this genre, women are no longer confined to a stereotype and plots are no longer constrained to the rational. I love the anything goes mentality and letting my imagination run wild.

I hope you enjoyed running with me and will consider picking up another book and coming along for another adventure.

Please visit Jenny at www.jennypenn.com, or send her a comment at jenny@jennypenn.com

Siren Publishing, Inc.
www.SirenPublishing.com

Printed in the United States
132441LV00008B/49/P

9 781606 011591